THE CLUB

Barney Alesi

Dedication

I am dedicating this book to my wife Rose, also known as my sweetheart, love of my life, and soulmate simply because she put up with hours and hours on end of being alone while I was in my man cave working on this book and I would be remiss if I did not mention the fact that she gave me the idea for the ending.

Acknowledgments

I want to give special thanks to several people who made it possible for me to write this book: Rose Alesi, my wife, who put up with me and listened to me for hours and hours on end as I complained about all of the problems I was encountering while writing this book; my nephew Michael Santo, Esq., who helped me out immensely in many areas of this book; my two daughters, Bonnie and Theresa, along with my son, Anthony, my grandchildren, Anthony, Tiffany, Jacqueline, Nicholas, Kaitlynn, and Patrick; my daughters-in-law, Sue and Denise, my granddaughter-in-law, Kati, and grandson-inlaw, Sal, my godchild Dorothea and her husband Buddy, I also want to thank my friends, who have listened to me moaning about my book and who deserve to at least be recognized: Bob, Maryann, Jimmy, Nick, Janet, John, Celeste, James and Barb.

Contents

Acknowledgments	v
Prologue	1
Going to the big city	3
The trial starts	11
The father's reaction	15
The website is set up	19
The Club is born	23
The first letter	25
It happens again	31
The Club logo is born	37
Paul's trial starts	39
Not such a nice guy	41
We have a problem	47
The Tod Williams trial starts	53
Taking back their stuff	65
The calm before the storm	75
Big news hits the papers	81
The day of reckoning is in sight	101
The day of sentencing	155
Setting the stage	171
The plan	183
Setting the place up	233
Looking for some wiggle room	289
Good news	351
The big day	363
Epilogue	369
About the author	371

John Harrison lives in Cincinnati, Ohio, in a modest home, with his wife Mary of twenty years, his daughter Wendy, sixteen years old, and his son John Jr., seventeen years old.

John came from a poor home, never going on vacation and doing without the things most other children had. His father worked in a factory and barely earned enough to feed his family and keep a roof over their heads, let alone go on vacations or afford any lavish gifts.

Growing up, John had very few toys and only one bicycle – a used one – that his father had bought from a bicycle rental shop and that he did not get until his thirteenth birthday. So, growing up under those conditions, John vowed to educate himself and work hard so that his family would not want for anything.

After high school, John got a job and worked his way through college, becoming an engineer. John had several jobs as an engineer before he got a good position at a large construction firm, where he has worked for the past twenty years, earning him enough money to take his family on vacations and to afford a few of the little perks in life.

John is proud and happy, and he looks forward to taking his family on a vacation each year. To add to the pleasure and excitement, John and his wife Mary always make the destination a surprise, and this year, it is to be a big one, John and his family live in Cincinnati, Ohio, and the trip they have planned is to New York City, to Madison Square Garden, to see the circus and some of the sites in Manhattan, and even a take trip to see the

Statue of Liberty.

John is very proud of his children, especially Wendy. She is smart, doing great in school, a straight-A student and on the school paper. After school, she works as a candy striper at the local hospital, and when her shift is over, she even volunteers to read books to some of the older patients who cannot read for themselves. She is also active in sports. She is just happy and full of life, and a sweeter little girl would be hard to find. John Jr. is also a straight-A student, doing great in school, and excelling in sports. He is even thinking of trying to play professional baseball or becoming an engineer like his father. So because their children are doing so good, John and Mary are more than happy to reward them with a great vacation.

Two weeks before the trip, John and Mary sit the children down to inform them of this year's destination. They wanted to wait, but for some strange reason, Wendy and John Jr. kept asking, "Where are we going this year?" It was as though they had an inkling of something big coming up.

"Okay… so… this year, and because you guys are doing so well in school, your mother and I have a surprise for you. This year, we are going to New York, because we heard that the circus was in town—"

Before John can say another word, Wendy and John Jr. jump up out of their chairs, screaming at the top of their lungs, "Yes!! Yes!!" They hug each other, spinning and jumping up and down.

"Okay, simmer down… And while we are there, we will also go see the Statue of Liberty."

At this, Wendy shouts, "Oh, I can't wait to tell all the girls in school!"

The night before the big day comes, all the bags are packed, and knowing that it's a 643-mile trip, and at least a ten-hour drive, John decides he wants to get an early start, so he informs his family that he wants to be on the road by 6 AM, and would like everybody up by 5 AM. The kids moan at this, so John says, "You know, if you don't want to get up that early, we can always cancel the trip."

"No! No!"

"Okay, then, it's all set. We all get up at 5 AM."

By 6:30 AM, they are on the road, and John tells them, "In addition to the trip, when we get there, we will get some lunch and do some shopping, and you guys can all get two new outfits.

John Jr. says, "Oh, good," but Mary and Wendy scream with joy.

"Okay, okay," John says, "let's all settle down. We have a long ride ahead."

Ten hours and a few stops later, they finally get to New York City. John parks the car, and they check into the hotel. As soon as they've done that, the first thing out of Mary's mouth is, "I'm hungry. I want a hamburger," and John Jr. says, "I'm hungry too," so they all head to the first hamburger restaurant they see.

As soon as they walk in, Wendy says, "I want to pick the table."

John says, "Okay, what do you want to eat?"

"I just want a cheeseburger with fries and a diet soda," answers Wendy.

Mary says, "You know what, John, I'll have the same, so I'll just go and sit with Wendy."

3

John goes to the counter with John Jr. to order the food, and asks him, "What do you want to eat?"

"I want two cheeseburgers with fries and an orange soda."

John orders the food, waits for it with his son, and when it's ready, they bring it to the table.

After about half an hour, they finish eating, and John says, "Well, we still have a few hours to spare. What do you say we take in some of the city sites? There are a lot of them to see, and we will only be here for five days, and that's going to go fast."

Wendy says, "Okay, but before we go, I need to go to the bathroom."

"Okay, go, and when you're done, we will leave and get our vacation started by doing some shopping."

"Okay, Dad, I'll be right out."

Twenty minutes later, Mary says, "I thought she was only going to be a few minutes."

John says, "Why don't you go and see what's taking her so long?"

Mary goes to check on Wendy, but when she gets to the ladies' room and walks in, she doesn't see her daughter. She starts to look under the stall doors to see if she can see familiar legs, but when she doesn't, she starts calling out, "Wendy, are you in here?" Not getting an answer, she calls out again, this time a little louder, "Wendy! Are you in here?" Still no answer. By now, the two persons who were in the stalls have come out, and Mary asks them, "Excuse me, did you see a young girl with long blond hair in here?"

They both shake their heads no. One woman says that there was no one in the bathroom when she came in, and the second woman says that the first women was the only one in there when she came in and that neither one saw a young girl.

Mary goes back to the table, thinking that somehow she may have missed Wendy while going to the ladies' room to check on her. Upon returning, though, Mary sees that Wendy is not there. Now she starts getting nervous.

John says, "What's going on? Where is she?"

In a raised voice, Mary says, "I don't know! She was not in the ladies' room, and I asked the two women who were in there if they'd seen her, and they both said they hadn't, and I can't find her. I can't find her! Where can she be? John, I've got a really bad feeling about this."

As she starts to cry, John says, "Okay, don't jump to any conclusions. Let's go one step at a time. Maybe she stepped outside. Remember, she is not used to seeing a big city."

They all go outside to search for Wendy, looking all around and calling out, "Wendy! Wendy!" Now John is getting concerned. They all go back into the restaurant and start yelling out, "Did anyone see a little sixteen-year-old girl with long blond hair? She went to the ladies' room, and now we can't find her!"

John tells Mary, "Please go back to the ladies' room and check again."

Mary goes back to the ladies' room, only to find that there is no one at all in there now. Mary starts crying hysterically, and John starts crying as well, along with John Jr. All three are now crying hysterically and calling out Wendy's name. John and Mary both start yelling out, "Where is my little girl? I can't believe that no one saw anything! I need help!"

With that, the manager comes over and tells John that has already called the police and that they are on their way. In no time, the police are there. The first thing they do is lock down the restaurant. At this point, Mary is still too distraught to speak, so John starts telling them what transpired, though he is also physically upset. There are now eight NYC policemen there: four of them start searching the premises, in and out, while two start questioning the customers and another two stay with John, taking his statement. They ask John, "Has she ever disappeared or done anything like this before?"

"No, No!"

"Sir, please understand we need to ask these questions."

Again, John answers the question, "No, she is a good girl. She has never done anything like this before. I'm telling you something happened to her. Please, help me!"

"Sir, we are here to help you. Please believe me. I can just imagine what you are going through. I have a daughter of my own, so believe me, I know what you are feeling."

At this point, Mary, still crying hysterically, passes out and falls to the floor. The police check her out and immediately call to have an ambulance come for all three of them. When the ambulance gets there, all three are given a shot to calm them down, and the officers questioning them suggest they take the ambulance to the hospital.

John says, "We do not want to go to the hospital. We want to stay here and look for our daughter, sir."

"Please believe me," says one of the officers. "We will continue to search for her and ask questions, I promise, but Mr. Harrison, what I need now is a full description of Wendy."

Still all choked up and hardly able to speak, John manages to reply, "She is sixteen years old, about five feet three inches tall, about one hundred and ten pounds, long blond hair. Blue eyes. She was wearing blue jeans, a pink top, and white sneakers."

"Mr. Harrison, I know this is hard, but you can't stay here. Either go home or go to the hospital, because we need to know where we can contact you when we need to, and please try to stay positive for the rest of your family. We will get in touch with you as soon as we know anything."

"Okay, we will go back to the hotel that we are staying at."

"I will have an officer escort you back. How far away is it?"

"It's only about fifteen minutes away."

"Okay, great. Officer Thomas will escort you back and stay with you awhile."

By this time, Mary and John Jr. are feeling a little better, so reluctantly, they all go back to the hotel along with Officer Thomas.

Three hours later, two detectives are knocking on the door. John opens the door and lets them in. "So, did you guys find out anything about my daughter?"

"Mr. Harrison," says one of the detectives, "please sit down. We need to talk, and it would be better if you were sitting."

Mary looks at John and says, "John, I don't like this."

"Mrs. Harrison," continues the detective, "please sit down."

"Why do you want us to sit?"

"Mrs. Harrison, we have some information for the two of you, but we will not say a word until the two of you are sitting,"

Mary says again, "I don't like where this is going," but both of them finally sit.

"Mr. and Mrs. Harrison, we checked all over the restaurant and found no trace of your daughter. We surveyed the entire area for three blocks each way and could not find anyone who saw anything. But there are a lot of cameras in the city, so we then went to see if any cameras picked up anything, and then we found something. We have a copy of the video of a man holding and escorting a young girl by her arm who meets your daughter's description. They were leaving the area behind the restaurant. We want you to look at it and tell us if this is your daughter or not."

Mary shouts, "No! I can't look."

John hugs her and says, "We need to know, one way or the other." John looks at the video, and starts crying, "Yes, yes, that's her. Who is the guy? Where did he come from? Do you have him?"

"Mr. Harrison, please sit and let me explain how this works. Right now, all we can do is put out an APB out for him and hope that someone sees him or knows him, and gets in touch with us, but until then, all we can do is hope for the best. I know it's hard, but believe me, we are doing our very best to get this guy, Mr. Harrison, you need to understand, this may take a while."

"I understand."

"And please try to stay here or close by, because we need to be able to get in touch with you when we need to."

"Okay, you got it."

"Please don't go out and try to find her on your own. That has never worked out in any case like this. Again, we realize it's extremely hard, but you need to trust us to do what we do, and I promise to keep you informed on everything."

Three weeks go by, with John extending his vacation, and at this point, Mary is on medication and is walking around talking to herself. She just keeps saying over and over, "How can she not be here? How can she just be gone? I don't understand." And John, half out of his mind himself, keeps calling the detectives every other day, trying to get some information.

By the fourth week, John needs to go back to work, but he continues to extend his vacation. Mary seems to be getting better and is adjusting to the fact that her daughter Wendy is gone. John Jr. is also settling down, and it seems as though the whole family is slowly getting back to as close to a normal a life as possible under the circumstances.

On the last night of the sixth week, there's a knock on the hotel door. John opens the door, and standing there are the two New York detectives who are working on the case. John nervously invites them in, restraining himself from shouting out, "Did you find her!!"

One of the detectives asks, "Is Mrs. Harrison here?"

"Yes, she is."

"Okay, we would like to talk to the two of you." They ask John and Mary to please sit.

Mary sits and starts crying. John hugs her, trying to console her, and says, "Mary, please, let's hear what they have to say before we go off the deep end. Okay, we are seated. So what is this all about?"

"Mr. Harrison, what this is all about is that we have in custody the man who was seen on the video taking your daughter. His name is Jim Tally, and he heard that we were looking for him, so he turned himself in. According to him, his story is that he saw your daughter standing outside of the restaurant and that is when he grabbed her, so he did admit to taking her. But then he says he changed his mind and let her go, and she ran away, and that he just got in his car and left, not wanting to get in trouble. The last time he says he saw her, she was running back to the restaurant, unharmed."

"But if you have him, then you should know where Wendy is," John says. "I don't understand; where is my daughter? if he said that he saw her running back to the restaurant, then where is she?"

"Mr. Harrison, you need to understand that this is his story. It does not mean that it's true. We still have an APB out for your daughter, Wendy. We just wanted to let you know what has transpired so far. Mr. and Mrs. Harrison, we cannot emphasize to you how important this is to us, and let me assure you that we are working on this as diligently as we can. The best way we can put it is that we are working on this as though it is our own daughter who is missing, and we know that we have not said this before, but in cases like this, the best advice we can give you at this time is to please hope for the best, but prepare for the worst."

It has now been a month and a half since Wendy's disappearance, and John needs to go back to work in Cincinnati. He knows that if he doesn't, he will be fired, so the next day, John and his family drive back home.

After two more weeks with no news, John decides to give the detectives in New York a call. The detective who answers tells John that there is some news and that a detective from the Cincinnati police department will be in touch with him to talk about what is going on with the case. "Mr. Harrison, he will explain everything to you about the problem with the case against Mr. Tally."

Two days later, John gets a call from a Cincinnati policeman, a Detective Tags, who asks him to come down to the local station house for a talk, and to come by himself.

John asks, "Why by myself?"

"Mr. Harrison, believe me, it will be better by yourself. Trust me. After the talk, you will understand, okay?"

John explains to Mary that the police want to see him alone, and she asks him, "Why do they want to see you alone?"

"I don't know. All they said is that it would be much better if I went down there by myself, so please, I'm telling you, let's not jump to conclusions. Let me go see what they have to say, and I promise you that when I get back, I will tell you everything."

An hour later, John is at the station house talking to Detective Tags.

"Mr. Harrison, please be seated," the detective says, and John sits. "Mr. Harrison, first off, remember that this guy turned himself in. He is a very shrewd individual. We checked him out and found out that this man served eight years for child molestation and then was given an early release because of good behavior. So he has been around the block a few times, but we at least now know who this guy is. But the reason I wanted to speak to you is that we need to start talking about the reality of things. We need to talk about the hard facts of the case that you are up against, because it's going get rough. Do you feel that you're up to it?"

"Yes, I'm up to it."

"Okay, then, before I start explaining everything to you, I need to warn you. Some of the facts in this case are going to be hard to talk about, so please don't think that I'm insensitive or uncaring, or have no sympathy for you."

"I understand."

"Great. So this is how it is. Unfortunately, Wendy has not turned up or been found, and the D.A. has a problem with the case because of the lack of evidence. The only thing we have is him on video walking with your daughter, but, it does not look like he is forcing her in any way. Then he said that he changed his mind and let her go, so do you see where we stand right now? It's a weak case, and the D.A. would like more evidence."

"Why don't you let me talk to him in a closed room for a few minutes, and I will find out the truth."

"Mr. Harrison, if it were possible, I would do that in a second."

"So without beating around the bush, you are basically telling me that without Wendy's body, we have no case."

"Mr. Harrison, unfortunately, that is the problem, but what I'm saying is that we need more time to try to build up a case against Mr. Tally."

"You know what, please don't call him Mr. Tally in front of me."

"Okay, from now on, I will refer to him as the defendant."

"That's better. Thank you."

"Okay, then. Now that you understand what the situation is, please know this: we will work on this case as hard as we possibly can."

"Okay."

"Mr. Harrison, thanks for understanding, and it will be much easier for you to explain to your wife than if it were to come from me."

"Okay, I understand. I will talk to her when I get home."

"Great, thanks for understanding."

When John gets home, he explains everything to Mary. All she can do is break down and cry, nearly passing out to the point where John has to hold her up.

"I'm sorry, babe, but I had to tell you the cold hard facts," says John. "Without her body, their hands are tied. And by the way, that piece of shit served eight years for child molestation, so they know who he is. They are just trying to get more evidence against him so that they can put him away for a long time. So he said to just have more patience and let them do their work.

Finally, after almost three months of the Harrisons pleading with the D.A., and after the D.A. informing them that they should not get their hopes up, the D.A. decides to press charges and bring Jim Tally to trial, even though he knows that without a body, he has a weak case. For one, there are just four witnesses, including the manager of the restaurant, who saw nothing except for Wendy, John, Mary, and their son in the restaurant and can only testify as to what happened after the disappearance.

The big day comes, and John and Wendy are back in New York for the trial. The court is in session, and the D.A. is charging Tod with kidnaping and murder, but because there is no body, the D.A. thinks that he is going to have a hard time getting a conviction. For the sake of the Harrisons, though, he feels that he needs to go ahead with the case.

The bailiff announces the judge's entry into the court. He asks everyone to please stand, announces that the court is now in session, with Judge Peter Williams presiding, and that everyone can be seated.

The judge speaks first: "Are both sides ready?"

The D.A. answers, "Yes, Your Honor," and then the defense says, "Yes, Your Honor."

"Okay, then let's get this case started."

With that, the D.A. gets up and begins his opening statement, saying to the jury, "Ladies and gentleman, today I will prove to you that Mr. Jim Tally is guilty of the kidnaping and murder of sweet, innocent, sixteen-year-old Wendy Harrison, and the very first thing I want to say is to

11

please keep in mind that Mr. Tally is a convicted child molester and served eight years for that crime. Even though we never found her body, through circumstantial evidence, I will prove this to you beyond any reasonable doubt that Mr. Tally is guilty. I have video evidence of Mr. Tally dragging sweet little Wendy away from the restaurant, never to be seen again, and witnesses attesting as to what happened in the restaurant and to Wendy's character. Thank you, Judge."

Next, the defense gets up. "Judge, before I start, I first would like to make a motion to dismiss this case due to lack of evidence. The only real evidence they have is a video showing Mr. Tally just holding her hand and walking. Mr. Tally did admit to taking Wendy, but then he said that he changed his mind and let her go and does not know what happened to her."

"At this point," says the judge, "I'm going to call a recess, and I want to see both sides in my chambers."

Once both attorneys are in the judge's chambers, he asks them to please sit. "Mr. Collins, what is the exact evidence that you have?"

"Well, Your Honor, first, we have a video of Mr. Tally dragging sweet little Wendy by her arm. I also have four witnesses: the restaurant manager, and the father, mother, and brother. And besides, Mr. Tally is a convicted child molester and served eight years for that crime, so he has done this before, and I feel is capable of doing it again."

"Okay, so let me see. You have a video of Mr. Tally taking Wendy, but he then said that he changed his mind and let her go, so all you have is the manager, the father, mother, and brother. What significant information does the manager have?"

"Well, Your Honor, he can prove that she was there in the restaurant."

"Okay, Mr. Collins, let me stop you there. First, let me say this: as a Judge, I do not hold the past of a person against them, especially if they paid society back for their crime. Also, the manager is not needed to prove that Wendy was there. You have a video for that. And as far as the father, mother, and brother are concerned, I can't see them bringing any more evidence but to attest to Wendy's character, and that I don't need. I'm sure that she was a sweet, innocent girl, but, not to be uncaring, you have no body, and without a body, you really have no case, and I have no other course of action but to grant the defense their motion to dismiss this case due to the lack of evidence. However, Mr. Collins, I will dismiss it without prejudice so that in the future, when you get more evidence, you can reopen the case."

"But Your Honor, how can you just dismiss Mr. Tally's past history of being a child molester?"

"Because I can, and even dough I don't need to explain it to you, I, in fact, did explain it to you. I do not hold a person's past history against them, especially when they already paid their debt to society, so this session is over. Let's go back to the courtroom."

Both sides return to the courtroom. The Harrisons immediately notice that Mr. Collins is walking with his head down and shaking his head back and forth. John turns to Mary and says, "Something's up. I don't like this."

"Me neither," answers Mary.

Finally, the bailiff announces the return of the judge back into the courtroom, and he asks everyone to stand. The judge enters and sits down, and the bailiff orders everyone to sit.

At this point, the courtroom is silent. The judge shuffles some papers around, and then he says, "First, let me say this: I have come to a decision on this case, but before I let you know what that is, I want to warn everyone that I will not tolerate any outbursts, and I mean any outburst. I have come to the conclusion that there is insufficient evidence to continue with this case, so I am dismissing the charges against Mr. Tally without prejudice so that if more evidence comes to light down the road, the trail can be reopened. Mr. Tally, you are free to go."

THE CLUB

After hearing the verdict, John jumps out of his seat, runs and jumps over the railing, and attacks Jim Tally while yelling out, "I'm going to fucking kill you! You're nothing but a piece of shit!" Four court officers quickly try to get John off Jim, but they have a hard time doing it.

After John is restrained, the judge warns, "Mr. Harrison, you can't react like that. You could end up in jail." The judge then issues a restraining order on John and warns him to stay away from Jim or end up in jail.

After the trial, months and months pass, but John still can't live with the loss of his little girl. Ignoring the restraining order, John vows to kill Jim if he should ever see him. He searches for Jim without any luck and eventually comes to believe that Jim has moved out of the country or is just staying out of sight. In his head, John still vows to kill Jim if their paths should ever cross.

It is now three years since the trial, and John decides it's time to put the past behind him and, for his family's sake, try to get back to a more normal way of life. He decides to go on a vacation, and again he finds out that the circus is back in New York. He thinks that for the sake of his family, they should try and pick up where they left off and finish the New York vacation that they started three years ago, so they decide to spend two weeks in the big city.

Soon, they are back in New York and settled into a nice hotel, and like the last time, John decides to take the family on a shopping spree. One hour into the shopping, and as fate would have it, who does John spot in front of a movie house, but none other than Jim Tally. John does not say a word to anyone; he just runs over and attacks Jim, punching him in his face, knocking him down, and then kicking him over and over while shouting, "I'm going to kill you!"

As John tries to strangle Jim, some people see what is going on and, not knowing the situation, come to Jim's rescue. They stop John from attacking and trying to kill Jim, and they call the police while holding John down. When the police get there and find out that there is a restraining order on John, he gets arrested, and he sits in jail for five months before his trial comes up. This puts a tremendous strain on Mary, who has to stay in New York, and on top of everything else, John is fired from his job, so now they have no income.

John decides against a jury trial, thinking that he will have a better chance to beat the charges with just a judge, but instead, the judge reprimands him, asking, "Mr. Harrison, did you forget that there was a restraining order on you?"

"No, sir."

"And did you realize that because of the restraining order, what you were doing was wrong and was about to get you in trouble?"

"Your Honor, at the time, I was so enraged that I was not thinking straight. When I saw him, all I could think of was what he did to my sweet little girl, and at that point, all I wanted to do was kill him."

"Well, Mr. Harrison, because of the restraining order and the things you were saying while beating on Mr. Tally, I have no recourse but to find you guilty."

At the sentencing, John is given five years, to be served at the correctional facility in Attica, New York. Mary is now forced to sell the house and move to New York so that she can be closer to John. This takes up most of their life's savings, and within a few months, she is forced to go on assistance. In the meantime, as fate would have it, John is sent to the same prison that Jim served time in for child molestation. While in prison, John finds out through the prison grape vine that while Jim was serving time there, he bragged about what he did to little girls and was almost killed in prison, because as bad as the prisoners are, most of them don't condone the raping and killing of children. Given a chance, they will kill child murderers and rapists. Because of this, Jim had to be put in a part of the prison that was safe for him, and it might have been another reason for his early release. The day John finds out about this, he goes crazy, but he finally consoles himself by saying over and over that what he did to avenge his daughter's death was a good thing, and he still vows that if he ever sees Jim on the streets again, he will kill him. On that day, John also vows to do something about child molesters and about how lenient the laws are pertaining to them, and he vows there and then to start a movement to get them changed.

While serving his time, John befriends one of the inmates by the name of Tom Reynolds, who just happens to be a computer whiz. One day, John is talking to Tom, bemoaning over what happened to his daughter and trying to figure out some way to get revenge. As John is talking, Tom gets an idea about starting a website that maybe could get some people to put up a big enough stink, and maybe find some new evidence so that the case can be opened up again.

Tom explains his idea to John and tells him about how powerful the Internet can be. Then Tom, along with John and Mary, work together for weeks to put together a website, Tom explains to Mary and John how to go about setting up a website.

THE CLUB

The website is set up

The website is up and running and is called *THE VIGILANTE*. It explains to people what happened to little Wendy and how unfair it is that a child molester can literally get away with rape and murder. It also details how the court system and some judges, who should be removed from the bench, let these child molesters get away with no more than a slap on the wrist, allowing them to go on their merry way. And even though there are laws in place to warn the people of their whereabouts and to keep track of them, in some cases, they slip through the cracks altogether. The website also asks the people to sign a petition to get the laws against child molesters changed, and to get the bleeding-heart judges now on the benches to get tough on these monsters and put them away forever.

The website is on the Internet for several weeks, without getting much action.

Tom explains to John, "You know, what you may need to do is to advertise the website somewhere, like maybe on the radio or in the newspaper, or anywhere that people can see that you have this website. Word of mouth alone is not enough to get it going."

"Yes," John says, "I realize that, but with me being in jail, there is no money going into the household, and right now, there is just not enough money to go to advertising the website on the radio or the newspapers."

John calls his wife and explains to her what Tom said about advertising the website on the radio or in the newspaper. "But knowing how tight money is, I can't see how we can afford that."

19

Mary tells John not to worry; together, they will figure something out. She comes up with the idea of having John Jr. print up some flyers and put them all around town, asking for donations, seeing that all the town knows what happened.

John Jr. tells his mom, "Don't worry. I will also get a part-time job after school to help out." John Jr. prints up a bunch of flyers on his computer that explain the family's problem, and he puts them out all over town. He also hands them out in his school for the students to bring home to their parents.

Soon, some money starts coming in. Mary can now advertise on the radio, and that seems to do the trick, because after a few weeks, the site finally starts getting some hits. The results are great: people are signing the petition, donating money, and also leaving some good feedback on the message board.

Two months later, the petition has thousands of signatures, and some people are now leaving nasty messages condemning the justice system on the message board. Also, word of mouth is taking over, and Mary feels that the radio ads are no longer needed. The site is really taking off, and the messages are now calling for the death of some of the judges and the killing of child molesters.

One night, out of the blue, there is a knock on Mary's door. It's two FBI men. They ask her, "Are you Mrs. Mary Harrison?"

She responds, "Yes. What's this all about?"

They hand her a court order and tell her that the website is getting out of control, calling for the killings of judges and child molesters, and that she can't do that because, according to the law, that is inciting people to go out and murder other people. They tell her that she must shut it down immediately, and if she doesn't, they will. They also tell her that she could get a stiff fine and possibly end up in jail.

Mary is outraged and scared silly, and she calls the prison and leaves a message for John to call her. When he does, she asks him what she should do. John tells her, "Let me check it out and get back to you." He then confides in Tom and asks him if he knows a good lawyer.

"As a matter of fact, I do. His name is Mike Santino, and he is really a great lawyer."

As soon as John gets a chance, he calls Mary and tells her that Tom gave him the name and phone number of a great lawyer by the name of Mike Santino, and to give him a call, Mary wastes no time and calls him. She explains the situation and who referred her to him, and Mike agrees to help. First, he suggests shutting down the website until he has a chance to check into it.

John is outraged and at his wits end, and he can't figure out what to do. Several weeks go by, and John knows that time is of the essence, because the longer the site is closed, the more support they will lose. John and Tom come up with an idea for a new website, so John calls Mike, and asks him if he could please come up and meet with him in prison. Mike agrees to come up to the prison and meet with John.

Once they are face to face, John explains to Mike the ideas that he and Tom came up with. Mike tells John that he will check the laws and get back to him, and he tells John about his disdain for the laws and judges involved with child molesters. Finally, he says, "Because you're a friend of Tom's, and the way I feel about the laws, don't worry about my fee. I just want to help."

"Okay, Mike, that's great!"

It's two weeks before Mike gets a chance to get back to the prison to meet up with John. Mike says, "John, I have good news and bad news for you." Mike explains to John that what he wants to do is very tricky and dangerous, and he must make sure that every word on the new website is carefully scrutinized, that every i is dotted and every t crossed, because he could end up in more trouble than he could ever imagine. Mike tells John he will be walking a very fine line and that he needs to think long and hard before he does this.

THE CLUB

The Club is based on the theory that in unity, there is strength. And its primary goals are to ensure the safety of children, to try to get the current child molester laws changed, and to get people to become, in a very subtle way, vigilantes and take the law into their own hands, getting rid of all the convicted or known child molesters, something that the current laws and some judges are not doing. And if club members get caught doing this, they will be backed up by other members, such as lawyers who will defend them free of charge, judges who will hear their case and in some way help out, or just the regular members, hopefully numbering in the thousands and possibly in the millions, who will serve on juries all over the country and acquit them. In the event that any member gets in trouble financially, they will also be given financial help from The Club.

The way The Club will work is, first of all, there will be no message board for the people to express their anger and get the site in trouble again. Instead, the site will be for information, posting a newsletter every month about the latest child molestations and the outcomes of those crimes, such as the investigations or trials. It will also include any new laws pertaining to child molesters, as well as news about the release of any molesters from prison and their current whereabouts.

There will be a yearly charge of $20.00 to join The Club, which will get cut down as the membership increases. This fee will get you a monthly letter and a bumper sticker. The money will be used to cover the expense of operating the site and to help defend any member who, after reading the monthly letter, takes the law into their own hands and gets rid of a child molester and gets caught.

Before the new website is set up, Mary and John Jr. again get some flyers out, again explaining what happened and asking for donations. This time, the money comes in a lot slower, but it's still enough to help get the website started and get some air time. While Mary and John Jr. try to get the money together for the website, Mary, John, and Tom work diligently on the first letter for the website, because they feel that the first letter will be the most important one. It must teach the readers to read between the lines and motivate them, to take action against child molesters – a call to arms, so to speak. The most important part of the letter will be the "Wouldn't It Be Nice" column. This will outline, suggest, or guide the members as to what to do, and motivate them to get more people to join The Club.

Hi, and welcome to THE CLUB. This site was set up to protect our children and educate our members as to what is going on in this sick world regarding child molesters. It will try to explain the insane laws on the books that desperately need to be changed and identify the bleeding-heart judges that need to be taken off the bench, because they let these monsters get away with the rape and murder of our innocent children with little to no punishment.

We will also, from time to time, be giving safety tips from known experts in the field of child safety on how to protect and educate our members and their children on what to do if someone tries to take your child somewhere against their will, or what to do if you see someone else's child being taken against their will. Every month, at the end of the letter, we will also print an up-to-date list of convicted child molesters and their current whereabouts so that our members can keep track of them. We'll also try to get some petitions going on changing the laws, and also to recruit new members to THE CLUB so that we can grow strong and get some teeth.

First, the disclaimer: we are not telling anyone to go out and do these things. We are only saying that because of all we said at the beginning of this month's letter, about how the laws and some judges let child molesters get away with their crimes, wouldn't it be nice if The Club had millions of members, including Judges and lawyers, so that we could go out and avenge our children's deaths, something the law is not doing? And wouldn't it be nice to be able to do this with the knowledge that if someone who did take the law into their own hands got caught and went to trial, that there would be a lawyer to defend them at no charge, or a judge who would be on their side? And wouldn't it be nice if there were enough members of this club that the chances would be good that a few would serve on the jury and acquit you?

❦❦❦

Again, the website really starts to take off, and people are joining up by the hundreds. In a few months, the membership is up to the thousands, and by the end of eight months, it's nearing the one-million mark.

Now, again, the radio spots are no longer needed because of word of mouth, and the money is also rolling in, and the newsletter is looking and getting better and better, real professional looking. But because of all the money coming in, the site now has to make everything legal. They have to hire a bookkeeper, get an accountant, and Mike, John's lawyer, gets all the rest of the papers together to make the website legal. Also, The Club is now giving all members bumper stickers.

Now, because of all the action the site is getting, the news media on the radio and TV are talking about it, and this is also helping to get new members. including the first two of many lawyers, Barney Cicale and Nick Alesi.

After about a year, it happens: a ten-year-old girl, Betty Sweeney from Cincinnati, is missing, and a convicted child molester, Ray Thomas, who was let out on early parole, is picked up and charged with the crime, thanks to an eye witness who saw Ray put the little girl into his car. Again, like so many times before, the little girl is not found. It's two months before the trial begins, and on the first day of the trial, the little girl's father, Tom Sweeney, manages to get a gun into the courtroom. He pulls out the gun and shoots Ray dead. Tom Sweeney, who turns out not to be a member of The Club, gets arrested and gets put in jail. Right away, the two new lawyers of The Club, Barney Cicale and Nick Alesi, come forward to defend Tom free of charge. They plan to claim temporary insanity: due to the fact that the father was so overwhelmed with rage, he did not know what he was doing, and therefore, should not be held responsible for killing Ray, a known child molester who should have still been in jail.

John feels that even though Tom is not a member of The Club, it would be a good idea to defend him. John contacts Tom and lets him know that all of his financial problems will be taken care of, and he also informs the two lawyers that The Club will cover all expenses.

The jury selection starts, and during selection, Barney and Nick ask many questions of potential jurors. One very important question is: Are you a member of any club or organization? When two of the potential jurors say yes and that one of the clubs that the two of them are members of is The Club, Barney and Nick are very happy, and the best part of it is that the prosecutors do not realize what is going on. The only thing now is that Barney and Nick are hoping that the two members of The Club will be on the jury, that they have read the "Wouldn't It Be Nice" part of the website's monthly letter, and that they have also learned to read between the lines and know what to do in the jury room.

Finally, the trial starts, and both the D.A. and the defense lawyers come up with great opening statements. The D.A. brings in four eyewitnesses who were in the courtroom when Tom shot Ray. The D.A. tries to prove that Tom knew exactly what he was doing, and that he planned the whole thing and executed it in cold blood.

Nick and Barney bring in their own witnesses, ten of them, in fact. One by one, Nick and Barney question their witnesses and bring out the fact to the jury that in the weeks leading up to the trial, Tom was very depressed and even suicidal. They also try to get the point across to the jurors that Tom is by no means a violent man.

The trial goes on for almost two weeks. Finally, both sides rest, and after the judge gives the jury their instructions, the jury leaves the courtroom to go and deliberate the case. The jury deliberates for two days, and finally, the announcement is made that the jury has reached a decision. Everyone is very quiet when the jury comes back into the courtroom.

The judge asks the jury foreman if the jury has reached a decision. The jury foreman answers, "Yes, we have, Your Honor," and he hands a piece of paper to the court officer, who in turn hands it to the judge. The judge reads the paper and hands it back to the court officer to return to the jury foreman. The judge then asks the jury foreman to read the verdict. The jury foreman stands up and says, "We, the jury, find the defendant NOT GUILTY ON ALL COUNTS."

All the people in the courtroom jump up and start clapping their hands and yelling, Yea! Yea! Yea!" Tom's family starts yelling and crying and hugging each other. The whole courtroom is going crazy; even Nick and Barney are giving each other high fives and hugging everyone.

After the trial, Barney and Nick call John and let him know the outcome of the trial and that two of the jurors were members of The Club. So when The Club puts out its monthly newsletter, in its "Wouldn't It Be Nice" column, the newsletter explains what happened in Ohio and the outcome of the trial, how happy John is because the two jurors did the right thing by getting Tom acquitted of the crime, and that wouldn't it be nice if this could happen more often, that the good guys win. John hopes that the members can read between the lines and realize that there were members of The Club on the jury and also the fact that one more child molester is off the street, that children are safer now, and that the public is finely starting to fight back. The Club also calls for all its members to urge more people to join, because John feels that The Club is finally starting to move in the right direction and is actually making a difference.

Over the next few months, the membership in The Club increases steadily, and The Club also has quite a bit of money. John is excited with the increase and hopes that soon his dream will be fulfilled of having many members in The Club being on juries, and child molesters being taken off the streets by members, and getting away with it, and doing this until the powers that be figure out what's going on. He believes that the people, in doing what they are doing, are making a statement that they want the lawmakers to listen and change the laws to protect innocent children and deal with these child molesters in an extremely stern way, because it is a proven fact that there is no rehabilitating child molesters. They never stop doing their thing. They get caught, go to jail, are let out, do it again, get caught again, and it goes on and on. In the meantime, our children are being molested and killed, and these animals keep walking free on the face of this earth to stalk, molest, and kill innocent children again and again.

THE CLUB

Unfortunately, it happens again. This time, it's two children, a ten-year-old girl, Betty Dickerson, from Texas, who was walking home from school, which was just five blocks from her home, and never made it home, and a nine-year-old boy, Neil Perry from California, who was taken from his bedroom sometime during the night. The parents found the boy missing when they went to wake him up for school and noticed that the window over the garage had been forced open.

The Club goes right into action and gathers as much information as it can on the two stories. Again, the two children cannot be found, and there are no leads. An Amber Alert is put out on nearly all TV and radio stations, and in all the newspapers. It seems that the whole country is looking for these two children.

In the meantime, John is released from prison early because of good behavior. The first thing he wants to do after seeing his wife and son is meet up with Barney and Nick. To John's delight, Barney and Nick inform him that The Club is growing in an unbelievable manner. It is getting hundreds of e-mails from members offering all kinds of help, including money, the willingness to go to anywhere, and free legal help. Even the lawyers Barney and Nick, who successfully defended Tom Sweeney in his murder case against that animal Ray Thomas, who molested and killed his daughter, are offering their help again.

John feels that The Club is now taking on a life of its own, and this is what John was looking for to begin with. John now feels that if The Club keeps growing the way it is, it will fulfill his dream of getting the all-too-liberal laws changed against child molesters. Even though the laws are different in each state, John would like to have all the state laws against child molesters changed to a national law that would be the same all across the country.

"By the way," he says, "seeing that I have the two of you here now, I have something I want to talk to you guys about. I think it's time that we got some official office space, and I want the two of you to start looking for a place so that we will have a nice place to work instead of working on our computers from our home."

The two attorneys agree that it's a good idea, and start their search for an office.

In the meantime, there is a break in the case in California. It seems there is an eyewitness who saw a little boy fitting the missing boy's description with a man at a gas station at about 3 AM in the morning. The eyewitness took notice only because she thought it was kind of late for a small boy to still be up. So now, at least, the police have something to go on: the description of the car, the man, and the location.

An APB is put out for the car and driver. It's three days before the car is found, but there is no sign of the driver or the boy. The next day, the police get a tip from someone who saw the story and picture of the car in the newspaper. The tipster recognized the decal of a small boy playing ball on the rear side window, and remembers seeing it on a car that was always parked at a summer camp that her child attended. The police check out the camp and find out that they have photos of all their employees and parents for ID purposes.

The police have the eyewitness who saw the car in the gas station take a look at the photos, and she identifies one of the employees of the camp as the man she saw that night in the gas station. Unfortunately, the man does not work there anymore, but the police now have a name, address, and photo of the man. The police rush over to the man's address, but he does not live there anymore, and the landlord has no idea where he moved to.

An APB and Amber Alert are quickly put out for the man and the boy. Within hours, the man is spotted in a supermarket. The police rush over there and pick him up. His name is Don Frei, and he was a groundskeeper for the camp, but he claims he is not the man that they are looking for and that he knows nothing about a missing boy. The police also find out that the missing boy attended the same summer school, and upon further investigation of the man, the police now find out that he is a convicted child molester who jumped bail in Utah while waiting for trial to start. Now the authorities in Utah want him back to face the charges that he skipped out on, but the police want to keep him in California for their case.

✣✣✣

Detectives now want to question all the children at the camp, and their parents, to see if Don molested any of them or if any of the children complained to their parents or anyone about this man. After questioning all the children, the detectives come up with additional information that they could use against Don. It seems that Don offered some of the children money to touch them, but the children could not comprehend or remember why, and only two of them remember getting money, but they don't remember Don touching them.

Talking to the parents of the two children, the parents seem to remember the children coming home with money, but that the children said that they'd found it, and only one parent went to the school to enquire if anyone had reported losing any money. No one had, so the parent ended up accepting their child's story.

Then, two days later, a great story hits the news. It seems the police caught and arrested a man, David Mudd, as the one who kidnapped Betty Dickerson in Texas while she was walking home from school.

What happened was David kidnapped Betty and brought her to his home, where he locked her in his basement and repeatedly molested her, day after day. Miraculously, one day, while David was at work, Mary escaped. She went straight to the first policeman she saw and told him who she was and what had happened to her, and before anyone knew what was going on, detectives were at the home, staking it out, and waiting for David to come home. When he did, they arrested him. He was then brought to the police station for a lineup, and there the little girl identified him as her kidnapper and molester.

Unbeknownst to everyone, though, Betty's uncle, Paul Dickerson, was a police sergeant in the very precinct where they were bringing David to be booked, and while David was in an interrogation room getting ready to be booked, Mary's uncle, Sergeant Paul Dickerson, went into the room and said, "Hi, are you comfortable? Can I get you anything to drink or eat?"

"No, no, that's okay. I'm not hungry, and I'm not thirsty."

"So, just between the two of us, David, did you enjoy what you did to this little girl? 'Cause she's kind of hot, and I am into that stuff myself. So tell me before the other detectives get in here. I would like to know whole story."

David just looks at him and says, "Are you kidding me?"

"Paul says, "No. I would really like to know."

"Well, I really don't want to talk about it."

"No, you're finished talking about it, David. I just wanted to know if you enjoyed yourself and if you had a good time."

"I'd rather not answer that."

"Okay, David. There is just one other thing I want to say to you. David, you have molested your last child. Do you understand?"

"What do you mean?"

"I mean I know that you have molested your last child. Do you want to know how I know?"

"Yes."

"I know because I am about to kill you, you son of a bitch," and with that, Paul pulled out his service revolver and put a bullet in the middle of David's head, killing him instantly. Other officers, hearing the shot, rushed into the room, and as they did, Sergeant Dickerson turned to them, handed them his gun, extended out his hands, and said, "You can arrest me now. I have been waiting to meet this son of a bitch ever since he took my niece." The officers were stunned, but they read him his rights, arrested and booked him. The story of Paul hit the news media, and they were all over it. No one could believe that a police officer could do such a thing.

The Club again gets all kinds of e-mail about the case and all kinds of offers of help. John cannot be happier that another child molester is off the streets, and again, the lawyers Barney and Nick give John a call and offer their help in defending Paul. Even though they are not licensed to practice law in these different states, Barney and Nick will travel to the different states and enlist or hire lawyers to defend Paul. This time, John thinks that it would be a good idea for them to do that, because of their experience defending Tom on his murder case against the child molester, Ray Thomas, especially since Paul is a police officer, and there are a lot of people who would like to see a police officer hung out to dry for any reason. There are now at least twenty other lawyers in The Club, and some of them are allowed to practice in different states. They offer their help in defending Paul. John thinks that it would also be a good idea to have Barney and Nick work with two more lawyers from The Club to get the experience of working with club members.

John calls Barney and tells him that he would like for him and Nick to defend Paul, and to get in touch with Paul as soon as possible, before he lawyers up with the wrong lawyer. John explains to Barney that The Club will cover everything, including his bills.

Barney somehow gets a phone call to Paul, and because Paul is not a member of The Club, he is puzzled as to why a lawyer from another state, one whom he does not know, is calling him and offering to help him at no charge.Barney explains quickly what is going on, and he tells Paul he will explain everything in detail when they meet with him. Paul agrees to at least listen to them, so Barney and Nick get in touch with Mark and Dave, two other lawyers from The Club, and explain what is going on.

The four lawyers hop on the first flight to Texas to meet with Paul. When they get there and meet and explain everything to Paul, he is all in for it.

Barney calls John and lets him know that they met with Paul. Barney explains that Paul is all in, that it's a big relief for him and his family, and that Paul thinks that The Club is a great idea. Finally, Barney says that Paul also wanted to thank John for coming up with it and that Paul wants to join The Club.

Barney tells John that he hopes that there will be at least one member of The Club who will be one of the jurors and that he wishes that there was an easier way to tell them apart from the other jurors. John tells Barney that he was thinking about that and that he has come up with a great idea for The Club, one he would like to get it patented. He tells Barney that he will let him know when it will be available, because he still needs to finish the design. "It's a lapel pin that the members will wear at all times and will identify them as members. In the meantime, please get started on Paul's defense."

The Club logo is born

It's a lapel pin that symbolizes the fact that in unity, there is strength.

It will be patented and will only be available strictly from The Club.

It will easily identify other members of The Club to each other.

Members must promise to wear their pins at all times.

Members must also agree not to talk to anyone in public, including other members, about what the pins signify or what their purpose is.

The club logo

Barney tells Nick about the pins, and he is overjoyed with this news, because it will make their job a lot easier to recognize potential jurors. "Please let me know when they will be available," says Nick.

"You got it," says Barney. He calls John, who informs him, "The pins are being manufactured right now, as we speak, and will be sent out as soon as possible to all the current and new members, along with the pledge card that they must sign stating that they promise to wear the pin at all times. Barney calls Nick and informs him that the pins are currently being manufactured and will be available soon.

All the old members, along with the new members, get their pins and start wearing them at once. It seems that there is a great, silent feeling of pride with all the members that is hard not to see. Maybe it's the proud glances they give each other as they pass on the street, or the feeling that they are not the only ones that feel the way they do about child molesters.

John conducts a secret interview with one hundred members and finds that they are all excited about the pins, because now the members can see for themselves how strong The Club really is, and it gives them a lot more confidence knowing that if they do get on a jury, there is a good chance that there are going to be other members there with them, or if they get themselves in any kind of trouble involving a child molester, that The Club will be there to help them.

John hears on the news that a child molester who was let out of jail was killed in New York in a drive-by shooting and that the police are looking for two men in a white car. An eyewitness told police that he saw two men in a white car shoot the guy and speed off, but the witness did not know what kind of car it was, nor did he get a plate number.

Before John gets a chance to call Barney to give him the latest news, he hears about two more child molesters killed, one in New Mexico and another in California. John calls Barney, gives him the latest news about the other killings, and tells him that they are going to need more lawyers familiar with the way The Club works. He tells Barney, "You and Nick should get together with about ten lawyers who are members of The Club and work with them. We already have six, counting you and Nick, so ten more should be enough for now, and explain to them that if they are not licensed to practice in said state, to hire someone to defend said defendant with our help. The way things are going, we are going to need them."

The next day, John finds out that Don Frei, the man who was arrested and booked by the police in California as a suspect in connection with the missing nine-year boy, while being held awaiting his trial, was killed by another inmate, Tod Williams.

The little boy was never found, and now the authorities feel that with the death of Don Frei, they never will.

John gets in touch with Barney and Nick in Texas and fills them in on all that has happened. He tells them that they should leave the two new lawyers, Mark and Steve, there to defend Paul and that the two of them should fly to California and meet up with two other lawyers, Dan and Lou, and Tod Williams, the inmate accused of killing Don Frei.

Barney tells John that they will get on the first flight to California and leave Mark and Steve behind to defend Paul.

Mark and Steve, the new lawyers, start the jury selection for Paul's trial, and they feel very confident because they have noticed that one of the prospective jurors is wearing one of the pins from The Club, but they hope that the prosecuting attorney does not challenge her. They get their wish; the prosecuting attorney does not challenger her, and the trial starts.

The trial lasts two weeks. Mark and Steve do a great job in Paul's defense, bringing in many good witnesses for Paul, but now it's in the hands of the jury. They hope the one juror with the pin does what she is supposed to do.

The jury is out for two days, and finally, the verdict is in. In the courtroom, it's standing room only; there is someone there from every media outlet. The jury foreman reads the verdict: "We, the jury, find Paul Dickerson NOT GUILTY." Pandemonium breaks out in the courtroom.

Mark gets on the phone as soon as he can and calls John with the good news about Paul's verdict John is thrilled and tells them that they did great job.

Mark tells John that he wants to be the one to call Barney and Nick, to give them the great news about Paul's trial. John says, "I have no problem with that. Knock yourself out. And while you're at it, you can also tell Barney and Nick that in three days, The Club will be five years old, and as of today we have reached two million members and are still growing strong." John also tells Mark that he plans to use them to train ten lawyers, because of the other killings, and he says that he will be in touch with Mark and Steve as soon as he gets things set up.

John decides that because of the way things are going, The Club is going to need a place to set up the new headquarters. The Club has the money, and instead of lowering the dues, getting a common meeting place would help out a great deal. John calls Barney and asks him if he remembers what he said about the idea of a headquarters, and Barney says, Yes, I do remember, and I think that it is a great idea."

"Okay, then, let's start looking for a place immediately."

"You got it, John."

In the meantime, Mark and Steve call Barney and give him the great news about Paul's trial Barney tells Nick, and the two of them go wild, and even get a little emotional. Barney tells Mark and Steve, "We need to celebrate, because – and I know that I said this before, but now I really mean it – I think, that we are finally starting to move in the right direction,

Mark and Steve agree, and Mark says, "Yes, we finally are, and yes, this definitely calls for a celebration. We have to plan one as soon as possible."

A week later, John finds a building in New York to buy, and he jumps on it. He gets in touch with Barney and Nick and tells them that he wants them to go there and take care of all the legal matters pertaining to the purchase of the building, and also, he tells them to set the place up the way they think it should be set up, including a meeting room, a classroom, and offices for the four of them, but that they must wait there until Dan and Lou, the second set of new lawyers, get there and take over the defense of Tod Williams.

Barney and Nick meet with Dan and Lou in Texas to plan out the defense of Tod Williams, who happens to be not such a great guy. He's robbed people, broken into homes when no one was there, shoplifted, stolen cars, and bounced a few checks. The only thing he has not done, until now, is kill or injure anyone.

Barney meets with Tod and explains to him who he is, who sent him, and who is going to pay all the bills. As he talks to Tod, he asks a lot of questions. Finally, Barney asks Tod the most important question: "Why did you kill Don...?" To Barney's amusement and surprise, Tod tells him he is a card carrying member of The Club and that he did what he was supposed to do as a member.

Barney feels that because of the past record of this defendant, this case is going to end up being a landmark case and will surly set a precedent for similar cases, so even though he feels that Tod is not the pillar of his community whom he would prefer to defend, he feels that he still has to do all he can to make sure he gets Tod cleared of this murder for the sake of The Club. He thinks, *The primary goal of The Club is the safety of our children, and if we have to defend a few undesirable people along the way, well, we will just have to live with that. We cannot lose sight of our final goal, and that is getting the laws against child molesters changed. That's what this whole thing is about.*

Barney and Nick leave Texas and head back to New York to buy the building for the new headquarters, and they leave Dan and Lou in Texas to talk to as many people as they can. Dan and Lou try to get some sort of defense going, but they are finding it very hard, because Tod, well, he just is not a nice guy. Anyway, Dan and Lou forge on and do the best they can.

Finally, it's time to select the jurors. Dan and Lou are hoping against all odds that they will spot some pins, but after questioning many jurors, they have yet to see any. Then there it is: Dan and Lou spot a pin on a woman and sigh breaths of relief. Now, they think, if only the district attorney doesn't get rid of her, they have a shot. All of a sudden, out of nowhere, they spot at least three more jurors wearing pins. Dan and Lou are on cloud nine, and now feel that they have a lock on this trial.

Meanwhile, John hears about three more killings in Washington, Oklahoma, and Nevada. He also hears something that disturbs him, about a reporter on a Las Vegas newspaper writing a story about the killings and saying that it seems like, all of a sudden, it's open season on child molesters and there is more to it than meets the eye.

John has mixed emotions about the whole thing, because he feels that this is part of what he wants, that the media eventually see what's going on and make it a big enough story to point out to lawmakers what the members of The Club are up to, and that they are saying to the lawmakers, "Change the laws against the child molesters or we will take matters into our own hands and do it for you."

Two days later, the Las Vegas story hits the wire, and now a few more papers are running stories about it and trying to figure out what is going on and why is there such a sudden rash of killings of child molesters. John, not knowing who killed these child molesters, doesn't know if they are members; all he knows is that after checking, The Club does have members in all three states where the killings took place.

Two weeks go by, and the police have not arrested anyone in any of the three states where the killings took place. John is happy about that, but now John gets a call from a friend of his, who he tells John that he heard about two more killings of child molesters, one in Arizona and one in Wyoming. John checks and finds that The Club has members in those states also. Then John checks further and finds to his delight that The Club is now close to having several members in just about every single state in the U.S.

The next day, sure enough, all the media outlets, talk shows, newspapers, and TV news shows, are talking about the new killings, and they are all saying the same thing: Why, all of a sudden, is it open season on child molesters? What is going on? John calls Barney and Nick and tells them what's going on, and they tell him that they have heard all about it. Barney asks John, "Well, do you think that this is what we have been waiting for?"

John says, "I hope so, but I really wanted this to happen when we had more members, because the stronger we are, the better the chances we have of getting the laws changed. But at this point, there is nothing we can do now but hope for the best."

In the meantime, in Texas, during the jury selection for the Tod Williams trial, while the district attorney is questioning the second juror wearing a pin – and this is after letting the first juror wearing a pin pass – says to her, "I noticed that there are a few of you people wearing the same kind of pin. Is it some kind of club or something? What does that pin represent?"

"It's just a club."

"What kind of club?"

"It's just a club"

"I asked you, what kind of club?"

"I don't know, just a club."

"Okay, I will ask you one more time. What kind of club?"

With that question, the juror began to get nervous. "I don't have to tell you. It's just a club for women."

With that answer, Dan and Lou got very nervous and think to themselves, *Here it comes. It's about to hit the fan.*

Now smelling blood, the D.A. asks the judge to instruct the juror to answer the question. The judge does so.

"It's a club to protect our children," answers the juror.

When the D.A. hears that, it is as though the hair on the back of his neck stands up. Here he is, trying to prosecute a killer of a child molester, and here is a juror who belongs to a club that helps women protect children. It's like, these two things don't go together. Protect your children?"

he says. "Can you explain it a little better?"

"It gives woman ideas on how to protect our children."

"What kind of ideas? Give me an example."

"Well… like, don't talk to strangers."

"That's the best example you can give me?"

"Yes."

"Okay, let's move on." Then the D.A. stops and points to one of the men who is wearing a pin. "I thought you said that it's a club for woman. Then why is that man wearing a pin? Do they allow men in this club?"

"I guess so."

"You guess so? So you really don't know."

"No, I don't."

"Can you give me another example of the pointers that you get from this club? And do you attend meetings? If so, where do you meet? Juror…?"

"We don't meet. It's a website we go on."

At this point, Dan and Lou get very, very nervous, and they are holding their breath with every question.

Now the district attorney realizes that the judge gave each side only four challenges and that he has already used two of them. There are three more jurors with pins on that he can see, and he has already let one on the jury. This makes him think real hard as to what to do next. "Your Honor," he finally says, "I think something is very wrong here, and I would like to stop the jury selection. Normally in a murder case, I would be allowed more than four challenges, but for some reason, you only gave us four. Because I have already used up two of my four challenges, and there are three more prospective jurors that belong to the same club, I have a problem with that. I would like to have time to check this website out, and on top of it all, I have already approved one juror from this club to hear this trial. So, Your Honor, I think that it is imperative that you grant me the time to check it out."

Dan and Lou both jump up at the same time and object. Dan says, "Your Honor, this is ridiculous. I've never heard of such a thing."

"Your Honor, a man was killed before he had his day in court, and I feel that for justice to be served here, I should be given some time to check out this website to see who I am dealing with, because if this is what I think it is, and you allow these club members to get on the jury, this trial would serve to be nothing more than a mockery of the justice system."

"What kind of problem are you having with these jurors?"

"Your Honor, I would rather tell you in your chambers, rather than in front of the rest of the prospective jurors."

Dan and Lou object again. The judge shouts, "I heard your objection the first time. We are still talking about the same request, so sit down and give me time to think about this. We will take a brief recess, and I instruct the court officer not to let any of the prospective jurors leave the courtroom. Okay, I will now meet with both sides in my chambers."

Once they are all in the judge's chambers, he says to the D.A., "Okay, let me hear what your problem is with these jurors."

"Your Honor, I don't know if you are aware of the fact that the man I am prosecuting is accused of killing a known child molester, and lately, I am hearing and reading in the media that it's seems like it's open season on child molesters. Because of the answers that I'm getting from this juror who is a member of this club, I'm getting a strong feeling that this website may have something to do with it, and I would like to have some time to check it out. If my suspicions are correct, I would like to request that you dismiss this whole jury pool and start with a whole new group.

Dan objects, saying, "Your Honor, again, I say this is ridiculous. I have never heard of such a request."

"Well, I must say that, to me, this is a first, but I can see the point that the D.A. is making, and it is an important one. Okay, tell you what. I will give you until tomorrow morning to check out this website. At that time, I will hear your argument, but keep in mind that if you've heard about this open season thing on child molesters, these prospective jurors may have also heard about it, and as far as the man who was killed being a child molester, they may have read something about him also. I want to see the three of you in my chambers tomorrow morning at 9 AM sharp.

Back in the courtroom, the judge tells the jury pool that he is calling a recess until 9 AM tomorrow morning, and he instructs the prospective jurors not to talk to anyone about what went on in the courtroom today.

THE CLUB

We have a problem

Dan runs to the first phone he can find to call John, telling him, "We have a really big problem. I think the D.A. is on to us." He proceeds to tell John all that went on during the jury selection.

John tells Dan, "Well, it seems that the pin idea has backfired on us, and we need a new plan fast."

Dan says, "At this point, John, I don't know what to tell you. I will try to come up with something and get back to you."

"Okay, Dan, you do that, and in the meantime, I will give Barney and Nick a call, let them know what's going on, and see if they have any ideas on what we can do."

John calls Barney, brings him up to speed, and asks if he has any ideas.

"Well, I think the first thing we have to do is tell the members to stop wearing their pins during jury selection, and do that as fast as we can. But we can't do it with an e-mail, because when the D.A. checks out the website, it will really tip our hand and possibly implicate us in these killings. It can't seem like we are actually telling the members exactly what to do. It's supposed to look like the members are doing this on their own."

John agrees. "Then what about sending all members a letter in the mail?"

Barney says, "That would be just as bad as an e-mail, maybe even worse. I think at this point the only thing we can do is keep on doing what we have been doing, and that is to just suggest something in the 'Wouldn't It Be Nice' segment. First, we wait until the story hits the papers, and it will, even if we have to help it. Then we say in the 'What's New' part of the newsletter that The Club heard about what was going on in the Tod Williams jury selection phase, and say that it's a shame that the D.A. is accusing the members of being up to something no good. Then suggest in the 'Wouldn't It Be Nice' segment of the web page that if the members are being harassed during jury selection because of the pins they are wearing, then maybe they shouldn't wear them during jury selection."

John tells Barney, "That sounds like a good plan. I'm calling our webmaster as soon as I get off the phone with you, and I'll tell him to start putting something together. Then we have to sit back and wait until it hits the fan."

At the same time, the district attorney heads straight back to his office and goes on the website, but in order to see and read the monthly newsletter, he has to join The Club, so he does just that. When he gets on and starts reading the newsletter, the first thing that hits him is the part about the wearing of the pins, that before they accept you as a member, you have to agree to wear the pin all the time. This gets his suspicions aroused about what he thought, that something was going on with the pins that these jurors were wearing. Then, when he gets to the "Wouldn't It Be Nice" segment, he can't believe what he is reading.

He says to himself, *I knew it! This is the proof I need. This is what all the media is talking about. These people are actually telling their members to go out and kill child molesters and not to worry about it, that The Club will protect them. Oh my God, I can't believe what I'm reading. It's like what the media is saying: it's open season on child molesters. I can't believe that they thought that they could get away with this. I can't wait until tomorrow with this news. I have to try to see the judge tonight, because, now, this case has taken on a whole new path.*

He prints out a copy and tries to get a hold of the judge to arrange a meeting with him ASAP, but when he does get in touch with the judge, the judge tells the him that whatever it is, it can wait until morning, that he is too busy to meet with him tonight. The D.A. insists and tries to tell the judge how important it is that he talk to him tonight, but to no avail; the judge tells him that he will see him in the morning.

The next day, Dan, Lou, and the D.A. are all in the judge's chambers at 9 AM sharp.

"Okay, Mr. D.A.," says the judge, "let's see what was so important that you wanted to see me last night."

"Your Honor, yesterday I said that I had a problem with some of the jurors, the ones who were wearing the same pins, and I'm sure when you see what I have, it will convince you that I had just cause to worry." The D.A. hands the judge the papers that he printed out from the web site, and he says, "Your Honor, I'm sure this will shock you as much as it shocked me, and back up the suspicions that I had."

The judge takes a long time to read all the papers. Finally, he says, "Okay, I have read all these papers, and what exactly are you accusing this website of doing?"

"Your Honor, it's about what all the media is talking about, about the fact that it seems like open season on child molesters. This website has something called 'Wouldn't It Be Nice.' This column is telling its members to go out and kill a child molester, and to not worry if they get caught, because The Club will probably have a member on the jury that will acquit them. They wear the pins to identify each other. Your Honor, I had to join to get all this information. I'm telling you, Your Honor, this club is out to kill all the child molesters in the country. God only knows how many members there are or how long they have been in existence. We have to shut them down and prosecute the founders of The Club and its members for murder."

✸✸✸

First," replies the judge, "if there is any wrongdoing here, I will be the one to decide that, and frankly, I do not see any wrongdoing here, least-ways, nothing that you can prove."

"Your Honor, you got to be kidding me. These people are guilty as sin. They know exactly what they are going to do before they even get on a jury. You must do something, or I will talk to another judge to confiscate their computers and records and charge them all with murder."

"First, you don't talk to me that way, or I will hold you in contempt. Second, I'm not kidding. Like I said before, I see no wrongdoing here, and if you want to talk to another judge, be my guest. The only thing I see these people doing is trying to educate people on protecting their children, and in the 'Wouldn't It Be Nice' segment that you speak of, all I see is a wish list, and everybody has a wish list. Don't you? Haven't you ever read about a heinous crime and said someone should kill that person? And if the person sitting next to you hears you and then goes out and kills that person, should they arrest you for wishing that, or should they arrest the person that did the killing? The members are all grown up people, with minds of their own, and are able to read anything they want into that wish list. If a member decides that after reading the 'Wouldn't It Be Nice segment, it's telling them to go out and kill a child molester, then it's the one who kills the child molester who should be arrested and tried for the crime. So, now, this meeting is over, and we should all go back to the courtroom.

Back in the courtroom, as the jury selection continues, the D.A. asks the judge if he can make a statement. The judge tells him, "Okay, make your statement."

"Thank you, Your Honor. I want the record to show that I am asking to preserve the record for the purpose of a possible appeal."

The judge says, "So noted. Let the record show that. Now let's get on with the jury selection."

The D.A. calls the juror that he was questioning the day before, when this all started. "Okay, let's get back to the question I asked you about the club that you belong to." As he asks the question, he notices that she is not wearing the pin. He says, "Wait a minute; where is the pin that you were wearing yesterday?"

"What pin?"

"The pin that you and several other jurors were wearing." The D.A. turns and points to the rest of the jury pool, and as he looks around, he notices that none of the jurors are wearing the pins any more. "Okay, I see what is going on here, but let me say this: it's too late to hide what's going on, and you and your cohorts are going to be held responsible for your actions."

Dan and Lou are just about to say something when the judge says, "Mr. District Attorney, you are coercing this juror. She is not on trial here. I'm telling you to stop with this line of questioning right now and get on with the normal line of questioning, and if I have to tell you again, I will hold you in contempt."

The D.A., not knowing what to do next, and without the pins being worn, has no idea who is a member or not. He just says, "Your Honor, I challenge this juror. I do not want her on the jury."

The judge tells the juror, "Okay, you're free to go, and thank you for your time."

❧❧❧

Now it's Dan and Lou's turn to question the next juror, but without the pins, they too are working in the dark, and they don't remember who was wearing the pins yesterday. Also, they don't want to ask the wrong questions so as to give the D.A. a hint as to whether or not they are questioning a member of The Club. So Dan and Lou go on and question the jurors in the normal way, with the knowledge that they have at least one juror already on the jury.

The D.A. is working in the dark, and according to the judge's instructions, he's not even able to question any of the jurors about his theory of what the pins and The Club represent, but he tries the best he can to get rid of any of The Club's suspected members with whatever questions he can ask.

Finally, the jury is selected, and the trial is set to start in the morning.

Dan and Lou rush to call John and tell him what happened with the jury selection and the fact that the members of The Club, because of what happened the day before, took it upon themselves not to wear the pins during the rest of the jury selection. That also left the two defense attorneys to work in the dark, but they are still happy with the fact that they have at least one member on the jury, if not more.

John says, "That is great news. You did a good job, but we still have to come up with a way of letting the members know what happened and to tell them not to wear their pins during the jury selection of a trial."

John calls Barney to give him the good news.

Barney says, "Wow, that is great news, and it also gives me a great idea about how we can tell the members not to wear their pins if they are

51

ever being picked for a jury. What we will do is, in the next letter on our website, in the section where we talk about the outcome or progress of child molestation trials, we put this story in it explaining how The Club members that were wearing their pins during the jury selection process were harassed, and that they decided on their own to take them off and not to wear them. Hopefully, the members reading the newsletter will read between the lines and get the message we are sending about not wearing the pins during jury selection."

John tells Barney, "That sounds like a great idea, because the pin idea that seemed great at the time has backfired on us, as far as the jury selection part goes. But I think it's still a good idea for the support and morale of the members."

Barney and Nick agree, because at this point, with the number of members in The Club nearing the three million mark, they can afford to take a chance and gamble on one of the prospective jurors being a member, rather than try to devise a scheme to identify a member and tip their hand to the D.A.

The Tod Williams trial starts

The trial starts, and both sides are ready to do battle. The D.A. knows what he is up against, and Dan and Lou know that this is a very important trial, because no matter the outcome, the D.A. is going to do all in his power to make sure that somebody in the right place hears his story and tries to blow the lid off what they are doing, especially if they win the case.

Dan tells Lou, "I wish we had more time to get more members. Right now, there are about three million members, and I would have liked to have had about five million before the lid came off, because that would give us a stronger hand dealing with the lawmakers."

Five days into the trial, both sides are pulling out all the stops. The D.A. is getting frustrated, because he can't bring up what's going on with the website. Every time he brings up anything about the pins, Dan or Lou object, and the judge grants the objection, admonishes the D.A. about going there, and threatens him with a contempt of court charge. Finally, both sides give their summations and hand it over to the jury. The jury is out for three days before they reach a decision.

As the jury enters the courtroom, it is standing room only; the court-room is packed with spectators and journalists from every form of news media.

The judge asks the jury foreman, "Has the jury reached a decision?"

The jury foreman answers, "Yes we have, Your Honor."

The judge asks how the jury finds the defendant.

"We, the jury, find the defendant NOT GUILTY."

53

The courtroom explodes with hoorays, boos, hand clapping, crying, laughing, and yelling; you name it, and it was going on in that courtroom.

As Dan and Lou are congratulating each other, along with Tod Williams, the D.A. comes over to them and says, "This is only the beginning. The two of you just helped free a murderer, and I would not be celebrating too much if I were you. I promise you this: you will be hearing from me."

Dan gets to the first phone he can find to call John, and gives him the good news. John is delighted, to say the least, but not too happy with what the D.A. said to Dan and Lou.

John now feels that this whole thing is getting closer to their objective, which was the original plan to begin with, and that was to bring the all-too-lenient laws pertaining to child molesters now on the books to the attention of the lawmakers to make needed changes, and he hopes that everyone in The Club is ready for it.

John calls Barney, fills him in on what is going on, and tells him that he thinks it's about to hit the fan and that it may be a good time to get together to make some sort of a defense plan. He tells Barney to get in touch with Nick and tell him that he would like the two of them to come to his office tomorrow morning. The next morning John, Barney, and Nick all meet and try to put something together, against what, at this point, they don't know, but they feel that they should come up with some kind of basic defense and take it from there.

John tells them, "You know what? Why don't you ask Don and Lou to join us tomorrow morning, and maybe between the five of us, we can come up with something."

Barney and Nick agree. Barney says, "Okay, I will get in touch with them and let them know to be here tomorrow morning."

"Okay, great."

The next morning, they all meet and try to put together some kind of plan. But even though there are five of them, they can't seem to come up with anything, because they just don't know what to plan for, so they all agree to just wait until they have something to work with.

In the meantime, John hears about two more cases of a child molesters getting murdered and the defendants getting off. John is amazed at this, because The Club, as far as he knows, had nothing to do with it. John checks into the two cases, which took place in Kentucky and Utah, and discovers that The Club has members in those states, but he can't say for sure if they had a hand in it.

Three weeks go by with nothing going on. John feels that they may have more time then they think they have before all hell breaks loose, and that maybe the D.A. can't do anything.

The district attorney, Philip Morrison, who was outraged by the decision of the jury to find Tod Williams not guilty, and also the actions of the presiding judge in that case, Judge Tony Ghetto, too outlandish to let go by unanswered, starts looking for a judge to side with him and get the website closed down and prosecute the guilty parties. In his search, he calls in every favor from anyone he has ever helped in the past, leaving messages for those he wasn't able to talk to, hoping for a callback.

Two days later, he gets a call from a friend of his about the message he left on his answering machine. It's a buddy he went to law school with, Larry Reynolds. "Phillip, how are you doing? Long time no see."

"Yes, I know, but I have been really busy with my D.A. work. They keep me busy. Anyway, Larry, not to cut you short, but I hope you're calling to tell me that you can help."

"As a matter of fact, I am. I have been reading the papers about what is going on with all these killings of child molesters, and I was talking to a judge friend of mine, Judge Oswald Tunis, about it, and he and I are outraged about the whole thing. I think he is looking to do something, and if you need someone to help you, I think he's your man. I can give him a call, and I'm sure he can help you out."

"Oh, that would be great!"

"Okay, I will call him, and if he can help, I will ask him to get back to you."

"Larry, I will owe you big time for this one."

"Don't worry. What are friends for, if not to help each other out?"

"Okay, Larry, thanks again, and I will be waiting and hoping for a call from him."

The next day, Phillip gets the call he is waiting for.

"Hi, is this Phillip?"

"Yes."

"Hi, Phillip, this is Judge Oswald Tunis. Larry Reynolds asked me to give you a call regarding what has been going on with the killings of child molesters and this website."

"Yes, Judge, I prosecuted a case of a suspect who killed a child molester while they were locked up together in the same cell. It should have been an open and shut case. Instead, the jury acquitted him. I'm sure it had a lot to do with a few jurors who belong to this club, which has its own website. It's basically telling its members to go out and kill child molesters and that the club will have their backs and will defend them free of charge. Your Honor, I went on that website, and it has this newsletter that advocates the killing of child molesters, and it tells its members that they will have an excellent chance of getting away with it. Because there are so many members, they stand a very good chance of getting one or more members on the jury and acquitting them."

"Well, you know what, Phillip? Oddly enough I have sort of been following this story ever since I saw another story about someone calling for open season on child molesters. After Larry called me and told me what was going on, I went on that website. I had to join to get the full scoop, and you are absolutely right about the newsletter advocating the killing of child molesters and telling people that they will have a very good chance of getting away with it. Tell you what, Phillip. I'm on your side. You get the paperwork started, and I will sign a court order for you to have all their computers and files confiscated, and to lock up the ones who are running that website. Then you can prosecute them, and we will see how sure they are of things turning out the way they think they will."

Phillip wastes no time in getting the paperwork started and getting it signed by Judge Tunis, and seeing that these killings are being committed all over the country, across state lines, the FBI gets involved with serving the court order, confiscating the website's computers and files, and arresting the owners.

Then, just when John is feeling good about the whole thing, his secretary comes in and tells him, "There are some men here from the FBI, and they want to talk to you."

Unnoticed by John's secretary, the FBI agents have followed her right into John's office, giving him no time to do anything, and before he knows what is happening, there were three FBI agents in his office.

One of the agents tells John, as he hands him a court order signed by a Judge Tunis, that they are there to seize all of his computers and files and to shut the website down immediately. They read him his rights and inform him that he is being arrested and will be held for questioning.

As they put the cuffs on him, John asks if he can call his attorney. They tell him that he can do that when they get him downtown to their headquarters. They ask him if there are any other computers and or files anywhere else in the building. John tells them no.

More agents, who were waiting outside, are called in, and armed with empty boxes and hand trucks, they start to dismantle the computers in all three offices: John's, Barney's, and Nick's, and also the secretary's.

As John is led away, he is really upset with himself, because now he realizes what kind of plan they should have come up with, that being to get rid of all the computers and files and store them in a different building. Then they would have had time for someone to go there and get rid of the files and clean out the computers. Instead, now he feels that he has handed over everything to the feds on a silver platter.

John tells his secretary, "Call Mike Santino, my personal attorney, the one who helped set up the website, to see if he can get me bailed out. Also, call Barney and let him know what's going on."

Before John is out the door, his secretary gets a hold of Mike and fills him in on what's going on. Mike tells her, that he will get on it right away, not to worry. "I don't know what they think that they are doing, but they can't do this. There is nothing illegal going on with the website." Mike tells her that he can't do anything until John is arraigned, to see if he can be bailed out and how much it will cost, that she should just sit tight and wait, that he is on top of it. Next, she calls Barney, fills him in, and tells him what Mike said.

Barney gets Nick on his cell, fills him in on the goings on with the FBI, and tells him that he agrees with Mike. Nick also feels the same way, that they don't have the right to just go in and do all that.

Barney tells Nick, "I think the first thing we have to do is get together with Mike. Then we should maybe get in touch with the judge from the Tod Williams trial to see if he can help us out, because it seemed like he was sympathetic to our cause."

Barney gets in touch with Mike, and he agrees to meet in Mike's office tomorrow at noon and discuss what to do next.

When all three meet, Barney fills Mike in on what went on in the Tod Williams case with Judge Tony Ghetto. Mike also feels that it would be a good idea to get in touch with the judge, and he suggests that they all meet for lunch. Mike gets the judge's phone number, calls him, explains to him that he would like to treat him to lunch and see if he could help them out. The judge agrees to meet with Mike.

The next day, all three meet with Judge Ghetto and explain the situation to him. To their amazement, the judge tells them that he is a non-card-carrying member of The Club. "The reason I did not join should be obvious. I feel that the present laws against child molesters are outdated and inadequate, and even though I don't condone murder, I feel that somebody, somehow, has to bring this to the attention of the lawmakers of each state, and possibly try to make it a national law across this country. Although it seems like medieval or barbaric tactics, I still feel that something has to be done, and all the legal protesting people have done in the past seems to have gone unseen, or has fallen on deaf ears, and all their effort has produced absolutely nothing. So maybe this tactic will work.

"As far as the child molesters are concerned, not to be callous or without empathy, I have no remorse for them, because I feel that they are broken machines that cannot be repaired, which has been proven time after time. They must be discarded, just as you would a broken machine.

"I will give you all the help and guidance I can, short of putting my signature on anything, again, because of the obvious. It would be better if I stayed in the background, behind the scenes.

"Your first step should be, as soon as possible, to get yourself to an appellate court to override the court order that Judge Tunis signed and the FBI executed. The judge who signed that court order had no right to do that. There was not enough evidence. I went on the website and read every single word, and although you are skating on thin ice, there is nothing there to warrant what that judge did."

Three days later, John is finally arraigned, and his bail is set at $50,000. Mike calls Barney and informs him that he does not have that kind of money. Barney says not to worry. The Club will put up the money. He makes arraignments to meet Mike later that day with the money. They meet, Mike gets the money, and then Mike goes to the jail to bail John out. John's trial is set for next month. Mike tells John that by then, all charges should be dropped.

John can't believe that the closing of his website is still in the news. It's in the news media like nothing ever before. It seems like everyone was waiting around for something big to happen, and this was it.

It's the biggest thing to hit since the Son of Sam and Ted Bundy killings.

It's unbelievable. All the headlines are saying the same thing, that a website is calling for open season on child molesters, and everyone who is anybody is on TV, radio, and in newspaper editorials and articles, putting in their two cents worth of commentary on the subject. Some are agreeing with it, and some are condemning it. All the talk is going from one end of the spectrum to the other, even though no one knows all the facts on why this all started.

Meanwhile, first thing in the morning, when Barney and Mike get to the steps of the appellate court house, and while trying to file the documents needed for the court to hear arguments to override Judge Tunis's court order that the FBI served and executed the day before on John, they find themselves surrounded by twenty reporters who somehow found out who they were and what they were doing there. The reporters ask them a thousand questions, and Barney and Mike keep answering with, "No comment."

Barney and Mike finally get past the reporters and submit their brief asking for a hearing and a ruling posthaste. For some reason, it appears to Barney and Mike that the courthouse clerks knew that they were coming. They can't put their finger on it, but something is definitely wrong. The clerk takes the brief, tells them to wait, and says that she will check to see how soon they can set up a hearing with a judge to hear their arguments and make a ruling. It takes fifteen minutes for the clerk to get back to them. She tells Barney and Mike that the first open date available for a judge to hear their argument will be in thirty days.

Barney and Mike cannot believe what they are hearing. Thirty days is a ridiculous amount of time to wait, especially when they asked for a hearing posthaste. Mike pleads with the clerk to double-check, and maybe even talk to a judge to see if they can get an earlier date.

The clerk says, "I don't think so, but I will try."

Another fifteen minutes goes by before the clerk comes back. She says, "Sorry, but there was nothing I could do. I even spoke to a judge, and the judge said that you were lucky to get a date as early as you did."

Getting nowhere at the courthouse, Barney and Mike decide to leave, go back to Mike's office, and try to come up with something. At Mike's office, they decide it's time to talk to Judge Tony Ghetto again, to see if he has any ideas on what to do next, because if they have to wait thirty days to get a hearing, it will put a huge hole, to say the least, in what The Club is trying to accomplish. Barney call's Judge Ghetto and sets up a lunch date that afternoon with him and Mike.

At lunch, Barney and Mike fill the judge in on what went on at the appellate courthouse that morning. The judge tells them that he will make a few phone calls and try to find out if anything funny is going on, and see what they can do next. He tells them that he will get back to them later today.

The judge calls Barney later that day and tells him that their feelings about the courthouse clerk was right. In fact, there is something funny going on there. The judge tells Barney, "After making a few calls, I found out that the D.A. from the Tod Williams trial just happens to have his uncle working in that courthouse, who just happens to be an appellate judge there, Judge Oswald Tunis. So, my thinking is that the D.A. took a guess that your next step would be to go to the appellate court, and he called his Uncle Tunis and asked him to give you a hard time and, if he could, to stop you altogether. Right now, you guys are between a rock and a hard place, and there is not much you can do. Let me make a few more calls and see if I can come up with something, and I will get back to you as soon as I can."

Several days pass without hearing from the judge. Finally, he calls Barney and tells him, "It seems that the D.A.'s uncle is the leading judge over there, and no matter what, he is determined to sit and hear your appeal, and I don't have to tell you what that means. So the only thing I can think of right now would be to try to take it to the New York State Supreme Court and see if they will hear your appeal sooner, and hope that Judge Tunis doesn't have a friend over there."

The next day, Barney and Mike are at the New York State Supreme Court, submitting their brief to try to get a hearing sooner than thirty days. The clerk accepts the paperwork and tells them that after looking at their brief, someone will be in touch with them to let them know if they will hear their appeal.

Eight days later, Barney finally gets a phone call from the New York State Supreme Court telling him that the court will not accept their brief and, therefore, will not be hearing their appeal, on the grounds that thirty days in this case is not considered a hardship for anyone.

Barney and Mike now think that they are getting paranoid, or that Judge Tunis may know more people then they realize. While Barney and Mike try to come up with something to do, they get a call from John. He tells them that he heard on the TV that in the past three weeks, there have been five more killings of known child molesters across the country, and that three more of the suspected killers were already tried and found not guilty.

John has no idea of how any of this happened, and he tells Barney, "I don't even know if any of the suspects or jurors are members of The Club. I think that with all the news about The Club, people may just be going out and doing this without bothering to join, knowing that they will get away with it. Also, without our computers, we have no idea if any of the people involved were members."

Barney tells John, "Well, we still have to figure out a way to get those files and computers back, especially now, with all this happening, because if this thing blows up altogether and does not end the way we want it to end, a lot of people will be in trouble. Somehow, we have to get control of how this thing will end to protect children and all the members, because while all this is going on, there are children still being molested and killed as we speak. It seems like just about every week you read about another child being molested or killed. You would think that with all the publicity this thing is getting about the fact that it seems like open season on child molesters, they would heed the warning and stop what they are doing, but they don't. This is just more proof that they can't be healed or rehabilitated and that, in fact, what we are trying to do is the right thing."

John tells Barney to get together with all the other lawyers and try their best to come up with something.

The next morning, out of the blue, John gets a call from Judge Ghetto.

"Good morning, John. How are you today? Guess who I had lunch with."

"I have no idea, Judge."

"Well, then, I'm going to tell you. Yesterday, I had lunch with a New York Senator, and it turns out that he is on your side and that he may be able to help you get a judge to overturn the court order from Judge Tunis and get your computers and files back.

"Oh my God, that would be great if he can do that."

"I figured that you would like that. So, for the time being, just sit tight, and I will get back to you."

John turns around and calls Barney to give him the news about the call he got from Judge Ghetto and about the fact that the judge met with a New York Senator. "He may be able to get a judge to help us out and get our stuff back."

Barney says, "I can't wait to let Nick and the rest the lawyers know what's going on."

Two days pass with no call from Judge Ghetto, and John, Barney, and Nick are going crazy thinking about nothing but the files and computers that the FBI have and what they are doing with them.

Finally, John gets the call he has been waiting for from Judge Ghetto. The judge tells John, "The Senator I was talking about knows Judge Alex Mohan, from the New York State Supreme Court, who will help us out. Have your attorneys draw up the necessary paperwork for the judge to sign."

John wastes no time. He tells the judge, "Thank you, thank you, thank you," hangs up and calls Barney, telling him what happened and to get on it ASAP.

Barney calls Nick, fills him in, and tells him to get down to the office right now. Barney and Nick fill out the papers, hop in the car, and head out to get the paperwork signed. When they meet up with Judge Mohan, he signs the paperwork and issues a new court order overturning the original court order that took their computers and files and shut down their website. He also orders that all the computers and files be returned immediately, that the website be reopened immediately, and that all information obtained from the files and computers cannot be used, that it must be destroyed or turned over to The Club. Barney and Nick are also delighted to find out that the judge supports what they are trying to do. He tells them, "If I can be of any other assistance, please let me know."

Barney immediately rushes down to the FBI building and presents them with the new court order while Nick goes to rent a truck and get some help. In no time, Nick and some help meet Barney with the truck at the FBI headquarters.

The FBI agents stall and take their time, telling Barney and Nick that the files and computers are all over the place, being worked on, but in time, and reluctantly, they start giving them the computers and files. While this is going on, the lead agent calls Judge Tunis and lets him know what's going on. The judge goes wild and says, "I will be right down there. Don't give them anything until I get there. I want to see that court order myself, and see what court it came from and what judge signed it."

The agent tells the judge, "We already started giving them the stuff back, but don't worry. I will stall them until you get here." He goes to Barney and Nick and says, "Look, you've got to give us time to locate all your stuff and get it together for you. Your stuff is all over the building."

Barney tells the lead agent, "Please hurry. I need my things as soon as possible, and remember, this court order was signed by a New York State Supreme Court Justice."

The lead agent tells him, "I don't care what you want. I said that I need some more time to find your things, so just keep your shirt on, and I will get them as fast as I can. And I don't care who the hell the judge is who signed that court order. My men and I can only work so fast."

"You know what?" says Barney. "If you don't comply with this court order I have, and hinder me in any way, you definitely will have a problem with me, and I will see you in court answering charges of obstruction."

"Like I said, it will only be a few more minutes. Why can't you just have a little patience and wait?"

Barney tells him, "I have waited too long already, so start giving me the rest of my stuff, or I will call my office and have them start drawing up the obstruction papers against you."

"Okay, I'll give you all your stuff."

THE CLUB

Taking back their stuff

Barney and Nick, along with the help that Nick brought, start loading everything. Halfway through the loading, Judge Tunis shows up and demands that they stop, and he wants to see the court order. Barney explains to the judge, "Your Honor, with all due respect, I will show you the court order, but I will not stop loading my stuff, and you can't stop me."

Barney shows the judge the court order, and Judge Tunis reads it, throws it back at Barney, and storms out, saying, "This is not over yet, not by a long shot."

They bring everything back to headquarters and start setting it all back up as they take inventory to make sure that they got everything back.

In the meantime, John gets on the phone with his webmaster, explaining to him what happened and to get the site up and running again as soon as possible.

John, along with Barney and Nick, start working on the "Wouldn't It Be Nice" letter to give to the webmaster. They want to make sure that they let the members know all that went on and that The Club won and got everything back and is back on track again.

Several weeks go by, and it seems like there is not much interest in people joining The Club. John attributes this to the fact that the website was off the net for the past month, and he hopes that now that the site is up again, enrollment will pick up.

John hears about two more killings of child molesters out west, one in Texas and one in New Mexico. John gets in touch with Barney. "Hi, did you hear what's going on in Texas and Mexico? There were two more child molesters killed, and you need to assign a couple of lawyers in case anyone gets picked up for the killings and needs defense."

Two days later, a man is picked up in Texas for one of the killings and is charged with murder. Barney calls Nick. "Hi. Please do me a favor and pick one of the teams of lawyers that you have ready and fly to Texas with them to set up a defense for this guy." Nick tells Barney that he will get right on it. At this point, all the lawyers in The Club have set up a list of all the lawyers they know from other states, so they go and check the list, and sure enough, two of the lawyers know several lawyers in Texas, so Nick picks those two lawyers to go to Texas.

The next day, all three get on the first plane to Texas and meet up with the suspect. Then Nick and the other two lawyers are shocked to hear from the suspect, that he doesn't need a lawyer from The Club, that he already has one, whose name is Salvatore Whine.

Nick tries to explain to the suspect where he's from and the special kind of defense work that he does, but the defendant tells Nick, "Yeah, that's the kind of lawyer I have."

Nick gets the address of the lawyer, goes to see him, and explains to him who he is and what he was there for. To Nick's amazement, the lawyer tells Nick that they have their own sort of club going on right there in Texas, about 300 strong, and that all of the members volunteer their services to defend those who've gotten themselves in trouble. "If need be, we all donate to help out with the expenses, and the members include people from all walks of life, regular people, lawyers, doctors, we even have a few judges, but most of the professional people are not members, for obvious reasons. It's nice that you came here to help, but you can go back home and be assured that everything will be okay here. We are self-sufficient, and in the event we do need help, be assured that we will ask for it.

"And by the way, I have a few lawyer friends in other states, Wyoming and Nebraska, and they also have their own group of people there, and they are also self-sufficient. I guess you people don't realize what you have started. The groups I told you about, I know exist, but I hear that there are other groups all over the country that are doing the same thing. But again, be assured that if any of us should need any help at all, we will not hesitate to get in touch with you guys."

Nick can't wait to get back to New York to fill John in on what's going on in the country. He still can't believe the words that he heard coming out of that lawyer's mouth, and he suspects neither will John. Nick lands in New York and wastes no time getting to the office to talk. As Nick is walking into John's office, he says to John, "Do I have an earful for you." He sits down and says to John, "Are you ready for this?"

John says, "So, tell me already."

"Well, when I got to Texas, the first thing I did was to go see this guy, and he asked me what I was doing there and who I was. I explained to him that I was a lawyer and that I was there to defend him. He tells me that he already has a lawyer, named Salvatore Whine, to defend him. I said to him, 'I'm from a special website called The Club, and we specialize in defending people like you.' He says, 'Yes, that's the kind of lawyer I have,' so I said, 'Okay, can you give me his name and address so that I can get in touch with him?' and he does that, so I went to see him." With that, Nick fills John in on all that happened, and Nick was right; John can't believe what he's hearing.

John doesn't know what to make of it, or what he should try to do about it, if anything. He feels like he set a baby monster loose, and now that monster has grown up and is uncontrollable, and can cause havoc all over the country if not working in unison. John has an uneasy feeling about this. He doesn't like not having control of the whole situation, and he feels that if he doesn't have total control, it could really get out of hand. "My God, what have I started? I never envisioned anything like this happening. Could people start taking the law into their hands for other reasons?"

Nick tells John, "Now, don't go off the deep end. Let's get in touch with Barney. All three of us will sit down and think about this. We have overcome adversity before, and we can do it again.

Nick calls Barney and tells him to get to the office as soon as possible. "Something has come up."

Barney asks Nick, "What's this all about?"

"It's too much to talk about over the phone. Just get here."

"I hope this is as good or as important as you are making it out to be."

"Just get here. The three of us have to sit down and talk."

"Okay, I will be right there."

When Barney gets to the office, Nick and John explain everything to him, and all three agree that something must be done about this, but just what and how is a mystery to them. All they know is that they have to come up with something.

John tells Barney and Nick, "Go home and think long and hard about solving this problem, and be back first thing in the morning with a solution. I will do the same, and no matter what, none of us will leave my office tomorrow until we have a solution."

The next day, hours go by, and it's nighttime before they come up with a plan. It's not the plan to end all plans, but nevertheless, it's a plan. John sums it up for everyone: "The plan is for Barney and Nick to go back to Texas and talk to Salvatore Whine, the lawyer defending the man who was arrested for killing a child molester there, to find out more of what their goals are and to see if their goals are the same as ours and if they are on the same track as us, or if they are on a different train altogether, going to a completely different place. All this information is important because, if their goals are different from ours, it would undermine all that The Club has done so far."

When Barney and Nick get to Texas, they get in touch with Salvatore to set up a meeting, explain the importance of this meeting, and ask if he can get all the lawyers in his group to attend the meeting. Salvatore agrees to this, and the meeting is set up for the first thing next morning.

In the meantime, while all this is going on in Texas with Barney and Nick, Judge Tunis is busy trying to get someone to listen to him. He puts a call in to a big shot lawyer friend of his in Washington, Larry Rockwood, who is also the district attorney there, and explains to him what he has discovered about what is going on with all the killings of child molesters.

Judge Tunis tells Larry, "You've got to help me out here. I'm telling you these people are out to kill all the child molesters in the world, and if someone doesn't stop them, they will succeed in doing just that. In fact, if you don't believe me, go onto their website, because it is now up and running again, and check it out."

Judge Tunis is surprised to find out that his friend may indeed know someone who can help him, as Larry says, "Okay, Judge, let me check it out, and if I also think that there is something funny going on, I will get in touch with a Senator I know and fill him in on the story."

Back in Texas, Barney and Nick are in Salvatore Whine's office at 9 AM sharp for the meeting they set up with him and the rest of the lawyers in his group. Once all the lawyers are there, Barney tells them, "First of all, I want to thank you for taking the time out of your busy schedules and meeting with Nick and me. We are here to sort of read your minds and to get an idea of what your goals are, to see if we are all heading in the same direction, and if we can all work together toward the same goal. We also want to explain why The Club exists and why it was started, because most people don't know why.

"John Harrison started this whole thing back in June of 2005. It was because of the fact that his daughter was abducted from a fast food restaurant playground. She was beaten, raped, and we believe that she was buried alive and left to die a horrible death. The body was never found, and this was done by a known child molester who was let out of prison early because of the prison being overpopulated. He was basically allowed to live and do anything he wanted so long as he got a job, did not move out of the state, and reported to his parole officer once a month.

"But remember, going to prison for his first offense of child molestation did not cure or rehabilitate him in any way, shape, or form, or stop him from doing what he did when he got out, and that was the taking of a little sixteen-year-old Wendy's life in a most horrible way. To this day, he still lives, and no one knows where he is. For all we know, he may have done it again, or is planning to do it again.

"What we are doing is trying to save the lives of children all over the country. The Club has interviewed dozens of psychologists to see if there is any evidence that child molesters can be cured, and ninety-five percent agree that they can't. Even a lot of the child molesters themselves agree that they can't be cured and must be put away for life, or executed if the child is killed in the process. But under no circumstances should they be let out once caught, tried, and convicted.

"This meeting is very important to us at The Club. Nick and I want to know what you are trying to accomplish here. Do you have a goal? Is it the same as ours, or are you just freeing killers because they killed a child molester? We also want to know if you guys will work with us by keeping us abreast of the goings on here, and work with us by following orders if need be. Because, if you guys are on your own, doing your own thing out here, then all the work The Club has done will be for naught unless you guys are on the same road as us.

"I will put it in one simple sentence: the main goal of The Club is to get the all-too-outdated and liberal laws against child molesters changed, and to keep it out of the hands of our bleeding-heart judges who keep letting these child molesters out on the streets to molest children again. That's all I've got to say. I would now like to hear what you guys have to say."

Salvatore says, "Okay, let's see if I got this right. You guys at The Club want us to continue doing what we have been doing, but to keep you abreast of our activities, and if we need help, we should not hesitate to ask for it. Also, you want us to follow your orders if a situation warrants it, and you want to know what our goal is, to see if it's the same as The Club. Did I get it all?"

Barney says, "As a matter of fact, you did."

Salvatore says, "Well, then, Barney, can you please give me ten minutes alone with my cohorts to discuss this?"

Barney says, "Absolutely. Nick and I will wait outside. Just let us know when you are done."

After about five minutes, Salvatore calls Barney and Nick back into his office. "Okay," he says, "we talked it over, and my cohorts and I agree that our goal is exactly the same as The Club. As far as everything else goes, the answer is yes, because, without The Club, we would have never thought of doing anything like this on our own, and now, by doing this, we feel connected to the main terminal of this movement and feel good about it. So, yes, yes, and yes to everything. Let's get started ridding the world of these bad guys."

༃༃༃

Barney says, "That's great, and the first thing on our agenda is to ask

70

you guys for your help in locating other groups like yours. The last time Nick and I were here, you said that you knew of at least two other lawyers who have a group like yours and are doing the same as you guys are."

Salvatore thinks and says, "Yes, I do know a few lawyers that are sort of doing the same as we are, or were thinking of doing it."

"Okay," says Barney, "then one of the first things I would like to do is to officially sanction you and your cohorts as representatives of The Club, and as your first task, I would like to have yourself or one of your cohorts go and talk to these other lawyers that you know and explain everything to them just the way I explained everything to you, hear what they have to say, and report back to me or Nick. And of course, now that your group is an officially sanctioned member of The Club, we will reimburse all your expenses. Just send us the bills."

Salvatore says, "Well, that would be great, because, up until now, we were each paying our own way."

Barney calls John and tells him that he has good news for him and will explain everything to him when he and Nick get back.

John says, "That is great news, and by the way, two little girls were molested while you guys were gone, an eight-year-old girl in Chicago and a nine-year-old girl in North Carolina. The eight-year-old was raped and killed, and the police are looking for the guy. The second molester was caught by two guys who heard the screams of the nine-year girl, and they beat him so bad that he died in the hospital. The two guys were picked up and are being held for manslaughter. I sent two of our lawyers to defend them. The papers over here have the front-page headline 'Still Open Season on Child Molesters.'"

Barney tells John, "Well, it looks like what we have been trying to do may be starting to work. I think that headline helps us, and I hope they find the other molester and that someone takes care of him. I just hope that all that we are doing is the right thing to do. Sometimes, I feel guilty feeling the way I do toward these child molesters, wishing them dead."

John tells Barney, "Are you kidding me? I thought we all passed that guilty feeling a long time ago, when we first started this, and how many experts have we talked to that all say the same thing, that there is no cure for the child molesters, that they must be put away for the rest of their lives. Don't go soft on me now, because now is when the going is going to get tough, and you know what they say about that."

"You're right. Someone needs to do something about these child molesters, and I guess we are the chosen ones, and I can't go soft now. I do know that we are doing the right thing."

John says, "I remember a close and dear friend of mine, Robert Brunkard. He once made a very profound statement to me that applies to just about everything you do in life. That is 'Let your conscience be your guide,' and in this case, if I don't follow through with this thing, my conscience would definitely bother me."

"Don't worry, John. I got that out of my system, and I'm on track now. Nick and I will see you tomorrow."

The next day, Barney and Nick take the first flight back to New York to meet up with John and explain everything to him. When they get to their building, they go straight into John's office, close the door, sit down, and stare at him.

"Well," don't just sit there and stare at me," John says. "How did you guys make out?"

Barney and Nick both start talking at the same time. John says, "Okay, the both of you, just calm down and speak one at a time."

Barney speaks first: "I can't believe how smoothly it went. We all thought we were going to have trouble with them or, at the very least, not know what to expect, but it all went unbelievably well. When we first got there, we called Salvatore and set up a meeting with him for the next morning in his office at 9 AM sharp. We asked him to invite the rest of the lawyers in his group, and he said that should be no problem. I said, 'Okay, then, Nick and I will see you in the morning.' The next morning, at 9 AM sharp, everyone was there. I started the meeting by emphasizing its importance. Nick and I explained why, when, where, and how this all got started, and how it led to the creation of The Club, and exactly what our goal or goals are.

"And they are all for it. They gave us no trouble at all. They just wanted ten minutes alone to discuss it amongst themselves, and in fact, they only took five minutes, and they called us back into the room. They said yes to everything, keeping us advised and up to date as to what they are doing, to ask for help if they need it, and to follow any orders we deem fit for them to follow.

"Then I came up with the idea that instead of Nick and I staying there and tracking down the other lawyers that Salvatore mentioned the last time we were there, I figured, seeing that Salvatore knew them, I would ask him or have him send one of the other lawyers to go and talk to them to find out where they stand. Then I thought it would be a great idea to set them up as a satellite unit out there, sort of an extension of our arm. So I hope it's all right with you, but I told them that I could sanction them as a representative of The Club and cover their expenses."

"That was a great idea," replies John. "I was thinking of setting up another office out west anyway, and now we have one. And as long as they have the same goal as us and are willing to follow our rules, it should all work out great. Now I feel that we are definitely on our way. If we get enough of these satellites set up, we will be home free. We will have enough power for the government to finally listen to us."

John breaks out a bottle of twenty-five-year-old Scotch and says, "This may not be the biggest event to toast to, and I hope that we will have much bigger ones, but this one definitely qualifies as one to toast to." With that, John pours out three shots, hands one each to Barney and Nick, and lifts his glass. Barney and Nick do the same. John says, "This toast is to the safety of all the children in the world."

All three clang their glasses together and say, "To the safety of all children," and down their drinks.

THE CLUB

The calm before the storm

While all this is going on in John's office, and all three are feeling great and toasting what they believe to be a huge step in their endeavors, Judge Tunis is still waiting for his friend Larry Rockwood to call him back.

The judge decides to call Larry back and see if he found out anything. Larry gets on the phone and tells the judge that he would like to have lunch with him in Washington, because he has some news for him. Judge Tunis says ok to the meeting.

Two days later, Judge Tunis and Larry meet for lunch, and the judge explains everything again to Larry about the trial, the web site, and what he thinks is going on. Larry tells Judge Tunis that he remembers that call, and also remembers reading something in the papers about what he is talking about, and if what he is telling him is true, and he has proof, it could be something that needs looking into. Larry tells the judge that he knows George Woods, who is a member of the U.S. House of Representatives, and that he would talk to him and explain what is going on. Larry tells Judge Tunis to give him a few more days to work on it and that he will get back to him.

Back in New York, John is checking the news wire to see if there is any news about the little eight-year-old who was raped and murdered in Chicago, and he reads that there may be a break in the case, that there may be an eyewitness. John thinks to himself that he has to keep an eye on the story.

Two days go by with nothing going on. Then Barney gets a call from a friend of his in Las Vegas who tells him that the reporter that wrote a story about a year ago with a headline that read "Website Calling for Open Season on Child Molesters" is at it again, and this time he claims to have gotten his information from an inside informant.

Barney tells him, "Please keep an eye on the story, and please keep me informed. I will see what I can find out at my end."

His friend says, "Okay, I will stay on top of the story and keep you informed."

Barney calls John and tells him about the call he got from his friend. John says, "That's just great. Now we have a spy among us to worry about. You better let Nick know about this and tell him to keep his eyes and ears open, and to keep us updated."

About a week goes by with nothing happing. Then it hits the papers and TV: a Las Vegas reporter breaks the news about a website that is calling for the freelance killing of child molesters. The article gives the name of the website, TheClub.com, and says that he wrote about this website about a year ago, but had no proof, and that this time he has an inside informant to back up his story. The article also calls for someone to investigate the website.

When John reads about this, he immediately calls Barney and tells him to get in touch with Nick and for both to check out the validity of the story as soon as possible and get back to him, again, as soon as possible. If the story is true, they will need to get together to discuss the matter.

Barney and Nick immediately check out the story and conclude that the story is indeed true. Barney calls John and says, "We have to get together today and discuss this so we don't get caught with our pants down again, like we did last time."

John says, "You are absolutely correct. I would like the two of you to be in my office this afternoon if possible."

Barney tells John, "Hold on." He checks with Nick and says, "Okay, John, we will be in your office this afternoon at 3 PM, if that's ok with you."

John says, "That would be great."

That afternoon, at 3 PM, all three meet in John's office. John speaks first: "Okay, what shall we do about this matter? Should we just disregard the story and hope that it goes away like it did last time, or should we take into account the inside informant he is talking about. And how the hell are we going to find out who it is?"

Nick says, "I think the first thing we should do is have a meeting with all the lawyers and employees we have, and see if we can find out who it is. Maybe whoever it is will tip their hand by being nervous or something."

Barney and John agree with Nick. John says, "I will get right on it, but in the meantime, I think we should download all the names and addresses of all the members from our computers onto CDs and hide them in a safe place. I would like the two of you to each assign one girl to download the names. Keep an eye on them so they don't have a chance to make a copy in case one of them is the informant, and also don't let anyone else know what's going on or what you are doing, because until we find this person, we can't trust anyone."

John tells his secretary, "I want you to send a memo to everyone, and I mean everyone, every single person that is connected in any way, no matter how trivial, with this organization, even our new satellite offices in Texas, that there will be a mandatory meeting next Thursday in our meeting room at 2 PM sharp, and anyone who does not attend will be fired or dealt with."

Barney and Nick get right on the task of downloading the member's names and addresses. Each select a computer operator to download the information they want, but first, they explain to each one that what they want must be done in one sitting, with no lunch break or bathroom break, so before they tell the girls what they want them to do, they tell them to go and have lunch and to visit the ladies room before they start.

When the girls get back, Barney and Nick explain to the girls what they want. Then they sit down next to each girl and watch everything they do, not taking their eyes off them for a second. After a few hours, the girls are done. Barney and Nick tell the girls that under no circumstances are they to tell anyone what they did, and if they do, they will be fired immediately. "Also," says Barney, "if anyone should ask you what you were doing, let either one of us know."

Barney and Nick bring the CDs to John. Nick says, "What are you going to do with them now?"

John replies, "I'm going to pack them up and send them to a friend of mine for safe keeping."

Barney says, "But if this hits the fan, won't the police check out all of your friends?"

"Not this one. This is someone I met a long time ago, and I don't think they can trace this guy. I have not seen or talked to this guy for over twenty-five years, but I know he will do this for me, and I also know that I can trust him. And on top of everything else, he owes me big time for something I did for him."

The next morning, John is on a pay phone trying to get in touch with his long-lost friend Bob Brunkard. The last place he knew of where Bob was living was in Florida. Luck is with John this morning, because he gets Bob's phone number without any trouble, and as John dials the number, he thinks to himself, *This is a break for me, because he has a listed number. Otherwise, I don't know how I could have gotten in touch with him. If it does hit the fan, they will be looking at everything I do.* Then he thinks, *Oh my God, I hope he's still alive.* Then John hears what he's sure is a familiar voice say hello.

John says, "Hello," hoping his ears are not deceiving him, "is this Bob Brunkard?"

"It sure is. And who is this?"

"Bob, this is John Harrison."

"Oh my God, is that really you? God, I've thought about trying to get in touch you so many times, but you know how it goes, you get involved in your own little world and forget to do some things. Anyway, where are you, and when will I see you?"

"Good, Bob. Unfortunately, we can't get together right now. I promise you we will, but right now, I can't say when. Bob I'm calling to ask you a very big favor."

"John, anything you want. Just tell me what you want or need, as long as it doesn't include killing someone."

"No, Bob, what I need you to do is hold a package for me, and don't tell anyone, not even your wife, that you got this package from me or even that you spoke to me. This is extremely important."

"Okay, John, but I've got to ask you one question about this package. Does it contain drugs? Or anything that can explode or harm me or my family in any way?"

"No. I promise, you there is nothing in the package that will harm you or your family. All I ask is that you keep it in a safe place, and no matter what, do not try to get in touch with me. I will get back in touch with you when I'm ready."

"Okay, John, send me the package, and I will do what you ask. I just wish that you could give me more information about this whole thing."

"Bob, I promise you that when the time is right, I will fill you in on the whole nine yards, and let me say thank you, thank you, thank you. You have no idea what this means to me. The package will be in the mail tomorrow."

"Okay, John. I will look for it. And please take care of yourself."

"You too, Bob. Bye for now."

John goes straight back to his office and gets the CDs ready to ship. He gets in his car, drives to the next town, and sends them off to his friend with delivery confirmation only, and he plans to check the delivery in an Internet café in a few days.

THE CLUB

Big news hits the papers

For the next two days, all is quiet. Then, just as John, Barney and Nick suspected, the story that the Las Vegas reporter was working on hits the papers again. This time, it's a two-page story, and it has all the details about The Club that were given to the reporter by his informant: The Club's strategy, its goals, names, dates, locations, and even addresses for the satellite offices in Texas. The reporter is calling for a federal investigation, and the article is still using the headline "Web Site Calling for Open Season on Child Molesters."

All the papers in town are carrying the story, and a lot of out-of-town papers and TV stations as well. Plus, it's on the news wire for all the country and world to see.

After reading and hearing the news, all three get together in John's office. John, Barney, and Nick all three agree that this time, they think that something is going to happen, and they try to prepare for the battle.

For three days, the news is all over the papers and TV news stations, and now some local politicians are getting into the act and calling for a federal investigation.

A few of the clerical workers, after reading and hearing the story, quit their jobs, but just when John hears about some workers quitting, one of the office managers comes into John's office, all excited, and says, "John, you are not going to believe this. I just checked our site to see if we'd gotten any negative e-mails after the story broke about us, but in the past two days, since the news hit, we've gotten over two thousand new members, and today looks like it's going to be the same. I can't believe it; our servers are burning up."

John doesn't know what to make of it. It looks like the story helped The Club instead of hurting it. Again, John calls Barney and Nick to his office. He tells them about what his office manager told him about the membership increase. "Well, what do you guys think about what's going on with the membership? What do you make of it? I know I can't figure it out. Do you guys have any ideas?"

Barney says, "No, but at this point, I don't think it's a bad thing."

"Neither do I," says Nick. "This is like the calm before the storm, and yet, this is part of what we have been waiting for, to get more strength, so I look at it in a positive way. If the membership keeps growing the way it has been for the past two days, and today looks like it will be the same, we will have the power you always wanted."

Barney says, "What I think we should do now is to just sit and wait for them to strike the first blow and then take it from there."

Both John and Nick agree, and in unison, as though rehearsed, they both say, "Yes, I think that is what we should do. In the meantime, enrollment in The Club is still going strong."

The rest of the day is quiet. All three men are in their offices thinking about what to do if and when something happens. But John can't sit still anymore, so he decides to see what's going on in the world. He checks the news wire, and what he sees blows his mind: almost everything on the wire, is about the article that the Las Vegas reporter wrote about The Club. Also, as John reads, he is still more amazed. He reads about two killings of child molesters in different parts of the country last night, and one more today, and on top of that, he reads that four registered child molesters actually went to the police demanding protection, but the police sent them all home because of lack of evidence. No one had actually threatened any of them. Two of the molesters threatened the police with lawsuits.

John calls Nick and tells him to get together with Barney and get all the information they can about the new killings, and to send some lawyers out from the pool to help the defendants.

Judge Tunis, after hearing and reading the story about The Club, puts in a call to his D.A. friend, Larry Rockwood, in Washington.

Rockwood's secretary answers. "District Attorney Larry Rockwood's office."

Judge Tunis says, "Hello, can I please speak to Larry?"

"Who may I say is calling?"

"Tell him it's Judge Tunis."

Larry picks up the phone. "Judge, how are you doing?"

The judge says, "What I want to know is how are you doing with what I asked you to do for me? And by the way, have you been reading the papers the last three days about The Club? The article was about what I came and talked to you about, and you were supposed to talk to George Woods from the House of Representatives about it for me."

"Yes, I have been reading the papers, and yes, I did talk to George about it, and yes, he said that he would check into it and get back to me, and I'm still waiting for his call."

"Well, now, with what this reporter wrote, and the fact that he is claiming to have an informant who is willing to testify, that should open the door for you and your friends out there to start an investigation."

"You're right, and now, with this in hand, I will give George another call. He should be able to do something right away. So let me call George again, and I will get back to you."

Back at the office, Barney and Nick are busy trying to get as much information on the new killings as they can so that they can get a few pool lawyers ready to go out and defend the defendants if need be.

While John is sitting in his office taking care of business, his secretary calls him. "Good morning, John. You have a call from Mr. Salvatore Whine from the Texas office."

John picks up the phone and says, "Good morning, Salvatore."

"Hi, John. You can call me Sal."

"Okay, Sal, what's up?"

"Well… I think I've got a story that you are really going to want to follow up on. A friend of mine just got back from Chicago, and he said that right now, they are investigating a story about a little eight-year-old girl who was missing, and something to the effect about them having a witness who saw the little girl getting into a car with a man. The police are now in the process of investigating this."

John says, "Yes, I remember reading something about that a week or so ago. Okay, thanks for giving me a heads-up. Good work. I will check into it and get back to you. Thanks again. I will talk to you later."

"Take care."

Again, John calls Barney and Nick into his office. He tells them, "This may or not be anything, but I just got off the phone with Salvatore Whine from our Texas office. He told me that a friend of his who just came back from Chicago told him about a story that broke there about a little eight-year-old girl who went missing a few weeks ago, and that they now have a witness who claims he saw the little girl get into a car with a man, and that the police are now investigating. So, along with me, I want the two of you to check into it and keep an eye on the story. Let me know if anything develops, and I will do likewise."

In the meantime, enrollment in The Club is still going strong. But then there is breaking news that one of the killers was caught in California, and he tells the police that he is a member of The Club and that he is not worried because the jurors will find him innocent and he will go free.

John, Barney, and Nick can't believe what they are reading and hearing. John says, "This guy can really hurt us. I think one of you guys should handle this yourself. Get down there as fast as you can and shut this guy up."

Barney says, "I will go."

Barney goes home to pack, and then he gets on the first plane to California to talk to this guy. He gets there about 5 PM and heads straight for the jail to talk to him.

Barney meets up with the guy, and the first thing the guy says to him is "What took you so long to get here?"

Barney says, "The first thing you have to do is to shut your mouth, and are you kidding me, asking me what took me so long to get here? As soon as I heard the story about you, I hopped on the first plane here. What do you think, we stand outside all the jails and wait for people like you to defend and just jump in? If you really want to help The Club, from now on, keep your mouth shut, and don't open it unless I tell you to open it."

The next morning at the office, Nick is checking the news wire, which is what John and Barney do every morning. Nick reads something about the little eight-year-old girl who went missing in Chicago, that the police now have a sketch of the man that the little girl was seen getting into the car with, and they also know the color and maybe the make of the car. Nick goes into John's office to ask him if he has read the morning news wire yet.

John answers, "No, not yet. Why? Is there something that I should know about?"

"Well, I don't know how significant this is, but there was some more breaking news about the missing eight-year-old girl in Chicago. It seems that the police now have a sketch of a man that the girl was seen getting into the car with. Also, they may have the make and color of the car."

John says, "That's good news. I hope the police catch that SOB, and I think we should keep a close watch on that story."

Back in Washington, Larry Rockwood gets the call from George Woods, who is a member of The House of Representatives, that he has been waiting for.

"Good morning, Larry. How are you doing?"

"I'm doing fine, George, and how about yourself?"

"I'm also doing fine. Larry, the reason I called you is about that website you wanted me to check on. Well, I checked it out, and based on what I have been reading and hearing about this website in the papers and on the television, it may qualify as something that needs looking into. What I would like to do is set up a meeting with this Judge Tunis here in Washington, and have him bring whatever information he has on the website. I will have a talk with him and then decide what to do next."

Larry says, "That is great, George. I will call Judge Tunis and tell him what you decided to do. I'm sure that he will be overjoyed with the news."

Larry hangs up with George, and he can't seem to dial the judge's phone number fast enough and quickly gets him on the phone. "Judge, this is Larry. I've got great news for you. I finally got a call from my friend George Woods, and he has agreed to meet with you and hear what you got to say, and to see what proof you have about that website you were telling me about."

Judge Tunis is elated, to say the least. He tells Larry, "As soon as I get off the phone with you, I'm dialing his phone number."

Judge Tunis calls George Woods and gets him on the phone. "Hi,

George, I'm sure happy to finally get a chance to talk to you."

"That's okay, Judge. So, when do you want to meet with me?"

"I would like to meet with you as soon as possible."

"Well, let me see. Today is Tuesday, and it looks like I'm free on Thursday. How about we meet then?"

"Tell me what time and place, and I will be there."

"Okay, how about 3 PM, my office, this Thursday."

Judge Tunis says, "That sounds great. I will see you on Thursday."

He then calls the Las Vegas newspaper with the reporter who wrote a story about the website and who is claiming to have a witness or proof or both of what is really going on at that website. His name is Bryan Kelly, and the judge asks to talk to him. He tells the reporter who he is and asks him if he really has proof.

Bryan tells the judge, "Yes, indeed I do have proof via a person who is working on the inside of the organization, who knows all that is going on inside The Club, and who is willing to testify and tell all."

Judge Tunis says, I have been trying to shut down this site for some time now, and in fact, I did shut it down for a while, but they managed somehow to get a judge in a higher court than me to override my court order, and they reopened their website. Since then, I have been trying to get someone with more power than myself to close down the site and investigate them. In fact, this Thursday, I finally have a meeting with a member of The House of Representatives who agreed to meet with me and discuss the situation with The Club's website, and I'm going to try to convince him to start an investigation. Like you, I believe that the website is inciting people to go out and kill child molesters without due process. But if you have someone on the inside who is willing to come forward and would be willing to testify, and if you decide to help me and maybe are willing to take a trip with me to Washington to meet with this guy, I'm sure that we can take these people down once and for all. I promise you that as far as I'm concerned, you can have the exclusive story to write in your newspaper. All I want is to do my job and close them down, and prosecute the guilty parties. But the only evidence I have is how I interpret what The Club is doing, but if you have someone on the inside who can corroborate that what I feel is actually going on there, then that would be the final nail in their coffin, and then we could bury them once and for all."

"I have to talk to my inside man to see if he would be willing to go to Washington with us. Let me call him and get back to you."

"Okay, but remember we only have one day."

"No problem. I will call him first thing in the morning and get back to you."

The next morning, Bryan calls his inside man and explains the situation to him. The inside man tells him, "You know, when you ran the first story about The Club in your paper, I was the one who got in touch with you and told you that you were right on the money in what you were writing about, that I am a member and actually work for The Club, that I'm on their payroll, and that I would be able to furnish proof that what you are saying in your paper is the truth. Then I asked you how much would the proof be worth to you. You thought about it for a few seconds and told me that if I really had proof and was willing to show it to you, you would give me one thousand dollars cash. Then you never got back to me and went ahead and printed the story without checking the proof I said I had. I gave you that information over the phone with the understanding that we were then supposed to meet. I was to give you the proof of what I said on the phone, and you were supposed to give me my money. Then, not only did you go ahead and print the story, you lied to your readers, saying that you had the proof that you did not have, and now you have the balls to call me with this cock and bull story about you going to Washington to speak to a member of the House of Representatives, and that you want me to join you so that I can show what evidence I have to him so that you can write another story. Well, I tell you what. You're fucking crazy if you think that I would help you out again after what you did to me, and in fact, you can go and fuck yourself."

"Okay, hold on a minute. I know what I did last time was wrong, but I never meant to screw you over. I'm still going to pay you the thousand dollars. It's just that I got so busy working on the story that I just forgot. I swear I never meant to screw you out of the money. Please believe me. I promise I will give you your money today. This is a really big story to me, and if I break it open, it could mean a Pulitzer to me. Please, please, you've got to help me. I promise I will give you just about anything you ask for."

"Well, now, that's interesting. Now you will give me just about anything I ask for. Isn't that swell of you to offer me just about anything. Well, tell you what, let me think about it and get back to you."

"Okay, but remember, I have to know today. In fact, I really need to know as soon as possible, like within the next hour."

"Let me think about it, and I will get back to you in an hour."

It's one of the longest hours that Bryan has ever gone through in his life, but the hour passes without a call. It goes to an hour and a half and still no call. He thinks to himself, *I will give him just a half-hour more. Then I am going to call him back.*

The half-hour goes by and still no call, so Bryan decides to calls his inside man back. He gets him on the phone. "So, what's going on? You said that you would call me back in an hour, and it's been two hours. So, what did you decide?"

"I need more time, another hour."

"Wait a minute, do you really have proof, or are you bullshitting me?"

"Oh, no, I'm not bullshitting you at all. I do have the proof, but if you're talking about this being as big a story as you say, and that you could possibly get a Pulitzer prize for breaking it open, then I've got to make sure that I get my Pulitzer, so to speak. So, sit tight, and I promise that I will call you back in about an hour."

"Okay, please do."

Finally, in about forty-five minutes, the informant calls back. "Okay, this is what I decided I want, and I want this in my hand before I step one foot on the plane to Washington. If this story is as big as you say it is, I want one hundred thousand dollars cash."

"Are you out of your fucking mind? Where the hell do you think I can get that kind of money? Did you forget that I work for a living?"

"No, I did not forget that you work for a living. That's the point. You work for someone who owns a newspaper, and that someone has a lot of money. Are you getting the big picture yet? Again, if this story is as big as you say it is, and you have the exclusive story, then the paper will sell a lot of newspapers and make a lot of money, so just go to them and ask for the money."

"Oh, man, you are killing me! I really don't want to do that."

"Okay, then, I'm not going to stay on the phone and debate this with you. That's my deal, take it or leave it. Call me back if you decide you want to do this." With that, the inside man hangs up.

Reluctantly, Bryan calls his inside man back. "Okay, I will go and talk to my editor and see what he has to say about this, but this I will say, if my paper agrees to go for this deal, they are going to want to see what evidence you have before handing you over one cent. Is that agreeable with you?"

"Absolutely. You get them to give me the money, and I will give you all the evidence you need for your story and all the evidence your pal, the judge, needs to shut them down, convict them, and lock them up for a long time. I will even agree to testify in court if necessary."

"Okay, then, I will get back to you."

As soon as Bryan hangs up, he goes into the office of his editor, Bill Franklin. He sits down and asks, "Bill, do you have a few minutes to discuss something?"

"Only if it's important."

"Well, as a matter of fact, I think it is very important."

"Then start talking, because right now I'm very busy."

"Okay, then, here it is. Do you remember that story I wrote about a website called TheClub.com, where I had the headline that read "Website Calls for Open Season on Child Molesters"? It was about how the website is inciting its members to go out and kill child molesters without due process. And do you remember that you told me that I better know what I'm talking about, that you did not want the paper to get sued? And do you realize that we did not get sued, so that told me that they did not want to go to court because of what might come out at the trial? And, also, do you remember telling me that if I could get proof that it would be one heck of a story, probably one of the biggest that you have ever seen? Well, what if I told you I have an insider from that website who is willing to come forward with hard evidence and even testify in court for a price."

"If he has really good evidence and is willing to work with only us, I guess it would be worth something. But remember, it would have to be ironclad evidence, no bullshit. Anyway, how much money is he asking for?"

"He is asking for one hundred thousand dollars."

"What?! Are you fucking kidding me?"

"No, I'm not. I'm telling you that this is going to be one of the biggest stories ever. I have this feeling that this website has influence over millions of people. Haven't you been reading your own paper, or other papers, or reading what is coming over the wires, or looking at television, or listening to the radio about all the killings of child molesters that have been going on over the past few years?"

"Yes, I have, but some judge already tried to shut them down, and he failed. The website reopened, because they could not prove anything."

"Well, that same judge is still trying to shut them down, and now, because of me and my insider, he thinks we have enough evidence to shut them down for good and prosecute the guilty ones. He wants my insider and myself to fly to Washington with him on Thursday to speak to a member of the House of Representatives and present the evidence we have to him so that he can get an investigation going. I don't think that the judge has that kind of money, and besides that, we will get the exclusive story. All the judge wants is to close the website down, arrest the people, and put them in jail."

"You know what? I think you may just have something here. Let me talk to the owners and get back to you."

"Okay, but time is short. We only have one day to put this together."

"I will talk to them tonight."

That night, Bill pleads his case to the owners of the paper and convinces them that it would be money well spent to get the exclusive story. The owners agree and tell Bill that he will have the hundred thousand dollars in the morning, but they reminded him that his job depends on this being, as Bill put it to them, money that will be well spent.

In the meantime, the news wire has a breaking story about a little girl's body that was found in Chicago, and authorities believe that it is the body of a little girl who went missing about a month ago, and it appears that the little girl had been raped and murdered. The police have stepped up the hunt for the killer, because they have found some evidence at the crime scene that they did not have before.

And at the newspaper office, first thing in the morning, Brian is waiting outside Bill's door. As soon as Bryan spots Bill, he grabs his arm and escorts him into his own office.

"Well," asks Bryan, "what happened last night? Did the owners go for it?"

"I'm telling you now, Bryan, if this blows up in our face, I'm go to fucking kill you, because, to get the money, I had to put my job on the line."

"Oh, great! Then they agreed to the deal."

"Yes, they did, but remember what I said: my job is on the line."

"Okay, don't worry about it. And by the way, did you read the news wire today? There is a breaking story in Chicago about a little girl's body being found, that she had been raped and murdered, and that the police found more evidence at the scene, so they think now that they have a good chance of catching the person responsible. I'm sure that this website that I'm working on is going to get involved in this if the police catch the killer. I'm telling you this is going to be one of the biggest stories this paper has ever run. I just know that it's the right thing to do. So, when will I get the money? I have to know when so that I can call my inside man and tell him it's a go."

"The owners are dropping it off this morning, but this is the way it's going to go down. Your inside man has to come down to the paper, show us what he has, and then, if it's what we hope it is, the paper wants him to sign a confidentiality agreement stating that he is handing over all the evidence he has, that it becomes the sole property of the newspaper, and that he does not have a duplicate set of this proof. If he refuses to do that, then the whole deal is off, because the paper doesn't want to pay for something and then find out that your man sold it to somebody else. If that's okay with you, then you can call your man and see what he has to say about it."

"That's great. I will call him right now and get back to you."

Bryan goes to his desk, calls his inside man, and gets him on the phone. "I'm getting your money this morning, but in order for you to get it, they want you to come down to the paper and show us what you got, hand it over, and then they want you to sign a confidentiality agreement."

"What?! What kind of a confidentiality agreement are you talking about?"

"Well, they just want to make sure that you are giving us all the evidence you have and not hold anything back to then try to sell it to somebody else."

"Oh, ok. I'm a lawyer. I know what they are looking for. Tell them not to worry. I will give them everything I have. By the way, if I give them all the evidence I have, what are we going to take to Washington with us to show that guy from the House of Representatives?"

"I don't know. I guess we will figure that out when you get here."

"I will be there in about an hour."

"Okay, see you then. Now I've got to call Judge Tunis and get all the details from him."

Next, Bryan calls Judge Tunis and gets the judge on the phone. "Good morning, Judge."

"Good morning, Bryan. So what's going on? I hope you have some good news for me."

"Well, as a matter of fact, no… I've got great news for you."

"So let me hear the great news that you have for me."

"First off, the inside man that I have has agreed to accompany you and me to Washington, and has agreed to tell all he knows."

"Okay, that sounds good, but is it just going to be his word, or does he have physical proof, like notes or letters etc.?"

"I don't know exactly what he has, but he is a lawyer, and he claims that he has the evidence that can shut them down and convict them."

"Then let's do this. I can't believe that after all that I have been through with these people, the time has come that I may actually have enough evidence to shut them down, arrest, and prosecute them."

"Okay, then, Judge, tell me when and where you want us to meet you."

"I want the two of you to be at the airport at 12 noon. We have to catch the 1 PM shuttle to Washington. I want you to show me the evidence that you have. Then, if all is well, the round-trip tickets are on me."

The inside man shows up at the newspaper and goes straight to Bryan's office. "Bryan, hi. I'm the one who works for The Club.com. We spoke a little while ago."

"Yes, yes, hi. Happy to meet you. First off, what is your name? You never gave it to me."

"My name is Lou Ratsky."

"Lou, what do you say we head straight to my editor's office and get this thing going? I, myself, can't wait to see what you've got."

"Okay, then let's go."

With that, the two of them head to Bill's office. They walk straight in, and Bryan says, "Good morning, Bill. This is Lou Ratsky, the gentleman I was talking to you about."

Bill stands up and the two shake hands as he says, "Good morning, Lou. I sure hope you have what you claim you have. Otherwise, a few of us are going to be very disappointed."

Lou says, "Good morning to you too, and yes, I'm sure I have the information that you are looking for."

"Okay, then, Lou, the first thing I would like you to do is to read this contract, and if it's okay with you, sign it. Then you can show us what you have. Or you can show us what you have and then sign it, however you prefer. I understand you are a lawyer, and if you are, you will understand that all it is saying is that in consideration of the sum of one hundred thousand dollars cash, the information, documents, or objects you have in your possession and are about to give this newspaper is or are complete and up to date, and are true facts to the best of your knowledge. It also says that you give up all rights to said information, documents, or objects, and to all the pertinent information, documents, or objects that may follow. Also, that all said documents, information, or objects will become the sole property of this newspaper, to do with as the newspaper deems fit."

Lou Reads the contract, signs it, turns to Bill, and says, "There you go, all signed. Now can I see my money?"

Bill tells Lou, "Well, okay, I will show you the money, but remember, I want you to show us what you have first. You have your copy of the contract attesting to the fact that the paper is prepared to pay you the money, so you don't have to worry about the money. The whole transaction will be taped, and you will get a copy."

With that, Bill picks up the phone, calls security, and tells them to bring up the money. In about a minute, three armed security men show up with an attaché case and hand it to Bill. He puts it on his desk, opens it, and all of them gaze at the money. Bryan speaks first: "Wow, that is beautiful."

"Yeah, yeah," says Bill, and he closes the case. "Okay, you've seen the money, so now let's see your proof."

Lou says, "Well, unfortunately, I can't show you the proof I have."

"What?!" shouts Bill as he jumps out of his seat. "If this is some sort of a joke, mister, you are going to feel very sorry."

"No, it's not a joke. Please sit down and let me explain. I was one of the first lawyers The Club hired, and right from the start, one of their biggest rules was that there was to be absolutely no talking on the phone or any kind of written correspondence of any kind, as to the mission of the website. Anything that had to do with the mission was to be discussed face to face, and there was to be absolutely no exceptions. Break this rule, and it was grounds for immediate dismissal and a fine, so what I realized from the very beginning was that these people are up to no good if they have rules like that. I decided from the get-go that I wanted to do something to protect myself, so I started taping the sessions every chance I could."

With that, Lou opens his attaché case and pulls out a case with six tapes in it. He says, "All the evidence you need to shut down that website and prosecute those people is on these tapes. You will hear exactly what the website was meant to accomplish. You will hear addresses, names, and dates of all parties involved. Plus, you have me to testify in court, and I will as part of our deal. You did not have that in the contract I signed, but if you wish, I will sign something to that effect."

Bryan looks at Bill and says, "What do you think?"

Bill says, "Before I decide on anything, I want to hear what is on those tapes."

Lou says, "No problem. I also have the player."

One by one, Bill and Bryan listen to all six tapes. Bill says, "I don't know. What do you think, Bryan?"

Lou says, "Listen, guys, as a lawyer, I'm telling you this stuff is dynamite. You can't get anything better than this. The only thing better than this would be if I had the video to go along with these tapes. You know what? Call that judge and ask him."

Bryan says, "Yes, that's a good idea."

Bryan goes to his office and puts a call in to Judge Tunis's office. After a brief wait, the judge answers. "Hello, Bryan. I've been waiting for your phone call all morning. I hope you have good news for me."

"Well, I think it's good. Here it is in a nutshell. The evidence my inside man has is six audio tapes that he secretly taped at meetings, and on them, you can hear people talking about the ultimate goal of The Club. They mention, names, dates, etc."

"Are you kidding me? That's great! I could not ask for better proof. I would like you and your inside man to meet me at 12 noon at the airport. Oh, and make sure you bring the tapes."

"By the way, Judge, my paper had to pay a lot of money for these tapes, and I don't know what the deal is as far as us, taking them to Washington, but I'm sure that it will be okay."

"Alright, then, I will see you at the airport."

"Okay. Bye."

Bryan goes back to Bill's office and tells them, "The judge said that the tapes are great, as he put it, so we are good to go. So, Bill, how is this going to work with the tapes?"

"It's going to work like this. We are going to make copies of the six tapes, the paper is going to keep the originals, and you can take the copies with you, but you have to sign for them. And remember, if these tapes get into the wrong hands, the hundred thousand, all the work you did on those stories, what the judge is trying to do, and the future revenue of this paper on the story that this paper will miss out on will go right out the window, along with both our jobs. So I'm telling you, you better not fuck this up."

As Lou and Bryan get ready to leave, Lou tells Bill, "Once I sign for the money, can I trust you and the paper to keep my money safe until I get back from Washington? I don't have time to do anything with it now. We have to go straight to the airport."

Bill tells Lou, "Don't worry. Sign for it, and we will give you a receipt, and you can pick it up when we get back. We will take good care of your money."

Bill signs a receipt for the money and gives it to Lou. He takes his receipt, Bill gets copies of the tapes, and then Bryan and Lou head for the airport. They get there at about 11AM, and they meet up with Judge Tunis at the ticket counter.

Bryan says, "Hi, Judge. This is Lou, the man I was telling you about."

"Yeah, let's find a table in the coffee shop. I can't wait to hear the tapes. If they are all that you say they are, I will purchase the tickets, and we will be on our way."

Bryan loads the first tape and hits play. The judge listens carefully to it. Then Bryan plays the second tape, and so on, until the judge has heard all six tapes. As he hears each succeeding tape, his eyes open wider and wider, and his head nods up and down, as if saying, "Yes, yes."

The judge practically jumps out of his seat, grabs Bryan, stands him up, and gives him a big hug. He then grabs Lou, stands him up, and gives him a big hug also. "You guys have no idea how much these tapes mean to me. They are great! I have been waiting for proof like this for a long time. Now, let's get those tickets. I don't want to miss the flight."

Finally, all three men are on the plane to Washington for their 3 PM meeting with George Woods, a member of the House of Representatives. They land with just enough time to grab a quick bite, and then they grab a cab to the office of George Woods. Once there, they are told to please wait, that Mr. Woods will be with them shortly. After a few minutes, they are told that Mr. Woods will see them now, and they are escorted into Mr. Woods's office.

As the three men walk into Mr. Woods's office, Judge Tunis is impressed, to say the least. Mr. Woods is a very distinguished, tall, well-groomed man with slightly graying hair at his temples. He wears a perfectly fitting, hand-made, expensive suit with coordinating tie and pocket hankie. The office smells of success and importance. The judge cannot help but notice the large picture window behind Mr. Woods's desk, framing the Lincoln memorial in the distance. There are pictures of all the presidents on the walls, along with pictures of all of the Washington landmarks and monuments, including the White House. In the corner of the room is a large American flag with gold fringe all around it and, on top, a golden eagle. Also on the walls are various diplomas and awards. The fine leather couches and chairs, along with a deep plush rug, complete the room.

"Good afternoon, gentleman. Please, have a seat. And which of you is Judge Tunis?" Judge Tunis stands up, extends his hand, and shakes hands with Mr. Woods. "Okay, Judge, I'm familiar with your plight and what you have been trying to do with this website, so let's hear what you got and see if I can be of any help to you."

Bryan loads the first tape, the second tape, and so on. Mr. Woods listens very intensely to all six tapes. Then he sits back in his chair and asks, "And which of you is Mr. Lou Ratsky?"

Lou says, "That would be me."

"Okay, Mr. Ratsky, let me ask you this: will you be willing to testify to all of this in a court of law?"

"Absolutely."

"Good, Judge. I think that as long as Mr. Ratsky agrees to testify, you definitely have enough evidence here to have someone look into what's going on with this website, and I think I have the perfect person to take a look what paperwork you have and listen to the tapes. That person is Justice Kurt Spencer of the United States Supreme Court, and if there is anyone who can do something, it's him. Just leave everything with me. I will get in touch with my friend Justice Spencer at the Supreme Court, show him what I got, let him listen to the tapes, and see what he has to say about this. Then I will get back to you. Is what I said agreeable with you, Judge?"

"The only problem I have is leaving the tapes with you, because they don't belong to me. The newspaper that Bryan works for owns them, and they paid a lot of money for them. I don't think that they would want them to get out of Bryan's sight. Is it possible I could come back with them when you get an appointment with Judge Spencer."

"No, that would be out of the question. If you want anything to get done, you must trust me with the tapes. If you want, I will sign for them and give you my personal guarantee that nothing will happen to them, nor will anyone but Judge Spencer see and hear them, and if so, I will get in touch with you first."

Judge Tunis asks Bryan, "What do you think, Bryan? Will your paper go for that?"

"I will have to call my editor at the paper to get his okay. That is not anything I can decide on my own."

"No problem," says Mr. Woods. "You can use my phone, or if you want, I have a small private office in the next room."

"Well, if it's okay with you, I would like to use the private office."

"No problem. Just go through that door."

Bryan goes into the next room, which is a nicely appointed office, small but nice. Bryan thinks to himself, *Boy, I wish my office was as nice as this.*

With the wishing part done, Bryan picks up the phone and gets Bill on the phone. He explains to Bill what's going on, and Bill tells him, "Kid, you are putting me in a tight spot. I don't know if I can allow that."

Bryan starts pleading his case: "Bill, there is no other way to do this. We've gotten this far, and we can't stop now. This man is a member of the United States House of Representatives, and he is willing to sign for them, plus give us his personal guarantee that no one but Justice Spencer from the United States Supreme Court will hear them. And if someone else needs to hear them, he will call us for permission first."

"Okay, Bryan, but remember, our fucking jobs are on the line, and that's for real, no bullshit. So I hope you know what the hell you are doing."

"I know what's on the line, and I know what I'm doing. Don't worry. It will be okay. Talk to you when I get back."

Bryan goes back into Mr. Woods's office. "Okay, Mr. Woods, you can hold onto the tapes as long as you sign for them and agree to only let Judge Spencer hear them, and no one else. And if the need does come up that someone else should hear them, you call us first."

"Bryan, you've got a deal. I will have my secretary type up a receipt for the tapes, and I will sign it."

Judge Tunis is all excited about what is going on. He says, "Mr. Woods, if you can do anything, I will be eternally grateful to you. All I ask is that you let no one else know about these tapes, except on the terms we discussed, because the paper I'm working with to stop these people and shut down their website paid a lot of money for those tapes so that they would have the exclusive story, and I also gave my word that I would take every precaution to make sure that no other paper would get the story first."

"Don't worry, Judge. The only ones that will be seeing anything or hearing the tapes are those that absolutely have to see or hear the evidence. You can assure the paper that you are working with that I will take every precaution to make sure that their story will not get out before they put it out. Tell them they have my word on that."

A week later, Judge Tunis gets the call that he's been waiting a long time for, from Mr. Woods. Mr. Woods tells him, "Judge, I spoke to my friend Justice Tom Spencer, who is a member of the U.S. Supreme Court, and he told me that he has heard about this website from someone else, and it has already sparked his curiosity in it. He said that he is absolutely sure that as long as your witness is still willing to testify, along with the tapes and evidence that you have, you have an excellent case and that you should submit your papers to the United States Supreme Court ASAP. Because of the seriousness of the situation, he feels that this website must be shut down and some people sent to jail. Again, he said that he is absolutely sure that they will hear your case.

THE CLUB

The day of reckoning is in sight

With the good news in hand, and all excited, Judge Tunis calls his friend Larry Rockwood, the Washington D.A., and asks him to do him a big favor.

"And what would that favor be?"

"I need you to prepare the papers to submit to the United States Supreme Court to check out that website."

"Okay, you got it, Judge. By the way, I'm staying over so that I can accompany you to the courthouse."

After going over all of the evidence that the judge brought, and listening to the tapes again and making sure that all his i's are dotted and t's are crossed, Larry and Judge Tunis head to the U.S. Supreme Court building to summit their papers.

After filing their papers, Rockwood puts in a call to Congressman George Woods to give him an update. The congressman's secretary answers. "Good morning. Mr. Woods's office."

"Yes, hi, this is Larry Rockwood. By any chance is Mr. Woods in?"

"Actually, he is, Mr. Rockwood."

"Oh, great, can I please speak to him?"

"You sure can. I will put you through."

"Thank you."

The secretary contacts the congressman in his office. "Mr. Woods, Larry Rockwood is on the phone."

"Okay, put him through."

"Mr. Woods," says Larry once the congressman is on the line. "How are you today?"

"Fine, Larry. What can I do for you today?"

"Well, I just wanted to update you as to what I was doing. Today, I filed the papers to the United States Supreme Court on that website that I spoke to you about at our last meeting, the one that Judge Tunis told us about."

"Okay, that's great. From what I heard on those tapes, that website needs to be shut down. And by the way, Larry, is your witness still ready and willing to testify?"

"Yes, he is."

"Okay, then, I guess that you are all set."

"I hope so, and Mr. Woods, thanks again for your help."

"You are welcome, Larry, and good luck. I will keep my eye on this."

"Thanks. Good bye."

With that done, Judge Tunis thanks Larry and heads back to the airport for his flight back home. As soon as he gets home, he starts his waiting game, that is, waiting to hear from Larry to see if he heard anything from United States Supreme Court, to see if they are going to hear the case or not. He reads in the newspaper that yet another accused child molester was killed before he had his day in court, and the killer was found not guilty.

He puts in a call to Mr. Rockwood, hoping that he is still in his office.

"Mr. Rockwood's office. Can I help you?"

"Yes, this is Judge Tunis. By any chance is Mr. Rockwood in?"

"Yes, Judge, he is. Hold on, and I will put you through."

The secretary calls Larry and says, "Mr. Rockwood, Judge Tunis is on the phone, and he wants to talk to you again."

"Okay, sure, put him through." Once on the line, Larry says, "Hello, Judge, how are you?"

"I just wanted to ask you if you read today's papers yet."

"As a matter of fact, I have not. What's up?"

"Well, just to point out how important the case of yours is, in my hometown paper, there is a story about another accused child molester in

Chicago that was picked up by the police and was killed right in front of the police station as he was being led into the station house for his arraignment. The man who shot him just stood there and let the police arrest him. He was charged with premeditated murder, and when his trial came up last week, he was found not guilty. So, you see, it's still going on."

"Okay, Judge, I will put a call in to my friend Judge Spencer. I will fill him in and ask him to try and push my case through ASAP."

"Okay, thanks again."

"Judge, while I have you on the phone, I would like to ask you a big favor."

"Sure, anything."

"Okay, and please don't take this the wrong way, but please don't call me with every incident involving a child molester, because I'm really busy, and every time you call me, it throws me off my game. I promise you that I will call you anytime I hear something."

"Oh, okay, I understand. I'll just wait for your phone call."

"Great, Judge, and thanks for understanding."

"You got it, and again, thank you for all your help."

"You are welcome, Judge. Good bye for now."

In the meantime, and unbeknownst to the judge, John, Barney, Nick, and Mike are up to their ears with cases of defendants to defend, because, now, people are getting so brazen that they are seeking out known child molesters, and not only are they killing them, but now, the ones who can't bring themselves to kill someone are beating them to the point that they are hospitalized in critical condition.

Two weeks go by with no call from Washington, and Judge Tunis is getting antsy. He tries to keep himself busy by watching television. Then, one night, Judge Tunis finds out about the new twist to things. He hears that now it seems that not only are people killing child molesters, but they are seeking them out and putting them in the hospital in critical condition, and the individuals responsible for the attacks are turning themselves into the police. People all across the country are calling for something to be done. Judge Tunis wants desperately to call Larry Rockwood, but then he remembers what Larry said about calling him.

Later that afternoon, in Washington, Larry returns to his office. When he gets there, he asks his secretary if there are any messages for him.

"Yes. Judge Spencer called, and he wants you to call him back."

"Okay, great. Please get him on the phone for me."

Larry's secretary calls the judge's office. "Good morning. This is Mr. Rockwood's office, returning the judge's call."

"Okay, I'll put the judge on."

Larry's secretary tells him, "Mr. Rockwood, the judge is getting on the phone."

Larry gets on the line. "Good morning, Judge. How are you doing, Larry?"

"I'm fine, Judge, and I hope I know why you called me. Is it about that website?"

"Yes, Larry, that is exactly what I called you about. I talked to my colleagues, and we decided to hear the case, so you will be getting a call very soon from our clerks informing you of the date that we will hear his case."

"Okay, Judge, that's great news."

As promised, Larry puts a call in to Judge Tunis and gives him the good news, thinking, *I'm sure that he will be overjoyed, to say the least.* He gets him on the phone. "Judge Tunis?"

"Larry, how are you?"

"I'm doing good, Judge. I have great news for you. I spoke to Judge Spencer, and he told me that very soon, I will be getting a call from one of the clerks from the United States Supreme Court giving me a date to hear my case."

"Oh my God! That's great...! I can't tell you how happy I am right now and how much I appreciate the help that you have given me. Thank you, thank you, thank you."

"You are welcome, Judge. Now, go and get some rest. I will take it from here, and as promised, I will keep you updated."

"Okay, yes."

"Judge, you have a good night now."

"I definitely will. Good night."

It's three days before Larry hears anything. Finally, on Monday, May 22, he hears from the clerk at the U.S. Supreme Court. She tells him, "Because of the seriousness of the situation, the court has decided to move your case to the top of the pile. They want to inform you that the date of June 2nd has been set aside to hear your case, at 9 AM. Please make sure that you bring all your evidence and make sure that you, and any witnesses you have, get here on time. The judges don't like to be kept waiting."

"Okay, that's great. And don't worry, I will make sure I'm there on time with my witness and that I bring all my evidence. Thank you. I have been waiting a long time for this day."

The next thing Larry does is call Judge Tunis. When the judge gets on the phone, Larry says, "Good morning, Judge."

"Good morning, Larry. What can I do for you?"

"I just wanted to let you know that I got a date for the U.S. Supreme Court to hear my case, and I wanted to let you know. The case is set for June 2nd, so I'm going to plan on getting to Washington on the June 1st, if it's okay with you."

"That would great."

"I just hope that your witness keeps his word and shows up."

"Not to worry, Larry. I will give him a call right now."

Next, Judge Tunis calls Lou Ratsky, his inside man. The judge gets Lou on the phone. "Good morning, Lou. Well, I finally got a date for the U.S. Supreme Court to hear my case, and I hope you're still willing to testify."

"Yes, I am, Judge."

"Okay, that's great. The trial is set for June 2nd, and I would like to be in Washington on the 1st. Is that okay with you? I will pay for everything."

"Okay, Judge I will be ready."

"Great, thanks. I will call you later with all the details."

Then the judge calls Bryan Kelly, the news reporter. Bryan picks up the phone. "Good morning, Bryan Kelly speaking."

"Good morning, Bryan. This is Judge Tunis. I'm calling to let you know that the U.S. Supreme Court is finally ready to hear the case, so you will be getting to write your story before you know it."

"That's great. What's the date?"

"It's June 2nd. I will be going to Washington on the 1st. I don't want to take any chances of not being able to get there because of weather or anything else. I will be going there with Lou."

"Okay, let me know where you will be staying, and I will meet you there."

"I will do that. Thanks."

Next, Judge Tunis tells his secretary to book two seats on the first flight to Washington for June 1st, and to book two rooms at the closest hotel to the United States Supreme Court Building for the 1st and for at least a week afterward. "Hopefully, I won't need the rooms that long, but book it that long anyway just in case."

On June 1st, at 7 AM, Judge Tunis and Lou are at the airport, waiting for their 9 AM flight to Washington. The flight departs on time, and before long, the two of them are getting the keys to their rooms. Judge Tunis tells Lou, "First, let's grab some lunch. Then we'll come back here to the hotel and go over what you are going to say to the justices. I want to make sure you don't forget anything."

Finally, it's Tuesday, June 2nd, the day that the judge has been waiting for. He is all excited. He can't believe that this day has finally come. All he keeps thinking about is how good it's going to feel when the court shuts down the website, arrest all the workers, and puts a stop to all the madness that's been going on.

At 8 AM, the judge and Lou are at the steps of the United States Supreme Court Building. The two of them just stand there in awe, thinking of what this court represents and what important decisions they have made over the years.

As the two of them stand there, the judge's cell phone rings. It's his secretary. She says, "Just to let you know, Judge, in case you're not up to date with the latest news, there was another beating of a child molester. It seems that he was beaten up by two men, and he ended up dying from his injuries. The two men were caught on tape doing this and were arrested and charged with murder, but they did not seem to care. In fact, they seemed cocky and indifferent about the whole thing."

"When did this happen?"

"Yesterday, Judge."

"Okay, we will see how cocky they and all the others are after Larry pleads his case to the U.S. Supreme Court. They just gave Larry more ammunition." Judge Tunis turns to Lou and says, "Well… are you ready for this?"

"I think so."

"No! no! no! That's not what I want to hear. What I want to hear is, 'Yes, I am absolutely ready to do this.'"

"I'm sorry, Judge. You're right. I am ready to do this."

"Are you sure?"

"Yes, I'm sure."

"Absolutely sure?"

"Yes, absolutely sure."

"Okay, that's better. Now, let's go up these steps and meet up with Larry."

As they ascend the steps, they can't help look up and notice the enormous columns that hold up the massive roof of this towering building, all leading one to believe or feel small and almost insignificant in the realm of things. They can almost feel the power that this building holds – it is just awesome – yet for some strange reason, they feel proud for being a part of it.

When they reach the top of the steps and approach the immense bronze doors, again, they can't help feeling impressed by it all. Going through the bronze doors and entering the building, they then notice the two tremendous sets of spiral staircases, again overwhelming them. Seeing a guard, Judge Tunis asks for directions to the main reading room in the court's library. Getting to the library, he is amazed by the size of it, and after taking it all in, the judge sees Larry sitting at a table, busy preparing his case.

Judge Tunis tells Lou, "Let's walk over and greet Larry." When they get to him, the judge says, "Good morning, Larry."

"Good morning, Judge. Good morning, Lou. So, Lou, are you ready to do this?"

"Yes, I am."

"Good. Just remember, all I want you to do is tell the truth about why and how you got the tapes, and answer any questions the justices have truthfully and to the best of your knowledge."

Larry goes over everything twice, asking Lou questions that he thinks that the Supreme Court Justices will ask him. He also makes sure they have all the tapes and that the tape machine is working. Just in case, Judge Tunis actually brought a second tape player with him. Now that Larry feels that everything is set, all the three of them have to do is sit and wait until they are called, which seems like it's taking forever.

After a while, a clerk comes in and tells the Larry that the main courtroom is now open, and that he will be happy to escort them to it. Judge Tunis and Lou follow Larry and the clerk into the Great Hall leading to the Courtroom. They are all mesmerized by the huge columns and the decorative ceiling. The closer to the door of the Courtroom they get, the faster their hearts beat, until they feel like they're about to pop out of their chests. Finally, they pass through the doors and enter the Courtroom. The judge is awestruck, and he wants to pinch himself, because he feels that he is dreaming, but then he doesn't, because he doesn't want to wake.

As Larry, the judge, and Lou are led to a desk by the clerk, Judge Tunis looks around at the bench with all the chairs, the flags, the high, decorative ceiling and walls, and the podium that Larry will be standing at in a few moments to argue his case, and now he truly believes that his heart is going to burst right out of his chest because of how hard it's beating. He sits down and, using all of his willpower and concentration, fights to calm himself down before Larry has to plead his case.

After about ten minutes, Judge Tunis finally calms down, and just as he is taking a long, deep breath, the court officer comes in and ask all parties to stand. Then he announces that the Supreme Court of the United States is now in session, Chief Justice Scala presiding.

All of the justices file in and take their seats. The court officer swears in Larry Rockwood and Lou Ratsky, and then the bailiff reads the docket on the case and calls up Larry to the podium.

Larry grabs all his papers and the tape player, walks up to the podium, and waits for Chief Justice Scala to speak first. After a few moments, Justice Scala says, "Mr. Rockwood, first, let me say that after reading your brief and what I and the rest of my colleagues have read in the papers, we are all in tune with your plight. Truthfully, I hope that you have the evidence that you claim you have so that we can close this website down and lock some people up, because if, in fact, this website is doing what you claim they are doing, they must be stopped as soon as possible. So, with that said, let me hear what evidence you have."

Larry begins to speak: "Thank you, Your Honor, and may it please the court, today, I stand before you to plead my case, a case–"

Judge Scala says, "Mr. Rockwood, you are wasting time. I told you that we are all aware of your plight, so please get on with your case and let us hear your evidence."

"Okay, Your Honor. I read a story in a Las Vegas newspaper about an unusual number of child molesters being murdered, and the reporter who wrote that story noted that it seemed like open season on known child molesters. This story, for some reason, piqued the curiosity of Judge Tunis, and he started following it, and as he did, he became more skeptical of it. And then, while questioning a potential juror, in one of the trials of one of the accused killers of a child molester, the district attorney in that case became suspicious of the answers that one of the jurors he was questioning was giving, something about a club that the juror belonged to. The D.A. became so convinced that something funny was going on that he asked for an adjournment so that he could check out this club.

"That night. the D.A. in that case went online and had to join the club in order to gain access to it. It was called The Club. After joining it and reading what they call a 'Wouldn't It Be Nice' newsletter that they produced once a month, he could not believe what he was reading. This club was advocating for its members to go out and kill child molesters, telling them that the lawyers from The Club would defend them free of charge and that due to the number of members in The Club, there would be an excellent chance that there would be a member on the jury who would acquit them.

❧❧❧

"Eventually, the accused killer got off. The jurors found him not guilty on all counts. That is when the D.A., Mr. Philip Morrison, got in touch with Judge Tunis, and that's when Judge Tunis decided to shut them down and prosecute its founders. He signed a court order shutting down the website, seizing all of their computers and records, and arresting the founders. He gave it to the FBI to serve and execute, which they did. But before any further action could be taken, a judge in a higher court singed a court order overriding Judge Tunis's court order, freeing all who were arrested and returning all of their computers and records, and then they opened up the website again and were back in business in no time.

"Since then, Judge Tunis has been trying everything in his power to get enough evidence to shut down that website again and arrest all the people again, and until now, he lacked the evidence. But then this news reporter said that he had evidence from an inside man, Judge Tunis picked up on that, met with that person, got the evidence he needed, and then got in touch with me. And now, as you will hear, I am confident that I have enough evidence to achieve my goal. I have with me today a witness, Mr. Lou Ratsky, who is an attorney and was a member of the law team in The Club, and who, after seeing and hearing what the goal of The Club was, decided to gather all the information he could to stop these people."

"Okay Mr. Rockwood," says Justice Scala, "let's hear from your witness."

"Your Honor, here is Mr. Ratsky."

Lou steps up to the podium and is sworn in. Then he says, "Your Honor, my name is Lou Ratsky. I am an attorney licensed to practice in many states. A colleague of mine introduced me to The Club, telling me that they stood for the rights of the people to get fair trials, that there was a lot of corruption in the court system today, and someone had to step up to the plate and do the right thing. So I stepped up, thinking that I was doing the right thing. After attending several meetings, I got the impression that there was more going on than met the eye.

"Then, one day, I was assigned a case with one of the older lawyers, and that's when I really got the whole picture. He told me why The Club was started and by whom. It seems that the founder of The Club, Mr. John Harrison, had a daughter who was kidnapped, raped, buried alive, and left to die a horrible death by a man named Jim Tally, and Your Honor, this I would never, ever want to experience for myself, and also, by the way, the man who was accused of having done it was let go due to lack of evidence, even though there was a video of the man pulling the girl by her hand. He claimed to have let her go. Plus, they never found the body.

"Not too soon after the trial, the girl's father, Mr. John Harrison, while shopping, saw Mr. Jim Tally coming out of a movie house, and he attacked him, shouting, "I'm going to kill you." Some people came to the aid of Mr.

Tally and held Mr. Harrison until the police came. When the police found out that there was a restraining order on Mr. Harrison, they arrested him, and Mr. Tally had to go to the hospital. While Mr. Harrison was in jail, he got the idea about the website, so that all child molesters would be killed, because, as he said, there is no chance of fixing them and the courts and bleeding-heart judges keep letting them go to keep doing what they do.

"So, after finding out all that I did, I decided that they would have to stopped, and I started gathering all the evidence I could. I taped all of the meetings that I attended, and you can hear on the tapes exactly what their intentions were."

"I assume that you have the tapes with you," says Justice Scala.

"Yes, I do, Your Honor."

"Okay, then let's hear them."

The justices listen to the tapes, and after hearing just three of them, Judge Scala says, "Okay, I think that we have heard enough." He looks at all the other justices and says, "Do you all agree?" and they all nod their heads in agreement.

He calls Mr. Rockwood back up to the podium. "Mr. Rockwood, normally we would go back to our chamber and discuss the evidence, but in this case, we all felt that if the evidence was as we feared, we would take action as soon as possible. So I can say this: at the conclusion of this hearing, we will take the necessary steps to issue a court order to shut down that website and arrest all that are responsible ASAP."

Judge Tunis stands up and says, "I want to take this opportunity to thank this court very much for their service."

Two days later, the FBI has in their hands the court order from the United States Supreme Court to close down the website, confiscate all their computers and records, and arrest all the officers of the corporation that owns The Club website.

Within hours, a bunch of FBI agents barge into John's office, and this time they are not so formal and dispense with asking John's secretary to speak to John. Seeing that they have been there before, they just split up and each go straight to John's, Barney's, and Nick's offices. They find John and Nick, but Barney is not in his office, so they hand John and Nick copies of the court order and arrest them. As John and Nick are led out,

John tells his secretary to call Mike and let him know what is going on.

While John and Nick are led away, other FBI agents are busy taking all the computers and records, and telling everyone else that the office has been shut down and that they will have to leave. John's secretary asks one of the FBI agents if she can make a call. He says, "Sorry, you have to leave right now or get arrested," so she leaves and goes home to call Mike.

As soon as John's secretary gets home, she calls Mike and fills him in. Mike can't believe that this is happening again, and tells her that he will try to get in touch with Barney and everyone else involved.

Mike gets in touch with Barney and tells him what is going on, saying, "You should meet up with me and then we will go to turn yourself in. It will be better than them picking you up and arresting you." Barney agrees with Mike, and Mike tells him to sit tight, that he will get in touch with the FBI and set up the surrender. Barney says okay.

Mike calls the FBI and tells them that his client Barney wants to turn himself in and that he will bring him in. "Just tell me where you want him to surrender himself." They tell him to come into the main FBI headquarters right there in New York City. Mike agrees and tells them that he will be there with Barney, today, at 3 PM.

Mike calls Barney and tells him that he will be picking him up at about 2:30 PM, because he has to be at FBI Headquarters at 3 PM to turn himself in. Barney says, "Okay, I will be ready by 2:30 PM."

"Okay, see you then."

At 3 PM, Mike and Barney are at the FBI Headquarters. Barney turns himself in, and as he is led away, Mike tells him, "Hang in there. I will start working on this right away and get to the bottom of it."

Before Mike leaves, he asks for a copy of the court order, and he is shocked to see that it was issued from the United States Supreme Court. He thinks to himself, *Oh boy, I think we are now officially in trouble.*

Mike heads straight to where John is being held, after a while, John is brought to the room that they led Mike to before. Mike tells John to sit down. "John, we are in trouble, really big trouble. This court order came straight from the United States Supreme Court, and I must tell you, there is nowhere else to go from here. The only thing we can do is to try to appeal this court order, but to tell you the truth, you would have a better chance of finding a snowball in hell before I could get this order appealed. We are just going to have to find another way around this. I am going straight back to my office to start working on this, to see if I can come up with something. In the meantime, like I told Barney, just hang in there until I can get something going. I will get back to you."

Mike goes straight back to his office and starts all the paperwork necessary for the trial, but he has no idea how he going to proceed. One of the first things he wants to do is find out what evidence they have. If there's one thing he does know, it's that if the United States Supreme Court is involved, it means that they have evidence to override the original court order issued by the previous judge, and this puts them right back to where the website was first shut down and John was arrested. At this point, Mike has a kind of uneasy feeling about learning what the evidence is, but whatever it is, he needs to know. So, one of the first things Mike does is submit the necessary paperwork to have all of the evidence the feds have turned over to him.

In the meantime, while all this is going on, there are stories all over the newspapers and TV about, child molesters still being killed, and the persons responsible for killing them are still getting away with it. All are calling for something to be done, because it seems to be getting out of control.

Mike finally gets the information he wants, along with the date of the arraignment. It seems that John, Barney, and Nick are being charged with accessory to murder before the fact. As Mike reads the information, he is shocked to read that Larry Rockwood, the D.A. who is prosecuting the case, not only has evidence, but it's in the form of an eyewitness, Lou Ratsky, who was one of the lawyers from the pool of lawyers in The Club. And to add insult to injury, the witness has audiotapes that he made of the meetings he attended.

Mike throws himself down in his chair and pushes his hair back in a stressful manner, staring at the ceiling. He is really upset with the whole situation and is at a loss as to what to do now with the evidence that the D.A. has.

Mike decides to go and see John, to fill him in on what's going on. He gets led into a visitor's room, with two chairs, one table, and no windows. Everything is gray: walls, chairs, and table. Mike feels that it's a very gloomy room and can't wait to get out of there. He sits down and waits for John to come in.

After a few minutes, John is brought into the room. Mike says, "Hi, John. You better sit down for this."

John says, "That doesn't sound good."

"Well… it isn't," Mike replies.

John sits down and says, "Let's hear what you got."

"Okay, John, here it is. The D.A. somehow was able to get the United States Supreme Court to hear his case, and he had the court order from Judge Alex Mohan overturned. So, the long and short of it is that we are right back where we were when the website was first shut down and the computers and records were taken, except, this time, they have more evidence then they had before."

John asks, "What kind of new evidence can they have that they did not have before?"

"First off, do you remember one of our lawyers by the name of Lou Ratsky?"

"Of course I remember him. He worked on the Tod Williams case with Dan. What about him?"

"Well, it seems that he turned state's witness and is telling all, and on top of that, it seems that he taped many of the meetings that he attended."

John stands up, stares at Mike, and shouts, "What the fuck are you saying?!!!"

"I'm saying that we are fucking screwed, that's what I'm saying. That son of a bitch piece of shit royally screwed us, and at this point, I don't know what to do. Right now, the three of you are being charged with accessory to murder before the fact, and the first thing I have to do is to go back to the office and try to figure something out. This is not the news I wanted to bring you, but it is what it is."

John sits back down and stares into space, turning his head left and right. Mike says, "John, I know this is a lot to take in, but like I said, it is what it is, and right now, you have to pull yourself together and try to help me come up with some kind of defense. But right now John… I'm going back to my office. I know it's hard, but try to relax for now. We have a few weeks to come up with something. Right now, I have to go and fill Barney and Nick in on all this bullshit, and I'm sure that they are going to react the same way that you did. Okay, I really have to go now. I've got a lot of work to do. I will keep in touch. Bye for now."

Mike next meets with Barney and then Nick. He fills them in, and both of them react just like John did, except Barney really went off the deep end and wanted to kill someone, and expelled expletives like Mike had never heard before, even when he was in the Navy. Mike told him to try and calm down, because he had to go back to his office to try and come up with something and had no time to waste, calming him down. "Okay, Barney," Mike finally said, "I'm out of here. Like I said to John, I will keep in touch. Bye for now."

Mike goes back to his office, sits down at his desk, puts his hands under his chin as though holding his head up, and stares into space, pondering what to do next. He stays that way for at least ten minutes, and then he starts hitting the books, looking for some direction.

Three days go by, and Mike makes at least twenty phone calls to his cohorts in an effort to find a path to go down, one with some sort of light at the end of it. Finally, Mike comes up with a plan, one with the only solution he can think of. After reading all the evidence and listening to the tapes, it seems that it's the only path he can take, because, at this point, he feels that the D.A. has John, Barney, and Nick by the balls.

Mike goes to see John in the jail where he is being held until his trial comes up. When he gets there, the guards lead him to that same gray room that he hates, but he tries to put himself into another place as he sits down and waits for John.

As John enters the room, and even before the door is closed behind him, he says to Mike, "I hope you came up with something, because I came up dry."

Mike tells John, "Sit down and let me explain what I came up with, and please, let me finish explaining before you say anything. John, I'm going to give it to you straight. I'm not going to hold anything back or pull any punches. So, here goes. I have read all the evidence and listened to all of the tapes, and first off, I have to tell you that the D.A., at this point, has got the three of you by the balls, and there is no way that I can see to come up with an intelligent defense other than saying that you were so grief stricken that you did not realize that what you were doing was wrong, and that all the things that you were doing were just to relieve your grief. I guess you can say that it's sort of an insanity plea."

John just sits there, staring at Mike, and in a calm voice, he says, "Are you fucking kidding me? You mean that this is the only defense that you can come up with?"

"Okay, John, were you not listening to me when I was talking, or what? Yes, that is exactly what I came up with. John, let me enlighten you about something. Lou has you on tape saying that you hope that the members of The Club 'go out and kill all those fucking sick bastard child molesters and rid this world of those fucking mutants, and the way people are joining, we will have enough of them to almost guarantee that there will be a member of The Club serving on the jury in all of those cases and set them free.' And John, those are your words, verbatim. So, John, if you don't like that defense, you tell me exactly what path you would like me to take, and I will take it."

There is just silence.

"Well, I'm waiting."

Nothing.

"I thought so. John, I don't think you realize how much trouble you are in. Let me put it this way: you are in deep shit, up to your neck and sinking. Maybe you understand that. Well, do you?"

"Yes, Mike, I guess I do. It's just hard to admit it. You are right. Let's go with the insanity grief thing."

"Okay, John. I will get things started. Again, I'm sorry, but there is no other way that I can see. Believe me, I did not just pull this shit out of my ass. I spoke to a lot of people and researched a lot of books before I decided on it, so just sit tight and hope for the best. There's one last question I want to ask you, and please don't jump down my throat. It's something I have to ask you even though I know the answer. Will you be willing to have a psychiatric evaluation? It's something to think about, because if they find you unfit to stand trial, you may get away with just a few years in a psychiatric ward."

John looks at Mike. "Let me put it this way. I will let you get away with asking me that question just this once, but if you ask me one more time, I will kill you with my bare hands. Do you understand that?"

"Yes, I do. So, right now, forget that I asked you that question and calm yourself down, and I will keep in touch. So, bye for now."

Next, Mike visits with Barney and then Nick, to fill them in on what kind of defense he plans, except, in their cases, he tells them that he will have to plead, that John was so grief-stricken that he was able to brainwash them into believing that what he was doing was the right thing to do, causing them to have a severe lack of judgement.

Barney and Nick, both being lawyers, agree with Mike that due to the evidence against them, there is not much wiggle room for a good defense. As Mike put it, it is what it is. Mike thinks to himself, *Well, that was easy, if only because, being lawyers, they understand.* "Okay, so, like I told John, hang in there, and I will be in touch."

Mike goes back to his office to work on some last-minute details, and as he walks into his office, his secretary greets him. "Good morning, Mr. Santino. I have a message for you from a Judge Ghetto. He would like for you to return his call."

"Okay, can you please get him on the phone?"

"Yes, Mr. Santino." A moment later: "I have Judge Ghetto on the phone."

Mike gets on the line. "Hi, good morning, Judge. What can I do for you?"

"Well, Mike, I have been reading in the papers and seeing on TV about the goings on with John, Barney, and Nick, who were arrested and locked up, and about the website being closed down. I just want you to know that if there is anything I can do, please don't hesitate to ask, because, as you know, I was and still am in allegiance with their plight."

"Judge, that's great. I will certainly keep that in mind, and thank you."

"You're welcome. And by the way, are you aware – and I don't know if this is just a coincidence – but did you hear that yesterday, right here in New York, there was a child molester killed, and the killer turned himself in. Do you know if any of the lawyers from The Club are still doing their thing?"

"No, as far as I know, all of the lawyers went their own way, but I will definitely keep my eye on that case. Thanks for the heads up."

"You're welcome. Bye for now."

"Bye."

Mike checks out the story about the killing on his computer, and he thinks that maybe he can somehow use this in the defense of John, Barney, and Nick, so he decides to keep a close eye on the story.

It's the day of the arraignment, and Mike sits it the courtroom waiting for John, Barney, and Nick. The courtroom is filled with reporters and spectators. Mike feels that it's like a three-ring circus, with TV news trucks outside, along with hundreds of spectators. All of a sudden, from outside, he can hear the spectators yelling all sorts of things, so he assumes that the three of them have arrived.

Finally, John, Barney, and Nick are brought in. When they come in, they are in handcuffs and prison jumpsuits. They sit down at the table with Mike, and he turns to them and says, "I know I don't have to remind all of you, but for your sake, John, all that is going to happen today is that the judge will read the charges against you and ask you how you plead. And remember, not guilty, okay?"

"Okay, Mike.".

After about ten minutes, the bailiff calls the court to order, asks everyone to stand, and announces that Judge Panini is entering the courtroom and that this court is now in session. After Judge Panini sits, the bailiff instructs the people to please have a seat.

The bailiff reads, "Your Honor, this is case number 1937, against, John Harrison, Barney Cicale, and Nick Alesi. All are charged with accessory to murder before the fact."

The judge asks all three to stand. "Do you, John Harrison, understand the charges brought against you by this court?"

"Yes, I do, Your Honor."

"And how do you plead?"

"Not guilty, Your Honor."

"And you, Barney Cicale, do you understand the charges brought against you by this court?"

"Yes, I do, Your Honor."

"And how do you plead?"

"Not guilty, Your Honor."

"And you, Nick Alesi, do you understand the charges brought against you by this court?"

"Yes, I do."

"And how do you plead?"

"Not guilty, Your Honor."

"Okay, then, I will set aside June 13 as the trial date, and June 11 and 12 for jury selection. Does either side have any objections to those dates?"

The D.A. and Mike both say, "No, Your Honor."

"Okay, so then, it's all set. I will see all of you on June 13, 2006."

On June 11, Mike is at the courthouse bright and early, waiting for jury selection to start. He looks around the room and thinks how boring it is – the only thing to break up the color scheme is the American flag – but he figures that it's good not to have too many distractions so that everyone can concentrate on the business at hand.

Finally, the jurors file into the room and get into their chairs, and then, after a while, the judge comes in, and finally, the process starts.

"Good morning, everyone," says the judge. "We will now start the jury selection, but before we begin, I want to let the D.A. and defense lawyers know that because of the scope of this trial, I will only allow two peremptory challenges for each side, with no exceptions. With that said, I just want to remind the prospective jurors that they will be under oath, and to make sure that they think of that before they answer the questions. Now, let's get started. Bailiff, please call the first juror."

The D.A. starts questioning the first juror as Mike sits there listening to every word from the juror's mouth and making notes for when he is ready to question that juror when his time comes. After the D.A. finishes with the first juror, it's Mikes turn, and this goes on and on for all the jurors, with all of the jurors giving what seem to be all of the right answers.

Then, while the D.A. is questioning the ninth juror, Mike doesn't like the answer he hears from one of the questions the D.A. asked. He makes a note to question the juror about her answer.

When it's Mikes turn, he tells her, "Hi. Let's get right to it. Okay, when the D.A. asked you about your feelings concerning child molesters, the same question that the D.A., as well as myself, asked all of the previous jurors, you answered a little differently. You said that you think that child molesters are sick and should be put in a hospital until they are healed and not held responsible for what they have done. Do you really think that? Let me ask you this: do you think that if they did get put into a mental institution that they could be healed or fixed so that they could be released to lead a normal life among us?"

"No. Like I said, I think that they are sick and need to be put in a hospital so that they can be healed, and not in an institution for the insane."

With that answer, Mike tells the judge that he would like to use one of his peremptory challenges on this juror. The judge says, "Okay," and he tells the juror, "Thank you for your service. You are excused from jury duty." Then he turns to the bailiff. "Bailiff, please call the next juror."

To Mike's surprise, the rest of the jury selection goes on without a hitch. All the questions that are asked by the D.A. and Mike are answered correctly or, at least, to the satisfaction of them both. Mike is sure that, at some point, he would have had to use his second peremptory challenge, but it never comes to that, but still, the little hairs on the back of Mike's neck are standing up. It all seems too easy, and Mike cannot figure out why. Nevertheless, both sides come away happy.

The judge gives some more instructions to the jury and reminds both sides that he will see them on June 13th, and to please be on time. With that, Mike and the D.A. head back to their offices to map out their plans.

June 13 arrives. In life, it seems that every time there is an important day coming up, a day that if you could, you would rather avoid than acknowledge and confront, that day always seems to get there too fast, and you never seem to have enough time to plan for it. Well, that's how Mike is feeling right now. The day has come for the big trial, and to Mike, it feels like it's the trial of century and that no matter how hard or long he worked on his defense, he did not have enough time. This all seemed to have been put on the fast track. But whatever Mike feels, there is no turning back now, and he has to pull out all the stops on this one.

Mike gathers his papers and heads to the courthouse. When he gets there, he can't believe his eyes. First, if it were not for the courthouse providing parking for the attorneys, he would not have been able to find a parking spot. In all his years of practicing law, Mike has never seen such a gathering of spectators, reporters, media trucks, photographers, and vendors with wagons full of souvenirs, people selling t-shirts with all kinds of sayings and pictures, a lot of which are not suitable for minors. There are even vendors selling food. There are kids with balloons with sayings on them like "Please protect me." It is literally like a three-ring circus.

Mike fights his way through the reporters, photographers, and spectators, and finally gets into the courthouse, where he finds that it's not very much different from what is going on outside, minus the vendors. Again, Mike has to fight his way through the courthouse to the courtroom itself. Once inside, he finds it a little less hectic. Mike sits down at his table and starts to prepare his defense, going over in his mind who the D.A. will call as their witnesses, and Mike is surprised to see on the disclosure papers that the D.A. sent him that all they intend to call as witnesses are Mrs. Tod Williams, Mrs. David Mudd, one psychiatrist, Dr. Thomas Nopis, and their star witness, Lou Ratsky, their inside man, along with the audiotapes he made of meetings he attended.

※※※

Mike feels that his witnesses, a psychiatrist, and the parents, grandparents, siblings, and friends of the children who were raped and murdered will offset all the witnesses that the D.A. has except for Mr. Lou Ratsky and his tapes. Mike feels that they have no choice but for John to plead extreme anguish and being so grief-stricken that he did not realize that what he was doing was wrong, so much so that he convinced Barney and Nick to join him in his quest for revenge.

Everything set up now, Mike sees the D.A., Mr. Morrison, come in with his entourage, and he looks over at them as they get themselves set up. Mike and the D.A. look at each other and nod their heads in greeting, like two gladiators ready to do battle to their death but still showing respect for each other.

Finally, the court stenographer and clerks enter the courtroom, followed, a few minutes later, by the bailiff. Once in the courtroom, the bailiff settles everyone down and explains the rules to all, and he warns everyone that he will have zero tolerance with anyone who tries to disrupt the proceedings and will have them ejected posthaste. Then Mike sees six police men and three court officers enter the room. The three court officers come up to the front, and the six police men stand at the rear. Now Mike realizes the magnitude of this trial.

Mike just sits and waits for Barney, Nick, and John to be brought in. Soon, a door opens, and all three are brought in, and they come and sit at Mike's table. Mike asks, "How are you guys doing?"

Barney says, "How do you think we are doing? Okay, I guess."

John and Nick both say in unison, "Okay, I guess."

John asks Mike, "Well, since I spoke to you last, has anything changed?"

Mike answers, "No, I'm afraid not, but I promise you guys that I will do the best I can with what I've got."

With that, the bailiff yells out, "All stand! The honorable Judge Phil Panini presiding. This court is now in session." After Judge Panini sits down, the bailiff tells everyone to please be seated. Then he announces to Judge Panini, "Your Honor, this is case number 1937, the people verses Harrison, Alesi, and Cicale, against the charges of accessory to murder before the fact."

Judge Panini sits quietly and looks down at some papers on his desk, turning a few pages and looking them over, and he continues to do this for at least three minutes, which, to Mike, seems like forever. At this point, you could have heard a pin drop in the courtroom.

Finally, Judge Panini looks up and all around the courtroom. Then he stares at the ceiling for a few seconds, and then at the people again. At this point, everyone is wondering what is going on. Finally, he says, "Ladies and Gentleman, I have something to say to every person in this courtroom, and I mean ever person, no exceptions. I want you to know that because of the underlying seriousness of this case, this court will show zero tolerance to anyone, and again, I mean anyone, who will try to disrupt these proceedings, and anyone who tries, will be dealt with to the full extent of the law. Okay, enough said about that. Now, let's get on with this trial. First, is the defense, ready?"

Mike stands up and says, "Yes, we are, Your Honor."

"And Mr. Morrison, are the people ready?"

Mr. Morrison stands up and says, "Yes, Your Honor, the people are ready."

Judge Panini then exclaims, "Okay, then let's get started. The jury has been sworn in, so let's start with opening statements. Mr. Morrison, for the people, you may start."

"Thank you, Your Honor."

Mr. Morrison stands up and walks toward the jurors. He looks at them and then tilts his head back, staring up at the ceiling for a few seconds, holding his chin as though he is thinking about what he is about to say. Then he tilts his head back down, now looking at the jurors, and starts speaking: "Ladies and gentleman of the jury, I will make this as short as possible and try not to bore you today. Because of the overwhelming evidence that the people have, you are about to hear a trial that will probably go down as the shortest murder trial in history. This trial is about three men who thought that taking the law into their own hands was the righteous thing to do, and in doing so, they are responsible for the useless and senseless death of many men, and to date, we are not even sure of how many. The last time we checked, it was at least twenty-five to thirty-five, and possibly many more. Not all of them have been brought to our attention, and this has been going on for many years. And to top it all off, because of these three men, all the killers got away with it. That's right, they got away with it. I will repeat it. All of them got away with murder, and just to remind you, most of the men who were murdered were sons, husbands, and fathers who were taken away without warning or reason, and in many cases, will be sorrowfully missed by their parents, wives, children, and grandchildren.

"Today, I will show you evidence, beyond any reasonable doubt, in an open-and-shut case, that these three men are guilty and have shown absolutely no remorse for what they have done, and knew exactly in preplanned moves that what they were doing was wrong and against the law. I will also show you that they were so cunning and so convincing that they convinced millions of people to join their website, called The Club, and fund their movement, and some were motivated to the point that they would go out and kill another human being. So, ladies and gentleman of the jury, after hearing all of my evidence, I implore you to search your soul and conscience to find all three guilty as charged. Thank you."

Judge Panini waits until Mr. Morrison is seated, and then he calls for the defense to make their opening statement. "Defense, are you ready?"

Mike answers, "Yes, we are, Your Honor." Mike gets up, thinking to himself as he walks over to the jurors' box, *I hope to hell I know what the fuck I'm doing here.* Finally at the jurors' box, Mike looks at the jurors. He looks left to right, looking at all of their faces, and then he goes back left, stopping for a few seconds at each one, looking into their eyes for some sign of compassion or anything else that might give him some kind of a good feeling about what he is about to do. In the courtroom, there is dead silence as Mike stands there looking at a juror.

Judge Panini shouts out, "Mr. Santino, do you think that we can get to hear your opening statement sometime today?"

Mike is startled, as well as many in the courtroom. He turns to the judge, and in between the smattering of laughter from several spectators, says, "Yes, Your Honor. I will start now. Ladies and gentleman of the jury, good morning. And to follow what Mr. Morrison said, I too will try to make this short and not bore you. First off, let me say right now, at the onset of this trial, standing here before you, I am not going to try to defend what these three men did as being right. That's right. I said it was not the right thing to do. My clients don't deny that what the people are accusing them of doing, they actually did. And knowing what evidence the people have and that is that they have enough evidence to make this an open-and-shut case, well, I don't think that it's that simple. There is a lot more to this case than what Mr. Morrison says there is. But what I will say is that I don't intend to defend my clients in the standard textbook manner that's called for in a case like this. However, I am going to go out on a limb and try this case in a different and unorthodox way by trying to make you understand and feel what my clients felt that brought them to the state of mind that they were in. Also, I will categorically state, right now, as I stated before, and that being due to the evidence that Mr. Morrison has, that I will not try to convince you of my three clients' innocence. I will, however, detail the macabre, morbid, deplorable, atrocious, grotesque, monstrous, and many more ways to describe what these men who were killed did. And remember this, all the men who were killed were convicted child molesters. They were not your normal, everyday, law-abiding citizens.

"And now the people say my clients are responsible for these men being killed, and as I said before, I will attempt to appeal to your innermost feelings of your consciences and perceptions of what the loss, loneliness, and sadness a parent experiences upon the loss of one of their children, such as what one of my clients, John Harrison, went through. So incomprehensibly grief-stricken was John that he was able to bring himself, and convince two of his cohorts to join him, to do what they did, and all three thinking that it was the right thing to do.

So, in closing, just let me say this: all I ask is that you pay close attention to my witnesses and clients, listen closely to what they have to say, and try to put yourself in the places of my clients. Try to feel their feelings of grief and sympathy for the children that they lost and how the parents felt, and if you can do that, then I'm sure that you will bring back a decision of not guilty due to insanity brought on by intense grief. Thank you."

Judge Panini, then says, "Okay, then, if everyone is satisfied with their opening statements, let's get this trial started. Are the people ready to start?"

"Yes, Your Honor."

"Okay, then, please call your first witness."

"We would like to call our first witness, Mrs. Frei, the wife of Mr. Don Frei, who, while incarcerated, was murdered by an inmate by the name of Tod Williams, who was a members of the website club that was put together by these people who are here on trial. And that man was found not guilty, because one or more members of this website just happened to be on the jury."

Just then, Judge Panini shouts out, "Mr. Morrison! This is sounding like your opening statement all over again. Cease what you are doing immediately and just call your witness. Is that clear?"

"Yes, Your Honor. The people call Mrs. Frei to the stand."

The bailiff opens the back door and shouts out, "Mrs. Frei, we are ready for you. Please take the stand."

She walks in, staring straight at the witness stand and not looking at anyone else. There is stone-dead silence in the courtroom, even though the courtroom is standing room only. Finally at the witness chair, she stands, the bailiff swears her in, and as she sits, Mr. Morrison approaches and begins to question her.

"Mrs. Frei, can you please tell this court who you are, why you are in this courtroom today, and how what happened to you has affected your life?"

"My name is Mary Frei, and several years ago, my husband, while incarcerated, was murdered by Tod Williams, a person who was a member of a website called The Club that advocated the killing of child molesters."

Mike shouts out, "I object, Your Honor. That has not been proven. That's what we are doing here today."

Judge Panini says, "You're right. That is what we are doing here today, so the objection is sustained. The jury is instructed to disregard that last statement. Okay, Mrs. Frei, you may continue, but please refrain from accusing anyone of being guilty of a crime that they have not been found guilty of."

"Okay, Your Honor. Anyway, the person who killed my husband was arrested and tried, but was found not guilty. I can't believe that they found him not guilty. I had to be treated for acute depression, and had to be hospitalized because of it. Also, my two children suffered from depression, and on top of everything else, when my husband was killed, his pension stopped, and eventually, I ended up losing my home, and all the things that I was making payments on were repossessed. I had to go on welfare to exist, because all I was getting was Social Security, and that was not enough for me to live on. Not only did I lose my soulmate, I lost everything else that mattered to me, and again, I had to be taken to the hospital emergency room, because I tried to commit suicide. And now, two years later, I am still in therapy because of it. This whole thing, just ruined my entire life to the point that there are no words to describe what I went through, and am still going through."

With that, the D.A. says, "I'm done with this witness, Your Honor."

Judge Panini now looks at Mike. "Defense, do you want to question this witness?"

Mike replies, "Yes, Your Honor." He gets up, walks to Mrs. Frei, looks at her, and says, "Mrs. Frei, I'm sorry for your loss and all that you went through but did you ever take into consideration the anguish, the agony, the distress, the torment, the misery, the heartache, the mental distress–"

The D.A. shouts, "I object, Your Honor. I believe the defense has made his point."

"Overruled. I know this case is very sensitive to all parties, so please try not to be so melodramatic."

"Okay, Your Honor," says Mike. "So, I say again, did you ever take all that I said into consideration, for the family that lost a child to a child molester and what the victim themselves went through, the horrible way that they were killed? Did you?

There is silence in the courtroom as Mike waits for an answer. Finally, she answers, "Yes, I have."

"Okay, great. I have one last question for you, and I know that this next question is going to be an extremely difficult one to answer, and I really wish that you try to answer it if you can. If, somehow, you were put into a situation where you had to choose, between losing your husband or one of your young children to a violent crime, which one would you choose to give up?"

The D.A. jumps out of his chair and shouts, "I object, Your Honor! That is irrelevant to this case."

"Sustained. Defense, I warned everyone at the onset of this trial that I will not tolerate anything that does not conform to the decorum of this case, and you just went over that line. The jury is instructed to disregard that last question. Now, get on with your questioning."

"I'm finished with this witness, Your Honor."

"Okay, does the D.A. want to recross this witness?"

"No, Your Honor."

"Okay, then, Mrs. Frei, you are excused."

The D.A. stands up and says, "Next, the people call Mr. John Mudd to the stand."

The bailiff goes to the back doors, calls Mr. Mudd, and asks him to please take the stand. Mr. Mudd gets to the chair, and the bailiff swears him in, saying, "Okay, you may be seated now."

The D.A. approaches Mr. Mudd. "Good morning, Mr. Mudd. Could please tell the court who you are and what were the circumstances that brought you to court today as a witness?"

"My name is John Mudd, and I am here today to tell this court what I went through after my father was murdered by a policeman in a police station while he was cuffed. My father never had a chance to have his day in court. This policeman took it upon himself to be judge, jury, and executioner. This happened about a year ago, and I had to live with my mother's deep depression, for almost a year, until, one day, when I came home from work, I could not find her. I looked all over the house. Then I finally found her in the garage. She was dead. She hung herself, and let me tell you this, finding a loved one like that is a sight that I wish no one ever has to see. My father was a kind and gentle soul, and did not deserve to be murdered like that, and that person is still walking around, because he got away with it. To that cop who killed my father, I want him to know that he ruined my family's life and is responsible for my mother taking her own life. To me, that cop murdered her also."

"I am finished with this witness, Your Honor."

As the D.A. returns to his desk, Judge Panini says, "Does the defense wish to question this witness?"

"Yes, Your Honor." Mike stands and walks toward John, all the time thinking how quiet it is in the courtroom. It seems that everyone in the courtroom, including the jury, is listening intensely, to every word.

"Good morning, Mr. Mudd. First, let me say how sorry I am to hear about all the grief that you went through."

"Thank you."

"Mr. Mudd, let me ask you this: do you know what crime your father was arrested for?"

"Yes."

"And would you please tell the court what that crime was?".

Mr. Mudd pauses before answering. "They said that he kidnapped a little girl and held her captive in his home and molested her, but that was never proven, because, like I said before, he never got a chance to have his day in court."

"Yes, I understand that, but when the little girl managed to escape, she showed a policeman where in the house he kept her, and she also identified him at the police station as the person who took her and molested her every day. Can you imagine just what that little girl went through every day?"

"Well, I guess, but I still say my father did not do it."

"Also, do you know why your mother left you father?"

"No."

"Do you think that it was because she knew what kind of man he was?"

"I don't know."

"Did your father ever say anything to you about liking little girls?"

At this, the D.A. stands and says, "Objection, Your Honor. Mr. Mudd is not on trial here."

"Sustained. Stay with this case, Mr. Santino."

"Okay. One final question. Knowing what this little girl went through, and if you could put yourself in her shoes and had the same chance to kill him, would you have?"

At this point, the D.A. again jumps up and shouts, "Objection, Your Honor! Again, it's irrelevant to this case."

"You're right. Sustained. Mr. Santino, I warned you about this line of questioning."

"I'm sorry, Your Honor. I have nothing more. I'm done with this witness."

The judge asks the D.A., "Do the people have any more witnesses?"

"Yes, we do. The people now call Dr, Thomas Nopis."

The bailiff calls Dr. Nopis. The D.A. is standing by the witness chair, waiting for the doctor. As Dr. Nopis sits, and after he is sworn in, the D.A. says, "Dr. Nopis, can you please tell this court who you are and what you here for?"

"Yes, my name is Dr. Thomas Nopis. I graduated from the Harvard Medical School's psychiatry department at the top of my class, and I am the senior member of the board of the Massachusetts General Hospital, which is considered the top hospital for the practice of psychiatry. I am also affiliated with several other prestigious psychiatric hospitals. Due to the fact that Mr. John Harrison refused to be seen by a psychiatrist so that he could be evaluated, I was asked to listen to the tapes of Mr. Harrison speaking and to also speak to Mr. Ratsky, who attended many meetings that Mr. Harrison spoke at, and give them my evaluation of Mr. Harrison as to whether or not he seemed insane and did not realize that what he was doing was right or wrong."

At this point, Mike is squirming in his chair and wants to jump up and object to something, but he feels that there is really nothing he could object to, so he just sits and squirms.

"And what was your expert determination, Doctor?"

"My expert determination is that Mr. Harrison, knew exactly what he was doing."

"Thank you, Doctor. Your Honor, the people are finished with this witness."

"Mr. Santino," asks the judge, "do you wish to cross?"

Yes, Your Honor." Mike walks up to the witness chair and stands there, looking at Dr. Nopis for a few seconds, not saying a word. Then, after what seems like forever, Mike says, "Good Morning, Doctor. I have only one question for you. Well, maybe two. First, how long have you been practicing?"

"I have been practicing psychiatry for twenty-seven years."

"Okay, thank you, Doctor. And my second question is, in all of your twenty-seven years, when was the last time that you were ever asked to evaluate a person to see whether that person was insane or not, without the person actually being seated in front of you?"

"Well, you don't really need the person in front of you to evaluate them."

Mike interrupts the doctor, asking the judge, "Your Honor, can you please instruct this witness to answer just the question I asked him, and not to give us his personal opinion on evaluating people?"

"Doctor," says the judge, "please answer just the question that Mr. Santino asked you. Also, the jury will disregard the last statement of the witness."

"Thank you, Your Honor," says Mike. "Okay, Doctor, can you just answer the last question, and would you like for me to repeat it?"

"No, that won't be necessary."

"Okay, then, Doctor, what is your answer?"

"No, I have not."

"Doctor, can you please be more explicit with your answer?"

"How much more explicit do you want me to be? I answered your question. I said no."

"What I mean by being more explicit, if you don't mind, is, and being that you did not answer the question when I asked you, I would like you to answer it in a complete sentence so that the jurors know exactly what you are saying no to."

Before the doctor has a chance to answer, the D.A. jumps up. "Objection, Your Honor!!! The witness has already answered the question."

"Overruled, Mr. Morrison," answers the judge. "It's no big deal. I can understand why Mr. Santino wants a complete sentence with the answer, so you are overruled. Doctor, please answer the question properly."

"Okay, Your Honor. No, in all of my twenty-seven years of practice, I have never been asked to evaluate the mental health of someone without that person actually being present in the same room as me. Is that a better answer?"

"Yes, it is, Doctor. I'm done with this witness, Your Honor."

"Does the people wish to recross," asks the judge.

"No, Your Honor."

Judge Panini asks the D.A., "Mr. Morrison, do the people have any more witnesses?"

"Yes, we do, Your Honor. The people now call our last witness, Mr. Lou Ratsky."

Once again, the bailiff goes to the back doors and calls Mr. Lou Ratsky. As Lou enters the courtroom, he is very nervous about something, and seems to be running to the witness chair, as though he himself is on trial. Mike can't figure just what's going on. He thinks to himself, *Something is not right here.*

Lou is sworn in, and the D.A. gets up and walks over to the witness chair. "Good morning, Mr. Ratsky."

Lou replies back, "Good morning."

"Mr. Ratsky, let's not waste the time of the jurors."

"Okay."

"Will you please tell the jurors who you are, what kind of evidence you have, how you obtained this evidence, and why?"

"Okay, my name is Lou Ratsky. I am an attorney who was just starting out and finding it very hard to make ends meet. One day, a fellow attorney told me about this website that was hiring lawyers, so I got the address from him and went over to see what it was all about. I was interviewed by an attorney by the name of Barney Cicale. He explained the job as helping out people who were wrongfully accused of a crime and could not afford an attorney on their own, and the pay was good, so I decided to go to work for them.

"I shared an office with a few other attorneys, and we all got along great. I was very happy there. I attended meetings where we discussed some of the cases that they were working on, and all seemed to be going well. Then, one day, I was assigned a case to work on, and that's when I realized what this job was all about, because that is when the other lawyers I was working with filled me in on exactly what was going on. It seemed that this place that I worked for was setting up some kind of club, hence the name of the place, which was The Club. And the long and short of it was that they were trying to set up a system to rid the world of child molesters, where a person who went out and killed a child molester got all the help they needed, including an attorney, money, and anything else that they might need."

While Lou is testifying, an aide of Mike's comes into the courtroom, hands him a note, and whispers in his ear, "I thought that you would like to know about this, Mike."

"Thanks."

Mike reads the note. It says that there was another killing of a child molester a month ago, and the killer went to trial this morning and was found not guilty, and the headline in the papers read "It Seems That They Are Still at It." Mike is surprised by this note, and he hands it to John to read. John reads it, looks at Mike, and hands it to Barney, who reads it and then hands it to Nick. He reads it and then hands it back to Mike. All three men are looking at Mike, shrugging their shoulders. By now, most of the people are looking at Mike and the three suspects, and it seems that no one is paying attention to the D.A.'s prize witness.

Judge Panini, noticing this, instructs Lou to stop speaking. "Mr. Ratsky, please stop your testimony. It seems that we have something more interesting going on in this courtroom than your testimony. Mr. Santino, would you like to share with the rest of this court what you have that's so interesting that it warrants the disruption of these court proceedings?"

"I'm really sorry, Your Honor. It was something extremely important to me, and it was also extremely time sensitive. Again, Your Honor, I'm extremely sorry."

"Mr. Santino, it seems that you have a lot of extremely important things going on, but maybe you should concentrate on the extremely important case that you are working on right now."

This prompts a little laughter from the spectators, and the bailiff shouts out, "Order in the courtroom!" and everyone settles down. Judge Panini then tells the witness to please continue with his testimony.

"As I was saying, The Club would supply anything the suspect would need. Then, as the trial progressed, I found out about the possibility of one of the jurors being a member of The Club, and they would either deadlock the jury or convince them to decide on a not-guilty verdict, thus setting the killer free. After that, I said to myself that what these people were doing was very wrong, and the more I checked into it, by letting them believe that I was totally with them, the more I was startled at what they were trying and in some cases succeeding in doing.

"It was then, that I decided to collect all the information on The Club that I could. I first started writing things down after each meeting, but I felt that I could not retain all that I heard, so I then decided that If I wanted to do this right, I would have to try and record some of the meetings. It was then that I went out and bought a small tape recorder so that I could record the meetings, and I believe that these tapes will tell the whole story, hopefully, enough to put these people in jail.

Mike jumps up to object, but then he thinks that it would only be an exercise in futility. Mike says, "Never mind, Your Honor," and sits down.

Judge Panini then asks Lou, "Do you have these tapes?"

Lou replies, "Yes, I do."

With that, Mr. Morrison stands up and says, "Your Honor, I would now like to submit evidence number one, in the form of six tapes."

"Okay, Mr. Morrison. Please hand them to the bailiff to play."

As the tapes are played, most of it is of no interest. After a few moments, Judge Panini tells the D.A., "Mr. Morrison, can you please speed up the tape to the incriminating parts that you say you have on these tapes?"

"Yes, Your Honor." The D.A. goes over to the bailiff and asks him to fast forward the tape until he tells him to stop. The bailiff speeds up the tape as the D.A. listens carefully. Then, finally reaching a portion of the tape that he was looking for, he tells the bailiff to please stop and play it at the regular speed, and then to pause it. "Your Honor, this is the portion of the tape that says it all."

"Okay, then play it."

The bailiff hits the play button, and what comes out of the speakers shocks the spectators, judge, and Jury, and the looks on their faces tell the whole story. On the tape, you can hear John ranting about child molesters and hear him clearly say, "I hope that the members of The Club go out and kill all those fucking sick bastard child molesters and rid this world of those fucking mutants, and the way people are joining, we will have enough of them to almost guarantee that there will be a member of The Club serving on the jury in all of those cases and set them free."

With that, Judge Panini says, "Okay, shut it off. I think that we have heard all we need to hear. What about Mr. Alesi and Mr. Cicale? Do you have them on any of the tapes condemning themselves?"

"No, Your Honor, and according to my witness, John was the only one to speak at these meetings, at least most of the time, and if anyone else spoke, it was to reiterate what John was saying and not on what we are here for. It was just incidental stuff about the everyday goings on at the office. On a few of the other tapes, you can still hear John going on about killing child molesters, but Your Honor, I think that the first tape you and the jury heard is the most important and critical tape I have. Your Honor, it says it all."

"Okay, then, Mr. Santino, do you want to cross-examine this witness?"

"Yes, I do, Your Honor."

Mike gets up and walks over to the witness. "Mr. Ratsky, after the website was shut down, what did you do to earn money?"

The D.A. jumps up. "Objection! Irrelevant, Your Honor."

Judge Panini asks Mike, "Mr. Santino, where are you going with this line of questioning?"

"Your Honor, I am trying to find out if there are other reasons as to why these tapes came out."

"What other possible reasons would there be?"

"To question the validity of these tapes."

"I can't see any path that you could go down to do this. Objection sustained. Now, get on with your questioning, and get off the path that you are on. Stay within the realm of this case."

"Okay, Your Honor. I have just one more question. Mr. Ratsky, you can answer the next question with just a yes or no. Did you receive any money for these tapes?"

Again, the D.A. jumps up. "Objection, Your Honor! What has that got to do with the evidence? As you yourself said, Your Honor, that has nothing to do with the validity of these tapes."

"Sustained. Mr. Santino, all I will say at this point is this is your last warning. Get off that path that you are on."

"Sorry, Your Honor. Nothing else. I'm finished with this witness."

The judge says, "Mr. Morrison, please call your next witness."

"Your Honor, the people rest."

Then, to Mike, the judge asks, "Mr. Santino, do you have any witnesses?"

"Yes, we do, Your Honor."

"Okay, then, you may now call your first witness."

"Thank you, Your Honor. I now call Mrs. Sweeney."

The bailiff again goes to the rear doors and calls Mrs. Sweeney. She enters the courtroom and heads for the witness stand amidst whispers from the spectators. Fighting tears, she sits. Mike walks up to her, and seeing the state that she is in, turns to the bailiff and asks for a tissue. The bailiff goes to a table, gets a tissue, hands it to Mike, and he, in turn, hands it to Mrs. Sweeney. Getting the tissue, she immediately wipes the tears from her eyes.

The D.A. stands up and says, "Objection, Your Honor. Mr. Santino hasn't even asked a question yet, and the tears are already falling. Your Honor, I think this is just an act Mrs. Sweeney is putting on."

"Overruled, Mr. Morrison. With a witness like this, you need to give them a little more leeway, so you are overruled. Continue, Mr. Santino."

"Thank you, Your Honor." Mike tells Mrs. Sweeney to take her time. After a moment or two, Mrs. Sweeney gathers herself and says to Mike, "I'm okay now."

"Good, now, can you please tell the jury who you are and what happened to you?"

"My name is Mrs. Sarah Sweeney, and my beautiful, precious little ten-year-old daughter, Dionn, was kidnapped, raped, and killed, by a degenerate monster, Ray Thomas."

At this point, the D.A. stands and bellows, "Objection, Your Honor. The defendant never had his day in court, because he was killed right there in the courtroom by the girl's father, so he was never proven guilty of that crime."

But before Judge Panini has a chance to say anything, Mike says, "Your Honor, this witness's testimony is crucial to proving the state of mind my client was put in, and is extremely important. I will show the continuity of this testimony to my case. The fact that this man was innocent or guilty, at this point, is irrelevant, but like I said, there will be continuity with my case."

"Okay, Mr. Santino," answers the judge. "I better see the continuity you're talking about. Objection overruled. You may continue, Mrs. Sweeney."

"Thank you, Your Honor. As I was saying, then, to top it all off, we find out that this degenerate monster was a convicted child molester who was set free by some bleeding-heart judge, no reference to you, Your Honor, and some all-too-lenient laws that allowed him to go free and walk the streets a free man."

"Okay, Mrs. Sweeney, you may continue."

"My beautiful little girl's body was never found, and my husband and I still cry almost every night over this, and we will never get over it. I know my testimony here today will never bring back my daughter. I am here to try to protect other children from a crime like this."

"Thank you, Mrs. Sweeney," says, Mike. "I'm finished with this witness, Your Honor."

"Okay. Mr. Morrison, do you wish to cross?"

"Yes, Your Honor." The D.A. approaches the witness. "Good morning, Mrs. Sweeney. First, let me say how sorry I am to hear about the horrible tragedy that you and your family had to endure."

"Thank you."

"Let me ask you this, Mrs. Sweeney. How did you feel when you found out that the man who was accused of kidnaping your daughter – and, Mrs. Sweeney, I know this is extremely hard for you, and if it gets too much for you, please let me know, and I will stop at once."

"Okay, thank you."

"Anyway, as I was saying, how did you feel when you found out that the man who was accused of kidnaping your daughter was picked up by the police? But before you answer that, just let me interject one thing, and again let me say one thing, I know this is hard, but the man that they picked up could never be accused of killing or raping your daughter, because her body was never found, and without her body, you can't prove anything."

Mrs. Sweeney starts crying, and raises her voice, saying, "No one had to prove anything to me. I know in my heart what my little girl went through. This man was a convicted child molester. What the hell did you think that he wanted her for? What the hell is wrong with you people? Does a house have to fall on you to see what is happening?"

"Okay, Mrs. Sweeney, please calm down. I warned you that this was going to be hard. I'm sorry, Mrs. Sweeney. All I'm trying to do is show you that you can't assume anyone is guilty until they have their day in court, and your husband denied Mr. Thomas of his day in court, because he murdered him."

Mike stands and says, "Objection, Your Honor. Mr. Sweeney was found not guilty of that crime. We are not here to reopen that case."

"Okay," says the judge, "Mr. Morrison, let me ask you the same question that I asked Mr. Santino: where are you going with this?"

"Your Honor, I am trying to establish a connection between the murder of Mr. Thomas and The Club website, and that is what we are doing here today."

"Okay. Mr. Santino, you are overruled."

"Thank you, Your Honor," says the D.A. "I am done with this witness."

The judge asks Mike, "Mr. Santino, do you have any more witnesses?"

"Yes, I do, Your Honor. I would now like to call Mrs. Mary Harrison."

Mary is called, and she takes the witness stand and is sworn in. Mike stands and walks over to her. "Good morning, or should I say, good afternoon, Mrs. Harrison."

"Good afternoon, Mr. Santino."

"Mrs. Harrison, please tell the jury who you are and what is it that you want to say here today."

"My name is Mrs. Mary Harrison," she says, now fighting back the tears that eventually come, and then continuing in a teary, sobbing, shaky voice.

"On June 15, 2001, my little angel of a daughter was kidnapped from a fast food restaurant."

Mike grabs her hands to comfort her and asks, "Mrs. Harrison, do you want to stop for a while?"

She exclaims, "No! I want the world to know what that animal did to my precious little girl." Then, mustering up all her strength and still crying, she says, "That bastard, after raping her, buried her alive to die a horrible death! And all I do every day, and all day long, is think of what my sweet little baby girl went through. And this monster had already been in jail for child molestation and was let out early for some stupid reason. He should have never been let out of jail in the first place, and if that was so, my sweet little girl would still be alive today. And due to the lack of evidence, because all they had was a video of him leaving with my little girl and him saying that he did take her but changed his mind and let her go unharmed, and because her body was never found at the time, they found him innocent. I will never forget when the verdict was read. My husband jumped over the rail and tried to kill him right there in the courtroom. My husband was stopped, and a restraining order was issued for him to stay away from that killer. It was at that point that my husband lost it. He vowed that if he ever found him, he would kill him, and I told my husband that I would help him.

"Several years later, we went back to New York, on vacation, and one night, while out shopping, my husband and I did run into him, and my husband went crazy and attacked him, but people, not knowing the story, got together and stopped my husband and held him until the police got there. My husband got arrested and went to jail for attempted murder, and because he violated the restraining order, he had to serve five years, while, to date, the man who did this is still out there walking around, free as a bird. Because of the fact that my husband got locked up, we lost everything. My husband lost his job, and I had no money to pay bills, so we then lost our house. To be near my husband, I moved my family to New York and then had to go on welfare to survive. That's what that man did to my family. And it was only due to a dog digging up the ground in a park that they found Wendy's body. An autopsy was performed, and they said that she had been beaten and raped, and they could tell that she was buried alive."

Now crying uncontrollably, Mary stops talking. The bailiff runs over and hands her a tissue. Mike asks her, "Are you okay? We can take a break if you want?"

"No. I'm okay now."

Mike says, "Your Honor, I'm finished with this witness."

"Mr. Morrison," asks the judge, "do you wish to cross this witness?"

"Yes, I do, Your Honor." Mr. Morrison walks toward the witness box, clasping his hands as though praying. He stops there and looks at her. "Mrs. Harrison, I am truly sorry for your ordeal. I wish that there was something I could do to soothe your feelings."

Mary shrieks out to him, "Yes, there is something you can do! Stop wasting time prosecuting my husband! And put all these sick bastard child molesters away."

At that point, the D.A., losing it for a moment, shouts back at her, "And as you so eloquently put it, do you think your husband and his cohorts are sick bastards too, for suggesting and condoning the killings of those child molesters?"

At this point, Judge Panini jumps in and shouts out, "I want everybody to stop talking right now! I will not tolerate this kind of conduct in my courtroom, especially by the D.A. This court is now adjourned until 10 AM tomorrow morning, and I want to see you, Mr. Morrison, and you, Mr. Santino, in my chambers right now!"

As John, Barney, and Nick, are led away, Mike says, "Sorry, guys, I really thought that we could have wrapped this up in one day. I guess I'll see you tomorrow."

As the courtroom empties out, Mike can hear all the commotion outside the courtroom in the hallway, reporters questioning spectators, photographers taking pictures, and people talking to each other about the case, and as some of the spectators pour out into the street and tell all, it gets just as hectic out there, if not more so. With all the TV trucks and their crews and reporters, you would think that there was a carnival going on instead of a trial.

In the meantime, Mike and Philip head toward Judge Panini's office. Once inside his office, Judge Panini asks them to please be seated. The judge sits, leans back in his chair, and stares at the ceiling for a moment, and then he looks down at them and says, "Gentlemen, I will make this short and sweet. If you ever had a chance to check me out, you will have found that I am a judge who does not mince words, and once I've warned you, I do not give second chances. Do you understand what it is that I'm saying?"

Both men answer, "Yes, we do, Your Honor."

"Okay, then, let me put it this way, and I am addressing both of you. Take this as your final warning. If either of you lose your cool and start yelling back at a witness or cross the line in any way, I will declare a mistrial. That will get me off this case that I never wanted in the first place, and you guys will have to start all over again with a new judge. Is that understood?"

Again, both answer, "Yes, it is, Your Honor."

"That is good. I can understand a witness under the stress that they are put in flying off the handle once in a while, but I don't expect that kind of behavior from a professional attorney, and I will not tolerate it in my courtroom. There is enough tension in this trial as it is without you guys making it any worse. So you guys can go now, and consider yourselves warned. No more of what went on, or any other funny stuff. Now go, and I will see you in the morning."

Mike goes back to his office and tries to figure out his next move, taking advantage of the break in the trial. He still feels like he is in between a rock and a hard place. He keeps doubting himself. He's not sure if he is going down the right road, but it seems that no matter how hard he tries, it always leads him back to the same road, and he thinks to himself, *I better stop, because if I keep going like this, I'm going to overthink this whole thing and screw it up altogether.*

The next morning, Mike finds himself back at the courthouse, and it seems like Groundhog Day to him. Just about everyone who was there yesterday is there again today, all the people, all the vendors, all the TV trucks with all their reporters, all the kids running around. At this point, Mike can't even say that he has never seen anything like this, because he saw it yesterday. He just thinks to himself, *It's like a freaking circus.*

Entering the courthouse, he finds that it's just as bad as outside, and the same as yesterday. Finally, after fighting his way through all the people just to get into the courtroom itself, he sits at his table, gets out his papers, and waits for everyone else to get there. It seems he's a bit early.

Finally, after about half an hour, Barney, Nick, and John are brought in, and they sit with Mike. A few minutes after that, the D.A. and his crew come in, and a few minutes after that, Judge Panini comes in. The bailiff calls for everyone to stand and says, "This court is now in session. The honorable Judge Phil Panini presiding." After Judge Panini sits, the bailiff tells everyone else to please be seated.

Judge Panini says, "First, let me say good morning to everyone, and let's see where we left off yesterday. Okay, Mr. Morrison, I believe that you were in the middle of questioning Mrs. Harrison. Do you wish to continue questioning her?"

"No, Your Honor. I'm done with her."

"Mr. Santino, are you also finished with that witness?"

"Yes, I am, Your Honor."

"Okay, then do you have any more witnesses to call?"

"Yes, I do, Your Honor. I would now like to call Mr. John Harrison Jr. to the stand."

Just as before, the bailiff goes to the back door and calls, "Mr. John Harrison Jr." John's son comes in, is directed to the witness stand, and sits.

Mike gets up and approaches John's son. "Good morning, Mr. Harrison."

"Good morning, Mr. Santino."

"Mr. Harrison, please tell the jury who you are and what you and your family endured."

"My name is John Harrison Jr., and I would like to let the jury know what my family and I went through after my sister was kidnapped, raped, and murdered. My family and I went through hell, living with the fact that the man who was responsible for it was walking around a free man, and still is, because they let him go. And then, one night, my father finally finds the guy, and upon seeing him, loses it and starts beating him up, and ends up in jail for five years, on top of everything else that we were going through. Then, like my mother said, it was only thanks to a dog digging up some earth in a park that we found my little sister's body and had to relive what happened all over. And now that they have my sisters body that they were looking for, they still can't tie her murderer to her death, and he is still free to this very day."

"Thank you, Mr. Harrison. Your Honor, I am done with this witness."

"Mr. Morrison," asks the judge, "do the people wish to cross-examine this witness?"

"Yes, I do, Your Honor." As he walks up to the witness stand, the D.A. says to John's son, "Mr. Harrison, I just have a few short questions for you, okay?"

"Yes, I guess so."

"First, let me say how sorry I am for the loss of your sister. Knowing how you and your family felt, and what you guys went through, how do you think the families of the men your father is responsible for killing felt?"

Mike jumps up, shouting, "Objection, Your Honor! That's call for speculation, and my clients have not been found guilty of anything yet."

"Overruled," answers the judge. "Sit down, Mr. Santino. Mr. Harrison, please answer the question."

"Only if I can answer it in my own way."

"Mr. Harrison, I am the judge, and this is my courtroom. I make the rules, not you. I will decide if you can answer the question, as you put it, in your own way. Mr. Morrison, do the people have any objection to giving this witness the latitude to answer the question in his own way?"

"Yes, we do, Your Honor. Please ask the witness to answer the question as I posed it."

"Mr. Harrison, answer the question that was put to you, or I will hold you in contempt of this court, and you can spend some time in jail because of it.

John thinks to himself, *Do I really want to do this?* Then he decides against it. "I will answer it, Your Honor."

"Would you like the D.A. to repeat the question?"

"No, Your Honor. I don't know how they felt. I never thought about it."

At that, the D.A. says, "I'm done, Your Honor."

"Mr. Santino," the judge asks, "do you have any more witnesses?"

"Yes, I do, Your Honor. I would like to call psychiatrist Dr. Randy Webster."

Once again, the bailiff goes to the back and calls, "Dr. Randy Webster."

The doctor enters, goes straight to the witness stand like he knows the drill, and sits down.

Mike walks over and says, "Good morning, Doctor."

"Good morning, Mr. Santino."

"Doctor, can you please tell this jury where you got your degree in psychiatry?"

"I attended and graduated from Harvard Medical School, Department of Psychiatry at the top of my class."

"So you graduated at the top of your class just as Dr. Thomas Nopis did. Could you please tell the jury just how that is possible?"

"I graduated the previous year and opened my own practice. I am also associated with Massachusetts General Hospital's psychiatric department, and I am affiliated with several other prestigious psychiatric hospitals throughout the country."

"So, Dr. Webster, according to my math, that means that you have been practicing psychiatry for 28 years. Is that correct?"

"Yes, it is."

"Thank you, Doctor. I have only one question for you, and that is, in all of your twenty-eight years of practice, have you ever been asked to evaluate someone without them physically being in front of you, or by looking at a video of them?"

"A few times, I have been asked to look at a video of someone, but that was only to see if they were a candidate for a psychiatric evaluation. But never to give my evaluation of them just by viewing a video of that person."

"Thank you, Doctor." Mike turns to the judge and says, "Your Honor, I'm finished with this witness."

"Mr. Morrison," asks the judge, "do the people wish to cross examine this witness?"

"Yes, we do, Your Honor." Before walking over to the witness, the D.A. ruffles through his papers as though he is looking for something but can't seem to find it. Giving up the search, he turns and walks up to the witness stand. "Good morning, Dr. Webster."

"Good morning, Mr. Morrison."

"Doctor, I also have only question for you. I find it really hard to believe that in all your years of practice, you have never been asked to evaluate someone without them being in the same room with you or by viewing a video of them. So my one question is how much did Mr. Santino pay you to come into this courtroom and lie while under oath?"

Mike jumps about three feet out of his chair and screams at the top of his lungs, "OBJECTION! OBJECTION! Your Honor, how dare the D.A. accuse the doctor of lying."

"Objection sustained. Mr. Santino, calm down."

"I'm sorry, Your Honor, but I have never heard a D.A. talk to a professional witness like that. It's uncalled for and rude."

"Mr. Morrison!" bellows the judge. "Mr. Santino is absolutely correct. That was rude and uncalled for. I want you to apologize to the doctor right now or face a severe contempt charge."

"I'm sorry, Your Honor, and I will apologize to the doctor. Doctor, I am really sorry. I apologize for accusing you of lying. I don't know what came over me. Again, I apologize. I'm sorry. It's just that I am into this case so much that I can't even think of the possibility of these men walking away free."

Mike again jumps up. "Objection! Your Honor, what is the D.A. doing, giving his closing argument?"

Judge Panini bellows, "Mr. Morrison, you are now finished with this witness. Please return to your table."

"Thank you, Your Honor."

"You should thank me," retorts the judge. "I was very close to hitting you with a fine. Remember, I don't give second chances." The judge turns to Mike and asks, "Mr. Santino, do you have any more witnesses?"

"No, Your Honor."

"Okay, then, Mr. Morrison, do you have any more witnesses?"

"No, Your Honor."

"Then are the people ready to close?"

"Yes, we are, Your Honor."

"And Mr. Santino, are you ready to close?"

"Yes, I am, Your Honor."

"Okay, Mr. Morrison, you may start your closing arguments."

"Thank you, Your Honor."

The D.A. walks very slowly toward the jury box, silently reading a piece of paper with notes on it. As he reaches them, he looks them over and hesitates a few seconds before speaking. Finally, he says, "Ladies and gentleman, good afternoon. Like I said at the beginning of this trial, because of the preponderance of evidence, it is going to be an open and shut case. In the last two days, I have given you overwhelming evidence to prove my case beyond a reasonable doubt. You have heard Dr. Nopis give his expert testimony as to the sanity of Mr. Harrison, that he is not insane and knew exactly what he was doing. You have heard Mr. Ratsky's testimony, about meetings he attended and taped, where Mr. Harrison spoke, and what he said at those meetings. And the best evidence in this case are the tapes you heard with the voice of Mr. Harrison himself advocating the killings of child molesters. You can clearly hear him saying on tape what his unambiguous intentions were, that he wanted people to go out and, as he so eloquently put it, 'kill those fucking sick bastard child molesters.' I'm positive that I have proved that Mr. Harrison and his cohorts are guilty as charged, and I have all the faith and confidence in the world that you will do the right thing and bring back a verdict of guilty. Thank you."

"Mr. Santino," asks the judge. "Are you ready to close?"

"Yes, I am, Your Honor." Mike looks over his paperwork, going over in his mind what he will be saying to the jury, but it seems like he's hesitating.

"Mr. Santino!" barks the judge. "Do you think, that you could give your closing sometime today?"

"Yes, Your Honor." Mike takes his time walking over to the jury, still going over in his mind what he will be saying. Finally there, he looks at the jury from left to right, looking into their eyes, trying to figure out if they are on his side or on the side of the D.A. Then he thinks to himself, *What the hell. Here goes nothing.*

"Ladies and gentleman, good afternoon. The people told you all about the preponderance of evidence they had and all about how Dr. Nopis gave his expert opinion on the state of Mr. Harrison's mental health just by looking at a video, something, by his own testimony and admission, he has never done before. You also heard, on tape, one of my clients, Mr. Harrison, expressing his desires as to the well-being of child molesters. I am not going to stand here before you and deny that Mr. Harrison said those things, or that Mr. Alesi and Mr. Cicale did not do these things. However, because of the witnesses I had, I do hope I made you understand why they did what they did.

"I hope that none of you have ever had a child murdered violently, or had one of your children beaten and raped and left to die, or had one of your children go missing and never knew what happened to them, never finding their body, having your mind go crazy with all sorts of scenarios as to what happened to them, but could you try to put yourself in their place and think of what state of mind you would be in, what kind of action you would want to take against the criminal that did it? And how you would feel if that criminal got away with it? What would you want to do to that criminal? There is no way that anyone could possibly know how a parent feels when one of their children is kidnapped, raped, or murdered. No way, no how.

"All I am asking you to do is dig deep down into your soul and just try to imagine the pain, the anguish, the despair, the hopelessness, the gloom, the desperation, and any other noun or word that you can think of that tries to describe what you would be going through. I don't think that there is such a word, one that would adequately describe what feelings you would be going through.

"If you can do that, put yourself in Mr. Harrison's place for just one moment. Then you would realize that Mr. Harrison could not have been in the right frame of mind to the point that he was able to convince Mr. Alesi and Mr. Cicale to join him in his quest, to do at that time what he thought was the right thing to do, and if I have shown you enough proof, so that you can put yourself in his place, then you must return a verdict of prolonged insanity due to mental anguish. Thank you."

As Mike returns to his table, Judge Panini starts to give the jury their instructions. Then he instructs the bailiff to escort the jury to the deliberation room and announcers, "This court is in recess until the jury arrives at a verdict."

As Judge Panini leaves, discussions break out throughout the courtroom. As John, Barney, and Nick are taken out, Mike says to them, "I hope I did right by you guys."

All three give him a thumbs-up sign, and John says, "You did the best you could, Mike. It's in the hands of the jury now."

Mike, not wanting to travel too far, decides to go to the corner restaurant to get a bite to eat and go over what he did today in court. As he fights his way out and onto the street, he is disgusted with what he sees going on both in and out of the courtroom. He thinks to himself, *My clients are facing jail time and the destruction of their lives, and these people are out here partying*. Reporters are interviewing anyone who will talk to them about what the verdict will be and why, and how they thought both sides did. Wading through the crowd, Mike finally gets to the restaurant, and it's no different than it was outside, so he decides to just get a sandwich and eat it in his car.

Mike finishes his sandwich, leans back in his car seat, and goes over the trial in his mind. All of a sudden, the ringing of his cell phone wakes him up. It's the court, notifying him that a verdict has not been reached, that the jury is going to be sequestered for the evening, and that the courthouse is closing and will reopen at 8 AM tomorrow morning. Mike shakes his head, trying to wake himself up, and the first thing he notices is that it's nighttime. Then he looks at his watch and realizes it's 6 PM and that he has been sleeping for five hours. He jumps out of his car, runs to the courthouse, and notices that everyone is gone. The only people that are still here are the news reporters and their trucks, and they are packing up all their gear, so he goes back to his car and heads home.

The next morning, bright and early, Mike is at the jail to see John, Barney, and Nick. A guard takes Mike to see them. Mike asks, "How was your night?"

"Well," replies John, "the only good thing was that we were all put in this same cell."

"That's good. Let's hope that good things keep happening today. I am going back to my office to wait for the call. In the meantime, if you guys need anything, call me. They will let you use the phone. Good luck guys."

Mike heads back to his office to try to take his mind off what is going on right now. He also has other cases to work on, but he can't seem to think of anything else. He just keeps going over the case in his mind, but he still feels that the path that he went down was the right one, so he settles down and works on some other cases.

At 4:30 PM, Mike's secretary calls him. "Mr. Santino, you have a call from the court."

Mike stops what he's doing and tells her to put it through.

"Mr. Santino, this is Mrs. Sara from the courthouse. I just want to inform you that the jury has not reached a decision yet and were sequestered again for the evening. They will reconvene tomorrow morning at 9:00 AM."

Mike stops what he is doing and heads for the jail to let the guys know what is going on. Again, the guard escorts Mike to see the guys, and he explains it to them. At first, Barney gets upset. Then Mike explains, "Listen up, guys. The fact that it's taking so long is a good sign, so just hang in there and hope for the best. I will see you tomorrow."

The next morning, Mike arrives at his office early and gets right down to work, just to keep himself busy. At lunch time, he heads over to the jail to fill them in on what's not happening, and again, he reiterates that it's a good sign that it's taking so long.

Back at his office, Mike keeps working. It's about 4: 45 PM when Mike's secretary calls him. "Mr. Santino, it's the courthouse calling."

Mike grabs the phone.

"Hello. Mr. Santino?"

"Yes."

"Mr. Santino, this is Mrs. Sara from the courthouse. I'm calling to let you know that the jury has reached a decision. Judge Panini is unavailable this evening, but will be in tomorrow morning, so the case will reconvene tomorrow morning at 9:00 AM sharp."

Mike drops everything and heads over to the jail, to meet up with the guys. "Well, I have good news or bad news, depending on how you look at things. The jury has reached a decision."

John jumps up. "What is it?"

"It doesn't work like that. You know that. We won't find out until tomorrow."

"Well, now I'm sorry that you told us this. I can't speak for Barney and Nick, but there will be no sleep for me tonight."

Barney says, "And do you think that I'm going to sleep tonight?"

Nick says, "Yeah, that goes for me too."

"I understand what you guys are going through," says Mike, "but at least the waiting is over, to a certain extent, and tomorrow morning, we will know one way or another, so do whatever you have to to keep calm. If it makes you feel better, say a prayer. Okay, see you guys tomorrow morning."

The next morning, bright and early, Mike gets to the courthouse, and to his surprise, there are only a few people and a few news trucks, with their reporters mulling around. There is no carnival atmosphere going on like there was on the first day of the trial. Mike is happy to see that, but as he enters the courthouse, it's a different story; it's only 8:30 AM, and the place is jammed, and inside the courtroom it's standing room only.

Mike makes his way to his table, sits, and waits for anyone else to show up. A few minutes later, the D.A., Mr. Morrison, arrives with his entourage. Finally, at about 8:55 AM, the court stenographer and bailiff arrive, followed by two court officers escorting John, Barney, and Nick. The three sit and exchange good mornings.

Mike asks John, "How was your night?"

"Well, needless to say, none of us slept last night."

Mike replies, "Well, let's just hope for the best, and that good things happen today."

After about twenty minutes, Judge Panini enters the courtroom. The bailiff bellows out, "All stand. The honorable Judge Phil Panini presiding. This court is now in session."

The judge sits, and so does everyone else. Judge Panini says, "Ladies and gentleman, Mr. Morrison, Mr. Santino, reporters, and anyone else in this courtroom that I missed, I just want to make it very, very, clear. As I said at the beginning of this trial, I will not tolerate any sort of disruption of this case in this courtroom, and as I also said, I do not give second chances, and I just want to make sure that all of you understand that before I bring the jury in. Now, with that said, bailiff, please bring in the jury."

The jury comes in and sits. Judge Panini asks the jury foreman, "Has the jury reached a decision yet?"

"Yes, we have, Your Honor." With that, the jury foreman hands a piece of paper to the bailiff to give to the judge.

Judge Panini reads it and hands it back to the bailiff to give back to the jury foreman. "And how does the jury find the defendants?"

"In the charge of accessory to murder before the fact against Mr. Harrison, we the jury find Mr. Harrison guilty as charged, in the first degree. In the charge of accessory to murder before the fact against Mr. Alesi, we the jury find Mr. Alesi guilty as charged, in the third degree. In the charge of accessory to murder before the fact against Mr. Cicale, we the jury find Mr. Cicale guilty as charged, in the third degree."

The courtroom erupts in low, whispered conversations. Judge Panini bangs his gavel on his desk so loud it startles everyone to silence. Judge Panini reminds everyone of what he said at the beginning of the trial and says, "This trial is over, and a decision has been made. I am setting June 23 for the sentencing. The suspects will be removed, and everyone must leave in an orderly manner." Judge Panini then gets up and walks out of the courtroom.

John, Barney, and Nick all look at Mike and shake their heads with disgust, disappointment written on their faces. John says, "Hey, Mike, don't let this get to you. You did the best you could. All three of us were talking last night, and we more or less came to the realization that we were fighting a lost cause. We were already expecting this decision today, so don't beat yourself up over it."

Mike shouts back, "Well, maybe you guys were, but not me. This is not over yet; I promise you that. Tomorrow morning, first thing, I'm going to submit an appeal." As Mike is talking to them, guards are putting handcuffs on all three. Mike tells them, "just remember what I said. This is not over yet."

The three are led away, and as Mike tries to leave the courtroom, he is stopped by reporters. They are all asking him, "What are your plans now?"

"All I will say now is that I plan to appeal the decision," he replies, but they keep shouting more questions at him. Mike just ignores them and pushes his way out of the courtroom. In the hallway, more reporters try to question him, but Mike just keeps on walking and pushing his way through the crowd. The reporters are talking to anyone who will talk to them. Outside, it's just crazy; it's pandemonium. Some people are cheering, and some screaming back at them. Then a fight breaks out between the two groups, and police have to move in to break it up and arrest people. Mike just heads for his car and gets out of there.

Back at his office, Mike ponders the thought of proceeding with an appeal, but he doesn't know what he can use to appeal the decision, not even a clue. Then he remembers what happened during the trial, when one of his aides came in and handed him a note about another child molester being murdered. Mike thinks that maybe he can somehow use this to appeal the case due to the fact that this person was murdered while John, Barney, and Nick were locked up and could not possibly have had anything to do with it, so Mike decides to investigate that murder.

First, Mike goes to his aide to find out where she got that information. She informs him that she got it from the newspapers. Mike decides to go to the newspaper himself to get the information, rather than send one of his aides.

Mike gets to the newspaper's offices and goes directly to the editor's office. The editor directs Mike to the reporter who wrote the story. Mike sits down with the reporter and gets all the details about the murder. It seems that a convicted child molester, who was just released from prison, was murdered right in his own driveway after getting out of his car and while walking up to his front door. The man who did it turned himself in and is currently awaiting trial for murder.

Mike gets his name and where he is being held. The man's name is Ervin Shift, and he is being held at the local jail. Mike heads over there to talk to him.

When Mike gets there and asks to speak to Ervin Shift, he's given a few papers to fill out. Then he is let into a small, dirty, light blue room that reminds him of the room he was in when he went to see John, except, that this room has one window with thick bars on it, one table with a steel ring on it, and two chairs. Mike sits and waits for Ervin, looking around at the chipped paint and worn tabletop, which give him a feeling that this room has been used quite a few times. It also brings back memories of the trial, and he hopes that this meeting will give him something to bring back with him so that he can get an appeal started.

The door opens, and two guards walk in with a small, slender man in handcuffs. Mike thinks to himself, *This guy does not look like a killer.* Ervin sits down across from Mike. One of the guards removes one of Ervin's handcuffs, and then they inform Mike that they will be just outside the door in the event that he needs them. They then leave and close the door behind them.

"Hi, Ervin. You're probably wondering who I am and what I'm doing here. First off, my name is Mike Santino, and I am a lawyer."

Ervin interrupts Mike, saying, "Save it, save it. I know exactly who you are. Your name is Mike Santino, and right now, you're defending John Harrison and two of his workers, and I know exactly what I'm doing." Ervin looks down at the floor for a few seconds. Then he looks back up at Mike. "I guess if there's anyone in this world that I can trust, it would be you. Let me start by saying I was a member of The Club until the website was taken down. As a matter of fact, I've been trying to meet up with you for some time now, and also, as a matter of fact, I don't think you guys have any idea what you have started. There is presently an underground network of The Club, so even though it's off the Internet, it is still very much alive."

Mike sits there in shock with his mouth open. He can't believe what he's hearing. He pauses for a few seconds, and for the first time in a long time, Mike is at a loss for words. He just does not know what to say, and he just sits there staring at Ervin.

Finally, Ervin, seeing Mike in a state of shock, says, "You mean to tell me that you did not know anything like this was going on?"

Mike replies, "Not a hint."

"Well, then, let me say this: two weeks after the website was shut down, this underground movement started, and it has spread like wildfire. Also, we have a plan. So don't you worry about me. You just go back and take care of the business of getting John and his buddies off. I have a bunch of lawyers ready to help me, some of whom were members of The Club, so like I said, you can go back knowing that I'm in good hands."

Mike tells Ervin, "Well, that's great news, and I will go back and tell John, but that's not what I was here for. I was here to see if I could somehow use your case to help out my case with John, but somehow, now, I don't think I can do that. Anyway, would you mind if I kept in touch with you, or is there anyone else that I can keep in contact with to keep track of what's going on with the movement?"

"I'm afraid I can't do that. We have strict rules. We can only have contact with one person and one lawyer in the group. This way, no one knows more than that, and so far, it's working great. And you know what they say, if it isn't broken, don't fix it, so it's staying that way. But to answer your question, the answer is yes, by all means, you can keep in touch with me. In fact, I'm the one who was assigned to get in touch with you, so all this works out well."

"Okay, Ervin, I hope it all works out in your favor, and I will be talking to you. Hopefully, you won't be in jail, but if you are, how do I get in touch with you."

"You don't. I will get in touch with you every so often, more often if need be."

"Okay, then, so long, and again, good luck."

Mike heads back to his office, astonished, and confused. *The whole reason I went to see Ervin was to help with my case with John, and now I don't even want to mention that I know Ervin. And if it is true, what Ervin said about the underground movement and that The Club is still very much alive, why were John Barney and Nick found guilty? And again, if what Ervin said is true, there should have been a few Club members on the jury to find them innocent, but I guess there were none.* Still confused, instead of going to his office, Mike heads home so that he can just sit on his couch in his study and concentrate on his next move.

Once home, Mike does just that: he sits on his couch, thinking, and thinking, and thinking. Finally, he comes to the conclusion that there was no other way that he could have gone in defending John, Barney, and Nick. He knows in his heart that it was the tapes that destroyed his case. They were such overwhelming evidence that blocked any other possible way to defend them, except for insanity. Then Mike thinks to himself, Well, that's it. It's over. I am now convinced, that I did the best I could, and we will all have to live with the outcome of the trial. And unless I get an epiphany, then and only then, will I do something. So, for now, as a good friend of mine once said to me, it is what it is.

The next day, Mike goes back to jail to see John and fill him in on what transpired with Ervin and all about the underground movement that has gotten started. Mike tells John, "I want you to sit tight and don't get in any trouble while locked up, because if I do come up with something that I can use for an appeal, I don't want anything to get in the way. So until the day of sentencing, stay out of trouble, and I will keep working on an appeal."

THE CLUB

June 23 comes around real fast, and as Mike heads for the courthouse, he keeps thinking of something he could have used for an appeal, but the more he tries to think of something, the more confused he gets with all the possibilities, with none of them attaining the height that is needed to effectively submit an appeal.

Mike finally gets to the courthouse with not much time to spare. Because of all his thinking about an appeal, he made a few wrong turns that ate up some time. Then, to top things off, he sees the same carnival atmosphere that was there at the trial, with all the media, the people, and entrepreneurs selling their wares. One shirt he sees has a picture of John with a noose around his neck. It all just sickens him, and once inside the courthouse, Mike has to fight his way to the courtroom. Once there, he finds it eerily quiet. Then he notices six court officers standing around, and he now knows the reason why the courtroom is so quiet. In all his years of working in courtrooms, Mike cannot recall a single time when he has seen this many court officers at a sentencing.

Mike sits down and gets his paperwork out. While doing this, he feels that all eyes in the courtroom are upon him and watching every move he makes. Ten long minutes later, court officers finally bring in John, Barney, and Nick and escort them to the table where Mike is sitting.

Finally, after twenty longer minutes of sitting, the court officer bellows out, "All stand. Judge Phil Panini presiding. This court is now in session." After the judge sits, the court officer announces, "Everyone, please be seated."

❧❧❧

Judge Panini looks around at all the people and just keeps staring at them. Then, after what seems like an eternity, he finally speaks: "First, let me make this absolutely clear. I will not tolerate a disturbance of any kind while the sentence is being read or after the sentence has been read, and keep in mind I do not give second chances. The first time someone acts up in any way, they will be arrested, and that is all I will say on that."

Then Judge Panini picks up some paperwork, reads it, and says, "Will the suspects please stand." They do, and he proceeds to speak: "Before sentencing you three, I want to say this: that in all my years on the bench, I don't think I have ever come across a more despicable, heinous crime such as the crimes the three of you committed. You have purposely and maliciously provoked people to go out and kill other human beings without any thought of the impact it would bring on their families and friends, and without even a thought as to why they did what they did or if they were unable to control themselves and possibly just needed some help. You just took it upon yourself to take matters into your own hands and resolve what you three thought was a problem that you felt no one else had the knowledge or expertise to solve. So, without any regard for the law or what the consequences of these acts would have on others, all three of you went out and did your thing.

"With all that said and done, I want to say that I have taken into consideration that none of you have been in trouble before, but due to the disdain that I feel because of the crimes that all three of you committed, I cannot bring myself to show you any remorse, compassion, or leniency, so I am sentencing all three of you to the maximum sentence that the law allows. John Harrison, for your involvement in this crime, I sentence you to serve thirty years of confinement in a state penitentiary without the chance of parole. Nick Alesi, I sentence you to serve thirty years of confinement in a state penitentiary without the chance of parole. And you, Barney Cicale, I also sentence you to serve thirty years in a state penitentiary without the chance of parole. And let me say this: I wish it were in my power to sentence the three of you to a much longer term, but unfortunately, I don't have that power. Officers, please remove the defendants."

Mike turns and looks at all three, and with outstretched arms, he says, "Sorry guys. I tried my best, but those tapes killed us. The only thing that would have made their case any stronger for them is if they'd had videos of you guys actually killing somebody. But I want you guys to hang in there, and I will still keep trying to look for something to come up with for an appeal."

John tells Mike, "Don't sweat it. We know you did the best you could, and that you will keep trying."

"Thanks, John. In the meantime, you guys just hang in there, and I'll give you some time to get settled in. And if by chance any of you come up with something, give me a call." With that said, Mike shakes hands with them, and then the officers put cuffs on all three and take them away. Mike heads home, depressed, and when he gets there, the only thing he wants to do is sleep to try and clear his mind.

Two weeks go by before Mike learns that the three of them are settled in, and the good news is that all three of them ended up in the same prison, in Attica Correctional Facility in New York, and that will make it a lot easier for Mike to visit them. Mike makes plans to visit them next week.

❦❦❦

The next day, while Mike is working in his office, his secretary tells him that John is calling from the prison. Mike picks up the phone. "John, how are you doing?"

"Fine, Mike. How are you doing? Listen, I'm just calling to let you know that the three of us were talking and we decided that you don't have to visit us that often, only if you hear something new or something comes up that would help us, and then, only if you felt like it. Otherwise, don't feel obligated to visit us that often."

"Okay, John, but just to let you know, I plan on coming up and visiting with you guys next week, but other than that, you got a deal."

"Great, Mike. That's a deal. Bye."

Two days later, Mike gets a call from Judge Tony Ghetto. "Good morning, Judge. How are you doing?"

"Great, and how you doing, Mike?"

"Oh, trying to keep busy."

"Mike, the first thing I want to ask you is do you tape your phone calls, or do you know if your phone is tapped?"

"No, Judge, I don't tape my phone calls, and as far as I know, my phone is not tapped."

"Okay, then, Mike, I've been reading in the papers about the case you are working on, and I was curious as to how things were going with it."

"Well, Judge, if you've been reading the papers, you know that all three were found guilty and the judge threw the book at them and gave them the maximum sentence that he could give them. Judge, the evidence they had was so overwhelming that there was not much I could do. They had John on tape practically confessing to the crimes. I tried my best."

"Yes, Mike, I know you did, but that's not really what I'm calling you about. As you know, in the past, I've tried to help John out, and I have my own sources of getting information. Last week, I got some information about an underground movement that has been started in regards to what John was doing. Have you heard anything about this?"

"Judge, you know what? How about I stop you right there, and how about we set up a meeting, next week, and how about I buy you lunch?"

"Okay, Mike, I understand. How about next Thursday at noon?"

"Sounds good."

"And since you're buying, you pick the restaurant."

"Okay, Judge. How about Laduchies on 5th Ave."

"Okay, Mike, next Thursday at Laduchies at 12 noon. Sounds like a plan. I will see you there, and seeing the mood that you are in, I will say ciao for now."

"Yeah, okay, Judge, ciao."

At that point, Mike wishes that he were in as good a mood as the judge is, but unfortunately, he isn't.

Mike gets to the restaurant early and asks the greeter for a quiet table in the corner, because he's having a business meeting. About ten minutes later, the judge arrives.

"Good afternoon, judge. How are you doing today?"

"Fine, Mike, and how are you doing?"

"I'm doing good, Judge. Thank you."

"So, what's good here, Mike? What do you suggest?"

"Well… I like the chicken Laduchi. They say it's to die for."

With that, the waiter arrives. "Good afternoon, gentlemen. Can I get you anything to drink while you are looking over the menu?"

Mike says, "Well, I know what I want. Do you need more time, Judge?"

"Actually, no. I think I'm going to go with the chicken Laduchi."

The waiter looks at Mike and asks, "And what about you, sir?"

Mike says, "I'm going to have the same thing, the chicken Laduchi, and with that, I will have a glass of burgundy wine."

The waiter turns to the judge and asks, "And what about you, sir? Something to drink?"

"Yes, as a matter of fact, I'll have a glass of burgundy wine also."

The waiter says, "Thank you, gentlemen. I will put your order in and bring you your wine."

For a few seconds, the two men sit and stare at each other. Finally, Mike speaks first: "So, Judge… I was really taken aback by your phone call last week, and I apologize for so abruptly stopping you from speaking, but as soon as you mentioned something that had to do with The Club and an underground movement about it, I got nervous and had stop you. I'm paranoid about people eavesdropping, even though I'm in my own office and on my own phone, and one of the first reasons is that I have a cleaning company that comes in and cleans my office every night, and even though I had them checked out before I hired them, you never know. So I still find it better to be prudent than not, especially when talking about The Club. The second reason is that several weeks ago, I went to visit a prisoner, and this prisoner told me a story about The Club being very much alive, that it went underground and is flourishing. Then, out of the blue, you call me and tell me the same thing, that The Club is still alive and that it went underground. That's the reason I was so taken back. Okay, Judge, I'm all yours and listening with both ears. I hope you have some good information for me, because, right now, I can really use some. I need something that will lift me up."

"Well, Mike, I think the information that I am about to give you will do just that. As I told you on the phone, I was sort of giving John some advice as to what to do and not to do in his endeavors. And with respect to The Club, I made suggestions to him where and when to go, and who to see, and in many cases, it helped him out immensely. The person I get my information from has his ear to the ground and doesn't miss a beat, and furthermore, his information has always been dead on and extremely reliable. The main reason this man came to me was the fact that he is sympathetic to their cause and wants to help their cause as much as he can.

"So, this is the story. This guy I know and have worked with before calls me and asks me if I know anything about The Club or if I know John, the one who started it all, because he heard that somewhere along the line I helped John out. How he knows this, I have no idea, but this man is amazing with all the information he gets. I told him, 'As a matter fact, yes, I'm aware of The Club, and I also happen to know John. I met him once or twice.' Then my man proceeds to tell me that something really big is going on with the underground movement of The Club, and if I know John or his lawyer, that he thinks that they would be interested in the information that he is giving me. The word is that they now have a retired Army general working with them, getting them all set up military style, like some sort of a covert or black ops operation, with ranks and passwords, etc., just like in the military."

"Wait a minute, Judge. Hold on. If this underground movement is so secretive, how is your guy getting all this information?"

"As a matter of fact, I asked him that same question, and he said that right now, he can't tell me how he's getting the information, but like I said, I worked with this man before, and he has never been wrong, and in the past, everything he has told me has been dead on. But he assures me that whatever is going on, it is something really big, and all he knows about it is that it has something to do with some kind of a camp, and as soon as he gets more information, he will get back to me. That's all the information he gave me. The only other thing he said to me was to let as few people as possible know about this for now."

"Okay, Judge. I appreciate you getting in touch with me with this. I'm going to try and get in touch with John and fill him in on what you told me. I'm pretty sure that this information will lift him up a little."

After lunch, Mike heads back to his office and tries to figure out how he's going to give this information to John. Being the paranoid person that he is, he swears that the room he talks to John in is bugged and possibly has a hidden camera also.

Mike decides that the best way to do this would be to go and see John and not speak aloud, but instead write everything down really small, so that if there are cameras in the room, they will not be able to see what they are writing, and then bring all the papers back to his office and destroy them.

Satisfied with his plan, and armed with a new notepad, the next morning, Mike heads off to the prison to visit with John and let him know what's happening.

Again, Mike is led to this gray, dingy room. He sits down at the table and waits for John to come in. As soon as John enters the room, Mike crosses his lips with his index finger, signaling John to keep quiet. Then Mike gives John a small note that he wrote before he got to the prison, telling John not to speak aloud but to write everything down really small, because the information he is about to give him is extremely important and he does not want anyone but John to know about this.

Mike and John exchange notes for over an hour. In one of the notes, John writes that he is having trouble containing his emotions and hopes that somehow whatever is going on with The Club will help him, Barney, and Nick get out of prison. The last note John gives to Mike asks Mike to please keep him up to date as to what's going on, and to tell the judge, and whoever the judge's informant is, "thank you, thank you, thank you." Mike writes back, "I will do that and I will keep you advised as to what is happening." With that, Mike packs up his notepad and heads back to his office to destroy the notes.

While all this is going on, there are reporters throughout the country reporting on the killings of child molesters and pointing out the fact that the killers are getting away scot-free, and this is still going on even though John and his cohorts were locked up, The Club's website taken down, and the offices shut down and dismantled, causing the local authorities all over the country to get nervous about what's going on with all these killings.

Another person who is reading the papers and watching TV is Judge Tunis, and he feels like he's having a bad dream and wants someone to wake him up from this nightmare he is having. It seems the more he reads, the worse the situation is getting. There are more and more killings of child molesters being reported as the days go by, and the judge now feels that he must do something, but he doesn't know exactly what to do. The only thing he can come up with is to give his friend Larry Rockwood in Washington a call and see if he's aware of what's going on, and maybe he can come up with an idea as to what to do.

The next morning, bright and early, Judge Tunis puts a call in to his friend Larry Rockwood in Washington.

"Good morning. Mr. Rockwood's office. Can I help you?"

"Yes, this is Judge Tunis calling, and if Mr. Rockwood is in and has a few minutes, I would like to speak to him."

"Okay, Judge. Please hold on, and I will check." The secretary notifies her boss: "Mr. Rockwood, there's a judge Tunis on the phone who would like to speak to you."

"Okay, yeah, sure, put him through. Good morning, Judge. How are you doing?"

"I'm doing fine, thank you, Larry. And how are you doing?"

"I'm doing fine also, Judge. What can I do for you?"

"Well, I don't know if you've been reading the papers or watching television, and I was wondering if you were aware of what's going on. What I'm talking about specifically is the rash of killings of child molesters that is going on."

"As a matter fact, Judge, I have read the papers and also heard the reports on TV about the killings. About six months ago, there was a killing right over here in Washington. The killer was apprehended and brought to trial and, like the others, was found not guilty. Unfortunately, I was busy and could not follow that closely, but now that you're bringing it to my attention, I realize that your concern in this matter is justified. It seems like it's starting up all over again. But I know you're calling me for a reason other than just to fill me in on current events. So, Judge, what can I do for you? How can I help you?"

"Well, Larry, I was hoping that you could speak to Judge Mohan, the one on the U.S. Supreme Court, and see if he can come up with something. I just feel that something has to be done with these people. They just can't keep getting away what they are getting away with."

"You're right, Judge. There must be something we can do. So, I tell you what I'll do. I'll give judge Mohan a call and see if he has any ideas. I will call him this afternoon and get back to you as soon as I can, and let you know if he came up with anything."

"Okay, Larry. Thanks. Talk to you soon."

"You're welcome, Judge, and I will get back to you as soon as I hear from him and have some information for you. Bye for now."

Five days go by with nothing much happening, and almost everybody goes along with their everyday chores, sometimes being mundane, sometimes being important, sometimes being exciting, sometimes being painful, etc., etc., etc., Almost everybody, but not everybody, because one person is plotting something really big and is working really hard putting the finishing touches to it, and that person is the retired general that Judge Ghetto was talking to Mike about.

The General, now finished with his plans, pours himself a long stiff one in celebration of the completion of his plans, raises the glass up in a congratulatory gesture, and says, "This is to all of the children who were raped, tortured, and killed. I put this plan into motion to avenge all of your tiny souls, and I hope and pray that it all comes together, fulfilling the dreams of the man who first started this, Mr. John Harrison, and possibly saving many young lives from horrific crimes perpetrated against them."

The next morning, one of the first things the General does when he gets up is to look for Judge Ghetto's phone number. He takes a shower, has his breakfast, and then, all excited, proceeds to call Judge Ghetto.

"Good morning. Judge Ghetto's office."

"Good morning. Is the judge in?"

"May I ask who is calling?"

"Just tell him it's the General."

"Well, I'm sorry, General, but the judge is not in right now. I can have the judge call you when he gets in, or if you want, you can call back."

"Okay, please have the judge call me back."

"Okay, General, may I please have your number?"

"That's okay. The judge already has it. Just tell him to call me back."

"Okay, I will tell the judge when he gets back."

"Thank you."

Several hours pass, and the General is finding it hard to keep himself busy while waiting for the call back from Judge Ghetto. Finally, hours later, and what seems like an eternity to the General, the phone rings. Hoping it's the judge calling, the General answers. "Hello."

"Hello, General. This is Judge Ghetto. You called earlier, and I am returning your call."

"As a matter of fact, I did, Judge. I finally finished building that boat I was talking to you about, and I would like to set up a meeting with you so that I can show you some pictures of it and explain further how I built it."

"Okay, General. How about dinner at Laduchies this evening."

"Okay, Judge, that sounds great. How about 6:30 PM?"

"Sounds good to me, General. I will see you at 6:30 PM at Laduchies."

"Okay, Judge. See you there. Bye for now."

Later that evening, the judge arrives at the restaurant a few minutes early and asks for a quiet table in a corner. Several minutes later, the General arrives and is escorted to the judge's table. The two men greet each other with a handshake and exchange pleasantries. As the General seats himself, the judge speaks first: "So, General, when I returned your call, I could tell by your voice that you seemed really excited and very anxious to talk to me. So explain to me now what all the excitement is about, because now you've got me all excited. And what the hell were you talking about building some kind of boat? I have no idea what that was all about."

"Good, Judge, it's all part of my plan, and from here on out, everything I do and say must be done in a stealthy and covert way so as not to be exposed. Judge, do you remember me telling you about the plan I was working on to help John and The Club out? Well, the reason I'm all excited is due to the fact that I just completed the final plans, and if all goes well, this plan could be executed perfectly, and hopefully and eventually, it will help John and The Club fulfill what they originally set out to do, and that was to change the antiquated laws pertaining to child molesters and take the power and decisions out of the hands of these bleeding-heart judges that continually set them free to molest children again.

'First of all, Judge, let me say this: I cannot over-accentuate or stress enough the importance of keeping all of our meetings extremely covert in order to pull this plan off. Any leak at all would be cause to abort the entire plan, and starting with this meeting tonight, we will have to make plans to meet somewhere else other than a public restaurant or place. We have to come up with a place for whatever future meetings we have that is as private and covert as possible. It cannot be any building or summer home or whatever that we own. And Judge, if you don't know of any such place, I have my own idea if you want to hear it."

"Absolutely, General. Since you put this plan together and you're so adamant about it being a covert operation, then, by all means, let me know what your plan is, and if I can possibly do what you ask, I will be more than happy to oblige you."

"Okay, Judge, I can understand where you're coming from. If I were in your shoes, I would be asking the exact same question. Also, Judge, please know this: I would have preferred to speak to John face to face, but for my plan to work, I need to preserve my anonymity with him. And again, for this plan to work, there must be very little contact with all parties involved."

"Okay, General, let me stop you right there. I must say, that I am getting extremely apprehensive, and to put it in a blunt way, you are scaring the shit out of me with all this talk about secret meetings in secret places and how important it is to do all this with covert operations. So why don't you just give me a brief synopsis of your plans so that I can decide whether or not I want to get involved with this whole thing."

"Judge, first off, let me ask you a question, and yes, Judge, I know I have a lot of firsts, but you will understand when I explain it all to you. I understand that you helped John and The Club out a few times, so what I would like to know from you is do you know what John was trying to accomplish? But before you answer that, let me tell you what I think he was trying to accomplish. John, from what I can ascertain from actually being a member of The Club, wanted to get the attention of lawmakers to have them change the current laws on the books pertaining to child molesters. So, now, I ask you, Judge, do you concur with how I feel, or do you have a different opinion as to what John was trying to accomplish with The Club?"

"Yes, I concur completely with you, and you are right that what John and The Club were trying to do was to have the current laws changed about child molesters. He told me more than once that he was trying to do just that."

"Okay, Judge… here it comes, and let me warn you that the plan I came up with is as extreme a plan as there could possibly be, but it's meant to get the attention of the lawmakers, and I can almost guarantee that this will do the job. So, as I will now explain, and briefly give you the synopsis of my plan, keep in mind what the goal is here; it is still meant to get the lawmakers' attention, to change the current laws that are on the books for these animal child molesters so they don't keep getting away with what they been getting away with.

"So, here it is, and Judge, if you don't want any part of this or you want some time to think about it, I will completely understand. The synopsis of my plan is really a simple one, but as I said before, and I know I said it many times, but as far as I'm concerned, I can't say it enough times, it's meant to shock the establishment and bring attention to what the goal of the entire plan is.

First off, let me say this, and this is the important part. I know that each state has its own laws pertaining to child molesters, but instead of fighting a lot of small wars, trying to change the laws in each state, I'm aiming to change the laws from a state law to a national law, and not have to deal with mayors or governors but go right to the top and deal with a Senator, and have him introduce a new bill to change the laws about child molesters and make them apply nationally to all child molesters. I know that there are a lot of Senators, so who do I pick? Well, what I decided was to take aim at a New York Senator, because that is where it all started. I plan to get in touch with him and explain to him what is about to happen so that he knows what is coming, and if he has any kind of a conscience, he will help me.

"My plan is to invite as many child molesters via the best means possible to a camp that I intend to set up with the help of my underground colleagues. The child molesters will be led to believe that if they attend this camp and stay for the duration, which will be six weeks, and pass a few simple tests, that their names will be removed from the national sex offender registry. But in reality, they will all be killed, and myself and all my colleagues who helped set this camp up will just disappear."

At that, the judge looks as though he's in shock. He stares at the General for a few seconds and then says, "Are you fucking crazy? Seriously, are you out of your fucking mind? And even if I agreed to this preposterous plan you concocted, how in God's name… But you know what, let me leave God out of this. How the hell do you plan on putting this all together and then, by some strange and outlandish method, getting away with it? The one thing I'm sure of is that if I do go along with this plan, it will definitely get the attention of somebody. Please tell me you're not serious."

"Judge, I am dead serious. I have been working on this plan for over a year. I have dotted every i and crossed every t, and I am absolutely positive that if I followed every single rule I laid down in the plan, this will work. But I can understand if you need some time, or if you want to back out. I won't blame you for doing so. It's a lot to swallow in one shot."

"General, I will really need some time to think about this if you are as serious as you claim you are. I know in the past I tried to help out John and The Club, and I would like to continue to help. Hell, I was the one who spoke to John and concurred with him that child molesters were like broken machines that could not be repaired and had to be discarded, to put another way, but this is just much too much for me to absorb and extrapolate all at once. I will definitely have to get back to you on this one."

"Okay, Judge. But just keep in mind that I was a general in the United States Army Special Forces and was trained to lead men into combat, and that included covert missions, so rest assured that I know what I'm doing. If you decide to go along with this and help me, I will meet with you and fill you in on all the finer details so that you will be able to see the big picture. In the meantime, we have to set up a means of getting in touch with one another – and here's that word again – covertly.

"The way we should contact each other is to use a prepaid throwaway cell phone, so as not to have our calls traced, and as far as meeting each other, the plan I have is to meet at a small airport outside of town that I will divulge if and when you decide to call me. Because I am also a licensed pilot and can rent out a small plane, we can fly around and talk without the worry of somebody trying to listen to our conversation. Are you okay with that part of the plan?"

"Okay, General, I will go along with that plan for now, until I decide what I want to do."

"That's good, judge. I took the liberty of purchasing two of those throwaway cell phones, and I'll give you one tonight with the number of the one I'm keeping so that when you decide what you want to do, you can call me. I will then let you know the name of the airport and where it is. We can meet, fly around for a while, and I can get into more of the details of my plan."

"General, I have one final question for you. If I did go along with this plan, do you have any sort of a percentage number of me getting caught…?"

"Judge, you will actually have a small part in this whole plan, although an important one. After your initial meeting with Mike, John's lawyer, you will be out of the picture completely, because all I need you for is to get the ball rolling by getting me a yes or no from John via Mike as to whether he wants me to implement this plan."

"General, before I leave, I must tell you that this has been the most significant, soul-searching, ethical, and moral meeting that I have ever had in my lifetime."

"Judge, I can understand how you feel, and I can appreciate that, because this meeting has also been one of the most significant, soul-searching, ethical, and moral meetings in my life too. In war, when I put a plan together, it's to kill the enemy, not my fellow citizens."

"Even though they are broken and can't be fixed, I still have some feelings for them, but if the government won't do anything to save our children from these monsters, then ethically and morally, as a judge, I feel it's my duty to do so, even though it goes against every moral fiber in my body."

"Judge, I could not have said it any better myself. Okay, Judge, I will leave first. Wait about ten minutes, and then you can leave, and if you need to get in touch with me, you have the phone. All I ask is that you call me one way or another, and thank you for listening to me. You have a good night."

"Bye for now."

Several days go by with nothing going on, and the General is finding it very hard to keep himself busy while waiting for the phone call from the judge. He finally decides to start a crossword puzzle, one of his hobbies that he enjoys. All of a sudden, the General's throwaway phone rings. He gets all excited because he is pretty sure that it's the judge calling him, which also means that all the plans he has made may finally come to pass.

"Hello, Judge?"

"Yes, it's me. It seemed like you were not sure who was calling you. Who did you think was calling you? You didn't give anyone else this number, did you?"

"No, Judge. It's just that I thought that you would have called sooner, and it seems like I have been waiting for your call forever. I decided to work on one of my crossword puzzles – that always helps me pass the time when I'm waiting for something – and just when I sort of settled into working on the crossword, all of a sudden, my phone starts to ring. Well, it's hard to explain, Judge, but the phone ringing startled me because I was deep in thought on my crossword puzzle. Well, anyway, Judge, what have you decided?"

"Well, General, I feel like President Truman must have felt when he gave the order to drop the atomic bomb on Hiroshima and Nagasaki knowing how many people it would kill."

"I know, Judge, but even though they knew it would kill a lot of people, they also felt that it would end the war and save a lot of American soldiers, which it did."

THE CLUB

"Okay, General, after a few sleepless nights, and may God forgive me for what I'm about to do, I have decided to help you."

"That is great! Judge, just keep in mind that we are doing this to protect all the children.

"I know, I know. I don't want to keep talking about it. Let's get this thing started. Just tell me what you want me to do next."

Okay, Judge, outside of town, due east about thirty miles, there is a small airport called Brookhaven Airport off William Floyd parkway in Shirley, New York. I rent planes out there every once in a while. I will meet you there at 8 AM tomorrow morning. I will rent the plane. We can either fly around or go to some other small airport where we can sit down and discuss what the plan is and what part you will play in it. And please remember this very important rule – I cannot overemphasize how important this rule is – absolutely no one should know where you're going or be following you. This is an absolute must. If at any time we schedule a meeting and you feel that someone has followed you or gotten wind of what you and I are up to, then this whole thing gets canceled and thrown into the wastepaper basket, because every step we take forward is predicated on the last step being successful. One misstep on our part, and it's all over. So, Judge, I will see you bright and early tomorrow morning at the airport. We will either fly around or fly to another small airport, sit down, and then I will explain the whole plan to you, step by step."

"Okay, General. I will see you tomorrow morning."

Bright and early the next morning, the General is at the small airport and has already rented a plane. With that part done, the General takes the keys and paperwork from the FBO clerk and heads out to the aircraft to start his preflight. Five minutes later, just as the General is finishing up the preflight, a car pulls up in the parking lot, and out steps the judge. The General waves his two arms up in the air, catching the judge's attention, and motions the judge to come over to him.

As the judge gets close to the General, the General speaks first: "Good morning, Tony, and by the way, from here on out, lets greet each other by our birth names. My name is Mike."

"Good morning, Mike. How does the weather look for flying?"

"It's a great day for flying. The weather is perfect."

"Well, Mike, let me tell you right now, I'm not a big fan of flying, especially in small aircraft, which, by the way, I have never flown in, and right now, I'm a little apprehensive about flying around in a small plane for the first time with the pilot having a conversation with me and not concentrating, on flying the aircraft."

"Okay, Tony, not to worry. I will fly us to a small out-of-the-way airport that I know that has a nice little restaurant. We will land there, go into the restaurant, sit down, have something to eat, and talk. Then I will fly you back. I won't fly around and talk, even though I can. Is that okay with you?"

"Yes, perfect."

"Tony, let's get started. Get in the plane. I will show you how to buckle yourself in, and then we're off. Okay?"

"Okay."

Within minutes, they are flying. The judge does not look too good; he just stares out the window. Thankfully, this is only a short flight. Once on the ground, the blood returns back to the judge's face. Then, finally in the restaurant, they find a quiet corner table and wait for the waitress to order. After ordering, the judge speaks first: "Let's get started. I'm dying to hear this plan of yours."

"Okay, Tony, but first, let me start by saying this: I have worked on this plan for over a year now, and I have to say that it is very complicated. But I do believe that if I stick to my plan and don't deviate from it in any way, it will work."

"Okay, Mike, so let me hear what you've got."

"First off, I know I explained to you what the plan was when we met at the restaurant, but let me give it to you one more time in a nutshell. I plan on getting as many child molesters as I can, convince them that I have the power to remove their name from the national sex offender registry. All they would have to do to get off the list is remain in this program for thirty days, sit through a few seminars showing them what they did was wrong and how they can turn their life around, and pass a few simple tests. But unbeknownst to them, I will actually be luring them into a false sense of security, and when they least expect it, I will kill them all with deadly gas while they sleep. So, Tony, that's the plan in a nutshell, but now comes the hard part, explaining to you everything that I will need for this plan to come together.

"I know I have a lot of firsts, but the one thing that I cannot stress enough will be the absolute agreement by everyone to practice complete secrecy. They are to let absolutely no one know what they're doing, not their wife, husband, mother, father, sister, brother, priest, rabbi, minister, etc., or any relative. Absolutely no one must be aware of what they are doing, and for any one not following this rule, the consequences will be devastating. Everyone must understand that, because, for all intents and purposes, we are entering into a war and must realize that people are going to die. If anyone leaks any information, some or all of the volunteers who are working toward the goal of The Club can get into more trouble than they could possibly ever imagine in their life, to put it mildly.

"As far as your part in this whole thing, it is not too complicated. I will basically need you as my liaison between John, his lawyer Mike, and myself, to keep John advised as to what is going on. Your first task will be to get in touch with John's lawyer, Mike, to see if he would hopefully work with us and maybe give some legal advice, but the single most important thing is the first meeting with John. This will be important, because that's when John will either put a stop to this or put his stamp of approval on it. That will be our first and biggest hurdle.

"With that said, I will now explain all the things I will need to get this plan going and open up the camp. One of the points I would like to bring up right now is this plan could possibly take up to a year to accomplish. It's going to be a work in progress. I must make sure I dot every i and cross every t, and every other proverb you can think of. I am going to have to investigate everyone involved, so everyone is going to have to have some patience. This plan cannot be rushed."

"Mike, I understand all that bullshit, so get on with it already."

"Okay, Tony, it's just that I want to make sure that you understand everything I'm doing."

"I understand, I understand, Mike. Now please get on with it."

"Okay, here it is. These are the things I will need to open up the camp. First off, all of the people that I do bring on board will have to be thoroughly screened to make sure that there will be no moles in the group. I am going to have to locate people with different skills, such as make-up artists, psychiatrists, lawyers, contractors, detectives, nurses, bankers, doctors, and judges. We will also need people on the inside, such as in the building department, so that they can issue false building permits and other various documents. All of these people I select to bring on board will have to wholeheartedly volunteer to pitch in to make this camp possible. Some of the people involved may need to have their appearance and fingerprints altered, but not surgically. That is when the make-up artists come into play. I have many slots to fill, and all the slots are specific and must be filled. I cannot leave one open slot, or this will not work.

❧❧❧

"We will also need money, lots of money, goods, and land, especially land with buildings on them, and if that happens, and we do get land with buildings on it, and we are able to use the buildings, the owners can always claim that they did not know anyone was using the property. To get all of this done, I will attempt to contact as many members of The Club as possible for their support and donations. Lawyers will be needed to draw up phony documents, such as contracts for the child molesters to sign, giving this whole scam credence to them.

"The accommodations we build for them, or modify for them, will be built as airtight as possible, with no windows, with the excuse that no one will be able to look inside and see what's going on. There will be automatic locks, and there will be plumbing installed in advance so that after a few days, when all the child molesters are feeling safe and secure and thinking about what they are trying to accomplish here, and we've given them a false sense of security, one night, when they are all asleep, we will trigger the automatic door locks and, through the previously install plumbing, pump a deadly gas into the building, killing them all as they sleep.

"Once the gas is turned on, all of the members who are involved in setting this whole thing up will just disappear into the night with complete anonymity. A letter will be left behind explaining everything we did to the authorities, and hopefully we will get the attention of the lawmakers so that they can change the laws that are currently on the books pertaining to child molesters. It will also have a warning that if nothing is done about this. the next uprising will involve bigger numbers. We will not rest until the laws are changed, and they should be aware that phase two has already been completely planned and will be very easy to implement.

"All of this, will be done as stealthily as possible, but to the child molesters, it must look like the real thing and not have any phony appearance to it. Everyone involved must have their own escape plan set in concrete so that no enforcement agency can ever trace any of the volunteers to this camp. I plan on this being the biggest scam of all time, but executed for a good cause.

"Okay, Tony. There it is. Now that you've heard the whole plan, what do you think? Are you in or out?"

"Mike, I thought we already covered that and that I said I was in."

"Good, Tony. I just wanted to make sure that you still felt that way. Well, then, we are all set, and the first official thing you have to do is this: I want you to get in touch with Mike Santino, John's lawyer, and fill him in on our plan and see if he will help us. What we need him to do is be our go-between so that we can keep John up to date, but even that contact will be very little. We don't want too much of anything, because that will bring attention to us, and that, we don't want. So, Tony, that will be your first assignment, and depending on what Mike says, it will dictate our next move. Well, I think our first official meeting went well, so let's fly home."

175

"Okay, Mike. I can't wait for that."

"Oh, don't worry. It's a piece of cake."

The flight home was smooth and uneventful, and the judge very much appreciated that.

The next morning, the judge puts a call into Mike's office.

"Good morning. Mr. Santino's office."

"Good morning. This is Judge Ghetto. Is Mr. Santino in?"

"Yes, Judge. May I ask what this is about?"

"It's about a case he was working on, and I was the presiding judge."

"One moment, Judge."

After a moment, Mike gets on the line. "Good morning, Judge. How are you doing?"

"I'm doing fine. Mike, I need to set up an in-person meeting with you about a case you tried in my court, and it's kind of important."

"Okay, Judge. Where and when do you want to meet?"

"Well, how about tonight? I will buy you dinner."

"Hold on, let me check my calendar. Okay, Judge, it looks good. Where do you want to meet?"

"How about my favorite restaurant, Laduchies, at 6:30 PM? Do you know where it is?"

"Yes, I've been there before with you."

"Yes, you are right."

"That sounds good, Judge. I will see you there. But keep in mind, Judge, I'm a big eater."

"No problem, Mike. You can eat all you want."

"Great. See you tonight."

The judge gets to the restaurant a little early, but at 6:30 sharp, Mike walks into the restaurant and heads over to the table. As he gets close, the judge stands up and the two men shake hands. Mike says, "Well, Judge, I can see why this is your favorite restaurant. I have always wanted to try this place, but never got around to it. It's got great ambience. I feel like I'm actually in Italy, with the music and pictures and all. It's a great restaurant. I will definitely bring my wife back here for dinner. I have to thank you for introducing it to me."

"Oh, no problem, Mike. Anyway, thanks for meeting up with me."

"No problem Judge. So, what is this all about?"

"Well, first off, let me apologize to you, because I got you here under a false pretense, the truth being that it's about your client John Harrison. He still is your client, right?"

"Yes, he is. Wow! Now you've really got me guessing. What is this all about, Judge?"

"First, I have to have your promise that you swear on whatever you hold sacred that what transpires here stays between the two of us. If you can't agree to that, then I will simply buy you dinner and a drink or two, enjoy a nice conversation about the weather and world affairs, and then we can bid each other adieu."

"Wow, that's a heavy statement for me to take in, and I don't even know what you're going to ask me yet... but before I swear to keep this secret of yours, can I have a hint, and maybe have some time to think about it?"

"Absolutely not. I must have your absolute promise of secrecy before I utter one word of the story."

"You say it's about John Harrison?"

"Yes."

"Okay, if I promise to keep secret what you are about to tell me, after hearing it, am I locked in to do anything, or can I just promise to keep my mouth shut and go on my merry way?"

"You will not be locked into anything, except not to divulge anything said here tonight. If you decide not to help, you are free, as you put it, to go your merry way."

"Well, okay, Judge. I promise to keep all that is said here tonight to myself, and I'm doing this only because it's about my client and good friend, John."

"Great! A few weeks ago, I got a call from this guy I know, and he happens to be a retired United States Army general whom I have great respect for. He informed me that what John was doing with his website is still very much alive, even though the website was shut down. He told me that it simply went underground and is thriving."

"Oh, wow!"

"I guess John will be happy to hear that."

"Yes, he will. So what does that have to do with me, and why all the secrecy? I mean, I guess that's good news for John and all, and frankly, you now have me really confused. I can't figure why you would want me to keep that a secret. Who would I possibly tell or talk about it with anyone else but John?"

"Well, that's not the secret. Before I explain it to you, please try to have an open mind and remember to keep your eyes on the prize, that prize being to have the laws changed pertaining to child molesters."

"Okay, I promise to keep my mouth shut and keep my eye on the prize. Now, please, fill me in on this plan of yours before I explode with antici-pation."

"Here it is. Hold onto your hat, because what I am about to tell you is a real Jim dandy of a plan, and will be hard for you to comprehend, but believe me, what I'm about to tell you is an actual plan that is in the works, and this is phase one.

"As I told you earlier, several weeks ago, I got a call from this retired United States general. He asked to meet with me, and at the meeting, he explained how he'd like to help John and proceeded to explain the plan that he has come up with. He guarantees that if everything works right and his plan comes together, it will get the attention of the lawmakers so that the laws that are currently on the books pertaining to child molesters will be changed.

"Rather than me explaining the entire plan, I will give you a brief syn-opsis of it, and if you like what you hear and are willing to go along with it, I will fill you in with the finer details. So, here it is. What the General is planning to do is to somehow induce several hundred child molesters to attend a camp that he will set up with the help of some of the mem-bers of The Club. He will convince them that if they remain at this camp and attend a few classes and pass a few simple tests, their names will be removed from the national sex offenders registry. But after several days, and unbeknownst to them, and just when they feel comfortable and safe, the General will give the order sometime in the middle of the night to lock the doors, seal them in, and gas them all to death. Then, he will leave a note behind explaining what has transpired and saying that if the laws are not changed, there are more plans already put together to do this again, and again, and again, if need be."

After hearing all this, Mike just sits there, staring at the judge in disbelief, not uttering a word, just staring. Finally, Mike says, "Judge, I am not really one that utters exclamatory words, but this is a fucking joke, right? You're fucking kidding me, right?"

"No, Mike, but as you exquisitely put it, I'm not fucking kidding you, and in a way that you will better understand, what I just told you is the truth, the whole truth, and nothing but the truth, so help me God."

"I'm sorry, Judge, but I'm going to need some time to digest all this and then get back to you with an answer."

"I'm also sorry to put you on the spot, Mike, but I'm going to need an answer tonight. I know it's a lot to take in, comprehend, and believe all at once, but it is the truth. What we can do is take our time eating dinner while you run it through your mind, and in the interim, I can answer any questions you may have. If need be, we can sit here as long as it takes, or until they throw us out, because my instructions were to get an answer from you tonight."

"Dammit! My gut tells me to get up right now and walk away, but I can't, because it's for my good friend John. I just can't see this plan turning out good. Right now, even before knowing any more about the plan, I have a thousand questions."

"That's okay, Mike. Ask away, and I will try to answer all of them the best I can, but before you get too excited, how about I tell you what your part in this whole plan is? It's not that much; it's just that you are part one of the first steps in the plan."

"Okay, why don't you do that."

"Fine. Mike, all you have to do is go and visit John, hand him a letter explaining the whole plan, and bring back his answer. That's it. That's all you have to do for now, and according to the General, you may have to do that maybe a few times, and only when absolutely necessary, just deliver a letter now and then and bring back an answer."

"Would I be able to read the letter?"

"Absolutely. Then the only thing you must do would be to return the letter to me so that I can return it to the General and he can destroy it himself. So, your part in this whole thing would be very minimal."

"My God… I can't believe that I'm about to say yes to all this, but I do feel very strongly about John's cause. That's why I decided to help him in the first place. So, okay, I'm in. What's next?"

"Well, what I need to do next is give the General your answer, and I guess he will tell us what his next move is. So, eat up and be proud. I'm sure that there are many people out there that feel the same way we do, but they don't have the balls to do anything about it. So let's toast to this historic event that we are embarking on, and may God forgive us for what we are about to do."

With that, the two men lift their glasses, tap them together, and both say "Amen" at the same time.

The next morning, the judge, using the throwaway phone, calls the General.

"Good morning, Judge. How are you doing? I hope you're calling me with some good news."

"As a matter of fact, General, I am. Last night, I met up with Mike, John's lawyer, and filled him in on your plan, but I have to say that he was quite taken back, to say the least. He kept asking me if I was kidding him and if I was serious or not. As a matter-of-fact, to quote him precisely, he said, 'Are you fucking kidding me?' and I answered, 'No, I'm not fucking kidding you. I am dead serious.' After about an hour of questions, and him beating himself up over the answer he was about to give, he finally gave in and said yes. I thanked him and assured him that his involvement in this whole thing would be minimal. So now that we've got Mike's yes, what's the next step?"

"Well, next, I would like you to set up another meeting with Mike and give him a letter that I will give you so that he can bring it to John to read. The letter will explain the whole plan, and let me say this now, before we go any further, there must be absolutely no copies made of any documents I make up unless I specifically give explicit instructions to copy them. Then, and only then, can copies be made of anything I write up. Is that understood?"

"Yes, General, I understand."

"Good. Anyway, after John reads the letter, Mike is to get John's answer, yes or no, but one way or another, the letter must be returned to me so that I, myself, can destroy it. If the answer is yes, we go to the next step.

If it's no, then it's all over, and it ends right there and then. So, here's what we do next. And by the way, where did you meet up with Mike when you spoke to him last?"

"We met at an Italian restaurant I like called Laduchies."

"And was there anyone else with you guys?"

"No, it was just Mike and myself."

"Okay, so make it a point to meet Mike at the same restaurant again, only this time bring your wives, but by no means have any of your wives see you hand Mike the letter. In the envelope, there will be a second letter addressed to Mike. it will explain to him what I told you about making copies of anything I compose, and also about returning everything back to you so that you can return it back to me and I can destroy it myself."

"Okay, Judge. Tonight I will put together two letters, and you can pick them up the night before the meeting with Mike. Just give me a call when you are ready, and we can meet at the airport, and I will give you the letters."

Two days later, the judge sets up the meeting with Mike and his wife at Laduchies. Then he calls the General and sets up a meeting at the airport to pick up the letters. Armed with the letters, the judge meets up with Mike and his wife at Laduchies.

Halfway through the meal, the girls go to the ladies' room. That's when Mike asks the judge, "Have you got the letter? If you do, now would be a good time to give it to me."

"Not now, Mike. When the girls get back. I will make a joke to you, stating the fact that I need to use the men's room and would you like to join me, just like the ladies do, and you can say, 'You know what, judge, as a matter of fact, I think I will,' and there in the men's room, I will give you letters. There are two of them, one for you and one for John."

"Why is there one for me?"

"It's just to remind you not to make copies of any of the documents and to make sure you return them to me so that I can return them to the General and he can destroy them himself."

"He certainly has lots of rules."

"Yes, he does. When we get in the men's room, I will go in the stall, and you'll get in the next stall, and I will pass the letters to you under the partition."

"Okay, Judge, but this seems too melodramatic to me."

"Maybe to you, but not to the General, and please wait until you are home or at your office alone to read your letter. And yes, you can read John's also."

Just then, the girls get back, and the judge does his thing. "You know what? Now I need to use the restroom. Mike, would you care to join me?"

"As a matter-of-fact, judge, I think I will."

The two of them get up and go to the men's room. They each take their separate stalls, and the judge slips Mike the letters. After that, the two men return to the table, finish dinner, and then both couples go home.

Once home, Mike goes into his study and reads the letters. Mike's letter explains to him that his visit is all about an appeal that he is working on for John and to make sure that there are no cameras in the room that might be able to read John's letter. Also, he is to make sure that if there is a guard in the room, that he's not standing behind John so that he can read the letter, pointing out that it is imperative that no one but John read the letter. The rest of the letter is just about not making any copies of anything he gets from the judge and to make sure to return all the papers to the judge unless told differently.

The plan

The next day, with doubt still in his mind as to whether or not he's doing the right thing Mike heads out to the prison to give John the letter explaining everything to him. Mike finally gets to the prison and goes through the normal screening process, checking his attaché case, going through the metal detector, and answering a few questions. Mike informs them that he is there to talk to John about an appeal that he is working on. Finally, he's led to the same room where he met with John the last few times. Mike sits down at the table, and while waiting for John to come in, he looks all around the room, searching for cameras or microphones. He finds none, and this makes him feel a little more comfortable. After a few minutes, the guards bring John into the room, shackle him to the ring attached to the metal table, and then one of the guards tells Mike, "If you need us, we will be right outside the door."

Mike replies, "Thank you."

John looks at Mike. "So, what's this all about? I hope you've got good news for me."

"Well, I'm working on an appeal, and I got some information I want you to check out to see if I got all of the facts straight." With that, Mike pulls out an envelope from his jacket pocket, hands it to John, and says, "Read this. It's an outline of the appeal I'm working on. Read it and let me know what you think of it."

John opens the letter. It reads:

VERY, VERY IMPORTANT.

John, by no means react to this letter in any way other than it being about trying to get an appeal going for you. What you are about to read may shock you, but just to let you know who I am, I am a retired Army general who has led stealth fighters into many undercover missions, so let me assure you that I know what I am doing. I have been following your plight a while now, about you trying to have the laws changed against child molesters, and I feel that this plan I have will light a fire under the butts of the people in charge who make up the laws of this country. It's not a complicated plan, but one that I am sure will work. I will not fill your head with all the details, but I will give you the pertinent information.

Basically, all that I am looking for from you today is a yes or no answer. Other than that, I will attend to the details, and hopefully, if it all works out, you will finally have some say as to the laws on the books pertaining to child molesters.

So, here it is in a nutshell: I intend to open up a fictitious camp for child molesters in a desolate area, in a rigged-up house, and entice child molesters to attend a four-week course about child molestation – they must do this without anyone knowing about it, or they will not be allowed to attend – promising them that if they complete the four-week course, their names will be secretly removed from the national sex offenders registry, enabling them to lead a more normal life without the restrictions put on them. In short, after attending one or two classes that I will have for them, one night, when they are all asleep, I will remotely lock the doors and gas them all to death. Then everyone on my team will disappear into the night with their preplanned escapes.

I have worked out all of the plans and will try to enlist some of the members of The Club, and in case you were not aware of this, The Club has gone underground and is going strong and getting stronger every day. In fact, I am the leader of the local chapter. It is all set up the very same way you had it when your website was up and running, and there are many chapters around the country. But above all, remember this: you are still the leader. If your answer today is no, it all ends here and now. There are many details I left out, but just to put your mind at ease, I plan to have lawyers ready to make up phony documents and make-up artist to disguise everyone. I also have people in the building department to cover up whatever I need covered up, etc. etc., and many law enforcement people to help out.

John, this will work. Like I said, all I need is a yes or no from you, and I will take care and handle all of the rest. My biggest problem is tracking down more members to get everything I need. One thing I would ask you is, by any chance, would you have a list of members saved somewhere, with their names and addresses, from when the website was up and running? If you do, please write down the information and give it to Mike so that he can get it to me. Also, if you have any questions, please write them down and give them to Mike. Do not talk aloud. If Mike has an answer for you, he will write it down. If not, then I will get back to you via Mike with the answer. And remember, I want very few words spoken, and then only in reference to your appeal.

John continues reading, lifting his head up every so often, looking at Mike with eyes wide open, and slowly moving his head back and forth in a doubtful motion, as though he is in shock and cannot believe what he is reading. Forgetting all about having to write everything down, John blurts out, "Do you really think that this will work?"

Mike looks at John sort of shaking his head back and forth and says, "I have been working on this appeal for a while now, and I think it has lots of merit. Otherwise, I would not be wasting my time traveling here and talking to you. It may be a shot in the dark, but right now, it's the only shot we have, so if you need time to think about it, I can do that, and you can give me your answer, yes or no, whenever you want to. Then I will go forward or not with the appeal."

"No, Mike, just hold on a minute. I just need a few minutes to think about this."

"What's to think about? Do you ever want to get out of here or not? Like I said, it's a shot in the dark, but it's the only shot we have. After all, you've got nothing to lose and a lot to gain by trying this."

At that, John grabs Mike's pad and starts to write, "What do you think are the chances of this plan working, and how much confidence do you have in the General? Who is he? Where did he come from?"

Mike takes the pad back and writes, "Judge Ghetto is the one who got in touch with me, and according to the judge, who had a few meetings with the General and had him checked out thoroughly, he is convinced that he is the real deal. If Judge Ghetto thinks that this plan will work, then I am with the judge, or I would not be here bringing you this information."

John writes back, "My God, this is a big decision. I could go down in history as the biggest monster of all time. How much time do I have to think about this and give the General an answer?"

Mike writes back, "The General is all set to go. As far as how much time you have, he did not elaborate on that, but I am assuming that he would like an answer as soon as possible. As far as I'm concerned, I really would like to make as few trips to this prison as possible, because the General is planning it so that Judge Ghetto and I will not be too involved should the plan go south. So once you give me your answer, unless an emergency comes up and I have to visit you, the judge and I will be out of the picture, and the General will be handling everything."

John writes back, "Okay, I guess, right now, I am looked upon as a monster anyway, for what I've already done, so it couldn't get any worse for me. I am going to say yes to the General, so let him do his thing, and hopefully, it will give me the results that I started out looking for. Personally, I cannot see a plan this complicated going smoothly and being completed in a satisfactory way with no one getting caught. By the way, you can tell the General that I did manage to save a list of some of the members before the website was shut down, but I don't know how easy it is going to be to get them. I sent them to a friend of mine, and I swore him to secrecy and to not let anyone, including his wife and family, know that I sent him a package to hold. His name is Bob Brunkard, and he lives in Florida. I don't remember his phone number, but the last time I looked, it was still listed, so you should be able to get it. If he needs proof that I sent you, tell him that the nickname we called him by when we all hung out was little Elvis. Also, he had a beauty mark on his left chest, and he stuttered whenever he got mad."

Mike writes back, "Okay, I will give the General your answer, and I am sure that he will be very happy to hear about the list that you managed to save. I'm sure that it will be a tremendous help to him, and I hope that everything goes your way." With that, Mike picks up all the papers, double-checks to make sure that he has everything, shakes John's hand, and says, "You take care of yourself, you hear, and I will be in touch with you." Mike then calls the guards back in and tells them that he is ready to leave. The second guard comes in, unshackles John, and takes him back to his cell, and Mike leaves the prison and heads home.

The next day, Mike gets in touch with Judge Ghetto and asks him if he would like to meet for lunch, just the two of them, just to catch up on things and talk about world affairs.

"That would be nice," says the judge. "We haven't seen each other for a while, and that's just as good an excuse as any to get together."

"Okay, Judge, how about lunch at that deli on Second Street that you like?"

"Sounds good to me."

"Okay, then, I will meet you there at noon tomorrow."

"Sounds good. See you tomorrow."

At 12 noon sharp the next day, Mike and the judge meet for lunch. They get seated, check the menu, and order drinks and their meals. The judge speaks first: "So, Mike, how is that appeal coming along that you were working on?"

"Well, I finally got an answer from one of the witnesses, and they agreed to be interviewed and, if need be, testify."

"I guess that's good news for you."

"Yes, it is. I just hope that this whole thing doesn't blow up in my face and make things worse for my client."

"I'll drink to that." The two men raise their glasses and tap them. "Here's to good luck."

While eating, Mike reaches down and, from under his pants leg, slips out an envelope that was held in place with a large rubber band. Under the table, he taps the judge's leg with the envelope. The judge, feeling it, reaches down under the table, takes the envelope, and discreetly brings it up and places it in his jacket pocket.

"So, Mike, is all the information for your appeal all together? Was your client excited about the fact that you're working on an appeal for him?"

"He was absolutely elated, to say the least."

"Is there anything you're missing that I can help you out with?"

"No, thank you, Judge. I think I got everything covered, and in fact, I even included some testimony I had with my client, so I am all set. Everything is there. All of my t's are crossed and my i's dotted."

"Okay, Mike, but remember, if you need any help, I'm here for you."

After lunch, the two discuss how good the food was and that they should do this more often. They pay the check, shake hands, and go their separate ways, wishing each other good luck and to have a nice day.

The next day, Judge Ghetto, using the throwaway phone, calls the General.

"Good morning, Judge!! Well, I cannot wait any more. Have you got good news for me?"

"As a matter fact, General, yes, I do. I would like to set up a meeting with you at the airport so that I can give you the paperwork."

"Okay, that's great, but tomorrow I am busy, and interestingly enough, what I have to do is deal with something that pertains exactly to what we are doing here today. I have to meet with my people and assign a lawyer to defend a policemen accused of murdering a child molester who turned himself in after the incident, but I could meet you the next day, at 8 AM, at the airport.

"I will meet you Thursday morning, at 8 AM, at the airport."

"Good, I will see you there."

On Thursday morning, Judge Ghetto gets to the airport at 8:15 AM, expecting to hear a lecture from the General. However, the General is nowhere to be found. Driving around the parking lot several times gets the judge nervous, because he feels that he is bringing unwanted attention to himself, so he decides to park and wait a while before calling the General.

Finally, after about twenty minutes, the General shows up, parks next to the judge, gets out of his car, and walks over to the judge's car. "Good morning, Judge. Sorry I'm late, but I had to make some last minute changes with lawyers on the case that I told you about. That took me some time to do, but I'm here now, so let's go rent a plane."

"Do we really have to do that General?"

"Absolutely. Remember, there is to be no deviating from the plan."

The two of them walk over to the operations building, rent a plane, check it out, and take off.

"Okay, Judge, how about we kill two birds with one stone?"

"And just what do you mean by that?"

"What I mean by that is let's take care of business and go and get some breakfast at a new restaurant that just opened at a small airport that I know. It's a great day for flying, so let's enjoy it."

"Okay. I got your letter back with the answers, so let's go and get breakfast."

"Great!!"

After they land, they proceeded to the restaurant. Again, they get a nice table in the corner so that they will have some privacy. After ordering, the judge hands the General the letter. The General, being anxious to know the answers, opens the letter as quickly as he can. As he starts reading, he seems excited. Then, when he gets to the part that says that John did manage to save the names of many members, he blurts out, "Oh my God! That's great. That will be of great help to me. This has made my day."

After breakfast and back at the home airport, the two sit in the plane and discuss what to do next.

"So General, what's the next step?"

"Judge, for now, your job is done, and hopefully, I won't need you anymore."

"Well, thank God for that. I wanted to help, but the stress was killing me, and I can't take all the suspense."

"Good, Judge, you can relax for now."

"Great."

With that, the two bid each other goodnight and go home.

The next day, the first thing the General does is pick up the phone and call information to try to get Bob's number, the person that John sent the CDs to. He gets the number, and then he thinks to himself, *Wow, that went well. I did not think that it was going to be that easy.*

Now armed with the phone number, the General dials the number. After the fourth ring, a man answers, "Hello?"

"Hello, is this Bob Brunkard?"

"Yes, and may I ask who's calling?"

"Well, yes, you may. I am a retired general from the United States Army, and I would like to meet with you in person and discuss a very important matter if that's all right with you."

"I don't know. You say you're a retired general? What is your name?"

"Well, I'd rather not say what my name is. It's not really important. What I will tell you is this: if this is Bob Brunkard, some time ago, a very close friend of yours sent you a package, and your friend asked me to get in touch with you to make arrangements to pick up that package. So if this is truly Bob Brunkard, you'll know what I'm talking about. Your friend also gave me some information about you to prove that he truly sent me. So, first, answer me this: do you know what I'm talking about?"

"Well, I've gotten a lot of packages, so I don't know exactly what you're talking about."

"Okay, Mr. Brunkard, will you at least have the courtesy to meet me in person and let me explain further? I am not out to hurt you in any way, shape, or form. It's just that you have something that I need that this very close friend of yours wants me to pick up."

"Well, okay, but when would you want to come here?"

"I could be there tomorrow afternoon if that's okay with you."

"Okay, would you mind if I called the police and have them send the policemen so that they will be here when you get here, just to protect myself? Because, to tell you the truth, to me this is a strange phone call."

"No, no, don't do that. How can I convince you that I mean you no harm or anything like that? If you are who you say you are, and you know what I am talking about, I just cannot mention names on the phone. That's why I prefer to meet you in person and explain my plight."

"Okay, but I am going to have my son here."

"That's okay. You can have your son as long as he's not a policemen or has anything to do with the law."

"No, he is a truck driver. He has nothing to do with the law, but he's a big guy, and I would like to have him there."

"That's okay. I have no problem with your son being there. If that makes you more comfortable, by all means have him there."

"Then I guess tomorrow will be okay. Call me when you get to the airport. If you want, I will pick you up."

"No, that won't be necessary. I'd rather take a taxi to your house. All I need is your address."

Bob gives the General his address. "Okay then, I will see you tomorrow."

"Yes, I will call you from the airport and let you know when I'm on my way."

"Okay, thank you. Bye."

The next thing the General does is book a flight to Florida. Then, bright and early the next morning, the General is at the airport boarding a plane for Tampa. It's not that long of a flight, but the General is squirming in his seat, thinking that the flight is taking forever. Finally, the plane touches down, and he scrambles off to look for a pay phone. He dials Bob's number, and Bob answers, "Hello."

"Hello, Bob."

"Yes, this is Bob."

"I'm sorry, I should've said Mr. Brunkard."

"That's okay. Is this the General?"

"Yes it is."

"It's okay, General. You can call me Bob."

"Okay, great. I am getting the taxi now, and I should be there in about one hour. Is that okay?"

"Yes, it is."

"Okay, I will see you then."

As the General pulls up to the house, he is searching his mind for additional ways of convincing Bob to give him the package that John sent to him. Even as he's walking up to the door, he is still searching his mind, but he keeps coming up with nothing new. Finally, he's at the door and is about to ring the doorbell, when the door opens and Bob says, "General?"

"Yes."

"Well, hello, and welcome. Please come in."

"Thank you."

Bob leads the General into the living room and points to a seat. "Please, sit, and just to let you know, my son is in his room if I should need him."

"No, that will not be necessary."

"Well, I just wanted you to know that. Okay, then, would you like something to drink? Coffee or water?"

"No, thank you. I had plenty on the plane. If you don't mind, I would like to get right down to it. The friend of yours that I was referring to is John Harrison. Do you remember him? Do you know who I'm talking about?"

"Yes, I do, and when you called, I knew exactly who you were talking about. But you've got to understand, when he sent me that package, he swore me to secrecy, so that's why I am so reluctant to speak to anyone about it. But you touched on a few things that interest me, and I said, 'I must check this out,' so here you are today. So, how do you know John?"

"Well, I know the judge who helped John, and first of all, I don't know if you know this, but John is currently locked up in prison, and what I am doing here is trying to help him out. It's a long story, and I'd rather not go into it, but he gave me a message to give to you to prove that it was him that sent me here. First, he said that when you guys were young, they called you little Elvis. Second, he said that you have a beauty mark on your left chest, and third, he said that whenever you get mad, or get riled up, you stutter, so I hope that this is enough evidence for you to release that package to me."

"This is all happening so fast. You have not been sitting here but five minutes, and you came right to the point and, I must add, very convincingly. And you say that this package will help John get out of prison?"

"Yes, I promise you that what I will do with that package will help John get out of prison. I won't lie to you; it is not definite that I can get him out, but I will promise that it will help. And time is of the essence. That is why I came right to the point and did not beat around the bush. So, have I convinced you enough for you to release the package to me?"

"Actually, you have. Not many people know about my stuttering problem or about the beauty mark on my chest, so hopefully, you're not pulling a scam on me to get this package."

"Like I said, I promise you, and I swear this is no scam. I really need that package to help John get out of prison."

"Okay, then, hold on, and I will get it for you." Bob disappears into the basement and comes up shortly with the package. He hands it to the General. "Here you go. I just hope that I am doing the right thing for my friend."

"Bob, be assured that you are doing the right thing to help your friend. Now, I have one more favor of you."

"And what is that?"

"Can you please give me a lift back to the airport?"

"Oh, I thought you had the taxi outside waiting."

"No, I would rather you drive me back to the airport."

"Okay, General. No problem. Let me get my keys, and I will be happy to take you back to the airport."

Bob gets his keys, the two of them get into the car, and Bob drives to the airport. The General says, "Just pull up to the terminal, and I will get out there. I prefer that you don't park and escort me to the terminal. After I get out, I would like for you to just drive away."

"Well, okay, if that's what you want."

"Yes, please, I would prefer it that way, and thank you very much for your help. I promise you that you are helping John, and again, thank you."

Bob pulls up to the terminal. "Okay, we're here."

"Thanks again, Bob. You were a tremendous help, whether you realize it or not. And one more thing, you probably will not hear from John or myself for a while, and for John's sake, don't try to get in touch with him."

"Okay, you got it."

"Because, if you try to contact John or myself, you could jeopardize what I am trying to do for John."

"Okay, General, like I said, you got it."

The General gets out of the car and walks away. Once inside the terminal, he goes over to the counter and checks in for his flight back to New York.

The next day, bright and early, the General calls his people and sets up an emergency meeting for 8 PM that same night. The General gets to the meeting place at 7 PM and helps in setting the place up. Slowly all of the members arrive, and the room is abuzz with all of the members talking among themselves, trying to figure out what this meeting is all about. At 8 PM sharp, the General calls the meeting to attention, banging his hand several times on the table before he can get all of the members to finally stop talking. Finally, everyone settles down, stops talking, and sits. Now that it's quiet, the General looks out at all of the members, who are all staring back at him in anticipation of what he is about to say and why he has called an emergency meeting, something that he has never done before.

"Welcome," the General says, "and I want to thank everyone for showing up tonight. But before I get to the crux of why I called this emergency meeting, I just want to review one very important point as to why we are all here in the first place and what our ultimate goal is, that goal being getting the much-too-lenient laws changed pertaining to child molesters. And one very important thing: we are a local club that is part of a larger movement, so sometimes, we don't get a chance to hear all of the news about children missing that is going on all over country. But, then again, most people do not hear about these stories about these children, because, most of the time, it's only in the local paper of the town where it happened, and the news is not spread across the country unless it's a child of a famous person. Then it will be all over the news. But just to bring you up to speed, as of today, there are three children missing across this country: a six-year-old boy in Oklahoma, who is still missing, an eight-year-old girl in Nevada, who is still missing, and a twelve-year-old girl in New Jersey, whose body was found in a trash container. In all of these cases, no one has been arrested. These mutant predator animals are still out there, and this is what we want to put a stop to. So, before I get started, keep what I just said in your minds. And lastly, here are some statistics to think about: for every thousand children, sixteen percent of them between the ages of fourteen and seventeen, across this country, will be victimized by child molesters, and the most vulnerable are the seven- to thirteen-year-old children, so let that sink in and keep you motivated.

"And now I want you to please bear with me, with all my rambling, because this meeting is probably going to go down as the most important meeting this club has ever had. The plan that I am about to explain to you is designed to change the course of our plight, so before I go any further, I will ask a few questions, and depending on your response, and then by a show of hands, I will proceed to the next step. Finally, if the majority of you approve of this plan, then and only then will I explain my entire plan. Again, let me make this clear. If the majority of the members here tonight do not agree with a few questions that I will ask you, then my plan will die here tonight, and if you do agree with me tonight, the last question I will ask is should we present this plan to the rest of the underground clubs for their approval, because, for this plan to work, we must all act as one and have one hundred percent of our members behind it. It's a plan that I have been working on for several years, and I believe this is what is needed to get the attention of the lawmakers in this country. I have run this by a few very intelligent people, and they all agree that, though being drastic, this should work to get the attention that we are looking for.

"Okay, then, here we go. This plan that I am about to explain to you was approved and signed off on by John Harrison himself, and also a prominent judge, and please remember this is all aimed at achieving The Club's ultimate goal. John and the judge, and a few other people that I cannot mention, all agree that this will speed up our ride to achieve our goal.

"To start with, I will explain my plan in a capsule form. I will give you enough pertinent information to allow you to make this very important decision, and if the plan gets approved by you tonight, then I will take questions and get into the finer details of the plan, and give you some definitive answers.

"The long and short of it is this: I plan to get as many child molesters as I can, by any deceptive means that I can come up with, to attend a camp with the promise that if they attend, and go to a few meetings on child molestation, their names will be removed from the national child molesters list and they will be able to live their lives in a more normal a way, and live happily ever after. At the camp, they will stay in a special sort of a hotel, or several small buildings, that we will build with special features, and once they are all there, after a night or two, when they least expect it, they will all be gassed to death while they sleep. We will all just disappear with pre-arranged plans and routs, leaving a letter behind explaining that we have many more scenarios like this one, and unless the laws now on the books about child molesters are changed, we will enact all of them.

"Before you ask any questions, I will give you just a few facts. I have planned to get help from our members with, legal matters, make-up artists to change our appearance, plumbers, electricians, etc., etc. I know you have many questions, but rest assured that I have all the bases covered. Okay, let's get started. If you have any questions, raise your hand, and I will recognize you and answer your question as best I can."

Surprisingly, only three members raise their hands. The General points to one of them and asks, "What is your question?"

"Well, when I first joined this club, I thought what we were all about was to defend anyone who went out and killed a child molester, and to put it bluntly, now you're suggesting that instead of defending the ones that are doing the killing, we ourselves go out and kill child molesters. I know that you ran this by a few people that you consider very intelligent, and also by John, the one who started The Club, but are you sure that it's a good idea to be involved in a mass killing?"

"I'll answer that question this way: the ones that are going out and killing the child molesters now, and who we are defending, are members of The Club to begin with, so to answer your question, there is really no difference. We are all members of the same club, and to put it right out there, we have been encouraging all members to go out and kill child molesters from the get-go, and if they got caught, we would defend them. So what I am suggesting is nothing new. We are all members of the same club and should all be on the same page. Did that answer your question?"

"Actually, yes, it did. I just didn't look at it that way."

Next, the General points to the second person with his hand raised. "Yes, what is your question?"

"My question is do you really think that we can get away with this? You really didn't give us many details. I will need more details before I can make my mind up."

"Okay, I understand your question, but before I can get into more details, I would still like to see by a show of hands if most of The Club is for it. Right now, out of maybe forty members that are here, only three of you had questions. Let me answer this last questions, and then I will ask for a show of hands, and if my plan is approved, then I will give you more details." With that, the General points to the third person who had his hand up.

"Well, you have big plans, and my question is where are we going to get all the money to implement your plan?"

"While, as I said at the beginning, I have all the details worked out already, I worked them all out before I called this meeting many months ago. Are there any more questions?"

No more hands are raised.

"Okay, then, now for the big one. With a show of hands, I want to see how many members think that this is a good idea and will back it. But before I ask you for a show of hands backing this plan, I want to say this: if most of you members raise your hands and approve this plan, the remaining members that refrained from raising their hands will be allowed to distance themselves from The Club by resigning, and swearing not to reveal this plan to anyone other than another member of The Club. And anyone who refrained from raising their hand will not be considered a member of this club. You are either in or out. There is no in between. So, before I ask for a show of hands approving this plan, please think about how you intend to vote.

"Okay, with all that said, I would like to know by a show of hands whether or not this club approves the plan that I have laid out."

Surprisingly, all members except one raised their hands. Then, a few seconds later, the one holdout raised her hand and said, "I will go along with the majority vote and approve the plan also."

"Okay, then, the plan I laid out has been approved. So now we can do this two ways. I can answer your questions, explaining some of the finer details, or you can learn them as we go along, because this is a very comprehensive plan, and there will be much work ahead of us, and I would prefer not to confuse you with all of the facts. But I did say that I would take questions, and explain some of the finer details, so does anyone have any questions for me?" The general looks around, and no one is raising their hands. "Okay, that's great. So we all agree that we will get the details as we go.

"Now I want to take this opportunity to explain something to the members of this club, because I am pretty sure that most of you are unaware of the fact that this is not the only club in existence. There are seven other clubs spread out across our country, and each one has its own name. By the way, we are number six. The goal of each club is exactly the same, and the leader of each club can communicate with each other via courier.

"So, the next thing I'm going to do is run this plan by the other clubs spread out across this country, and hopefully, they will come on board and help us out, but it will not change the course of this club on the plan that we have just ratified. Hopefully, we will get the backing from the other clubs, but if not, we will pursue this course on our own. And for the last time, can I get a show of hands approving what I just said.?"

Again, every single member raises their hand.

"Great!! Now, the next thing I'm going to do is to start giving you some of the pertinent information that I was talking about. Unbeknownst to you is the fact that John made copies of the names and addresses of some of The Club's members, and before he got locked up, he sent them to a friend of his for safekeeping. John divulged this information to me via an intermediate. I then managed to get the CDs, and after briefly looking through them, I found out that there are about 200,000 members' names and addresses on the CDs. So one of the first things I'm going to ask you members to do is help me sort through the names and see how many of them have the qualifications that we are looking for, and to see if they will help us out. We will need help in many areas, from many different occupations, and we will also need to ask them for donations. Hopefully, with the help of the other clubs, we will have no problem raising the money we need to put this plan into action and complete it. So the first hurdle that we have to overcome is getting in touch with all these members and getting the help and money we need to get this plan started.

"The next step is for you members to go home and digest what has transpired here this evening, and also, I need to notify the other clubs and bring them up to speed as to what is going on here. So, as they say, stay tuned, and I will get in touch with you for the next step. Also, I want to thank all of you for attending this meeting tonight."

The next morning, the General gets on his computer and dictates a complete outline of his plan and what had happened the evening before at his club's headquarters. He puts all this on a flash drive and then proceeds to get in touch with his courier via a disposable cell phone. Along with the flash drive, the General includes seven disposable cell phones to pass on to the other clubs, because, now that the General has started implementing his plan, he wants each club to use a disposable cell phone for communications between each leader of the individual underground clubs. Also, each club has its own courier. That is how the underground clubs keep in touch with each other, but the general now wants to change that because of his plan, but he explains to the other clubs that the couriers can still be used.

On the flash drive, the general also explains that part of his plan is to execute it as stealthily as possible, and that he wants his original flash drive to go to each succeeding club in the underground network. After the last club in the underground network has had a chance to read the information on the flash drive, the flash drive must be returned to the General so that he may destroy it as part of his plan. If any of the leaders of the other clubs have any questions, they can get in touch with the General via the disposable cell phones.

Two weeks go by without a word from anyone. Then, one morning, the General's disposable phone rings. On the phone is one of the leaders of one of the other underground clubs.

The General answers the phone. "Hello."

"General?"

"Yes."

"Hi, I am the leader of the Virginia underground club. I have something I want to run by you, but I suggest that you sit down before I explain it to you."

"Oh, okay. I am actually sitting now. So, now that you have my attention, go ahead. Talk to me."

"Okay, here it is. I received a phone call from several of the other clubs, and we all think that this plan of yours will make a tremendous difference, but this is what we came up with. Why just do it in your state? Why not have all the clubs do it in their respective states? Then, instead of 300 to 500 child molesters, it could be 3,000 to 5,000 child molesters that we get rid of. Then I think we may get their attention. In fact, I am absolutely positive that we would get their attention. The only thing is you gave us an outline of what you intend to do and said that you will give us instructions on how you would want us to help out, but if all of the clubs do get in on your plan, we would need to know all of the finer details in order for each club to be part of the big picture. We suggest, and by we, I mean several other club leaders, along with myself, think that we should have a meeting with all of the leaders and you, and you could explain exactly all of the details of your plan to us. So, what you think?"

The General sits there, dumbfounded, not believing what he has just heard. "Oh my God, I never thought of it on that scale, but let me say this: I have worked on my plan for several years now, and like I said, I never thought of it working on a much larger scale. I would need some time to sit down and think about this, because I'm afraid that due to the intricacy of my plan, it may not work on a larger scale. There are so many things that could go wrong with my plan working in just my area. For what you are describing, it would be compounded tenfold. You've got to give me a day or two to think about this."

"Okay, we can do that, but if you think that doing it on a larger scale would mess it up, then don't worry about it. We would not want to mess up all the work and planning you put into it. If need be, we will do it your way. We just figured that if we are taking a chance, why not go all the way."

"Let me run it through my mind and get back to you."

"Okay, General, you got it. Bye for now."

The General takes the next two days to ponder the expanded plan, going over and over it, and then, finally, he comes to a decision. He decides that if everyone follows his plan explicitly and to the letter, it should work fine, just as it would work in his own area. But he feels that it's too big of a decision to make on his own and that he should at least run it by John, so he decides to call the judge and ask him to get in touch with Mike, and ask him to make a trip to the prison and ask John what he thinks of the expanded plan.

That night, the General calls the judge. The judge, sitting at home, hears his disposable cell phone ringing, looks at it, and while shaking his head, reluctantly answers. "Hello."

Judge, I'm glad I got you. How are you doing tonight?"

"I was doing just fine until this phone rang. I'm afraid to ask. What do you want, or what can I do for you?"

"Well, Judge, something has come up, something really big, and I'm going to need John's approval on it."

"Oh my God, oh my God, I'm afraid to ask you what this big change to your plan is."

"Well, Judge, to put it in a nutshell, I got in touch with all of the other clubs to seek their help with my plan, but then they got back to me with a more sophisticated plan, and I want to run it by John. So I would need you to get in touch with Mike and ask him to please take a trip to see John and get his approval on it."

"General, I think that I'm starting to regret the decision I made to help you. I thought it would be a one-time thing, but now you want me to do it again, so I'm getting a feeling that this is going to be a steady thing. And don't get me wrong, I still want to help, but I feel that I will be getting too involved with your plan. So, tell you what. How about I give my disposable cell phone to Mike and ask him to give you a call, and you can try to convince him to go and see John."

"Okay, Judge, I understand how you're feeling and you being reluctant to take this next step. So, I guess, if you would, please give your phone to Mike and ask him to give me a call. But please don't tell him what it's about. Let me try to convince him."

"Okay, General, I will see him tomorrow and give him my phone."

"Thank you, Judge. I appreciate it. Thank you."

"Okay, bye."

It takes two days before Mike calls. The General answers the phone. "Hello, is this Mike?"

"Yes, is this the General?"

"Yes."

"Well, I finally get a chance to speak directly to you and not go through the judge. What can I do for you, General?"

"Well, Mike, I know you don't like to get too involved, but I need a really big favor, and rather than go into the details of what it's all about, I would simply ask you if you can deliver a note to John in prison for me."

"Should I ask you what's in the note, and like before, would I be able to read it if I want to?"

"No, Mike, I would prefer that this time, you do not read it. It would be a fairly short note, and I would just need a yes or no answer to from John."

"I know what the first note was about. Is it about the same thing or something different?"

"Well, Mike, I won't lie to you. It's basically about the same thing, just that the plans have changed a little. Would that be sufficient enough information for you to do me this favor? And remember, all this is for John, to help him achieve what he's started out to do."

"Okay, General, I'm in this deep, so I guess that I can't get into any more trouble than I got into with the first few trips I made to the prison for you."

"Great! We will do the same as we did the last time. I will compose a letter for you to bring to John and see if he will sign off on it. We will also use the same precautions we did the last time. Do you remember them?"

"Yes, make sure that there are no cameras in the room that can see the letter, make sure there are no guards standing behind John who can read the letter, and make sure I return everything to you so that you can destroy it. Is that it?"

"Yes, it is. Okay, Mike, I will compose the letter and get back to you when it's ready to show John, so just hold onto the phone. Thank you and bye for now."

A few days later, the General calls Mike. "Hello, Mike?"

"Yes, General?"

"Yes, how are you doing?"

"I'm doing good."

"Okay, Mike, I have the letter ready. Are you still in?"

"General, against my better judgment, yes, I'm in."

"Okay, good. Good, Mike. The next step for us is to meet up so that I can give you the letter. What I did when I met up with the judge was to meet him at an airport about thirty miles south of town, called Brookhaven airport. Do you know where it is?"

"Yes, I do."

"Okay, then how about we meet up at 9 AM at the airport tomorrow?"

"General, that sounds good, but let me tell you this: I love John. We've been friends for many years. We've worked together, and I will do just about anything to help them out. But you've got to understand that I still have a life to live, and I cannot keep taking chances on ruining my family's life by me going to prison, so I will do it this one last time, and that will be it. If you need to get some information to John, you will need to find another way."

"Okay, Mike, I completely understand."

"Then, General, I will see you at the airport at 9 AM tomorrow morning.

"Great, and thank you."

The next morning, they meet up at the airport. Mike gets the letter, turns around, and goes home. The next morning, he goes to prison, goes through the same procedure, and finally gets to see John.

John reads the note, looks up at Mike, and asks him, "Did you read this?"

Mike answers no. Then, trying to throw everyone off, Mike says, "Well, John, that is all that they are offering you. All I need from you is to give me is a yes or no answer."

"I think it's a crazy move, but it's the one move that I think will get me out of here. I can't see any other plea working for me, so tell them that my answer is yes."

"Mike says, "Okay, John, I will give them your answer." With that, Mike leaves and goes home.

The next morning, Mike calls the General and sets up a meeting at the airport at 9 AM the next morning. Mike gets there early and waits for the General. At 9:05 AM, the General finally gets there. Mike gives the General his paperwork back and says, "John has agreed to the plan."

"Great! Now I can get my plan started."

Mike says, "I did not hear that, and I know nothing about a plan."

The General says, "I understand, Mike. Thank you for all your work, and I promise that I will not ask you or get you involved any further in this plan."

The next morning, with his mind finally made up, the General gets his disposable cell phone, and calls the leader in Virginia.

"Hello."

"Hi, this is the General."

"Hi. So, what's the good word?"

"Well, first off, let me tell you that John has given us an answer, and that answer is yes, so we can now go ahead with the expanded plan. I've been going over and over in my mind the conversation we had a few days ago, and I finally came to a decision. I think that if I had a meeting with all of the leaders and they followed my plan explicitly and to the letter and assured me that they would not deviate one iota from my plan, and if all the leaders agreed to my terms, then, and only then, would I be willing to hold a meeting and explain my entire plan from top to bottom, leaving nothing out. So, seeing that you contacted me as a spokesperson for the other clubs, then I would like for you to check with all the other clubs and get back to me. If they all agree unconditionally to my plan, then I will set up a meeting with all the clubs and get this plan started."

"Okay, General, you got it. I will do it and get back to you. Bye for now."

"Bye."

It takes Virginia two weeks before he can come up with a date for the meeting that all of the other club leaders can attend. Finally, the General gets the call that he has been waiting for.

"Hello, General?"

"Yes."

"Hi, this is Virginia."

"Hi."

"Okay, it took me awhile, but I finally got a date for the meeting when all of the other club leaders could attend."

"That's great! And what's the date you guys came up with?"

"May 3rd. That's about two weeks from today, so if that date's good you, all you have to do is tell us what time to be there."

"Let me check my calendar, and I will get back in a little while and give you a time."

"Okay, then. Bye for now."

"Bye."

The General checks his calendar and sees that May 3rd is good for him also. He decides that 7 PM would be a good time, so he gets his phone and immediately calls Virginia back. "Hello, Virginia?"

"Yes."

"Hi, this is the General. Okay, that date is good for me also, so I'd like to set up the meeting for 7 PM at my headquarters. You have the address, right?"

"Yes, I do, General."

"Okay, then, please get back to me when all the other clubs are all set for the meeting and everything is finalized."

"You got it, General. I will call you when everything is finalized."

"Great. Bye for now."

The two weeks seem to drag by, but what seems to help the General is the fact that his club is busy defending a man who killed a child molester, and it seems that this child molester had been let out of jail twice before after he was arrested for child molestation. The Club member that The Club was defending, after turning himself in, said to the police, "That animal needed killing because the authorities are not doing their job. So I had to do it for them." The Club was busy digging up evidence for the trial, trying to show that this man should not have been walking the streets after being arrested the first time on child molestation charges.

The day finally arrives, May 3rd. At 6 PM, the General is going over all of the points of his plan in his head to make sure that he covers them all, and he tells himself that he should try his hardest to convey his absolute confidence to everyone that his plan will succeed. He has only one hour left to go over it in his mind, or so he thinks, but at 6:30 PM, some of the leaders from the other clubs start arriving.

The General positions himself at the door so as to greet all of the leaders as they arrive. Finally, at 6:55 PM, the leader of the last club arrives. The General now thinks to himself, *This is now a surreal time. All of the years I spent putting this plan together are about to culminate into one big push toward achieving John's dream, ridding child molesters from the streets permanently.*

The General takes the stage as the leaders settle down and quiet engulfs the room. The General starts his speech by welcoming all of leaders. Then he says, "First, I want to say thank you for showing up tonight, and promptly, may I add. I have a lot to say, and I want to make sure that I do not leave anything out, so at the onset, I want to say this: if at any time during the explanation of my plan you do not understand it, or any part of it, I implore you to please raise your hand so that I may clear it up for you. I do not want to go to the next phase, or the next step, if there is someone who does not understand the previous step. I have worked many years on this plan, and I sure don't want to screw it up now by leaving something out or forgetting to tell you something. So, what I intend to do is start at the very beginning and go slow, making sure to touch all of the bases. And any time someone needs a break, please raise your hand, and we will take a break, because this meeting may last a while. That is also why I supplied food and drink, so all of you can remain comfortable.

"Okay, first, we are all here for the same reason, and that is to make sure that all the children and future children are protected from child molesters, and to fulfill John's dream. So now, for the last time, and by a show of hands, let me know if you are still all in and, after hearing the entire plan, will promise to back this plan to the best of your ability."

Everyone raises their hand, and the General continues. "Okay, I know that all of you know my basic plan, so what I'm going to do now is go through my plan step by step, with all the finer details, and like I said at the beginning, if anyone gets lost, please, please, raise your hand, and I will set you straight."

The General explains his plan to everyone and then goes on to explain, "Unbeknownst to you guys and myself, I later found out that John had made copies of the names and information of almost 200,000 members and saved them on CDs. When I found out about this, and explained my plan to John and said that I would need those names because of all the help I needed to execute my plan, well, I did get those names, and that's going to be a big part of our plan. The first step will be to divide these CDs and try to make contact with all of the names on them, to see if they're still alive, to see if they still feel the way they did when they joined The Club, to see if they would be willing to help us by offering their services if they are proficient in any of the occupations we need help in, or to donate money, or buildings, or land. It is not going to be easy finding all of these people we need, but I will say this: one of the biggest things we need is money, because with money, you can do anything.

"I think by now everyone here has gotten the gist of my plan as to why we need all of the different people we need. So, moving on, after getting in touch with the members on the list and getting pledges and commitments from all of them, what we need to do is get as much money as we can pledged so that we can buy property or abandoned buildings in desolate areas or, even better, get them donated by the members. But one very, very important thing that I must mention here: any money pledged must, and I stress the word must, be picked up in person by one of your members, and again, I stress the word 'must.' The money must be in cash, no ifs, ands, or buts about it, and we must also do this under assumed names, and with altered appearances and fake paperwork, and it's up to the member who is talking to this person to set up some sort of a code with the member who is donating whatever so that they know who you are when you get there to collect the money.

"We will also get help from our lawyers and, hopefully, people working in the building department. These are must haves in order for our plan to work once we get the land or buildings. Then we can refurbish them into hotels that will house the child molesters. These hotels or buildings will be built or refurbished to certain specifications, with the help of the members, because the ultimate goal is to have all of these child molesters in there. And after they feel comfortable, they will then all be gassed to death via special plumbing that was installed by our members. Then, as planned, we will all disappear into the night, according to our preplanned escape routes.

"Just a note here: each step forward in this plan is predicated on the success of the previous step being satisfactorily completed one hundred percent, and under no circumstance will I accept anything less. One failed step stops everything, and I mean everything. The whole plan gets discarded and thrown away, and everybody goes home. It would be the end, period.

"Now for some of the finer points, and how we expect to get away with all this. This is why I mentioned the need for make-up artists. They will be extremely important. We will all have our appearances changed. We will all act like actors on a movie set. We will even have our fingerprints altered, or wear rubber gloves, and even have the souls of our shoes altered, and under no circumstances will we touch anything without having our fingerprints altered or wearing rubber gloves, and if this does happen, whatever was touched, no matter what, must be completely destroyed. I want it so that once the make-up artists are finished with us, our own mothers would not recognize us.

"I am going to rely on all of my training as a general in the United States Army to pull this whole thing off. This will be a stealthy and covert operation. That's why every order I give must be carried out precisely as I give it. If everyone does this, then the whole operation will be a success.

"Okay, I think I touched on just about every point of this plan. What I'd like to know now is does anyone have any questions?"

No one raises their hand.

"All right, then, moving on. This is how it's all going to go down. The plan will be broken down into three stages, and after each stage, there will be a meeting here with all of you leaders. After the plan goes into action, I do not want the cell phones or couriers used. From then on, we will meet face to face so that everyone gets the same instructions, from my lips to your ears, so that it doesn't get disarranged by the courier or the recipient of a phone call who then has to relay it. Only in an emergency, or if time is of the essence, can cell phones be used, but until that time, we can still use the throwaway cell phones.

"Okay, then, this is how stage one is going to go down. I have in my possession thirty-three CDs with approximately 200,000 addresses on them. Tonight, I will hand out four CDs to each club, and I will keep five for my club. You will take the CDs back to your clubs and have your people get busy contacting all of these members. Like I said, see if they are still alive, see if they still feel the way they did when they first joined The Club, see if and how they would like to help us, see if they have any land or buildings to donate, and most importantly, how much money they would like to donate, but last, and most significant is, do not divulge any part of this plan to any member right now. The most information you can give them at this time is that we are working on something big, and when it's finalized, we will get back to them and invite them to attend a meeting that will be held at each respective club. By the way, if someone wants to donate money immediately, then by all means, have someone go out and get it, but make sure it's according to my plan about disguising themselves, and as far as the meetings, it goes without saying, that they will have to be staggered so that I can make them all feel comfortable.

"One final thing. I would like from each of you a weekly report due on each Monday as to your progress, delivered to me in writing, without you guys keeping any copies. I want the only copy so that I can destroy it after reading it, if necessary. Every piece of information you get will be saved on a CD, and those CDs will be locked away every night by you leaders. This plan will be tweaked as we go along and as I see fit, and I hate to keep saying this, but another important thing is seeing that the Virginia leader got all of you together, then he will be the go-to guy for any information, and he can get in touch with me. And from this day on, when communicating with each other, we will only address each other by an avatar name. Absolutely no real names will be used, so please pay attention. I am now going to assign all you leaders your avatar. New York, we will be One and will be the headquarters. Texas, you will be Two. California, you will be Three. Illinois, you will be Four. Florida, you will be Five. Ohio will be Six. Massachusetts, you will be Seven, and Virginia, you will be Eight, and remember, Eight will be the go-to for any reason, and Eight will then get in touch with me. So, now that we got that out of the way, and everyone here knows how to get in touch with the other clubs, does anyone have any questions on that subject? If not, I will now hand out the CDs."

No one says anything or raises their hand.

"Okay, then, you guys are welcome to hang out for a while. Have something to eat and drink, and remember, while all this is going on, we still have to defend the people who are going out and ridding the world of these sex offenders that are hurting and killing our children. Thank you and have a safe trip back home."

The meeting lasts for at least another hour, with all the leaders eating and drinking and holding their own little meetings amongst themselves. Finally, the last leader leaves. Then the General finally leaves, pondering what he has just started.

The next week drags by for the General, who is waiting for Monday to come so that he can get the first reports. Finally, Monday comes, and when the General gets the reports that he has been waiting for, he sees the money donations look okay, but there is no sign of anyone donating property or buildings. This is a little discouraging to the General, but he dismisses it as just being too early in the plan, and being realistic, he thinks to himself, *Hey, it's only the first week, but at least the money looks okay.* Between the eight clubs, they have managed to collect $20,000 cash in one week, so again, he thinks to himself, *That's not so bad; in fact, I think that's pretty good for the first week.*

In the next few weeks, the club manages to collect $132,000, but there's still no sign of anyone offering land, though they did get lots of professional people wanting to help. That's all well and good, but according to the leaders, they are about halfway through the CDs, and at this rate, the

General thinks that he will only get about $240 to $250,000, and he thinks that it will be not be enough money to execute his plan.

The next two weeks are all the same as far as the money goes, and some members are still offering their professional help, but again, no land or buildings, and no way will this plan work with the amount of money that is being generated.

Finally, on the tenth week, the General gets some good news from Virginia (now known as "Eight"): "It seems that a member has an abandoned hundred-room hotel that she would donate to us. The hotel is located on the outskirts of town and is kind of private."

"Okay, good. I kind of thought that we would run into something like this, so I have a plan for that also. What I would like you to do is have your attorney set up a fake charity called Child Safety in America. Tell them to make it look legal, with legal-looking papers. Then have her donate the hotel to that charity. Tell her to say that the Child Safety in America Foundation contacted her for a contribution, so she decided to donate the building to that association. This way, when it hits the fan, they cannot backtrack it to her and find her guilty of any wrongdoing."

"Okay, General, I will get the lawyers working on that ASAP."

The General can't wait to get a look at the building. He is now in a happy place.

Then, the following week, more good news: someone has a piece of property that he would donate to The Club, so the General tells Eight, "Okay, that's great! Let's do the same thing that we did with the hotel. We can use the same paperwork that we used for the acquisition of the hotel, and again, this would put the benefactor in a safe place."

But by now, the clubs have all but exhausted the names on the CDs, and so far, the total cash that has been collected is about $237,000. The General thought that by now, the clubs would have collected a lot more money than they have, so he now thinks that he will have to go to plan B. He calls Eight and explains the situation, that he thinks he will need to go to plan B, and asks him to set up another meeting of the leaders of all the other clubs so that he can explain plan B to them.

Eight asks the General, "Well, can you tell me a little more about plan B?"

"No, I will explain it all at the meeting."

"Okay, G, you got it. As soon as I can get everybody to agree on the same date, I will get back to you."

"Sounds good. Talk to you then. Bye for now."

Several days go by before the General hears from Eight.

"Good morning, General. Well, I set up the next meeting for this Friday at 7 PM, if that is okay with you."

"Yes, as matter of fact, that would be perfect, because I am busy the rest of the week. Okay, Eight, that's great. I'll see you and the other leaders on Friday at 7 PM."

On Friday, the General is in Virginia, and at 7:05 PM, he walks into the meeting room. Just as before, all the leaders are busy talking among themselves, trying to come up with some reason for this meeting. The General positions himself in front of the group and starts talking: "Good evening, and thank you all for showing up tonight. Tonight is going to be an important meeting. I know I told you that we were in stage one. This is still stage one, but it will be plan B of stage one due to the results of our endeavors in the past two months. I had to make some changes because I thought that by now, we would have raised a lot more money than we did, and from the information I get from you leaders, we have all but exhausted the list of names on the CDs. Hence, plan B.

"I know at the beginning we had intentions, or the plan called for, eight buildings to either be built or refurbished, but because of how sparsely the money donations came in, I am forced to revise my plan and have only two buildings. One building that we could use is an old hundred-room hotel right here in Virginia that a member donated to us and that we accepted under a fake charity that we had our lawyers draw up legal-looking papers for called Child Safety in America. We did this so that these benefactors could not be held responsible for what we intend to do with their donations.

"Okay, so I will make this short and sweet. This is plan B in a nutshell. At this point, we are down to two buildings, so unless things change drastically, we will be working with just two buildings, but what we need to do now, before we go any further – and I know you probably don't want to hear this – but what we need to do is call everyone on the CDs again and try to squeeze out a few more dollars from everyone before we go to stage two. So, I want to thank everyone for attending tonight. Please go back to your headquarters and try to get some more money. Thank you, good night, and have a safe trip home.

"One last thing before you all leave."

Everyone stops in their tracks and turns to face the General.

"A few days ago in Texas, an eight-year-old girl, on the way home from school, was kidnapped, raped, killed, and left on the side of the road like a bag of garbage. The man who took the little girl was seen putting her in his car forcibly, and after describing the man to the police and looking at mug-shots, the witness identified the man as a sex offender who was released out of prison just one month ago. The young girl had two brothers who found out about this. They somehow tracked this man down, killed and mutilated him. Then they got hold of a list of sex offenders in their area, hunted four of them down, and killed them, and they are now on the run. I want to ask Two, the leader of the Texas club, to somehow try and find these two brothers and help them out. And if any of you other leaders can help out, I would appreciate it. We must try to find the two brothers and help them out. Remember, this is what we're all about. So now, in closing, I want to thank everyone for attending tonight. Please go back to your headquarters and try to get some more money. Thank you, good night, and have a safe trip home. Also, Eight and Two, before you leave, I need a few words with the two of you."

While everyone starts leaving, Eight and Two hang back and approach the General. Eight asks, "What's up, sir?"

"Well, Eight, seeing how you popped up as sort of the spokesman for the other clubs, what I would like for you to do is keep a check on the other clubs, and when all of the people on the CDs have been called again, please get back to me with all of the totals, and then we will take it from there. And while you are here, get me a list of addresses of all of the head-quarters."

"Okay, General. You got it."

"Thank you, and also what I want from you two guys is for each of you to set up a meeting, Eight, with you to see the hotel, and Two, with you to see the land in Texas."

"Sounds good, General. When would you want to meet?"

"First off, I don't want fifteen people talking to fifteen other people. That's just too many people in my book. So, if you don't mind, I would like you, Eight, and you, Two, to go back to your headquarters and come up with a date that is easy for you. Two, you let Eight know, and he, in turn, will let me know the dates, and I will make it my business to make sure I meet each of you on the respective days. Do you guys have any questions?"

They both answer, "No problem, General."

"Great!! Then we are all on the same page. The less people talking to each other, the better the chances of us not getting caught."

A few days later, the General gets a call from Eight.

"Hello, General, this is Eight."

"Hello, but remember, whenever we are talking on the phone, I am not the General. I am G. In person, you can call me General, but on the phone, I am just G."

"You got it. Anyway, Two got in touch with me with his date. I could meet up with you this Wednesday at 10 AM, and Two said that he could meet up with you on Friday at 10 AM, if this is okay with you."

"Yes."

"Okay, I will get back to Two and tell him to expect you on Friday. G, by the way, do you want us pick you up at the airport, or are you driving?"

"I will be driving."

"Okay. When you get here, I will take you out to check the location."

"Okay, Eight. Get back to Two and set it up.

"Great, G. Bye for now."

"Bye."

On Tuesday morning, the General sets out for Virginia, planning to spend the night there in a hotel room and meet Eight in the morning. On Wednesday morning, the General is up early. He goes down and has breakfast. He's all excited about seeing this hotel. After breakfast, he heads to the headquarters of Eight, meets up with him, and both of them get into Eight's car and head out to see the hotel. It's about an hour's drive from headquarters, on the outskirts of town. The approach to the hotel is a long, winding dirt road. Finally, after what seems like a ten-minute ride, up pops the hotel.

The General cannot believe what he is seeing. The distance from town, the dirt road, it is all perfect. It's as though the General built it himself, and the closer they get to the hotel, the more the General can't believe what his eyes are seeing. The hotel is pristine. Even most of the landscaping is in good shape, except for the lack of water in the pool. It looks like, with just a little sprucing up, someone would be able to check in, and the closer he gets, he realizes that it is going to need less and less refurbishing. The windows are all boarded up, and hopefully, the glass is still there and intact.

They finally pull up to the front door, and the General gets out of the car. He just stands there, turns around, taking it all in, and then he heads for the door, only to find that it's locked. With that, Eight hands the General a bunch of keys.

"Where in the hell did you get these keys?"

Eight explains to the General, "When you agreed to check the property out, I took the liberty of meeting with the member to get the keys, because I was already out here checking it out and noticed that the doors were locked."

"Okay, that's all well and good, but did you go as yourself, or did you wear a disguise like you were instructed to do whenever we meet up with someone outside of our headquarters."

"Well, sir, you will be happy to know that I did wear a disguise."

"Okay, you had me worried there for a second, because, at this point, we can't afford to take any chances." The General makes a mental note to himself to address the issue of someone doing something on their own.

With that, the General is at the door. He unlocks it and walks in, and as soon as he does, he can hardly contain his excitement. The place is dusty and full of webs, and it has a mildew smell, but other than the obvious, the whole place looks intact.

The General says, "We need a flashlight."

Eight tells the General, "You know what? I brought a big spotlight, because I figured that we would need it."

Eight gets the spotlight, comes back, and then he and the General proceed to check the rest of the hotel out. The General checks every single room, all of the bathrooms, and the light fixtures, knocking on the walls to see how solid they are. He checks the kitchen and basement, and he is amazed beyond belief at what he is seeing. This hotel can be refurbished for next to nothing, and now he is really excited. This place is absolutely right.

"I love it!" he shouts. "This is definitely a keeper and will work great in my plan. Now, let's lock it up and get out of here." With that, the two men get into the car and head back to headquarters.

The General tells Eight, "This is great. I just hope the property that I'm going to see on Friday has ten percent of the potential of this hotel."

"Well, I hope so, sir."

"I hope so too. Well, I'm out of here. I'm going to head to Texas today. I want to spend a night or two there before my meeting with Two."

"Okay, General. Good luck and have a safe trip."

"Thank you. Bye-bye." With that, the General drives off and heads to Texas.

When the General gets to Texas, it's late. He gets a room, takes a shower, and goes straight to bed because he needs to get an early start in the morning. The General is up by 7 AM. He gets dressed and goes downstairs for breakfast. After breakfast, the General goes back to his room, packs, checks out, goes to his car, sets up his GPS, and heads to Two's headquarters.

It's a half hour drive to Two's headquarters, and it's about 9:45 AM when the General gets there. Two is outside waiting for the General. The General gets out of his car and greets Two: "Good morning."

"Good morning, General. Do you mind if we use your car? Mine is not running so good, so I don't want to take a chance with my car, because the property is about an hour outside of town.

The General replies, "No problem, as long as you know where it is and can direct me, or, if need be, I have a GPS."

Two gets in the car, the General sets up the GPS with the information Two gives him, and the two of them drive off. Two explains to the General that the information he gave him for the GPS will only take them to a main crossroad, and that they will have to find the rest of the way following the directions of the landowner that he got over the phone and wrote down.

After about two hours of driving, several U-turns, and resetting the GPS three times, they find themselves on a main paved road, with what looks like a small dirt access road going into the woods. The General turns into the woods and continues driving. After about five minutes of driving, and almost getting a stuck several times because of the condition of the dirt road – there are many holes and soft spots – finally, the woods open up to a beautiful, large open area of about two to three acres.

The General stops the car, and both of them get out. The General just stands outside of the car and slowly turns and scans the entire area. He does this for about ten to fifteen minutes without saying a word, just slowly turning and looking. Then he starts walking the perimeter of the property, checking every single inch. He finally turns, looks at Two, and says, "So, what do you think of it?"

"Well, General, I don't know exactly what your plan is or what you have in your mind, but as far as being a place that would be hard to find, I think we found it."

"You know what? You are absolutely correct. I do believe we found the right place. I can't believe how perfect this place is for what I have in mind. Between this place and the hotel, I am pretty sure that we are all set to go to stage two."

Both men get into the car, and they drive off, the General saying aloud, "I sure hope that we can find this place a lot easier next time."

"I hope so too, General."

The General drops off Two and gives him a heads up: "You should be hearing something soon, because, when I get home, I'm going to give Eight a call to set up a meeting so that we can get stage two started."

"Okay, General, I will keep my ears open."

Two days later, the General calls Eight. "Good morning, Eight."

"Good morning, G."

"The reason I'm calling is that I would like an update on the progress of calling the members on the CDs again."

"As a matter of fact, G, we are just about done. In fact, we should be finishing up today, and you will be happy to know that so far, we have picked up another $80,000. If you want, I can give you a call later on today when we are finished, or I can print it up and run it over to you."

"I'll tell you what. That won't be necessary. If you tell me that you're just about finished and that you picked up another $80,000, for a total of

$317,000 so far, at this point, I doubt that it's going to get any better, so what I'd like for you to do is to set up a meeting at my headquarters with all of the leaders so that we can get stage two started."

"Wow! That sounds great! Any particular date?"

"No, just make it whenever it's convenient for all of the leaders."

"Okay, G, sounds good. I will set it up and get back to you."

"Great. Talk to you then."

It takes three days before the General gets a call from Eight. "Hello."

"Good morning, G. This is Eight."

"Good morning. So, did you manage to do what I asked you to do?"

"Yes, G. I set the meeting up for this Thursday, if that's all right with you."

"It's absolutely all right."

"Good. I set it up for 7 PM."

"Great. So I will see all of you guys on Thursday at 7 PM."

"Before you go, G, I have some good news. The two brothers in Texas who killed those child molesters were caught by the police and are currently being detained. But we at least now know their names, and Two is currently making plans to meet up with them to come up with some kind of a defense plan."

"Okay, that's good news. I just hope we can help those guys out."

"Me too, G."

"Okay, then, I'll see all of you on Thursday."

"You got it. see you then."

"Sounds good."

Today is Tuesday, and the General thinks to himself that he has only two days left before the meeting, and he wants to make sure that he has all his ducks in a row. He takes out his master plan and starts going over it very carefully, reading stage two over and over, until he cannot keep his eyes open, so he decides to go to sleep.

The next morning, the General gets up, has breakfast, and then decides that the entire day will be spent going over and over the plans. Then, and only then, will he be confident enough to put it into action.

Finally, it's Thursday morning. The General spends most of the morning and just about all the afternoon jotting down notes for his speech tonight. He feels that up until now, all that was done was basically groundwork, but now, the real thing is about to start, and he cannot wait until 7 PM tonight.

On Thursday night, at 6 PM, the General is anxiously awaiting everyone to arrive. Finally, some of the leaders start rolling in. By 6:45 PM, all of the leaders have arrived. The General stands up front and waits until everyone has settled in and quieted down.

At 7PM, the General clears his throat and the place quiets down completely. "Good evening. I want to thank everybody for showing up tonight, and I know I keep saying this, but this is going to be an important meeting, and as these meetings progress, they will all become more and more important, so again, thank you for showing up tonight.

"Tonight, we will start stage two of our plan. This is where the tire meets the road, so to speak. First, let me tell you who, and what, we will need to get the show on the road. Some of the things that we will need first are make-up artists, a surveyor, and a general contractor. We will need to borrow a truck and get someone to drive it. We will need plumbers, carpenters, Sheetrock installers, workers to spackle the walls, laborers, mason workers, roofers, landscapers, painters, and electricians. We will need donations of lumber, plumbing supplies, mason supplies, electric supplies, paint, landscaping supplies like bushes and such, and any other building related items that you can think of. We also need building tools like cement mixers, nails, windows, doors, etc. Well, you get the picture. I could go on and on. Just think of what you would need to erect a building, and all the stuff that you thought of would be all the stuff that we will need to get the job done.

"So that you guys don't get overwhelmed, I am going to break down the list according to what stage of construction that we are at. We will take small steps first. I want all the cash that was collected, and all the cash that still needs to be collected, brought to my headquarters ASAP. I want it all in one place. I will assign one of my workers to act as treasurer. All expenses will be submitted to her, but must be approved by me.

"The first two people, that we will need are a surveyor and general contractor. Once we get the surveyor and general contractor, I will check out the hotel in Virginia with the contractor and get a list from him as to what we need to get it to the condition that I want it to be in. Then, along with the surveyor and contractor, we will check out the property in Texas and do the same thing as to a list of what will be needed to construct a building that we can use.

"If all that goes well, what we will need next is a make-up artist and a truck and driver. Then, moving on from there, all that will be discussed at the next meeting. Essentially, this will be your homework. That's it, and remember, all correspondence must go through Eight, and please make sure that you explain to any of the volunteers that all we want from them is their services, and if need be, we will pick up any expenses incurred. So let's go home and get this ball rolling. Good night."

Two weeks later, the General gets a call from Eight.

"Good morning, G. I'm calling to let you know that we have two surveyors and three general contractors that are willing to help, and will donate their time without any compensation. Plus, all the cash has been collected and all The Clubs are ready to bring it to you and turn it in."

"Okay, that's great, and where are the volunteers located?"

"The two surveyors are located in Ohio and Florida, and the general contractors are in Ohio, Illinois, and Virginia."

"Okay, that's beautiful! We can finally get this thing going. This is what I would like for you to do for me. Please get in touch with the general contractor in Virginia and set up a meeting at your headquarters, but before you do that, I need his name so that I can get him checked out by one of my members who is a detective. If he checks out okay, then I will meet him there at your headquarters and take him out to see the hotel."

"His name is Scott Johnson, and when will you want to meet up with him?"

"Well, seeing that he is doing us a favor, let him decide what day would be good for him."

"Okay, G, I will do that and get back to you."

"Okay, you do that. Bye."

The General immediately calls the detective in his club and asks him if they can meet for coffee. The detective says, "Absolutely. When and where do you want to meet?"

"How about in a half-hour, at the diner around the corner from The Club?"

"You got it. See you in a half-hour."

"Great. Bye."

The General heads right over to the diner and waits there for the detective. Fifteen minutes later, the detective arrives, they shake hands, and the General says, "Thank you for meeting with me."

"No problem, General. What can I do for you?"

"Well, there is someone I would like you to check out for me. He is in Virginia, and his name is Scott Johnson. I would like for you to get me whatever information you can on him."

"And how soon would you want this information?"

"ASAP."

"Okay, General, I will go back to my office and check it out right now and get back to you tonight."

"Well, at least have a cup of coffee."

"That's okay, General. I drink too much coffee anyway. If you called me to meet up with you and want this information ASAP, it must be important."

"As a matter of fact, it is extremely important."

"Okay, General, then I'll jump right on it and get back to you."

"Thank you. Talk to you later."

The General leaves the diner, gets in his car, and just as he's ready to drive off, his phone rings. He answers it. "Hello."

"Hello, G. This is Eight. I just got off the phone with Scott Johnson, the general contractor in Virginia, and he said that he is retired and can meet up with you anytime you want."

"Okay, but that will have to wait, because, right now, I'm having him checked out. Until I get that report, I will hold off on meeting up with him."

"Okay, G. Let me know, and I will get in touch with him then to set up a meeting."

Later on that night, the General gets a call from the detective."

"Hi, G. I got that info for you about that Scott Johnson."

"Good. So, what did you find out?"

"Well, General, he is seventy-one years old, he has lived in Virginia for the past fifty years, he had his own business as a general contractor. He is now retired, with no police record, and he has never even had a traffic ticket, and no affiliation with any antigovernment organization. To me, he looks like an all-around upstanding citizen."

"Great! That is just what I was hoping for. Thanks."

"No problem, G. Ask me anytime."

"I probably will do that. Thank you again."

The General hangs up and immediately calls Eight. When he gets Eight on the phone, he tells him to set up a meeting ASAP with Scott Johnson and to then get back to him with the information."

"You got it, G."

The next day, the General gets a call from Eight, who tells him, "The meeting is set up for Tuesday at 1 PM at my headquarters."

"Good. I will be there around 12 noon."

"Okay, G. See you then."

On Tuesday, at 12 noon, the General is at the headquarters in Virginia. Eight tells the General how enthusiastic this guy seems to be about the whole thing, and the General replies, "Good! I can't wait to meet him."

At 12:45 PM, Scott Johnson gets there. The general introduces himself and asks Scott to have a seat. "Scott, before we go any further, I just want to explain something to you. I want you to make sure that you know what you're getting into and why we are doing this."

Scott interrupts, saying, "Save your breath, General. I've been a member of The Club for many years now, and I know exactly what John and you guys are trying to accomplish. I am in one hundred percent. I hate those sons of bitches that are molesting and killing our children. I will do whatever it takes to get rid of those bastards."

"Well, I guess I know where you stand, and you are exactly the person that I was looking for, so if you're ready, let's get in my car, and I will take you to the site and explain what I am looking to do."

"Sounds good, General."

Thirty-five minutes later, the General pulls off the main road and onto a dirt road that never seems to end. Finally, after driving on this dirt road for a while, they come to an opening, and there in the opening is this large building with some shabby landscaping. It looks like just what it is: an old, abandoned hotel. Up to this point, Scott was quiet, but now he finally speaks: "Okay, then, what do we have here?"

"What we have here is an old, abandoned hundred-room hotel that I would like you to take a look at and let me know what we would need to get it back into operating condition, with a few additions that I have in mind, and also what kind of a workforce and tools you would need to accomplish this."

"Let's take a look at what you've got. I will assess the condition of the building and let you know what I would need."

With that, the General gets his flashlight, unlocks the front door, and the two men enter the building. As Scott starts to assess the building, he tells the General that this may take a while and that maybe he would want to wait out in the car. The General says, "Absolutely not. I know you're capable, but I want to make sure that you check out everything."

"Okay, General. Then let's get started."

Scott starts his inspection by explaining to the General, "Whenever I check a job like this, I always start the same way as I would if I was putting the building up, and that would be to start at the foundation. So the place that I want to start with is the basement, to check out the foundation. General, please show me the way."

"Absolutely. Follow me."

The two of them head down into the basement, and Scott starts his inspection. Within moments, the General is impressed by Scott's attention to every detail of the foundation. He scours every square inch of it. "Well, General, everything looks good down here, so now we can go to the first floor and check that out." Again, Scott scours every square inch of the first floor, looking at the floors, plumbing, light fixtures, walls, doors, and windows.

As Scott is checking the kitchen, he comments to the General, "My God, how long has this place been locked up?"

"I don't really know."

"Well, I will tell you one thing. This kitchen looks like it could be fully functional with just a few hours of cleaning. So far, General, I'm impressed. I guess we can go check out the second floor now."

Again Scott checks out the second floor with the same intense scrutiny as he did in the basement and the first floor, and again, Scott is impressed with how pristine everything seems to be, except for some webs and dust. "Okay, General, so far so good. So it's on to the third floor."

Once again, Scott impresses the General with his thoroughness, and again Scott finds everything in excellent condition. "Well, General, it looks like you got yourself a nice building. With a little elbow grease and a few bucks, you can get this place up and running in no time. The only thing left to check would be the roof, but even if that has to be replaced, that will not be a big deal. I can go home tonight and write up a list of everything I need to get this place going. But you mentioned at the beginning that there were a few things that you wanted to add."

"Okay, Scott, knowing what you know now, if we went back to headquarters and I told you what changes I wanted, would you be able to add it to the list without coming back to inspect this building?"

"Absolutely. Before we leave, I just want to take a few measurements."

"Okay, Scott, take your measurements, and then we will go back to headquarters, and I will explain the additions."

"Okay, General. Give me a few minutes, and I'll be ready to go."

Scott takes his measurements, the General locks up, and the two head back to headquarters.

Back at the headquarters, the two men enter the building. The General shows Scott to a small conference room, closes the door, turns to Scott, and says, "Scott, you may want to be seated for this."

Scott, with a confused look on his face, replies, "Okay, then." He sits down and says, "I'm sitting. So what is all this mystique about?"

The General takes a seat across from Scott, stares up at the ceiling for a second or two, and then slowly brings his eyes back down to Scott, finally making eye contact. "Scott… as a member of The Club, I'm sure that you are aware of the goal of this club that was set by its founder, John, that being to change the current laws pertaining to child molesters and change them to a much stiffer set of penalties than what is currently on the books.

Is that truly the way you feel today?"

"Yes, sir, that is exactly how I felt when I joined The Club, and is exactly how I feel today."

"Scott, is there any line that you would not cross to obtain this goal?"

Now Scott looks up at the ceiling, as though he is deep in thought. Finally, he brings his eyes down and makes eye contact with the General. "Well, except for killing or injuring a member of my family, no, there is no line that I would not cross to obtain the goals of this club. I cannot portray or express to you how much I hate child molesters. I hate them, with every fiber of my being. There are no words in the English language that could adequately describe my disdain and disgust of these people. So now that I have sort of signed on the dotted line and explained how I feel about these animals, can you now please, please tell me what the hell is going on here and what it is that you want me to do?"

"What I want you to do, in addition to getting the building up and running, well, the long and short of it is I want you to install a system that will lock the front door so that there will be no way for the people inside to escape, and then expel a deadly gas into all of the rooms, killing all of the inhabitants. I know you said that you would do anything to help this club, but would you have a problem doing that?"

"Is that what all this crap was about? I absolutely would not have a problem doing that, and in fact, it would be a very easy thing to do, because the entire building is heated with hot air, and that means that all of the ducting needed to accomplish your task is already there. And as far as locking the front door, that I can do by installing a remote control lock, and the easier way to keep them from escaping via the windows would be to install quarter-inch plexiglass or bars on all of them. That would be a lot cheaper than installing remote electric locks on all of the doors."

The General just sits there and smiles. "That makes me very happy to hear that. Okay, then, if that's the case, what I'd like you to do is go home, write up a list of what you need, as far as materials and manpower, and about how much you think it would cost and how long it will take."

Scott stands up. "I will work on this tonight, and I should have it finished by tomorrow or, at the latest, the day after."

"Okay, Scott. For now, I will have Eight get in touch with you. I don't want you calling us."

Scott asks the General, "Who is Eight?"

"Each one of our clubs has a number assigned to it, and his club is number eight. We use names very rarely, for security reasons. If you are going to be working with us, I guess you should start learning our procedures, and consider that lesson number one."

"Okay, I got it. I will wait for Eight to call me."

Later that day, the General instructs Eight that for the time being, he should get in touch with Scott.

"You got it, General."

The next day, Eight calls Scott. "Good afternoon, Scott. This is Eight."

"Good afternoon. I'm afraid that I am going to need a little more time, because of a few of the people who were supposed to get back to me with prices have not gotten back to me yet, so right now, I'm stuck waiting for them to get back to me."

"Okay, Scott, no problem. I'll give you a call tomorrow."

"Sounds good."

The following day, Eight calls Scott back. "Good afternoon, Scott. This is Eight."

"Good afternoon. Well… I finally got the calls back that I was waiting for, and I have the information you guys want. Now, I can give you the information over the phone, or if you want, seeing that I only live a few minutes from you, I can print it up and bring you over a copy."

"Okay, Scott, tell you what. Why don't you print it up and bring it over to me. But Scott, and this is very important, keep just one copy for yourself, and that copy must be saved in a secure and safe place, and bring me one single copy. Also, make sure that this information, cannot be found anywhere but these two copies."

"Okay, Eight, I will see you in about an hour, and I have a few things on the list that I want to go over with you."

"Good, Scott. See you then."

Two hours later, Scott arrives at Eight's headquarters. Eight answers the door and welcomes Scott in. The two men, go into the conference room and sit. Scott hands the list to Eight, who opens it and begins to read it. After reading the list, Eight asks Scott, "What on this list do you have questions about?"

"Well, there is nothing on the list, but one of the questions I have is that I'm going to need electricity, and who is going to get it turned on and sign for it?"

"Okay, Scott. Anything else?"

"Yes, what about water? We will need that working, but that's it right now. Unless something comes up when we start this, that is it, because before we can start anything, one of the first things we will need is electricity."

"Okay, Scott. I will give this to the General and then get back to you."

"That would be great."

After Scott leaves, Eight calls the General. "Good afternoon, G. This is Eight. Scott was here and dropped off the list. How soon do you want it?"

"Good. ASAP. I'll drive up there tomorrow."

"You got it, General."

The next day, the General arrives at the headquarters of Eight. The two men go into the conference room, sit down, and Eight hands the General the list. The General takes about ten minutes to read it, going over it a few times. "Wow! This is great news. According to this list that Scott gave us, and according to a few notes he put on the list, it seems that it won't cost that much to accomplish this whole thing, aside from the obvious workers, like a carpenter, electrician, plumber, etc., etc., and about 20 workers. It looks like it will cost about $30 to $40,000. I can live with that. I would like for you to set up a meeting with Scott as soon as possible so we can get this thing going."

"Okay, General, I'll get ahold of him right now."

Eight calls Scott and asks him if he could come over, that the General wants to have a talk with him. Scott tells him that he will be there in a few minutes. Eight tells him, That's great. We will wait for you."

Later that night, the General, Scott, and Eight settle down in the conference room, and the General begins to speak: "Okay, Scott, I went over the list, and I am delighted with your findings and cannot wait to get started. First, I want to address two of the items that you had concerns about, that being electricity and water. As far as the water goes, I want to get a large water tank on wheels so that we can fill it up and bring it over to the site and hook it up to the building. As far as the electric goes, I want to get a large generator, large enough to operate the entire building. I do not want any sort of outside source for this; we must be completely self-reliant and self-contained. That is a must. So, with all that said, the very first thing I want to do, Eight, is for you to get your club and also to get the other clubs to check if anyone can donate or lend us a large generator. After that would be the large water tank on wheels. Then I want to line up all of the tradesmen and workers that are needed. One last time, Scott, are you sure you want to get involved in this?"

"Absolutely, General."

"Okay, then. Eight, starting tomorrow, I want you to get in touch with the rest of the clubs and put the word out as to what we need, like a truck, including the driver, and all the tradesmen we need. Once you've gotten everything lined up, get back to me, but remember the very first things would be a generator and water tank."

"Okay, G."

Three days later, Eight calls the General. "Hi, G. Eight here. You are not going to believe this, but we already have more volunteers than we need or can use. We even have two members who are in the trucking business and who said that we could use their trucks. Also, there is a member who rents out construction equipment and who has a large water tank on wheels and a large generator that would generate enough electricity for the entire building. And most of the volunteers said that they would be willing to travel, as long as we reimburse them. And as far as the truck and construction equipment go, the owners said that we could take them out of town, if need be. The only problem I see with these items would be getting them back to the owners at the end of the operation."

"Eight, that would not be a problem. We would simply assign someone to return them on the night of the operation."

"Okay, I guess we could do that. And as far as the tradesmen go, we have more than we can use. We also have members who own their own businesses. Two own electrical supply houses, one owns a plumbing supply house, and two members own lumber yards, and all of them said that they would donate most of what we need. So, G, as far as I'm concerned, we have all the bases covered. The next move is yours; just let me know when you want me to start doing things, and I will get the ball rolling."

The General can't control himself, and he shouts, "Oh my God! That is great news. Okay, Eight, what we need to do next is to have the lawyers get that phony charity set up so that we can get the hotel and land. Then we can get started. So get in touch with your attorneys and get that done first. When that is done, the next thing I would want you to do is get in touch with Scott. Tell him about all the volunteers and ask him how many tradesmen and workers he needs. Call them and find out when all the volunteers can make it, even if we need to pay for their transportation. Just let me know the day and time."

"Okay, G."

Several days go by before the General hears from Eight.

"Good morning, G. Eight here. I've got great news for you. First off, my attorneys got the charity started, and you will find this hard to believe, but they actually got the charity registered, so it is now a legal charity that cannot be traced back to us. I have no idea how they did it, but they did. So, as far as that part of the operation, we are all set. And as far as the meeting goes, I got in touch with Scott, explained what was going on, and asked him who and how many workers he would need. I also explained to him about the trucks, construction equipment, and suppliers, and he seemed all excited about it. He gave me a list of who and how many. I got in touch with all of the parties and set up the meeting for this Tuesday coming up, at 7 PM, and the best part is that all the parties involved are local and there was no problem with travel expenses."

"Okay, Eight. So that is this coming Tuesday at 7 PM?"

"That's correct, General. And by the way, as long as I have you on the phone, I got a call from Two, and he told me that the two brothers that killed those child molesters have their trial starting. The lawyers are working their case, and after picking the jurors, seem confident of winning the case."

"Oh my God, with all this good news coming in one phone call, I don't know if I can stand this much joy all at once. I may overheat. I'm going to need to sit down and gather myself."

"Well, G, I'm glad that I made your day. Enjoy it, and I will see you on Tuesday."

"You got it."

Tuesday night arrives. The General arrives early and is happy to see that some of the volunteers are already there. The General looks around, trying to spot Scott. After spotting him, the General approaches him and asks if he would accompany him to the conference room so that he can have a few words with him. Scott agrees, and the two head into the small conference room.

"Okay, Scott. Being that you are the general contractor, I just want to run this by you. What I would like to do at this point is introduce you to all the volunteers here tonight and give you one of our disposable phones so that you can contact Eight and so that he can then get in touch with the people you need in the sequence that you see fit to get the job done. Other than myself, you will be in complete charge of the job from start to finish, checking with me only on obviously important decisions. So, before we go out in front of the volunteers, I just want to make sure that you're onboard with all of this."

"I am absolutely onboard. That would be the best way to go about this."

"Okay, then, let me give you the extra set of keys to the hotel. Go out there and get this thing started."

By now, it's after 7 PM, and everyone who should have been there is there. The two of them walk to the front of the room, and the General begins to speak: "Good evening, everyone, and I want to thank each one of you very much for attending tonight. This meeting is going to be a very significant one, because it marks one of the biggest steps that we must take in order to reach out goal. But before I get into it, I just want to give you this. By now, all of you volunteers and contributors know the number of the headquarters in your jurisdiction, and if any of you don't know, please get that information tonight. So. if at any time during this process you have a question, get in touch with that person. If they don't have the answer for you, they will get it and get back to you.

"Now, with that out of the way, standing up here at my side is Scott. Scott is a general contractor, and he has agreed to donate his time for this project. In order to get in touch with each one of you, he will be contacting Eight, and Eight will, in turn, get in touch with you whenever he needs your services or products. It will be a lot easier that way to keep track of who is doing what. To explain what we will be doing in a nutshell, we will be renovating a one-hundred-room hotel that one of the members has graciously given us permission to use. We will all be working together as a family. Absolutely no outsiders will be permitted on the job site. After this meeting, you will be taking your orders from Scott, unless something unusual comes up as far as safety or security. Then, and only then, will you hear from me. So, for now, that will be all you need to know. The one last order that I will give for now is that I want each one of you leaders of your respective clubs to know that I will be giving each club a $5000 petty cash box so that you can purchase items that you need right away. Also, and extremely important, before any of this starts, I want each leader to go out and purchase several boxes of rubber examination gloves and regular work gloves. These are to be given out to every worker who goes on this job site. These gloves must be worn at all times, and if any individual touches anything without a glove on, everything must stop, and whatever they touched must be cleaned or destroyed, no ifs, ands, or buts. We will also have portable toilets at the job site, because I do not want any DNA left on the site. I hope you will understand what I mean by that. It could spell the difference between success and failure. Remember, no DNA of any kind left on the job site."

The General turns to Scott. "So, Scott, do you have anything you want to add?"

"No, General. What I am going to do is take another ride out to the job site, give it one more look, and then start making my plans according to who and what I need first."

"Okay, then, before I end this meeting, does anyone have any questions?"

No one raises their hand.

"Then, this meeting is over, and the next person you hear from will be Scott. And thanks again to all of you for attending this meeting."

The next day, bright and early, Scott wastes no time and heads out to the job site to check it all out again. This time, he brings an extra-large spotlight and tape measure so that he can check things out more carefully. After several hours of Scott looking, touching, inspecting, measuring, and sniffing, he feels that he now has enough information to get this thing started, so he locks up and heads home.

As soon as Scott gets home, he calls Eight. "Good morning, Eight. This is Scott."

"Good morning, Scott. What can I do for you?"

"Well, I just came back from the job site, gave it another look-see, so now I know exactly what I need to get started. As soon as you can gather the workers and supplies I need, I will be good to go."

"Okay, Scott, I'm ready to copy. What is it that you need to get started?"

"The number one thing I need is a large generator, because we must have electric. What I need next are one plumber, one carpenter, one electrician, about twenty helpers, and a whole bunch of cleaning stuff, like spray cleaners, plastic bags, brooms, mops, etc., etc. And as far as tools go, tell the tradesmen to bring their own tools. But the generator is the number one thing; that is a must. And please get back to me and keep me advised as to how soon you can get the generator, because the sooner you get it up and running, the sooner I can get up and running. Oh, by the way, last, but not least, we will need one or two of those outdoor toilets, at least at the start."

"Okay, Scott, I will get back to you ASAP."

The next morning, Scott gets a call from Eight.

"Good morning, Scott. This is Eight."

"Good morning, Eight. What is the good word?"

"The good word is that you are all set. I've got everything set up for you. Just let me know when you are ready."

"I can start this afternoon."

"Okay, then, this is the way it will all go down. First thing is I am having a large generator delivered to the job site. All the tradesmen you requested have their tools packed and are already to go. I've got twenty-five workers with a whole bunch of cleaning supplies. I included just about everything I could think of to clean something. Just tell me what time you want everyone there. So that it does not look like a parade going into the job site, I am going to give everyone a different time to get there so as to stagger their arrival. What I need to know now is what time will you be getting there? Once I know that, I can take care of the rest. I know that you want the generator to get there first."

"Okay, let me see, right now, it's 10 AM. I could be at the job site by 12 noon. If you can, have the generator there by 12:30 PM, that would be great. Next would be the porta-potty, and don't forget the water tank. Then have the workers and cleaning supplies arrive after that. Then all the tradesmen. Oh, and please don't forget extra gas for the generator. Remember, without gas, it's just a paperweight."

"Okay, Scott, you got it."

By 11:30 AM, Scott is already at the job site, removing some of the wood off of the boarded-up windows. Then he remembers that he needs ladders, so he calls Eight and lets him know about the ladders and that he will need at least two twenty-foot extension ladders and about three six-foot folding ladders. "Oh, and tell them not to forget food and water, at least for today."

Eight tells him, "Not to worry. I will take care of everything."

"Great, thank you, Eight."

At 12:30 PM, Scott hears a truck coming. He turns toward the sound and is happy to see it's the generator. He thinks to himself, *Now, we can really get started.*

The driver sees Scott and pulls up to him. "Okay, where do you want this thing?"

"It's going around on the side of the building, where the electric is hooked up."

"You got it, boss."

"Oh, and make sure you wear your gloves. Do not touch anything else. Just drop it off there, and we will hook it up."

With that, the driver backs the generator up and drops it off. "My boss told me to ask you if there was anything else that I could help you out with."

"No, not now, but thank you."

"Okay, then take care."

At 1:20 PM, three vans pull up, and out pour about twenty-five workers, who start unloading the cleaning supplies right away. Scott can't believe what he is seeing. He is not used to seeing such enthusiastic workers. One approaches Scott and introduce himself as Pete, and says that he is the foreman. "Okay, Scott, where do you want us to start?"

"Naturally, I would like you to start inside, but it's still kind of dark in there because I still need to remove a lot of wood from the windows, and I still need to get the generator going. But see what you can do for now, and I guess you can start by bringing all of the supplies inside. Start in the kitchen and do whatever you can until I can get you some more light. But remember, no one touches anything without gloves on. That is an absolute must.

"Scott, the gloves were already handed out, and every member was instructed as to the importance of wearing them."

At 2 PM, three more vans pull up. One is the plumber, one is the electrician, and the third the carpenter. The three men introduce themselves to Scott, and as though it was rehearsed, all three simultaneously say, "Where do you want me to start?"

Scott tells the electrician, "First thing we need to do is get that generator going."

"Show me where it is, and I'll get it going."

"It's right over there, on the side of the building." Scott points in the direction of the generator. Next, he instructs the carpenter, seeing that he has ladders, "I'm sure happy to see that you brought your ladders."

The carpenter replies, "You know what they say: never leave home without your ladders. Besides that, I was told that you needed them."

"Okay then. You can help me remove the rest of the wood from the windows." Then Scott tells the plumber, "I wanted you to start checking the plumbing, but I am waiting for a water tank to arrive, so without that, I guess you can't check it."

"Why do you need a water tank?"

"Because the water was turned off when the building was boarded up."

"Scott, let me check it out first. I am pretty sure that you can cancel the water tank. I am sure that I can get the water going for you."

"Oh wow! If you can do that, you will make my day."

"Scott, consider your day made."

Fifteen minutes later, the plumber approaches Scott and says to him, "You can cancel the water tank. We now have running water."

Scott looks at him and replies, "I cannot take much more of this good news today. You guys are overwhelming me. Thank you, thank you, thank you all."

At 2:30 PM, while everyone is doing the best they can, all of a sudden, there is the sound of a generator running. Scott drops what he's doing and runs over to where the generator is. Seeing it running, he claps his hands in victory. "Will this run the whole building?" he asks the electrician.

"Absolutely. I am going to go inside now and start checking the electric."

"That's great." Scott goes back to work helping the carpenter remove wood from the windows.

Ten minutes later, the plumber approaches Scott. "Okay, now that I got the water running, I'm going to go in and start checking the water lines. If it's okay with you, I'm going to ask the cleaners to keep an eye open for leaks."

"No problem, you can do that."

At 7 PM, Scott calls everyone together and has an impromptu meeting. "Okay, guys, I think we can call it a day. I cannot tell you how happy I am seeing how far we got today. We got electricity, we got water, we got the whole first floor clean, including the kitchen, that we can now cook in thanks to the plumber. He not only turned on the water, but he also, turned on the gas, so starting tomorrow, if you want to bring some food to cook or heat up, you can do that. Just remember, you must clean up after yourself. I just want to let you know the only difference tomorrow will be that I would like everyone to get here a little early. You can work it out amongst yourselves. What I would like is for you workers to be here by 9 AM, and the rest of you a little after that. Okay, guys, great job today. If no one has any questions, I will see you tomorrow morning."

No one has any questions.

"Okay then. See you tomorrow."

For the next two weeks, the work progresses without a hitch, with the General stopping in now and then to check on the progress. Then, on his last visit, Scott tells the General that he and the crew are almost finished, and that the only thing that still needs to be done is to install the plexiglass on the windows, and the hotel will be ready to go. The only thing left after that is what kind of gas they are going to use and where they are going to get it from.

The General tells Scott, "Well, I had this idea. I thought about hooking up the exhaust from the generator to the ductwork, but then I remembered that we need to take it away on the night of the operation, so that would not work. Then I came up with the idea of having a few of our members in disguises go out and purchase about five or six old cars. As long as they are in running condition, we could then bring them here and hook all their exhausts together, and then feed it into the ductwork of the building. Then all we would have to do is make sure that they all had full tanks of gas, lock the front door, stick the note on the door, start all the cars, and disappear into the night. But before we celebrate, I want to check with our members and see if any of them would know whether or not that would work. If they say it would work, then I think that would be the way to go."

Scott replies, "Sounds like a plan to me, and personally, I think it would work great!"

"Okay, Scott, I will work on that, and you finish up the building."

"You got it, General."

Two days later, the General gets a call from Eight. "Good morning, G. I just got a call from Scott, and he told me that the building is all ready to go. He even had the plumber hook up pipes so that all of the cars' exhausts could be connected together. He also checked things out and suggested that we use ten cars, so that's how many pipes he hooked up together. He also had the electrician hook up a large twelve-volt blower that would take the exhaust from all of the cars and pump it into the building. This, he said, would guarantee that enough carbon monoxide would get into the building to do the job."

"So, let me make sure that I'm hearing this right. You're telling me that the building is ready to go. Is that what you're telling me?"

"Absolutely, G. That is exactly what I'm telling you."

"Oh my God!! That is great news. So now one of the last things we need to do is to get a make-up artist and two of your members who know a thing or two about cars, get some make-up on them, and go out and buy ten cars for cash, with an open registration, that are in good running condition. Then we'll bring them over to the job site and get them hooked up so that we can check everything out. But remember, they must wear gloves. I don't want any fingerprints or DNA of any kind left behind on these cars. I cannot stress the importance of this. They can tell the sellers that they don't like germs, or whatever. Then – and this may be a little more difficult than what we've accomplished so far – I would like for you to try to get twenty-four-hour security for the building. We need someone there with a cell phone, so they can get it touch with us should something happen. If you could do that, it would be the topping on the cake, because, after what we have accomplished, the last thing we need is for someone to vandalize the building."

"You got it, G."

"Thank you, and what I will do tonight is put a plan together for the building in Texas and give you a call tomorrow."

"Okay, G. Talk to you then."

That night, the General puts a plan together for the building in Texas. After spending $30,000 dollars on the hotel, he only has $287,000 to build in Texas, so one of the first things he wants to do is talk to Scott.

The next morning, the General calls Eight. "Good morning, Eight. This is G. What I would like for you to do, if you can, is to get in touch with Scott and see if he could meet with me in your headquarters this afternoon. I want to run a few things by him about building in Texas, so give him a call and get back to me."

"Okay, G. You got it."

Two hours later, Eight calls the General back and tells him that Scott can meet with him at 7 PM tonight.

At 6:30 PM, the General arrives at the headquarters of Eight. A few minutes later, Scott arrives. The General, Scott, and Eight all go into the conference room and seat themselves at the table. The General speaks first: "How you doing, Scott?"

"Great, General. I'm sure by now you've heard the good news."

"Absolutely! That was great news, but now I want to talk to you about the next phase of this operation, and that is the building in Texas. Now, I don't expect you to go to Texas; I just want to get your input about a few things about building there."

"First, General, not to cut you off, but I am retired, so I would have no problem going to Texas to supervise the building, just as long as you have a place for me to stay, and feed me."

"You know what, Scott? I wasn't planning on that, but you did such a great job here that I would have no problem doing that for you. I can set you up over there in a nice, comfortable place."

"Okay, General, with that out of the way, shoot some questions at me."

"Well, the biggest problem I have is money. All I have left to spend putting up the building is $287,000, and what I want to know is, by putting in just the bare essentials, can you put up a building with 100 rooms, a small kitchen, one large combination dining and meeting room? Just essential lighting, and basically you know the rest of what is needed."

"Okay, General, I will go home and work on this tonight. How about we meet back here tomorrow at about 6PM."

All three agree to do that.

At 6:PM the next night, all three are at the table in the conference room. This time, Scott speaks first: "Okay, General, this is what I came up with. I'm pretty sure that I can do what you want with the amount of money you have, but it's not going to be easy. I mean, this building is not going to be much more than a movie set. First, there will be no foundation. I will build all the framing right on the ground. I will build the walls with twenty-four inch on center, instead of sixteen inch on center. I will use the thinnest wallboard there is, no insulation, just some PVC pipe for water, just the bare wiring for electric, and no doors on the rooms. The only thing in the kitchen for cooking will be a stove with an oven. As far as the combo eating and meeting room goes, there will only be round tables and folding chairs. Also, for windows, they will only be quarter-inch plexiglass panels, built into the walls, that will be unbreakable. It will be a two-story building, with fifty rooms on each floor. There will be only two bathrooms on each floor, and they will only have a sink and toilet bowl, and they will be hooked up to a small cesspool. All this will be predicated on members donating a lot of stuff, like lumber, electrical supplies, light fixtures, sinks, bowels, etc., etc. I will need that generator again, and this time, we will definitely need a water tank. If only I was able to get the same crew that I had, and that I know I can't have, but it would be great."

The General just sits there, staring at Scott. Then he just breaks out into a smile from ear to ear. "Well, Scott, you once again have made my day. Eight, you heard what Scott said. So what do you think you can do for him?"

"General, first thing tomorrow morning, I will be on the phone with Two and see what we can work out. Also, I will get in touch with the last crew just to see if any of them might be available to go to Texas, and then get back to you."

"Great! I will talk to you then."

Three days later, Eight calls the General. "Good morning, G. I got some good news for you today."

"Good, I'm always in the mood for good news. So, what is it?"

"Well, first off, you can use the same trucks, with the same conditions as last time. Just put fuel in them. Also, the heavy-duty equipment renter said that you can use the generator again, and anything else he has, just transport it there yourself and then return them. As far as the rest of the crew is concerned, Two said that he has two electricians, one plumber, three carpenters, four wallboard guys, a lumber yard, an electrical supply house, and a plumbing supply house. All said that they would donate as much as they could.

"The rest of the stuff we need, we would probably have to buy ourselves. Two also has a list of volunteers, including make-up artists, lawyers, doctors, people and working in the building department. Also, some of the most valuable volunteers that I can think of are two building inspectors, and by the way, all of the professional volunteers have their own tools and ladders. So, that's it, G. Let me know what you want me to do, and I will get back to Two and let him know what we decided."

"Okay, Eight. Tell you what; tell Two to put all of the volunteers on notice that we will be calling them soon with a date to start. In the meantime, I will make arrangements for myself in Texas and then get back to you."

"Okay, G. Talk to you later."

Two days later, the General calls Eight. "Good morning, Eight. Okay, this is the deal. I happen to have a friend of mine in Texas who owns a ranch with several nice bunkhouses that are clean and comfortable, with all of the amenities. He has two of these bunkhouses that I can use; each one has four bedrooms. I will be there, starting this Saturday, so call Two and let him get started lining everyone up. First, check with Scott and find out whether or not he is up to staying in a bunkhouse with me. Also, there are six more beds available for anyone of the old crew that would want to bunk there. Rather than me give you a list of who I need, first check with Scott if he is into going to Texas and staying with me. Then get a list of who he will need and see if we can get them here, and then get the rest from Texas. You can reach me in Texas when you get things squared away."

Saturday afternoon, Eight calls the General. "Good morning, G. How's the weather out there in Texas?"

"Hot as hell. I don't know how these people can live here year round. Anyway, what's the good word?"

"Well, the good word is this. Scott has agreed to join you in your bunkhouse, and he will be there tomorrow. He wants to check out the land to see exactly what he needs. I could not get, any of the old crew to go to Texas, but we do have the use of the trucks that we used last time, with drivers, and you can have that big generator and a huge water tank with a gas operated pump that we can use. Also, anything else that we need, as long as he has it, then we just need to get them there and back. I made arrangements with two of my workers to do that, and they will be staying in one of the bunkhouses. We just need to feed them. Also, Two has lined up everyone else we would need. He has lined up four carpenters, two electricians, three plumbers, a lumber yard, an electrical supply house, a plumbing supply house, and a mason supply yard that will donate just about everything you need. Luckily, one of the inspectors who is willing to help us has jurisdiction in the area where the land is, so everything is looking good and all set. All I need now is a list from Scott to give Two so that he can get the ball rolling."

"That is beautiful, Eight. Talk to you later."

"Bye, G."

Sunday morning, bright and early, Scott and the General head out to the site. They spend several hours there, with Scott taking measurements.

"Okay, General, everything looks good. I know what I need now. We can go back, and you can get in touch with Eight. I can write up a list so that you can tell them, or I can talk to him directly.

"When we get back, you can call him and give him the list yourself. That way, nothing will be missing."

"Okay, General."

With that, the two men head back to the bunkhouse. When the two are inside, Scott sits down and makes up a list of what he will need. Then he calls Eight. "Good morning, Eight. This is Scott. I got the list of what I will need."

"Okay, what will you need?"

"The first thing I will need is lots and lots of lumber. Just tell the owner of the lumber yard that I will need 2x4s, 2x6s, 2x8s, siding, enough nails to nail everything together, Sheetrock with the screws, tape, spackle, and roof shingles, enough to build a two-story, hundred-room building. Whatever he can donate will be greatly appreciated, and I guess we will have to pay for the rest. As far as help goes, at first, I will need all of the carpenters with all of their tools, drinking water, porta-potty, and food, and that will get us started. After that, you can line up the electrical supply house and plumbing supply house; I will need their help and or donations next, because that's what I will need before I put the Sheetrock up."

"Okay, Scott. I will see what I can do and get back to you. Oh, the G wants to speak to you." Scott passes the phone to the General.

"Eight, once you get things set up, I want you to have Two set up a meeting with all of the volunteers involved with this building, just like the meeting we had at your headquarters, so that I can, run the plan by them to make them aware of what they're getting into and to see if they want to continue."

"Okay, G. I got you."

Finally, after two days, Eight calls the General. "Okay, G. Two got in touch with all parties involved and set up a meeting for this Wednesday at 7 PM at the Texas headquarters, and everything here is ready to roll. I just need your okay, and they can be there in two days."

"That's great! See you Wednesday night."

Wednesday night, at 6:30 PM, the General arrives early to make sure that everything is all set up by 7 PM. By the time the meeting starts, every-one is there.

The General walks up to the front of the room, and as though a switch is thrown, everyone in the room stops talking. The General begins to speak: "Good evening, everyone, and welcome to the Texas headquarters of The Club.

"Not too long ago, I had a meeting similar to the one that we are about to have tonight, and it is very important that you listen to every word I say, because, later on tonight, when I'm finished explaining everything to you, I am going to ask you whether or not you still want to have any part of the plan that I will have just explained to you. It will undoubtedly be one of the most significant decisions that you ever had to make in your life.

"Okay, so keeping in mind why we are all here, I will get right to the core of my plan. What I plan to do, with the help of all you volunteers, is to construct a building with one hundred rooms, with each room having the ability to sleep two men. We will then try to lure child molesters there, and only child molesters, via the telephone, with the numbers that we will get from the national sex offender registry. We will explain to these molest-ers that this will be sort of a camp, set up to help them out. We will tell them that if they attend this camp for two weeks and listen to a few semi-nars about sex offenders, and if they then pass a few tests, their names will be removed from the sex offender registry. Then they will be able to live a more normal life and not have to worry about registering every time they move. Then the most important thing that we will tell them is that they absolutely cannot tell anyone about this, no ifs, ands, or buts, because it is a secret government test project, and if word gets out, all hell will break loose and the camp will be completely disassembled, and they will never be able to have their name removed from the national sex offenders registry.

"So now that you have that information, here is the rest of the story. Once we get the child molesters into his building and let them attend a seminar on the first night, then, once they're all asleep in their beds, the front door will be locked and bolted so that no one can escape from the front door. There will be no other way to exit this building. We will then start up ten cars, all parked behind the building, and have all of their exhausts hooked up to a blower that will blow the carbon monoxide from the ten cars into the building via the ductwork we installed, killing them all. Then, we will remove whatever equipment that has to be removed, and before departing, I will place a note on the door for the authorities to read the following day, when it will be too late to save anyone. The note will explain what we did and why we did it, and if they do nothing about the laws, we have bigger and better plans already in the works and ready to go.

"Now, another important thing to keep in mind is that we already have a hundred-room hotel in Virginia that is all set up and ready to go. Everything is there, including the cars with full tanks of gas. The two sites, the hotel in Virginia and the building here in Texas, will be activated on the same night, so if you do the math, we will get rid of at least 400 child molesters in one shot. I know that this is a lot to swallow, so I will give you a few minutes to talk amongst yourselves. Then I will come back, and with a show of hands, I will see who's in and who's out, and if we can go ahead with this plan."

As the General starts to walk away, one of the volunteers in the back stands up. "Excuse me, General. As far as I'm concerned, I know what I'm here for and what I would like to do, and I myself don't need any time to think about it. And I'm pretty sure most of us feel the same way I do."

"Okay, then, with a show of hands, does anyone out there need time to think about this?"

No one raises their hand.

"Okay, then, by a show of hands, how many of you out there are ready to vote on this now?"

Everyone in the audience raises their hand.

"Well, I guess we don't have to wait. So, once again, by a show of hands, how many of you sanction this plan?"

Again, every member raises their hand.

"Well, I guess it's a go. Before I go any further, does anyone have any questions? If you do, now would be a good time to ask."

No hands go up.

"Okay, great! Your respective members will instruct you volunteers as to what, when, and where to go or do. I want to thank you all very much, and I hope the decision we made tonight will help to save many children's lives. Good night. Scott, Eight, and Two, if you guys can hang back, I want to go over a few things with you."

In unison, as though they'd all rehearsed it, the three men say, "No problem, General." They look at each other and laugh. Scott says, "Well, that went over well. Now I'm glad we rehearsed that."

The four of them retreat to the conference room, where they all sit. The General says, "Okay, so it looks like everyone is on board. So, this is the way it needs to go down. First off, Two, did any of your members find a member out here in Texas who rents out heavy construction equipment?"

"Sorry, General, but the answer to that is no."

"Okay, then we will need to get them here from Virginia. Eight, what I would like you to do, seeing that we cannot get what we need here in Texas, is to make arrangements to bring them in, from Virginia. Scott, what do you need first?"

"I need a backhoe with a plow, the large water tank, the one with the pump, and that large generator again."

"Well, that generator needs to stay where it is. We will need to try and get another one for this job site."

"Then the only other thing I would need would be a couple of out-houses, unless you want to rent them here."

"No, I don't want to rent anything here, so I guess we need to bring them here also."

Eight says, "I guess you want me to get on it right away, General, and I guess you want them here ASAP."

"Yes, you guessed right. I want to get this thing started yesterday."

"Okay, General, as soon as I'm done here, I will get started on that. Also, I'll sit down with Two and set up a schedule with all of the volunteers, like we did in Virginia. I will make sure that they understand, and I'll go over the whole thing about no DNA left behind. I will set everything up with Two so that the work coincides with the delivery from Virginia, and that date I will know as soon as I set everything up in Virginia."

"That sounds good. I'll be in my bunkhouse. Just keep me advised."

"You got it, General."

All four get up and leave the room.

Two days later, while Scott and the General are sitting in the bunkhouse having breakfast, the General's phone rings. "Hello."

"Good morning, General. Did I wake you?"

"Yes, you did Eight, and now I am pissed off at you."

"Can I ask you why?"

"Because I was having this nice dream that there were no more child molesters in this world, and that we got rid of them all, but now you woke me up to face reality. So that's why I'm pissed off at you."

"Well, then the news I got should make you feel better."

"I could use some good news."

"Everything you wanted from Virginia, including the outhouses, water tank, and generator, are on the job site already, so the next move is yours and Scott's."

"That is great. We will choke down our breakfast, and you tell them we will be out there ASAP. I seem to be using that term a lot lately."

"Yes, you are, General. Would you mind if I went out to the site now and waited there for you guys?"

"Absolutely not. You can go there, and we will meet you there as soon as we can."

Scott and the General finish eating, jump in the car, and head out to the sight. As soon as they get there, Scott jumps out of the car and heads over to the guy standing by the backhoe. "You know how to work this thing?" he asks.

"Yes, I do."

"Give me a few minutes to measure a few things, and I'll let you know where you can start."

"Okay, I'll wait here."

With that, Scott goes back to the car and gets out his tape measure. Then he asks the General if he would give him a hand with the measuring.

"No problem."

"Okay, great. Just follow me, General." Scott walks over to a point in the open field, looking for a marker he put there when he came out by himself. He finds it and then says to the General, "I just want you to stand here and hold this end of the tape measure." Scott cleans around the marker and then walks away, letting the tape out, until he seems, to the General, like he's a mile or so away. Scott stops, looks around, and finds a second marker that he put there. Again, with his hands, he cleans the area around the marker so that it's more visible. Then he proceeds to walk back to the General, taking in the tape. He tells the General, "Just keep standing here," and then heads off in a new direction, looking for another marker. Again, he finds it and cleans around it. This time, he motions to the General to come over to him, and the General proceeds to walk towards him. "Okay, General, one last time, just stand here and hold onto this end of the tape." Scott now walks in another direction and finds the fourth marker. He proceeds to clean around it, and then tells the General, "Okay, we are done here. Now I can tell the driver of the backhoe what area to clean so that we can get this thing going."

Scott calls the backhoe driver over and explains to him where to start and exactly how he wants the land to look like.

"You got it, boss."

Then Scott tells the General that the next thing he is going to need is lumber, and lots of it, followed by carpenters, laborers, and then the rest of the stuff, like electrical and plumbing supplies.

"Okay, that would be Two's job. I will let him know." The General then calls Two over, and tells him to see to it about getting the rest of the building supplies and whatever else Scott needs.

"Okay, General, I will go back to my office, and get right on it.

Two hours later, the land is all cleared and leveled to Scott's satisfaction. Then, as Scott is looking everything over, he hears truck engines, and he turns to see three trucks. Two of the trucks are loaded with lots and lots of lumber, and the third truck is loaded with electric and plumbing supplies.

Scott looks over at the General, who is standing next to him, and both men smile at each other. Scott says to the General, "Boy, I cannot remember any time in my building career getting my supplies this fast. All I need now are the carpenters and laborers. As soon as the words leave his mouth, Scott hears more engine sounds, and he turns to see two vans pulling in with carpenters and their workers. Scott walks over to them. and welcomes them.

One of the carpenters asks Scott if he has any building plans he could see, and Scott says, "Yes, I have plans, but they are in my head, and I will tell you them so that they will then be in your head."

Scott asks the two carpenters to sit in his car for a few minutes. The two comply, and all three of them, plus the General, all get into Scott's car. Fifteen minutes later, all four men get out of the car, and Scott says, "Okay, guys, so you got the gist of it, right?"

"We got it, Scott. We will take it from here." With that, the two carpenters instruct their men as to what to do. Then they get out their rulers and go to work.

The General tells Scott, "You got this. If you need me, I'll be at the bunkhouse."

"Okay, General."

That night, when Scott returns to the bunkhouse, the first thing that happens is the General asks him, "How did it go?"

"General, you are not going to believe this, but these guys are unbelievable. We actually finished the first floor. Tomorrow, we start on the walls, and General, the way these guys work, we will be done in no time."

"That's great news. I can't wait until it's built."

Three weeks later, as Scott leaves to go to the job site, he tells the General, "Today, we will likely finish up the building. Then all you would need to do is buy the cars and hook them up to the plumbing that is already there. All I need to do is hook up the front door lock, finish up a little landscaping, check everything out, and then we are done. All you will need next are the child molesters."

"Oh my God, I can't wait for you to get home tonight and tell me that. In the meantime, I will get in touch with Eight so that he can get in touch with Two so that they can buy the cars and get them hooked up."

That night, Scott gets home and looks at the General. "Well, General, my work is complete."

The General jumps up, runs over to Scott, and gives him a big hug while almost tearing up. Then, with his two hands, he grasps Scott's hand, and while shaking it, the General thanks him numerous times. "You have made my day, and I can't wait until tomorrow morning to go check it out."

"And the good news is that most of the building supplies were donated. The rest we had to pay for, but you still have about $25,000 left to accomplish your goals."

"That's great. That's perfect. It could not have worked out any better. I'm elated."

The next morning, the General goes out to the job site with Scott to check things out. He checks out the entire building and finds everything to be in perfect order, including the plumbing for the cars. He thinks to himself, *This building is perfect for what I need.* He turns to Scott and says, "You did a great job. This is exactly what I wanted. Let's go to town. I want to buy you a drink."

The two head into town and look for a nice place to have a drink.

That night, the General calls Eight to give him the good news, and he tells him to set up a meeting ASAP with all the leaders and, seeing that he is already in Texas, to have the meeting in Texas.

"Okay, General."

"And let Two know that he can send a couple of guys out to buy the cars and get them out to the job site and hook them up, but please remind them to wear gloves."

"Okay, General."

The following week, the meeting at Two's headquarters with all the leaders is set up, and as usual, the General gets there early and waits until all the leaders are present. Then he begins to speak: "Good evening, everyone. I want to thank all of you for a job well done. I am here tonight to tell you that we are now ready to start stage three. It seems like it was only yesterday that we started this at stage one, but we are finally here at stage three. The next part is going to be fairly easy. First, what we need to do is get some paper signs made up welcoming the child molesters, but leaving off the words child molesters. Instead it will read, 'Welcome to your life-changing camp. This radical camp will change your life once you complete the course.'

"So, stage three, we are here at last. Now, this is what we need to do next. We have at our headquarters the national sex offenders registry. Using this list, we will contact just child molesters in this area, no one else. We will tell them that this camp is a radical new concept that was put together by leading psychiatrists, and that it will remove their name from the national sex offenders registry so that they can lead a more normal life. They will also be told that under no circumstance are they are to tell anyone about this camp, or they will not be allowed to attend, and that they will need to stay at this camp for two weeks, listen to a few seminars, take a small test

248

at the end, and if everything goes right and they pass the test, their names will be removed from the list. But we need to stress the point that under no circumstances must they tell anybody about this camp, or they will be prohibited from attending the camp. All they will need to bring to the camp are several changes of clothing, a pillow, and a blanket. Everything else that will be needed will be provided free of charge, and one of the biggest things is that there will be absolutely no cell phones, iPads, or any other contraption that they can use to communicate with anyone outside of the camp, and their bags will be inspected upon arrival. If anything is found, they will be prohibited from attending the camp and will receive a $500 fine.

"We will make a list of all of these child molesters who wish to attend this camp and tell them that we will get back to them with a time and date as to where to meet. We will then give them a desolate place to meet, where we will pick them up with a bus and then transport them to the camp. There, we will set up a welcoming party, with the signs we had printed up hung on the walls. The camp is set up to house 200. It has one hundred rooms, which can each sleep two, and that will be the number that we will have to stop at. Once we get them there, the first night, we will have an impromptu meeting to put them at ease. Then, that night, when they are all asleep, we will do our thing, which you all are aware of, but just perchance there are any of you out there who do not know what will be done next, please raise your hand now."

No hands go up.

"Okay, once the deed is done, we will need four men in trucks, who will be assigned to disconnect the generator and water tank and return them to Virginia. So, are there any questions at all? One last thing, by a show of hands, does everybody know their job?"

Every single person raises their hand.

"This meeting has now ended. Starting tomorrow, please start calling our child molesters. Later on tonight, I will be going to Virginia so that I can hold a similar meeting with the group there. Then, when we have all our ducks in a row, I will set a date when all of this will go down. Thank you and good night."

Two days later, The General is at the headquarters in Virginia, waiting for all of the members to arrive. By 7 PM, all of the members are seated and waiting for the General to start speaking. Finally, he does. "Good evening, everyone. Welcome, and thank you for coming. The first thing I want to do is thank you for all your hard work. Without that, we would not be where we are, and where we are is stage three. Yes, that's right, we are at stage three of our plan. A few days ago, I had a similar meeting in Texas, and I told them the same thing that I am about to tell you guys."

The General gives the same speech, verbatim, that he gave in Texas, finishing with, "And I told the members in Texas that as soon as they get their list compiled, and you guys do the same, I will then set a date for all this, to come together and culminate into one hell of a night for our cause. So, again, like I told the members in Texas, and like I'm telling you guys, the next move is yours. I'll be waiting for your call telling me that you have all of the child molesters lined up. And now, by a show of hands, do any of you have any questions?"

No hands go up.

"Okay, then. Thank you for attending tonight, and good night."

Two days later, the General's phone rings. "Hello."

"Good morning, G. Eight here. G, I got some great news for you. This morning, my members started calling. All of the child molesters in our area, and every one of them that we spoke to, jumped at the chance to go to this camp."

"My God!!"

"Within a few hours, we had to stop calling them, because we already had our 200 child molesters ready and willing to go to this camp and comply with all of our rules. Also, I just got off the phone with Two, and he told me that they are experiencing the same reaction from the child molesters in their area."

"Damn, Eight, we got 200 at each place this fast? Well, Eight, I just got an idea. Seeing that this is going so good, I would like to take advantage of the situation. Scott informed me that we did not spend all of the money. I checked with my member, the one I assigned to keep track of the money, and she notified me that we have $25,000 left. So how about we do this? Check with the volunteers who supplied the beds for us for both locations and try to get another hundred beds, and some kind of nightstands, at each site, and put one bed and one nightstand outside of each room, in the hallway. Even if we have to pay for them, if we can accomplish this, then we can fit 300 at each location."

"Okay, G. I'll get right on it. Oh, and by the way, I don't know if you've been keeping up with current events, but there have been three killings of child molesters, one in Florida, one in Illinois, and one in New York. Fortunately for us, we have headquarters in all three of those states, and they are on top of the situation, getting ready to defend the men who killed them. Also, some more good news: Two advised me that the ten cars have been purchased and are on site, hooked up, full of gas, and ready to go."

"Eight, this is turning out to be a great day. Get on those beds and then get back on the phones and round up another hundred child molesters for each site. When this is done, please get back to me."

Later on that day, the General's phone, rings again.

"Good afternoon, G. Eight here again. G, I cannot believe how smooth this is going. I got in touch with the members who donated the beds, and that's a done deal. We can even get the nightstands from them. There were two members who supplied them, and both of them said the same thing, that it would take two days for them to get the beds and nightstands and that the day they get them, we could pick them up and bring them to the sites. They also said we would need to pay cash for them. I told them no problem. I, along with Two, have already assigned drivers to pick them up when they get in, and to deliver them to their respective sites. Also, Two and I got the other hundred child molesters for each location, so G, as soon as we get the beds in place, we will be ready to roll."

"Great. Now I need to sit down and double-check everything, and set a date. Thanks for the info. Talk to you later."

Four days later, Eight calls the General again. "Good morning, G. By now you should know who this is."

"Yes, I do."

"Well, G, today is the day we have all been working toward. I just got off the phone with Two, and he told me that they are all ready to go; all of the beds and nightstands, are in place, and they have 300 child molesters all ready to go. I am happy to say that I am also in the same position and also have my 300 child molesters ready to go, so all we need now is for you to set a date."

"Okay, Eight, while you guys were working on that, I was busy over here double-checking my plan. First of all, as far as the date goes, today is the seventh. So one date that would work great for me would be the thirteenth, and ironically, that date falls on a Friday. I think that Friday the thirteenth, would be an appropriate and befitting day to pull this off, but to do this on the thirteenth, we need to pick them up on the twelfth, because when we start those cars up, it will be after midnight, and that will make it Friday the thirteenth. This is the way it's going to go down. First off, each of you need to acquire a bus with a driver. Then I want you guys to work on this together. I want each of you to set up enough pickups as necessary, just as long as you get all 300 of them there. Set the time for each pickup two hours apart. That will stagger their arrival and give the workers at each site time to welcome them and inspect their belongings, to check for items that are banned. A good place for them to meet at would be in a corner of a large parking lot, like in a shopping center, and what would be a great idea would be to give yourself time to pat all of them down before they get on the bus, and then again when they get there. Please call Two and tell him to do the same. We want to make sure that no one ties to sneak anything on board that they could communicate with."

"You got it, G."

"Also make sure you tell each one what they can bring, and remind them about the secrecy of this camp. This plan should work out fine, and don't forget to have snacks and drinks to welcome them. Also, both of you need to assign someone to take the water tank and generator off the site in Texas, and just the generator in Virginia."

"G, that has already been set up. That's a done deal."

"Great! So while you guys are busy doing that, I am going to work on the letter that we are going to leave behind."

"Okay, G, you got it. And by the way, we both have the bus and driver already lined up."

"Great!"

On the ninth day of the month, the General gets the call that he has been waiting for.

"Good morning, G. We are all set at our ends. Everything is in place.

We have 600 child molesters scheduled to be picked up two hours apart at a quiet corner in a large parking lot of a major shopping center. Each first pickup is scheduled for 10 AM, second one is at 12 noon, 3rd pick up is for 2 PM, and the last pickup is for 4 PM, so that means that by 5:30 or 6 PM, all of them will be where they are supposed to be. Then we will check them all in, give them a snack and something to drink, and hold a meeting to go over a few things, explain to them that tomorrow will be an early day, with lots of seminars, and inform them about an 11 PM lights out, with no ifs, ands, or buts."

"Sounds good. Then, just to let you know, I will be there at 7:30 AM tomorrow. Please advise everyone else to also get there early, and please advise Two to do the same, just as I will do, on the twelfth. We must check everything out before the first bus gets there."

"Okay, G, no problem. I'll see you at 7:30 AM on the twelfth."

"Bye for now."

On the twelfth day of the month, at 7:30 AM, the General walks into the hotel in Virginia. The place is already abuzz with people double-checking everything. The General decides to take one last look at everything for himself, but first, he calls Eight over to talk to him.

"What's up, G?"

"What I want you to do is tell all of your members, and call Two and let him know also, that today I want you to address the child molesters as guests. You got that?"

"Yes, General, I got it, and I will call Two right now."

The General resumes his inspection. He starts on the top floor, checking every room, every window, all of the vents, making sure that they are not blocked, checking the bathrooms, and the extra beds and nightstands in the hallways. He works his way down to the first floor and checks the kitchen. He makes sure all the signs are up welcoming everyone, checks the meeting room, making sure that there are enough chairs and tables for everyone, and the last thing he checks are the cars parked behind the hotel. He checks all the connections, and even starts each one up for a few seconds to make sure that they are all running.

By now, it is 10:30 AM, and the first bus should be getting there very soon. Right now, the General is nervous. He searches out Eight and asks him if he's heard anything from Texas. Eight informs the General that everything is on scheduled and working out just fine, and that he should try and relax. Eight thinks to himself that he has never seen the General, acting like this, but then thinks that the General has been working on this plan for a long time, so he can understand why he's nervous. If he were in the General's shoes, he would be nervous also.

"Oh, Eight, one last thing, and please notify Two about this also. A thought just popped into my mind as I was checking out the cars out back. I think it would be a good idea to have a car mechanic stationed here, and one in Texas, just in case the cars don't start."

"That's a good idea, General. I'll get right on it."

At 11:15 AM, the first bus pulls in, and the first of the guests walk in the door. The General can hardly control himself. He can't believe that this day has finally arrived, and even though he is seeing it with his own eyes, he can't believe how smooth everything is going. The members are acting very professionally, welcoming all the guests as though they were long lost friends. They are really making the guests feel very comfortable as all of their belongings are checked and then as they are seen to their assigned rooms. Then, as one of the last guests is being checked in, the members searching his bag find a cell phone. The child molester seems truly surprised. "Oh my God!! I can't believe that I forgot that. I'm sorry. I'm really sorry."

The member tells him to hold on, goes over to Eight, and asks him, "What should I do?"

"Well, he looked like he was really surprised, so let him go, but let's keep an eye on him. Make sure that you check his bag good."

The General also saw what happened, so he comes over, excuses himself, and tells the guest, "Tell you what; seeing what just happened, if you still want to attend this camp, would you be willing to submit to a strip search?"

"No problem."

The General tells him, "Please follow me," and he decides to do the strip search himself. After he finishes the strip search and finds nothing, the General lets the molester go to his room.

By now, the second bus has arrived, and everything goes off without a hitch. Everybody is doing what they should. Then the General asks Eight, "Have you heard from Two?"

"Yes, I have. The fourth bus just pulled in, and everything is going great over there."

Just then, the third bus pulls in, and that also goes well. By now, the General has calmed down. Finally, the fourth and final bus arrives, and everything goes very smoothly. Right now, the General is floating on air.

It's now 8:30 PM. The General goes over to Eight. "Now that they are all in, please have someone go around and tell them to come downstairs to the meeting room for a snack and drink, and to attend their first seminar, and let's try to keep them there until about 10PM. This way, they will have about an hour to settle in. The plan is, at 11PM, we will put the lights out. Then, at 4 AM, we will lock the front door, start up the cars, put the letter on the front door, hook up the generator, take it away, and all of us will get the hell out of here. So when you get a chance, call Two and give him all that information."

"Okay."

The General sees some of the workers bringing in the snacks and drinks, and decides to help them out. Ten minutes later, while working, Eight gets a call from Two.

"Hi," says Two. "How is everything going over there?"

"It's going great. All of the guests are already in their rooms, and we are now in the middle of setting up the snacks and drinks for them."

"Oh wow! We are just about to do the same thing. We are just bringing out all the snacks and drinks. So far, everything is going as planned. What I need to know now is, has G made up his mind as to the times everything is going to go down?"

"As a matter of fact, he has. This is the way it's going to go down. At 11 PM, the lights go out. Then, exactly at 4 AM, the front door gets locked. We then hook up our generator and take it away, start up the cars, put the letter on the front door, and then get the hell out of there. The only difference for you is, after you lock the front door and start up the cars, you need to put the letter on the front door and then hook up not only your generator, but also the water tank. You then need to take them away and get the hell out of there."

"Eight, can I ask you a question?"

"Sure."

"Tell me, are you nervous or having second thoughts?"

"I was nervous yesterday, but you know what? All I need to do is think about what these freaks do to our children, and I snap right out of it."

"You know what? You're right. Okay, good luck, and I guess I will talk to you after 4 AM."

"You got it."

At 3AM, the General decides to call Two himself. "Good morning, Two."

"Good morning, G. What's up?"

"Well, I just wanted to check on you myself. How is everything going? Is everything on schedule?"

"Yes, it is, G. We are all set to go at 4 AM. Right now, ninety-five percent of the guests are asleep, and we are just waiting for 4 AM to get here."

"Are the drivers there to take away the water tank and generator?"

"Yes, they are. In fact, they are already hooked up. All we need to do now is disconnect them."

"That's great. Just remember, I want you to call me when you guys are leaving."

"You got it, G."

"Okay, talk to you later."

At 3:55 AM, the General tells Eight, "Let's get this show on the road. Please get all of our members who are still here out of the building. In the meantime, I'm going out back to start up the cars, disconnect the generator, and have the driver take it away. Then, after you give me the all clear that everyone but the guests are out of the building, I will lock the front door, secure the letter to the front door, and then get the hell out of here."

At 4:15 AM, the General gets a call from Two.

"Good morning, G. We are on the road, and everything went great. The water tank and generator are on the way back to Virginia, the cars started up good, all of my members are on their way home, the front door is locked, and the letter is on the door."

"Okay, that's great! If we did everything right and didn't forget anything or leave any DNA behind, there will be no way for the authorities to trace anything back to any of us. The last thing I need to do is to call the police in Texas and Virginia when I get home tomorrow and tell them to go and check things out at the locations. Then it's time to sit back and watch it hit the fan, and hope that all we did was not in vain, and that it will result in getting the laws pertaining to child molesters changed."

The next day, the General calls the Texas police, first speaking to a policeman, then a sergeant, then a lieutenant, and then finally, after convincing them that this call is extremely important, getting the chief of police on the phone. The General asks him if he has a pen and paper, and explains to him again that this is not a joke. "It is very important that you write this address down that I am about to give you."

"I'm listening. Give me the address."

"It is 391 Forest Drive Rd., San Antonio, Texas."

"Okay, I got that, and what exactly am I supposed to find at this address?"

"That, I can't exactly tell you, but I can tell you this: you better bring a lot of body bags, and I mean a lot."

"Okay, wise guy, I hope you realize that I got your phone number, and if this is a joke, I will make sure that you spend a lot of time in jail."

"I understand, Chief, but please do yourself a favor and check that address out." The General then hangs up.

Next, the General calls the police department in Virginia. He goes through the same routine that he did in Texas before he is able to get the police chief on the phone. After many convincing words, he finally gets the chief to agree to write down the address and go out and check it out.

"Okay, what's the address?"

"It is 2133 W. Willow Street, Roanoke, Virginia, and I'm going to tell you the same thing that I told the chief in Texas."

"Texas? What does Texas have to do with this?"

"You'll find out. Anyway, bring a lot of body bags when you go."

"Wait a minute. Who the hell is this?"

"Someone who you will never find. Good bye."

It takes three days before the news hits the airwaves and the papers. They are all reporting the same story, about two mass killings of 300 men at each of two locations, totaling 600 victims. It seems like they were all murdered by the same means, carbon monoxide poisoning, which was administered by hooking up ten automobiles to a single intake that was then pumped into the building, killing all 300 at each location. One of the two mass killings was in Virginia, and the other was in Texas. The authorities said that whoever was responsible for this evidently constructed or renovated these buildings for the sole purpose of killing these men. It seemed like there was only one way out, by the front door, and that was bolted and locked shut. These men had absolutely no means of escape. The organization that took responsible for this action is called The Child Safety In America Foundation. They left a letter on the front door explaining why they did this. It was to have the laws pertaining to child molesters changed. They claim that the current laws on the books are insufficient and outdated for the acts that child molesters commit. Also, they claim that child molesters are often just given just a slap on the wrist by liberal, bleeding-heart judges, or given just a short jail term and then released to go their merry way and be free to molest additional children. It has been reported by numerous authorities that these men who are committing these acts against children are nothing more than broken machines, and must be dealt with accordingly. There are even stories of child molesters themselves saying that they cannot be helped, nor can they stop themselves from committing these horrific acts on children. According to the authorities, the letter also said that if nothing is done to change the laws to keep these monsters off the streets, and done within a reasonable amount of time, then they have bigger and better plans already in the works to help the lawmakers change their minds. Also, if the authorities do decide to change the laws, it must be the same for the entire country, not just the individual states. The authorities in Texas and Virginia are asking for anyone with any information on these acts to please contact them right now. The authorities in both states are saying that right now, there is a full-scale investigation going on at both locations. The FBI is also looking into this to see if any federal laws were broken.

Other people are also looking at the news, and along with some very important people is Judge Tunis, who is outraged by what he is seeing and hearing. "SON OF A BITCH!!! This time, they've gone too far! These people are fucking crazy. This must end. This time, I'm going to stop them for good." He picks up his phone and puts in a call to his friend, the D.A. in Washington, D.C., Larry Rockwood.

"Mr., Rockwood's office. May I ask who is calling?"

"Yes, good morning. This is Judge Tunis. Is Mr. Rockwood in? And if he is, please tell him that I need to speak with him and that it's urgent."

"I'm sorry, Judge, but Mr. Rockwood is in court. If you want, I can have him return your call as soon as he gets back."

"That would be fine. Just tell him that I am at home, waiting for his call."

"Okay, I will do that, Judge."

"Thank you. Bye."

The judge is now in combat mode. He is pacing the floor and racking his brain, trying to figure out just what he can do to stop the people who were responsible for this horrific and sick act. He just keeps looking at the clock, which, to him, has not moved in the past hour, trying to figure out who it could be who did this. He thinks, *Is it the same people? Does John have anything to do with this? Is there a new movement going on here?* Then he thinks to himself, *I need a drink. I need something to calm me down*, so he pours himself a large glass of Scotch whiskey and downs it all in one shot. Then, while choking, he thinks to himself, *What the hell is wrong with me? What am I trying to do, kill myself? I hardly ever drink. Then I go and do something stupid like that.*

While trying to regain control of himself, the phone rings. He picks it up.

"Hello, Judge?"

"Yes. Larry?"

"Yes, Judge. Are you okay?"

"Yeah, I'm okay now. I just drank something too fast."

"Oh, okay. So what can I do for you?"

"Have you seen the news today?"

"Actually, no. I had a very busy morning. So, no, I have not seen the latest news, but I guess you are about to tell me. What is it?"

"Those bastards are at it again. They just killed 600 men."

"And just who would these bastards be?"

"Don't you remember? John, the website, The Club, the guy we put in jail for killing child molesters?"

"Oh, that John. Yes, I do remember, but he and his cohorts are currently locked up, aren't they? So how can you claim that they committed this crime? What you are telling me is that you think that they are now responsible for killing 600 men in cold blood, is that what you are telling me?"

"Yes, that is exactly what I'm telling you, and in my heart, I know they did it, and it's all over the news."

"Oh my God! Where and when did this happen?"

"It happened about three days ago."

"Judge, tell you what. Let me check into it and get back to you."

"Larry. Please see what you can do."

"Okay, but there has to be more to this story. If what you're telling me is true, that you think that the same group is responsible for killing these men, then we've got a much bigger problem than we thought we did. Okay, like I said, let me check into it and get back to you."

"Thanks. Bye."

The judge has nothing to do to keep himself busy while waiting for Larry to call him back. He tries reading a book, but can't get into it. He takes out an old puzzle from his closet, but that doesn't work either. As a last resort, he tries going to the movies, which he hasn't done for at least twenty years, but that doesn't work either.

By the third day, he is climbing the walls. Finally, he decides to take the bull by the horns and calls Larry.

"Good morning. Mr. Rockwood's office."

"Good morning. This is Judge Tunis. Is Mr. Rockwood in?"

"Yes, he is, Judge. Just a minute, and I will get him on the line for you."

"Judge, good morning. I had plans to call you later on today."

"Well, sorry, Larry, but I could not wait anymore. These people have been a thorn, in my side for a while now. It's driving me absolutely crazy, and I want to put an end to it. So, did you find out anything yet?"

"As a matter of fact, I did. I spoke to the chief of police in both cities, and both of them said the same thing. Evidently, whoever was responsible for this act were professionals. They did not leave one scrap of evidence behind. The police combed the area at both locations and came up with nothing, not one single thing, and the organization that left the letter does not exist. On top of that, the two sites involved were supposedly donated legally. So, right now, the ones who donated the sites can't be held responsible, but the police in both states are looking into that more closely. Hopefully, they will come up with something, and as soon as I hear anything, I will get back to you."

"I don't understand. How can someone do this and not leave one shred of evidence behind?"

"Right now, the only thing the police have to go on at both sites are the cars, but all of them were bought with open titles, and the sellers don't remember who they sold the cars to."

"I guess I'm just going to have to sit back and wait for something to break. Thanks anyway."

"Talk to you later."

"Bye."

Two weeks pass, and the judge is relentless in his endeavors to get some information on the events in Texas and Virginia, but all his efforts are in vain. The police are stumped. They are at a dead end, with no leads. They have even offered a $10,000 reward for any information, but there are no takers.

In the meantime, Eight puts a call in to the General. "Good afternoon, G. This is Eight."

"Good afternoon. What's up?"

"Not much. I just had an idea, and I wanted to run it by you."

"Okay, run it by me."

"Well, I was thinking that we did a pretty good job, and so far, nothing has been traced back to us. The only thing we have left that could connect us to anything is our phones, so I thought it might be time to have everyone turn in their old phones and issue new ones, just in case we overlooked something."

"You know what? That's a good idea. Get on it right away. I will destroy mine. Have everyone else bring them to you, and you personally make sure you destroy every single one at the same time you hand out new ones. But don't forget to call Two and have him do the same. In the meantime, I don't want anyone calling anybody for at least six months unless it's an absolute emergency. Is that understood?"

"You got it, G. I'll talk to you in six months. Bye for now."

Two weeks go by, and Judge Tunis is still having a hard time accepting the fact that the people responsible for the two mass killings are getting away with it. Then, to add insult to injury, he hears on the news that two brothers in Texas were found not guilty in the killings of several child molesters. Hearing this puts him just about at the end of his wits. Then, out of the blue, his phone starts ringing. He thinks, *Thank God, something to take my mind off of things*. He answers.

"Hello, Judge?"

"Yes."

"This is Larry."

"Hi, Larry. I hope you have good news, because I'm going out of my mind."

"Well, I don't know if you would call it good news, but it's an idea that one of the Senators proposed to me, and I thought that you would like to hear this."

"Okay, so what is it?"

"First, as you know, the killings in Texas and Virginia have led the investigators in those two cases to dead ends, with no leads, not even with a reward that was upped to $50,000. So, this is the idea: we want to invite the phony charity, The Child Safety In America Foundation, that got the two sites as donations, to come forward and talk to us face to face and let us know just what kind of changes they want to see with the laws pertaining to child molesters. Even though the laws are different in each state, maybe, with a little pressure from the federal government, some of the states might consider changing some of their laws. This way, maybe, they might slip up, and we could get them or get some evidence."

"You know what? That may not be a bad idea."

"Well, I'm glad you think so, because we are working on it. I thought that you would like to know about it, and I'll keep you posted."

"Okay, Larry, thanks for the call. You made my day. I will finally be able to get a good night's sleep."

"Great. Bye."

The Washington D.A., believing that it was locals who committed the two crimes, thinks that it would work out better if the D.A.s in Texas and Virginia put ads in their own local papers, rather than him doing it from Washington, so he puts a call into both. He explains to them his plan about putting an ad in the local papers, on the local radio stations, and on national radio, asking for the ones responsible for the killings to please come forward and set up a meeting with their local D.A., and sit down and have a face-to-face meeting. At the meeting, the killers could detail exactly what changes in the law that they are looking to make, and the D.A.s could explain to them that if the changes are not unreasonable, something might be done to help them out and to stop all of the killings. Both of the D.A.s think that it's a great idea. Right now, they are both at dead ends, so any ideas that might give them some help are better than no ideas at all. They both agree and say that they will get on it ASAP.

"Okay, that's great. Just do me one favor. If anything happens, please get back to me and let me know what's going on."

"You got it. Bye for now." With that, the two D.A.s set it up for the next morning.

The next morning, the news is all over the local newspapers and radio stations in Texas and Virginia. It's also on TV nationally.

One person who sees it is the General. While checking out the news on his TV, he thinks to himself, *That may not be a bad idea, but I need to sit down and think this through so that I don't waste a good situation.*

That night, as the General sits at his desk, trying to put some kind of a plan together, he gets a call from Eight and Two telling him of the news. He explains to them that he has, in fact, seen the news on TV and was just about to sit down and devise some kind of a plan that would help their cause.

The General decides that because John is already in prison and they can do no more to him, the best plan would be to suggest to the D.A.s that they go and talk to John, seeing that all of this was started by him.

The next morning, the General, using his disposable and untraceable phone, puts a call into the D.A.s office in Texas and explains to him that he was the one who is responsible for the two mass killings that got rid of a lot of child molesters, and that he and his cohorts were simply picking up where John Harrison left off, who is currently incarcerated in a New York prison. "We did this because we believe that what he was doing was the most righteous thing to do, and we will support him until the end, whatever that end may entail. So, if you want to know what changes John wants, I suggest that you visit him in prison and speak to him face to face, and whatever his wishes are, we will abide by them. In plain English, if he wants us to cease what we are doing, we will completely oblige him." With that, the General hangs up.

As soon as the General hangs up, the D.A. tries to put a trace on the call, but to no avail. Slamming the phone down in frustration, after calming down, he calls the D.A. in Virginia and explains to him what transpired and that the phone the General was using was untraceable. He bemoans, "After all that, we are right back where we started, in a dead end alley. I guess I'll call the D.A. in Washington and fill him in on what just happened, and let him take it from there."

"Good idea. Talk to you later."

"Okay, bye."

The Texas D.A. calls the Washington D.A. and explains everything to him. "So what do you think we should do?"

Larry says, "What we should do is exactly what the phone caller suggested. We do go and talk to this John Harrison, face to face, and hear what his story is. At least it's some kind of a lead. It's a hell of a lot more than we had prior to this."

"Okay, that sounds good, but who's going to be the one to go visit him?"

"You know what? I will go visit him and hear what he has to say, and then I'll get back to you."

"Okay, talk to you later."

"Bye."

Larry does some checking to find out what New York prison John Harrison is in. Armed with that information, he is on a plane the next day, heading toward New York to visit with John. Once there, he meets up with the warden and explains who he is and what he is doing there. The warden sets him up in a private meeting room within the prison.

While this is going on, John is advised that he has a visitor. He is confused, because he has not made any plans to see anyone, nor did he expect any visitors, but being inquisitive, John agrees to the visit. John is then led to the private meeting room. As John walks in, Larry stands up and extends his hand. John, with a confused look on his face, extends his hand, and both men shake. Larry tells John to please have a seat, and he begins to explain who he is and what he is doing there.

As Larry is speaking, John is just sitting there with a befuddled look on his face. He tells Larry, "Hold on there. Can you repeat what you just said? I want to make sure that I heard you correctly."

Larry repeats himself and then explains further, "Well, your people, your followers, the ones who, according to them, will do whatever you ask them to do, told us that they were only picking up your crusade where you left off. So seeing that you started this whole thing, they are now throwing it back into your lap. Now you have a chance to end it. Now is your big chance. Explain to me what changes you would like to see, as far as the prosecution of child molesters go. Tell me, and I will write them down and present them to the proper authorities, and maybe we can get this whole mess resolved to your satisfaction. What do you think? Do you want to take advantage of this meeting and explain to me what changes you would like to see in the law?"

John just sits there, staring at Larry. Finally, he says, "Pardon my expression, but you just dumped a whole bunch of shit on me that I was not expecting. Yes, of course I want to take advantage of this meeting, but I need to think about it, and I really believe that I should speak to my attorney before I go any further, so if it's all right with you, the next thing I would like to do is speak to my attorney and then have him get back to you."

"Well, John, I'm afraid that I will not be able to do that. This is a one-shot deal, take it or leave it."

"You know what? This is not my first rodeo, and I do not trust you guys, so tell you what. I am going to leave it. If you are not willing to meet with me after I speak to my attorney, then I don't want any part of this deal."

Larry, easing back a little, says, "Okay, wait a minute. Maybe there is something I can do. I'll make a couple of calls and will try to set up another meeting after you speak to your attorney and he calls me back."

"Oh! Now you can do it. See, that's what I mean about you guys. You are all full of shit."

"No, we are not. We just try our best to get bad situations resolved. I'm sorry you feel that way. In any event, we could probably go on and on about this, but let's end on a good note. You speak to your attorney, and I will wait for his call and then take it from there."

"Okay, that sounds good." Both men shake on it, and then John adds, "Before you leave, can you see to it that I can make a call?"

"Yes, I will speak to the warden."

"Good."

John is then escorted back to his cell. Before Larry leaves the prison, he asks to speak to warden and asks him if he could please give John the opportunity to use the phone. The warden agrees to let John make a phone call.

One hour later, a guard comes to John's cell. "Hi, John. The warden said that you could make a phone call, so please come with me." The guard escorts John to an area where there is a bank of phones. John picks one of the phones and proceeds to dial his attorney, Mike Santino.

"Good morning. Mr. Santino's office."

"Hi and good morning. This is John Harrison. Is Mike there? This is very important."

"Just a moment. I will see if he is in."

Mike picks up the phone. "John! What's the good word? It's not very often you call me. What can I do for you?"

"I need to see you. I can't explain over the phone, but it's very important that you come and visit me."

"And how soon would you want me to come and visit you?"

"How about yesterday?"

"I get the picture, John. I am busy as hell tomorrow, but for you, I will change my plans and come and visit you."

"That's great, Mike. I will see you tomorrow."

"Good."

The next morning, bright and early, Mike is at the prison in a special room just for prisoners and their lawyers to meet. After waiting about ten minutes, a guard finally escorts John into the room, shackles him to the table, and leaves the room."

"John, I can't wait for you to tell me what was so important that you have to see me as soon as possible."

John begins to explain: "Well, yesterday, a guard comes into my cell and informs me that I have a visitor. That took me by surprise, due to the fact that I was not waiting for or expecting anyone. First off, they took me to a special meeting room, almost like this one. That was also a surprise to me, because these rooms are only used for attorney and prisoner meetings. Anyway, I walk into the room, and this guy that I have never seen before stands up and puts his hand out to shake. Being a gentleman, I did likewise. After we shook, he asked me to take his seat. I sat down, and then he hit me with why he was there. I knew something was going down, but never in my life did I think it would get this kind of result. I imagined it all different. So, anyway, this is the gist of it. This guy introduces himself as the Washington, D.C., D.A., Larry Rockwood. First thing that goes through my mind is, 'What the hell does the D.A. from Washington, D.C., want with me?' But he then proceeds to explain everything to me."

John explains the whole thing to Mike, who says, "Wow! This is what you were looking for all along. It's what you been waiting for. Your day may have finally arrived.

"Yes, I know that, Mike, but what I need now is some advice from you."

"Okay, John, listen up. First of all, you have to deny any knowledge of what happened. You did not plan this or approve of this, but if whoever did it is saying that they will follow whatever instructions you give them, and if this D.A. really wants to do something, you tell him that if he really wants to stop what's going on, at the this point, the only person that you would be willing to talk to – and seeing that you want the laws changed to be national – would be to speak to a United States Senator, because if anybody could change a law, he would be the one to get the ball rolling. And by the way, it would be a good idea this time, seeing that you are in a good bargaining position, to include the release of you, Barney, and Nick. If not a full release or pardon, then at least let out on time served. So, John, that would be my advice to you, and you're only going to get one chance at this, so stick to your guns. And by all means, let me know what happens."

"Okay, Mike. Just one more surprise for you."

"And what would that be?"

"The surprise is that I told him you would be calling him."

"Do you have his number?"

"Yes, I do. I brought it with me. Here it is. So now it would be appropriate for me to say to you, let me know how you make out."

"Okay, John. I will let you know."

As soon as Mike gets back to his office, he calls the Washington D.A.

"Hello?"

"Hello, is this Larry Rockwood?"

"Yes, it is. Who is this?"

"My name is Mike Santino. I am John Harrison's lawyer. You went to see him yesterday. Well, he told me what you said and offered him, so from now on, anyone involved in this situation with him must talk to me first."

"I can do that. So, what is he offering? What changes is he looking for?"

"Well, he is offering you nothing personally. What I'm offering you is a message to take back with you, and that message is that John will only talk to a Senator, through me. Nothing against you personally, but that's the message. So, get in touch with a Senator that you know, or one who would be willing to get involved in this, and give him my phone number, and that's it. That's all I have to say to you today."

"Not so fast, Mr. Lawyer! You're not making any demands! I am making the demands! So you will talk to me, and only me, understand?"

"Okay, Mr. D.A. It's going to sound like I'm hanging up on you now, but in reality, I'm just telling you to go and fuck yourself, and unless you get a Senator involved in this, there will be no talking. Have good day." Mike hangs up on him.

Larry, who is now totally pissed off and disgusted, calls Judge Tunis. "Good afternoon, Judge. Guess what just happened to me."

"Larry, right now I'm not in the mood for games. What happened?"

"Well, you know about how I left off with John Harrison, that he wanted his lawyer to represent him from now on."

"Yes, I remember. So what's new?"

"What's new is that his lawyer just called me, and to cut to the chase, he basically told me to go fuck myself and that John would not speak to anyone but a Senator, because a Senator has a lot more clout as far as getting a law changed than a D.A."

"Well, Larry, I feel bad for you, but we cannot let personal feelings get in the way, so what I would suggest to you is to swallow your pride and speak to that Senator you know, and see if he would be willing to go and talk to John. If not, get back to me, and I will see if I can do something on my end."

"Okay, Judge."

"Bye, Larry. Just keep me advised."

While all of this is going on, somehow, the news media find out about what's going on with the two mass killings, and they are having a field day with the story. They are all reporting basically the same thing, that the original website, TheClub.com has never gone away, but instead has gone underground, and that authorities believe that The Club's followers are responsible for the two mass killings in Texas and Virginia. The current story now is about the D.A.s in both states being up a blind alley, with absolutely no leads, and now attempting to convince John Harrison, who is currently incarcerated and who was the original founder of The Club, to get his followers to cease and desist with the killings. But instead of John's followers cutting back, this story seems to have lit a fire under their butts, and is rallying them further into John's quest, and they've been going out and killing more and more child molesters. Since the story broke, there has been eleven killings across the nation, and now there seems to be an outcry by the citizens for government intervention. The people are saying that something must be done about this, that the government cannot just stand by any longer and just sit and watch as these people are being killed and their killers are getting away with it.

In the meantime, Larry puts a call into a friend of his, Senator Sam Adams, to see if he can set up an appointment.

"Good morning, Senator Adams's office."

"Good morning. This is Larry Rockwood, Washington D.A. Is this Senator in?"

"Yes, he is. May I ask what this is in reference to?"

"Actually, no. Just tell him who is calling, and that it's extremely important that I speak to him."

"Okay, Mr. Rockwood, please hold, and I will check whether or not he will speak to you."

Soon after, the Senator is on the line. "Larry! How the hell are you?"

"Fine, Senator. I'm calling to set up a meeting with you on something that I feel is extremely important."

"Well, Larry, if you feel that you want to meet up with me on something that is extremely important, how can I refuse you? When would you want to meet?"

"How about this afternoon, or, if not, tomorrow morning?"

"Well, Larry, today I'm really busy, and it would be impossible to meet, so let's make it for tomorrow morning at 10 AM, my office. I will clear my calendar. Is that okay with you?"

"Absolutely. I'll see you tomorrow morning at 10 AM sharp."

"Okay, thanks. Bye."

The next day, at 10 AM sharp, Larry is in the Senator's office.

"Good morning, Larry." Both men shake hands, and the Senator asks Larry to please have a seat. "So, Larry, what is it that has you all excited?"

"Do you remember a few years back, that whole episode we had with a website called The Club, where they were advocating going out and killing child molesters, and saying that the killers would get away with it, even if they got caught and had a trial?"

"As a matter of fact, yes, I do remember that."

"Well, I'm sure that you've been reading the papers lately, and I'm sure that you've read about the two mass killings in Texas and Virginia."

"Yes, I have."

"And I'm sure that you know that whoever did it left a letter at each site."

"Yes, I do. Okay, Larry, let me stop you right there. I know all there is to know about the two killings. What I'm hoping for now is that you have something new to add, because this has become a serious problem."

"That's what I'm here for. We had no leads in the case, and my friend Judge Tunis, for some reason, seems to have a personal vendetta against these people and has been on my case to do something for what seems like forever. So I came up with this idea about putting an ad in the local media for whoever did this to come and meet face to face and see if we could resolve the situation in a satisfactory way for both sides."

"So what happened?"

"Last week, the Texas D.A. got a call, but it wasn't to meet in person, but rather some instructions on what to do next. He was told to go and talk to John Harrison. You know who he is, right?"

"Yes, I do."

"Well, the person on the phone said that they were merely picking up where John Harrison left off, so they suggested that we go and talk to him, and they said that whatever John wanted them to do, they would respect his wishes one hundred percent. The caller also said that if no one goes and talks to John, then, like the letter said, they have bigger and better plans already worked out that would kill a lot more child molesters, much, much, more. So last week, I went to speak with John. When I first walked into the room, John seemed like he was happy to see me. We shook hands, I introduced myself, and we sat down. John told me that he was extremely happy to see me there, and he proceeded to tell me that this meeting has been a long time coming. I said, 'Okay, I can understand that, so I'm here today, and I am anxious to hear your story, and hopefully, there's something I can do for you.' He said, 'I hope so, but now that you are actually here, I'm having second thoughts about talking to you without my attorney here.' I tried to assure him that this was just an informal meeting, just to get the bare facts of what he was looking for, and I said, 'You tell me.' 'Okay,' he said, 'the bare facts are that I want the laws pertaining to child molesters that are on the books now to be changed.' I told him, 'Okay, what are the changes you're looking for? Tell me, and I will write them down and bring them to Washington and hopefully do something for you.' All of a sudden, John says, 'Excuse me. Like I said, I know you traveled a long distance to get here, and I appreciate it, but I just got this overwhelming feeling that I should have my attorney here. Like I said, this was a long time coming, but I feel a few more days could not hurt, so at this point, I would like to end this meeting until such time that my attorney can be present.' I said, 'Are you aware that I came all way from Washington, D.C., and you were happy that I was here, so I don't understand why all of a sudden you want your attorney here.' 'I can't explain it,' he said. 'I just got this feeling that my attorney should be here, and that's what I want, and I would appreciate it if you would respect my wishes, and if you really are sincere that you want to help me, then please respect my wishes. Give me your phone number, and I will have my attorney get in touch with you.' So I gave him my phone number and headed back to Washington. The next morning, I get a call from John's attorney. As I tried to set up an appointment with John and his attorney, his attorney rudely cut me off, saying, 'Hold on, Mr. D.A., not to disrespect you, but at this point, I advise John to speak to no one but a Senator or higher. I said to him, 'No, you hold on, Mr. Lawyer. I came all the way from Washington, D.C., to speak to John, and now you're blowing me off. That's not how it works. I came here to get John's demands and return to Washington with them,' and then his attorney politely told me to go fuck myself, saying that the only thing that I was going back with was with a message for any Senator who would be willing to meet up with John and him. Then he rudely hung up on me. So that's what I'm doing here today, trying to convince you to meet up with John."

"Okay, Larry, let me stop you there. As a matter of fact, the last couple of days, I have been talking to my fellow Senators, and apparently, this has gotten to be a big deal. They are all aware of what is going on, because they have gotten a lot of letters from their constituents asking them to do something about all the killings I myself have gotten twenty letters from my constituents asking me to do something about it. They feel that it's time that the government stepped in and got involved and did something to put a stop to the killings, so we are all well aware of the situation. And, as I said, so are our constituents. They want something done yesterday. My fellow Senators have already started doing something about it. We were actually thinking of putting a Senate investigations committee together to check into it. So if what you are asking me for is to meet up with John, the answer would be yes. Just give me his attorney's phone number, and I will have my secretary set up the meeting, and I will take it from there, because at this point, this seems to be the only avenue we have."

"I've got his phone number right here. Look, Senator, I know that you're busy, but please try to keep me in the loop."

"You got it, Larry."

"Okay, thanks.

"Just give me a few days to get this meeting lined up, and I will get back to you with what progress I've made."

The next morning, the Senator's secretary calls Mike's office.

"Good morning. Mr. Santino's office. Can I help you?"

"Yes, good morning. This is Senator Adams's office. If Mr. Santino is in, the Senator would like to speak to him."

"Please hold on, and I will check to see if Mr. Santino is in." Mike's secretary says to him, "Mr. Santino, there is a Senator Adams on the phone, who would like to speak with you."

"Okay." Mike picks up the line, and his secretary says, "Senator, Mr. Santino will speak with you."

"Mr. Santino?"

"Yes."

"Senator Adams here."

"Yes, Senator, how are you, and what can I do for you?"

"Well, the long and short of it is, the D.A. from Washington, D.C., paid me a visit yesterday. It seems that he went to New York to speak to your client, Mr. John Harrison, who is currently serving time for a serious crime and who seems to be currently involved in the latest escapades on child molesters that seem to be increasing every day. It is also my understanding that in the middle of the interview, your client decided to lawyer up. I also understand that according to your client's wishes, Mr. Rockwood got in touch with you, and also that you were extremely rude to him. To put it in his own words, you told him to go and fuck himself."

"Senator, as a matter of fact, I did tell him that exactly. I spoke to him that way only because he came across with an attitude to me, and Senator, I don't like people with attitudes. Attitudes serve no purpose. All they do is get in the way and block progress. I just spoke to him according to what his attitude dictated to me. I just informed him that my client would speak to no one but a Senator, and he sort of took offense to that and came back at me with severe attitude, so hence, my attitude back at him. I told him once more that my client would speak to no one but a Senator, and then he hung up the phone."

"Okay, Mr. Santino, let's move on and get past this. I told the D.A. that I would be more than happy to go visit your client and see what he has to say. In fact, if you don't mind, I would like to bring a stenographer so that if this goes anywhere, it will all be on record."

"Senator, I have no problem with that. In fact, I was going to suggest a stenographer."

"Okay, then all we have to do is set a day and time."

"Senator, I know that you are a busy man, and I have no problem with whatever time is good for you."

"Good, then I will have my secretary get in touch with your secretary and set up the meeting."

"Okay, Senator, when the meeting is set up, I will also call the prison so that we can get a nice, private room."

"Sounds good to me, Mr. Santino."

"Okay, then, Senator, I will see you when our secretaries set it up."

"Okay. Bye for now."

On Tuesday morning, Mike's secretary informs him that the meeting with the Senator and John is set for this Thursday, two days from today, at 10 AM. Mike says, "Okay thank you."

Mike calls the prison and informs them about the Senator's visit and requests a private room. Two days later, at 10 AM sharp, Mike is at the prison. They escort him to the warden's office, Mike is surprised to see that the Senator is already there, along with the stenographer. The Senator gets up to greet Mike, and both men shake hands. As the Senator asks Mike to please take a seat, the warden picks up his phone and asks to have the prisoner sent to his office.

While waiting for John to get to warden's office, the Senator says to Mike, "I hope we can really solve this today, because the killings are getting out of hand."

"I agree with you, Senator."

With that, a guard escorts John into the warden's office, and shackles him to a heavy chair that looks like it's bolted down to the floor. The wardens then stands, excuses himself from the room, and says, "I guess you guys can take it from here. There is a guard outside of the door. Just let him know when you're done, and he will escort the prisoner back to his cell."

The Senator speaks first: Mr. Santino, Mr. Harrison, are you guys all set and comfortable?"

Mike answers, "Yes, we are."

"Then I guess we can get started, and just for the record, will Mr. Harrison be answering the questions directly to me, or will you be speaking for him?"

"Mr. Harrison can speak directly to you. If I feel he's saying something that can harm him, I will stop him."

"Sounds good. So let's get started. Okay, Mr. Harrison, you asked for this meeting, so the floor is yours. Let me hear what your demands are."

John says, "Mr. Senator, as I told the D.A., this meeting has been a long time coming, and I feel that I only have one shot at this, so I want to make sure I do it right. So, here goes. First off, before I let you know the demands, I must tell you what started this whole thing. While on vacation with my wife and children, and while eating at a fast food restaurant, my daughter needed to use the ladies room. When she did not come back after ten minutes, my wife went to check on her and could not find her. My wife and I frantically searched the restaurant, in and out, screaming out her name, 'Wendy, Wendy, Wendy,' all over, inside and outside of the restaurant, to no avail. And to this day…" John pauses, fighting back tears. He stops talking for about thirty seconds.

Mike asks John, "Are you all right?"

John answers, "Yeah, I'm okay. Anyway, since that day, we have never seen our sweet little girl again. Someone called the police, and they started investigating it, questioning everyone in the restaurant, and after viewing the restaurant video tapes, it turns out that a stranger kidnapped her. They spotted the stranger holding my sweet little girl's hand and pulling her away. It turned out that later on, from that video, he was picked up. His name is Jim Tally, and he was brought to trial. And by the way, let me interject one very important thing now. During the trial, it came to light that he was a child molester, that he was out on parole because the prison that he was incarcerated in was overcrowded, so he was let out on time served. Then he claimed that he thought she was lost and wanted to return her to the restaurant, but she told him that she was not lost, so he let her go and just walked away. Because there was no body found…" John again needs to pause, fighting back his emotions. "…her body was never found, and no other evidence found. He was let go due to lack of evidence. When I heard the verdict, I could not control myself. I jumped over the rail and attacked him and threatened to kill him, and because of that, I got a restraining order put on me. Then, a few years later, I decided to return to New York to sort of finish the vacation that was cut short, and one night, while I was out shopping with my wife and son, I spotted Jim and went crazy and attacked him. Some people, seeing what is going on and not knowing the situation, came to Jim's rescue, pulled me off him, and called the police while holding me down. When the police got there and found out that there was a restraining order on me, I got arrested, was tried, and found guilty of violating the restraining order and attempted murder, and got sentenced to five years. Then, while serving my five-year sentence, as fate would have it, my cellmate Tom Reynolds knew who Jim Tally, because while Jim was incarcerated waiting for his trial to start, he made the mistake of confessing his crimes to Tom. And you know how the prisoners feel about child molesters, so Tom beat him up, almost killing him. Luckily for Jim, a guard was nearby and saved his life. While I was in jail, I met up with Tom, who knew a lot about computers, and because of what Jim got away with – and Tom told me about Jim's confession – he felt bad for me, so he decided to help me out. That's when I started the website. And ever since then, I have been on a crusade to rid the world of child molesters, because of the inadequate, lame, antiquated laws, and all of the bleeding-heart judges letting these child molesters out early for idiotic reasons. So now that you have all of the particulars, here are my demands, short and sweet. But just a quick prologue before I start: I want you to know that I have investigated every possible way a child molester can be cured, and there is no way on God's green earth that a child molester can be cured, and that even comes from a child molester's own mouth, so under no circumstances do I want to address that issue here today. So here we go.

"Number one. Whatever changes are made to the laws involving child molesters must be national. I don't want each state having the option to change them.

"Number two. For the first offense of child molestation, if the defendant is found guilty, they get a mandatory twenty-five-years sentence, with no chance of parole, and while committing the act, if the child is severely injured with permanent disabilities or murdered, they get a mandatory death sentence, with no chance of appeal, and the sentence must be carried out within thirty days, without exceptions.

"Number three. Second offense of child molestation, if the defendant is found guilty, they get a mandatory life sentence, with no chance of parole, unless the child is severely injured with permanent disabilities or murdered. In that case, the defendant gets a mandatory death sentence that must be carried out within thirty days, without exceptions.

"Number four. All child molesters are treated this same way, absolutely no exceptions, for any reason.

"Number five. I want to be released from prison, along with my two codefendants, Barney Cicale and Nick Alesi. If not completely exonerated, at least released on early parole or released as time served. This rule, or any of the rules above mentioned, are absolutely and positively not negotiable.

"Well, that's it, Senator, the long and the short of it, and I hope in my heart you take these rules back to Washington and implement them into law. If you do that, then and only then will I tell my followers to cease their actions. If not, then I can't be held responsible for their actions, and a lot of people are going to be getting hurt or killed. That responsibility will rest on you and your cohorts' shoulders alone."

"Well, I must say, Mr. Harrison, that was precise, complete, and eloquently presented, and I am impressed. But I must say this: you are not leaving us much room to move. Usually, when a bill is presented in the Senate, there is always a little wiggle room, but not in your case. It seems like you are steadfast in your resolve with these changes that you are looking for."

"Senator, you are absolutely correct in your evaluation of my demands. I will say it now: for the record, I will not budge one iota on any of my demands. As they say on the streets, it is what it is, and Senator, I am done talking. I have nothing more to say. I will answer any questions you have, though."

"From what you just unloaded on me, I guess I have no questions. Like I said, you left me no wiggle room. So I guess we are done here. I will take these changes you are suggesting back with me and present them to my fellow Senators and see if we can come up with something, But, remember, this changing of a state law into a national law is an extremely tough thing to do. These changes that you are asking for will be almost imposable to do. I just want you to be aware of this, but know this: I promise to go back to Washington and give it my best shot. if I can do anything, I will get in touch with your attorney, Mr. Santino."

"Thank you."

Mike asks the Senator if he could ask the warden to give him a few minutes with John.

"I'm sure that would be ok, but I will talk to the warden anyway."

"Thank you, Senator."

With that, the Senator and his stenographer leave the warden's office. Mike tells John, "I need to ask you a question. Would you consider any changes on any of the demands you made?"

"Absolutely not."

"Okay, that's what I wanted to hear. If the Senator does call me and wants to make any changers, I will not call you."

"Right."

"Okay, then, we are done." Mike opens the door and tells the guards that he is done with John and that they can escort him back to his cell. Mike and John shake hands. "Talk to you later, John."

"Okay, by for now."

"Bye."

When Mike gets back to his office, he decides to call the General and set up a meeting at to advise him as to what has transpired. The General agrees, and the next morning, the two meet at the airport. Rather than rent a plane like they normally do, they decide instead to just sit in the car and talk.

"Okay, Mike, what's going on? Leave nothing out."

"Don't worry. I will explain everything to you." Mike repeats every syllable uttered at the meeting."

"So, Mike, what do we do next?"

"What we do next is wait. We wait for them to get in touch with us."

"Okay, but I'm going to work on a plan to sort of push them a little."

"Okay, you can do that. Otherwise, as soon as I hear something, I will get in touch with you."

The two leave. The General goes home, and Mike heads back to his office.

In the meantime, it's business as usual within the world of child molesters. Across the country, in the following week, there are six children molested. Two of them are found dead, and three child molesters are killed. The news media seems to be jumping all over the news, and now their editorials are calling for something to be done about it.

Back at the General's house, he is busy trying to come up with some kind of a plan that will light a fire under the Senator's ass. He is up most of the night trying to come up with something. All of a sudden, it clicks. The usual expression is, "It was like a light bulb going on in his head," but in this case, it is like a very large nuclear explosion going off inside his head. He realizes that when he was in the service, on active duty, he trained and led men into black ops missions, so he thinks to himself, *Why not set up a black ops mission, enlisting the help of any of the members in The Club. We have thousands of phone numbers. We can call them and see if there are any ex-military men who would be willing to volunteer for a stealth mission to help our cause and rid the nation of convicted child molesters. And who knows, there may be some men already trained in black ops missions.* Now it seems easy. In fifteen minutes, the General puts a plan together in his head, and he then picks up his phone and calls Eight.

"Good afternoon, G."

"Good afternoon, Eight. What I'd like you to do for me is to set up a meeting with all The Club leaders. When you get everything set up, just get back to me with the date and the time. Set it up at your headquarters like we usually do. I will explain everything at the meeting. So, I'll just wait to hear from you."

"You got it, G."

A month goes by with no word from the Senator, but there are two child molester killings and more editorials from the media, who are now clamoring for the government to step in and do something, saying that it's getting out of hand. This is music to John's, Mike's, and the General's ears. The General feels that the pot is starting to simmer, and hopefully, it should not be too long before it begins to boil.

Two days later, on Tuesday morning, the General gets a call from Eight, who informs the General that the meeting he wanted is set up for Friday night at 7PM at his headquarters. The General replies, "Great! I will see you Friday night."

Friday night, at 6 PM, the General is at the headquarters of Eight. At 7 PM sharp, the General heads up front, and as soon as he gets there, the room quiets down. "Ladies and gentlemen, I want to thank everyone for attending tonight. Like all of our meetings, this is an important one. I'm sure that all of you are up to date as to what's going on with the meeting that John had with a Senator in which he explained to the Senator the changes we wanted made as far as the laws pertaining to child molesters are concerned. The Senator brought with him a stenographer, who recorded every single word. But that was six weeks ago, and as of today, we have heard nothing, not one single word, whether or not they are working on something or talking to somebody about it. We've heard absolutely nothing at all. So I devised this plan to light a fire under their asses, and considering what our last operation was, this plan that I put together should not shock anyone. I just feel that even though we warned them that we had bigger and better plans to execute, we really don't, because to try to get away with something like that again would be suicidal. So I devised this other plan. I have with me tonight, the original disks with all of the members' names and phone numbers. Like before, I am going to hand them out to you. Like before, I want you guys to call these numbers, again, just like we did the first time, and try to enlist ex-military men, especially snipers, lots of snipers, because eighty to ninety percent of them will be used as snipers. I would like them to voluntarily join us in this covert mission. The mission will be to get all of these men together and train them in sniper and covert operations. Even if we have to pay some of them or help them with their bills, I will train them, and after training them, we will then travel from city to city, killing as many child molesters that we can, and hopefully getting away with it. Then we'll randomly move to another state and do the same thing there, etc. etc. I will do this until the pot starts boiling, and what I mean by that is that the news media is starting to get on the government's case about these killings, so that would be like the pot simmering. So if we were to turn up the heat, the pot will begin to boil. But it seems our Senators don't give a shit, so by doing this, and getting the news media all stirred up, that should help the Senators give a shit. First, I want to see by a show of hands who is okay with this plan."

Just about everyone raises their hand.

"Okay, and now, by show of hands, who is not okay with this plan."

Three members raise their hands.

"Okay, like in the past, if the three of you want to opt out of this plan, you are welcome to do that, but remember, if you decide to rat us out or stop us in any way, you will be dealt with severely. At this point, I'm going to hand out the CDs and ask you to go back home, hit the phones, and, as usual, get in touch with Eight so that he can collate the information and then pass it on to me. Any questions?"

One member raises his hand. "What about us? If we wanted to personally volunteer, would we be able to do that?"

"Absolutely. So long as you have someone at your headquarters who can take over your duties. Any other questions?"

No hands are raised.

"Okay. then it's a done deal. Good night everyone. Again, thank you for attending tonight, and remember, together we will win this battle." With that, the General goes over to Eight. "I'm going to hit the road and head back home, and I'll be waiting for your call."

"Okay, good night, General."

"Good night, Eight."

Two weeks later, the General gets a call from Eight.

"Hello, G?"

"Yes."

"Good afternoon, G. Well, I got some good news for you. We have finished the list, and I think you're going to be very surprised by the results. We've got about 400 ex-military men who are willing to take you up on your offer of getting involved in stealth fighting. In fact, there are sixty of them who were actually part of black ops units, and about twenty of them are instructors in covert warfare. They said that they would be more than happy to help you train the rest of the men, and one of them said that he has a 500-acre ranch that you could train on. None of them want any kind of monetary help, and all but a handful said that they could start any time you're ready."

"Oh my God! That's great news. There's a couple of things I have to check on back here, and then I will get back to you. In the meantime, have these men on standby."

"You got it, G. Oh, and by the way, a few of them said that they may have been on a mission or two with you."

"You know what? That could very well be, and that would be very interesting. Anyway, I will get back to you, Eight."

"Okay."

The General calls Mike.

"Mr. Santino's law office. May I help you?"

"Yes, you may. Can I please speak to Mike?"

"May I ask who is calling?"

"Just tell him it's G."

"Okay, Mr. G. Please hold on."

Moments later, Mike is on the line. "General, what can I do for you?"

"Well, I hope there is something that you can do for me."

"And what would that be?"

"It would be, to tell me that you heard from our Senator friend."

"Sorry, General. I have heard absolutely nothing, not a single word."

"Okay, that's what I thought you would say. Well, I don't want to talk on the phone too much, even though my phone is untraceable. Can we meet up at our usual meeting place, say tomorrow morning, at the same time?"

"G, you're killing me. John is my personal friend, and I really want to help him, but please keep in mind that I have a practice to run."

"I do, Mike, but you know that I would not be asking you unless it was very important."

"Okay, G. I will see you tomorrow."

"Good, see you then."

The next morning, Mike gets to the airport first. Ten minutes later, the General shows up, parks his car, and walks over to Mike's car. He gets in and says, "So, how are you doing?"

"I'm doing fine, General. So what's this all about?"

"Well, like I said, it's about lighting a fire under that Senator's ass."

"Okay, and just how do you plan on doing that?"

"Very simple. I will make it short and sweet. First off, I already started this, because I knew that the Senator would not get back to us, so I put together this plan. Do you remember when we left the letters on the doors in Texas and Virginia that threatened the lawmakers that if something was not done, we had bigger and better plans already worked out to implement? Well, as you know, we did not have any other plans, so I am going to get an army of snipers and black ops people, and I already have about 400 of them lined up. I will train them, and then we'll go from state to state, killing child molesters. Plus, we'll put in some fake phone calls into the newspapers, pushing them to get on the government's case about all the killings. Then I think that the Senators may do something."

Mike just sits there, staring at the General, not saying a word. Finally, after what seems like eternity, he says, "You know what, General? I really think that there is something wrong with you. What you're talking about is like starting a war. Do you seriously think that you can get away with this?"

"Yes, I do. I did things like this many times when I was in the service. I led many covert missions that always worked, one hundred percent. I never lost one single soldier on any of my missions, and that was on the front lines, so doing this should be a walk in the park. Out of courtesy, I figured I'd fill you in as to what I was planning on doing, because I'm doing this to the push the Senators into doing something, and you are the one they will be calling. So, I thought that you should know what's going on, even though you're not involved directly in it."

"Well, okay, General. I'm glad you decided to fill me in. By the way, does John know anything about this?"

"No, but if he approved of our last two missions, I'm sure he would approve of this one. But if you want to go visit him and fill him in, I would feel much better doing this with his blessings. But that's neither here nor there; I am doing this for the cause that John started, and I always finish what I start. I started this for John, and I intend to finish this or die trying."

"General, at this point, all I can say is I wish you luck, and I don't know if it's appropriate, but Godspeed also."

With that, the General gets out of the car, goes to his car, and drives back home, while Mike returns to his office.

As soon as the general gets home, he calls Eight.

"Hello."

"Good morning, Eight."

"Good morning, G. What's up?"

"What's up is, do you remember what our last conversation was about?"

"Yes, I do, G."

"Okay, then what I'd like you to do is get the ball rolling. I still have some money left, so what I'd like you to do is to get in touch with all those volunteers. You said there were about 400."

"Yes, that's correct, G."

"Okay, get in touch with them and then get in touch with the one who has that property where we can train. Make sure that it's still a go, and I know this is a lot of work, but we need to know the sizes of all the volunteers so that we can get them some sort of stealth uniforms. Check with the members and find out if any of them have access to weapons, night vision items, and survival rations and gear. I would like you to get all this set up ASAP."

"Okay, G. I will call the other sites and get right on it, and I'll get back to you when it's all set up."

"Thanks."

Next, the General, decides to sit down and start working on the plan so that he can accomplish these missions in a safe way. He thinks back and searches his mind, and tries to recall the many covert missions that he was on and led, and he thinks that there are many things that he did on those covert missions that he can apply to the missions coming up. He is up till the wee hours of the morning planning this, until he cannot keep his eyes open, and he decides to go to sleep and continue in the morning.

The next morning, the General begins working on his plans again when his phone rings. "Hello."

"Morning, G. This is Mike. I just want to say I'm sorry if I was abrupt with you yesterday. I know your heart is in this cause and that you're trying to do what's best for John, so at this point, I decided not to tell John, because I feel he has enough on his plate right now. So, again, I want to wish you good luck and Godspeed."

"Okay, thank you, Mike."

It's three long weeks before the General hears from Eight.

"General, I got great news for you. I can't believe how everything is just falling into place. We have 405 ex-military men ready to travel at a moment's notice. It's also a little scary that some of them were like little kids going to an amusement park. One of the members is a retired arms dealer, and he said that he could get you any kind of weapon you need, and as many as you want. Also, another member has a military surplus business and can get you everything else you need except weapons. He has uniforms, tents, food, night vision goggles, first aid kits, and everything else you could possibly need for what you want to do."

"Oh wow! I can't believe this phone call. You have definitely made my day. I know I keep saying that, but you never fail me. You always come through. What I need now is two days to get my affairs in order over here. So, let's see… today is Thursday. How about we set this up for Monday at that ranch where we can train. Also, get in touch with the military surplus guy and tell him to put an order together for 410 men for a covert mission. If he is any good, he will know exactly what we will need. We will need everything for several missions, except for guns. Then get in touch with that arms dealer and have him get us 410 sniper rifles."

"Okay, General. I'll get it started."

"Thanks. You know what, Eight? Hold on. I just had a thought. Just put everything on hold, because I want to check something out before we do this. I will get back to you."

"Okay, G."

The General is having second thoughts about the covert missions. He thinks that there might be an easier way to get this accomplished, rather than go out and wreak havoc on the nation. He decides to give the papers a call and maybe stir up some shit with the government. He decides to call his local paper, and he gets the chief editor on the phone. "Good morning. Is this the chief editor?"

"Yes, it is."

"And may I have your name please?"

"Yes, it's Tom."

"Okay, Tom, please listen to me carefully. This is not a hoax call. I am as serious as a heart attack. First off, I'm sure you're familiar with the two mass killings in Texas and Virginia."

"Yes, I am."

"And are you familiar with the notes that were left on the doors at each site?"

"Yes, I am."

"Okay, then I am the one responsible for those two mass killings, and I left letters on the doors explaining to the government that this was done to try and have the laws pertaining to child molesters changed. And by the way, you can check all this out if you don't believe me. But eventually, we had Senator Sam Adams meet up with a man by the name of John Harrison, who is currently incarcerated. The two of them talked, John gave him some changes in the laws that he would like to see made, and the Senator said that he was going back to Washington, D.C., to see what he could do. That was a little over three months ago, and we have not heard one single word. So, to sort of twist their arm, I put together a plan that will wreak havoc on this nation and kill thousands of child molesters. So please believe what I say; this is not bullshit. If you do not believe me and ignore this phone call, whatever follows will be on your head. Just remember that."

"Yes, I understand. Okay, so let's say you convinced me that you are who you say you are. What do you want me to do?"

"I want you to get together with all the news media and try to get that Senator to do something. I am attempting to pursue this course before I wreak havoc on the nation. That's it in a nutshell."

"Well, there has been a lot in the papers about the killings, so even if I didn't believe you, it could not hurt for me to, as you put it, stir up some shit."

"Thank you, Tom. The last thing I would like to tell you is that I would like to see this started within the next three days. Otherwise, my havoc plan goes into action."

"Okay, I got it."

"Thank you. Bye for now."

Two days later, while watching television, the regular programming is interrupted with a special announcement. It's all about the phone call that the editor got from someone claiming to have committed the two mass murders. It also mentions the Senator by the name of Sam Adams, and that over three months ago, he had a meeting with John Harrison, who, according to their records, was the original founder of a website called The

Club. This website encouraged people to go out and kill child molesters in the hope that those who did so would have a very high chance of getting away with it, even if they got caught. The caller also went on to warn of an impending plan of havoc that he intends to put into motion, killing thousands of child molesters, as he put it, but instead, he called the reporting paper in an attempt to get them to get together with the rest of the news media so that they can try to convince the Senators to do something before he sets his plan of havoc into motion. Every newspaper, radio station, and TV station across the nation now has petitions ready to be signed and sent to the U.S. Senate in the hopes that they will do something to stop these killings.

The General checks out a few other channels and sees that they are all on the same page, with editorials demanding that Senator Adams do something. Later on that day, he goes out and purchases several newspapers, and most of them now have headlines about how the people are calling for something to be done and that the government must step in to stop these killings. The General is now feeling good, and he thinks that this may actually work and that he will not have to go the havoc way.

That night, the General gets a call from Mike.

"General, have you seen the papers? Are you watching TV?"

"Yes, I am."

"And do you see what's going on? Somebody called the newspaper."

"Yes, that someone was me."

"I thought that you had that other plan that you were going to put into action."

"I still do, but I gave this one more chance before I started that other plan. So I called the papers and laid it on the line to them, and now, hopefully, it's working. I think, at this point, we just sit back and see what happens."

"General. I'm glad you decided to try something else before implementing that other plan. Okay, then, I guess we'll just sit back like you said and wait. I'll talk to you later."

It has now been more than three months since John had that meeting with the Senator, and he still has not heard a single word from them, but the plan that the General implemented with the newspapers has picked up momentum. Thousands of people are signing the petitions across the nation, and more and more editorials are seen in the papers and heard on radio and TV.

Then, three weeks after the General's plan was put into action, the news blitz and editorials become more and more prevalent, also claiming that they now have almost 3,000,000 signatures on the petitions from all of the news media that they sent to the Senate, addressed to Senator Sam Adams.

Two days later, Mike gets a call from Senator Sam Adams. Mike takes the call. "Good morning, Senator. What can I do for you?"

"Mr. Santino, I will make this short and sweet. First, let me tell you this, and please believe me. I have been seriously lobbying with my fellow Senators about this whole situation, and I need to sit down with you, face to face, and have a serious discussion on this whole thing."

"Okay, Senator. So where and when would you want this face-to-face sit-down meeting?"

"Well, it needs to be as soon as possible, because, as I'm sure you've seen in the news media, the people are up in arms, and as a Senator, it is my duty to keep my constituents happy. The only problem I have is that besides this situation, I have other things to do as a Senator, so I would really appreciate it, and it would make things a lot easier, if you could come to Washington, D.C., and meet with me."

"Well, Senator, if that would speed things along and make it easy for you, I can do that. What about tomorrow afternoon?"

"That sounds good. In fact, we can do lunch, just the two of us."

"Okay, so where do you want me to meet you?"

"I'd prefer it if you came directly to my office, and then we could go to lunch from here."

"Okay, Senator, I will see you tomorrow at 12 noon."

"Thank you very much, Mr. Santino."

"No problem, Senator."

The next morning, bright and early, Mike is at the airport booking a flight to Washington, D.C., and by 11:45 AM, he is in the Senator's office. At 12 noon sharp, the Senator comes out of his office, walks over to Mike, and greets him. "Mr. Santino, good morning."

"Good morning, Senator."

"Mr. Santino, I would like to apologize. I thought that we could go to a nice restaurant and have some lunch while we discussed the situation. Unfortunately, I am so busy today that I cannot afford that luxury. Instead, may I suggest that we go downstairs to the cafeteria. The food is not that bad, but I'm sure we can find a nice quiet table in the corner so that we can talk."

"No problem, Senator. Whatever works for you, I'm fine with."

"Okay, then, let's go."

The two of them walk down two floors to the cafeteria. The Senator escorts Mike to a corner table, and the two of them sit. Mike is a little confused because normally when you go into a cafeteria that's located in a commercial building, you go up to the counter and either get your food or order it, but in this cafeteria, they have waitress service, something that Mike has never seen before. The waitress walks over to a table, greets the two of them, and hands them a menu. The Senator suggests that they order first and then get to down to business. Both of them order just a simple sandwich and a soda.

"Mr. Santino, like I said on the phone, I am honestly lobbying for Mr.

Harrison, but I am having a real hard time convincing my fellow Senators of accepting all of the changes that Mr. Harrison wants. As a lawyer, I'm sure you know and understand that whenever you submit demands for whatever, you always go overboard and leave a little wiggle room, so basically that's why I wanted to speak to you. There is absolutely no way I can convince my fellow Senators to accept the demands as Mr. Harrison presented them to us, no way, no how, in hell. You've got to speak to Mr. Harrison and convince him that if he wants any changes made, he must give us some wiggle room."

"Okay, Senator, I understand where you're coming from. I will speak to John and get some ideas from him and, as you put it, get you some wiggle room, but can you give me some kind of a hint as to where you would want that wiggle room?"

"To be truthful, and blunt, we would like to see a little wiggle room in all his demands."

"Okay, Senator, I'll go speak to him, but I can't make any promises."

Just then, the waitress delivers the food. "Great," says the Senator, "the food is here. Let's eat so I can get back to work and you can go back home and talk to Mr. Harrison." The two men finish their meals, Mike heads home, and the Senator goes back to his office.

Mike wastes no time; the next day, he's at the prison, but this time, he is not escorted to the warden's office, but rather to the room that he normally uses when he meets with John. After about a ten-minute wait, two guards escort John into the room, shackle him to the table, and leave, first explaining to Mike that they will be just outside the door and that he should knock on the door when he is finished.

As Mike is getting himself seated, John speaks first: "Well, I hope this is a good meeting, because I've been reading in the papers and seeing on TV all about the news media getting on the government's case about our cause."

"John, I have good news, and I've got bad news."

"Give me the bad news first."

"Okay, I'll give you the bad news first, and I'll get right to the point. Yesterday, I flew to Washington and met up with Senator Adams. He told me that he has been lobbying with his fellow Senators, about the changes you want to see made. He explained to me that in Washington, D.C., there is never a bill presented to the Senate that does not contain wiggle room, and he went on to tell me that the changes that you are demanding do not have any wiggle room. To quote the Senator verbatim, 'There is no way in hell that this bill will be passed the way it is. If John refuses to make any changes in his requests, this bill will never see daylight. It will never stand a chance to come up for discussion with the Senate. First of all, let him know that he is extremely lucky that my fellow Senators are even talking about it. Does he realize how hard it is to get a new law put in place? It's next to imposable, I'm telling you. I have been trying to lobby for this bill all this time, and all my talking is falling on deaf ears.' That's exactly what he said, word for word. So that's it, John, and to be honest with you, it's at least a start. So think about it. Sit down and try to come up with a couple of changes that you can live with. The one thing I encourage you to stick with is some sort of release from prison for Barney, Nick, and yourself, because this will be your one and only chance to do something about that. So, like I said, think about it. Go and have a good talk with yourself to see what changes you can live with. When you're ready, give me a call. I will sit down with you and go over them. So, you got homework to do tonight. And cheer up, John; this is as close as you gotten so far for your cause."

"Okay."

"Let me say by for now. Talk to you later." With that, Mike knocks on the door and explains to the guard that they are finished. The guards come in and take John back to his cell, and Mike heads home.

Two days later, Mike gets a call from John. "Good morning, John. How are you doing?"

"I'm doing okay."

"John, have you given any thought as to our meeting the other day, and did you do your homework?"

"Yes and yes. I sat down and thought real hard about all that I have gone through to get to this point, all of the heartaches and sacrifices that all of my loyal followers have also gone through, so to be this close to my goal and throw it away by being stubborn and bullheaded would be foolish. So, yes, I did my homework and gave it some real deep thought, and I came up with some changes, and to put it in their vernacular, I gave them some wiggle room."

"Okay, John, I can probably get there later on this afternoon or tomorrow afternoon."

"That won't be necessary. I know you've got your practice to run and you don't need to be running back and forth to the prison, so I can give you them right over the phone if that's okay with you."

"Oh! We can do that. Let me get a pen and paper, and I'll write it all down."

"Okay, Mike. Let me know when you're ready."

Mike gets a pad and pen ready. "Whenever you're ready, John, you can start."

"Okay, Mike, here we go. Number one will stay the same; any changes must be national, and the law must be the same in all the states. Number two, first offense of child molestation gets fifteen years, no parole. If the child is permanently injured or killed, mandatory life sentence, no parole. Number three, second offense of child molestation, mandatory life sentence, no parole. If the child is permanently injured or killed, the molester receives a mandatory death sentence, with no appeals, that must be carried out within thirty days. Number four, every child molester is treated the absolute same way in all states. Number five, and there is absolutely no wiggle room on this one, I want Barney, Nick, and myself released from prison within thirty days of these changes going into law. I would accept the release of the three of us under any reasonable circumstances. I would like complete exoneration for the three of us, but we would settle for early parole, being released as time served, or, as the last resort, being released on home arrest with an ankle monitor for a while. So that's it. What do you think of that, Mike?"

"I think that's reasonable. They can't say that you didn't give them any wiggle room. I will present this to the Senator, and as soon as I hear anything, I will get back to you."

"I will be waiting for your call."

"Okay, John. You take care now."

"Bye."

As soon as Mike hangs up, he asks his secretary to try and get Senator Adams on the phone. A few minutes later, she informs him that the Senator will be getting on the phone shortly. Mike picks up the phone and says, "Hello, Mr. Santino."

"Yes, please hold on. The Senator will be with you in a moment."

"Mr. Santino, good morning. How are you today?"

"I'm fine, Senator. I spoke to John a few days ago, and he called me back this morning with some changes in his demands. I can read them off to you when you're ready."

"Mike, let me stop you there. I never talk business over the phone, if you know what I mean. I'm afraid that if you want me to move forward on this, I am going to ask you to come to Washington to meet face to face with a stenographer. That is the only way we can do this. If I was not so busy, I would be more than happy to come to you, but right now, I've got too many things going on here."

"Okay, Senator. I'm a little busy myself here, so how about I come out there the day after tomorrow, say around noon, and we can go to our favorite cafeteria."

"Sounds good, Mike. I'll see you in two days in my office."

"Okay, Senator. I will see you then."

Two days later, once again, Mike finds himself at the airport bright and early, booking a flight to Washington, and once again, he finds himself in Senator Adams's office, waiting for him. Finally, the Senator comes out. "Good morning, Mike."

"Good morning, Senator."

Both men shake hands, and the Senator says, "So, Mike, I hope you're hungry, because today's blue plate special in the cafeteria is a deluxe cheeseburger with all the trimmings."

"Oh, that's my favorite meal too."

"And if you don't mind, I would like my secretary to join us so that she can write down and document everything."

"That's okay. I've got no problem with that."

"Then let's go get ourselves a couple of the blue plate specials."

With that, the three of them go downstairs to the cafeteria and find their special table in the corner. The waitress comes over and takes their order. The Senator speaks first: "Mike, I hope that you brought me some good changes so that I can get started trying to get them implemented into law."

"Senator, as I told you, I went to speak to John and laid it all out on the table for him. I explained to him how things work here in Washington, that there is never a bill presented to the Senate without any wiggle room in it, among other things.

"Mike, we need not go there."

"Well, then, Senator, let me get right down to it."

"Okay, here we go." The Senator asks his secretary if she is ready, and she answers yes. "Okay, Mike, you can start whenever you're ready."

"Number one stays the same; any changes must be national, the same in all the states. Number two, first offense, fifteen years, no parole, and again, if the child is permanently disabled or killed, mandatory life sentence with no parole. Number three, second offense, mandatory life sentence with no parole. If the child is permanently disabled or killed, mandatory death sentence that must be carried out within thirty days. Number four, all child molesters will be treated absolutely the same way. Number five stays the same; John, Barney, and Nick, get released from prison on whatever terms you deem fit. And their release should be no later than thirty days from when the bill is signed into law. That's it, Senator. What do you think?"

"Well, right now, I can't answer that question. I will bring this information back to my fellow Senators, see what they think about it, and get back to you. I will say this; John at least took the first step by compromising some of his demands, and at least now I have a little wiggle room. So, like I said, I will take this back, present it to my fellow Senators, and we'll take it from there. As soon as I hear anything, I promise I will call you."

"Okay, Senator. I know you've got other things on your plate, but try to do this ASAP."

"You got it, Mike."

"Great! Now, hopefully, I can get to the airport in time to catch my flight back home."

When their lunch is over, Mike heads back to the airport and back home.

Two days later, Mike gets a call from the General.

"Good morning, Mike. It's been a little while. What's the latest news?"

"Well, two days ago, I went back to Washington and spoke to the Senator and gave him John's revised list of demands. He said that he would take it back and present it to his fellow Senators, and he hopes that he will have an answer for me ASAP."

"Okay, and you say that was two days ago?"

"Yes, two days ago."

"Well, Mike, I'm getting a little tired of them dragging their feet, and I came up with a plan that will light a fire under their ass."

"General, if your plan involves breaking the law in any way, shape, or form, please don't let me know what it is. If you feel you have to do something, then, by all means, go ahead and do it, but please leave me out of anything that's illegal. Other than that, I will help you out as much as I can."

"Okay, Mike. I hear you loud and clear. I will do what I feel I have to and not involve you in the details. So you have a good day and stay out of trouble."

"Thanks, General. I will try to do that. You take care, okay?"

"Bye."

Later on that day, the General puts a call into Eight. "Good morning, Eight."

"Good morning, G. What can I do for you today?"

"Remember that meeting I had where I handed out the discs with the phone numbers, and I explained that I had a plan to light a fire under the Senator's ass?"

"As a matter of fact, yes I do."

"And do you remember calling me with the good news that you had all these members who would volunteer, and other members who could get all the supplies that I would need to carry out the new missions that I detailed at that meeting, like guns, night vision goggles, uniforms, etc. etc.?"

"I do, G."

"Well, I think it's about time to put the plan into action. What I would like you to do is get in touch with the members who were willing to volunteer, and also start getting all the things that I asked for. Just remember, what I am looking for are snipers, lots of them, or anyone who will be willing to learn how to become a sniper. I am looking to get at least 150 of them. You can explain to them that we will supply everything and, if need be, help them out financially. Then get in touch with the member who had that big piece of land that we could train on, and get that all set up for me."

"Okay, G."

"Also, I would like for you to do something special for me."

"Just name it, G."

"I want you to get a list of every single child molester in the United States, sorted out by state they live in and the town in that state. That is extremely important for this plan to work. That is a must, and it must be done first. We will not be able to do it once we get started."

"Okay, G. You got it. I will get in touch with everyone this afternoon and have them start getting together the volunteers and items that you are looking for and need, and I will start today with getting all those names that you want. Is there anything else?"

"No, at this point, nothing else. Get those volunteers and get me the stuff I need, including that list that I am asking for. When you have everything set up, with all the information that I'm looking for, then get back to me."

"Okay, G. Will do. Bye for now."

Two weeks go by, and there is no call from eight, but this just gives the General more time to finalize the details of his plan. Then the General hears very disturbing news on the TV. It seems that the bodies of two eight-year-old girls were discovered that morning in a local dump. Both little girls had been raped and beaten to death. The police are investigating, following up on two of the victims' classmates' statements that they saw the two little girls get into a car willingly while walking home from school. Police are pleading with anyone who has information to come forward.

The General sits there in disbelief, not wanting to believe what he has just heard. This infuriates him to the point that he cannot wait any longer, and he wants to initiate his plan immediately. He picks up the phone and calls Eight.

"Good morning, G. What I can do for you?"

"I want you to tell me that you have all the information I want."

"Well, G, right now, I have about three quarters of the information."

"Okay, Eight, let me put it this way. Have you seen the news today about the two little girls that they found?"

"As a matter fact, G, I have seen that. It was very disturbing."

"Well… that's what I'm trying to put a stop to, so please try to finish up getting the rest of the information I need by tonight, because that's only the beginning. Once I get the information, I then have to implement everything."

"Okay, G. I promise I will finish up tonight and call you first thing in the morning."

"Please do that, because we need to stop these sons of bitches."

"You got it, G."

"Okay, bye for now."

The next morning, bright and early, the General's phone rings. "Good morning," he says to Eight.

"Good morning, G. I was up real late last night, but I managed to get all the information you need. I managed to enlist 160 snipers, most of them Navy seals, some Marines, and some Army. As far as registered child molesters listed in the United States, there are a little over 300,000 of them in the USA, and I broke them down by state, city, and town. I have to say there are a lot of names."

"That's okay. We will work through them. Tell you what; let me sort this out in my mind, and I will get back to you."

"Ok, G. Talk to you later."

With the information in hand, the General sits at his desk and starts to work on his plan. Before long, he realizes that he has been working on it for six hours. He thinks to himself that he is only about halfway done, so he decides to take a break and get something to eat. After eating, he resumes working on his plan. By the time he is finished and happy with the plan, it's 3 AM in the morning, and he is extremely tired, so he hits the bed.

First thing in the morning, the General puts a call in to Eight.

"Good morning, G."

"Good morning, Eight. Last night was my turn to work late. I was up until 3 AM working on my plan. Anyway, that talk is for another day. What I want to do now is get the ball rolling."

"Okay, G, I'm ready to copy."

"Good. First thing I'm going to need from you is the list of child molesters, as you broke them down, and the names of all the snipers, but those lists must be brought to me by personal courier. That would be too much information to take a chance with e-mail or over the phone. After I get the lists, I will get back to you with what we need to do next.

"You got it, G."

"Great. Bye for now."

"Bye."

Two days later, the courier drops off the information to the General, who wastes no time getting into it. He works late into the night, shuffling papers around until he is satisfied with the plan, and again, the General is dead tired when he hits the bed.

The next morning, bright and early, the General is on the phone with Eight. "Good morning, Eight."

"Good morning, G."

"Okay, Eight, this is what we need to do next. First, get in touch with the 160 snipers. Make sure that they know what they are getting themselves into. If they all agree, or at least 150 of them do, then I will need to get enough sniper rifles and ammunition for all of them. You can get them from the arms dealer you said you contacted. Next, we will need some sort of stealth clothing. You know, mostly black clothes, nothing too obvious."

"Okay, got you, G."

"The next thing will be a piece of land with a building on it that we can train on. Hopefully, we have enough money to cover everything. Get that going, and when you've gotten it all together, get back to me. In the meantime, I will finalize my plan."

"Okay, G. Talk to you later."

The General takes this opportunity to go over his plan. Two days later, he gets a call from Eight.

"Good morning, G."

"Good morning, Eight. How are we doing?"

"Very good, G. I have 156 snipers lined up. I placed an order with that arms dealer for the rifles and ammunition, and he needs just two days to get them to us. And by the way, they will all be untraceable, so even if one gets left behind, we need not worry. I also lined up a piece of land with a building on it that we can use. It's sort of secluded, and best of all, it's right near you in Upstate New York."

"Oh, that's great. Now, the next question is are all the men ready to travel?"

"Yes, they are."

"Good. Then the next thing is to set up a meeting at that place. How about we make it for two weeks from today, at about 7 PM, and I will explain my whole plan to them."

"Okay, G. I will set everything up and get back to you when it's all done. Then I will give you the location of the land."

"Great."

The next day, the General gets a call from Eight. "Good morning, G. Your meeting is all set up for July 4th at 7 PM."

"Good. Now all I need is the address."

"The address is 9115 Rural Road 231. By the way, don't try to put it in your GPS; it will not find it. What you need to do is, while going north on Rural Rd. 231 from the New York State Throughway, you need to check your mileage. When you pass the old boarded-up diner on your left, then proceed exactly two and a half miles. You will see an opening on your left. It will be a dirt road. There will be a tree on the left side with a yellow circle painted on it. Then you will know that you are on the right road."

"Oh boy, this sounds just like the place I was looking to get for the training. This is a good thing. I will see you there."

"Okay, G."

Two weeks later, the General arrives at the place thinking that the directions that Eight gave him were right on the money. He also hopes that everyone else found the place. When he finally gets to the end of the driveway, it opens up into a large open field with a small bungalow and a large barn. Eight is standing outside the barn, waiting for the General. He parks his car, and as he's walking to the barn, Eight waves him on to join him.

"Good evening, G."

"How are you doing, Eight?"

"I'm doing great! Everyone is here. I thought that maybe one or two would have backed out, but none did. They are all here."

"That's great. Let's go inside and get this meeting going."

Both men walk inside, and to the General's amazement, just about everyone is sitting on the floor. The General looks at Eight, who raises his arms up and shrugs his shoulders. He looks at the General and says, "I forgot to get chairs. Sorry, sir."

"No problem. As long as everyone is comfortable."

"Well, G, at least I set up a table for you up front."

"Thank you, Eight." The General walks up to the table, looks at all of the men, most of whom are sitting on the floor, and smiles. "Hi, all, and welcome. I'm happy to see that all of you made it. You know what? If this meeting was not so important, it would be funny seeing most of you guys sitting on the floor. But enough with the humor; let's get down to the nuts and bolts of this meeting."

The General stands there, staring out at the men. He waits a few seconds before speaking. Finally, he says, "First off, before I get into the details, let me give it to you straight so that there is no doubt as to what you men are getting yourself into. In a nutshell, what I will be asking you men to do is go out and kill child molesters in cold blood. So think about that for a minute, and if you want, you can get up and leave right now, and I will not think any less of you for doing so. And not to get too dramatic, I will give you that minute now." With that, the General sits down on a chair that was at the side of the table.

Dead silence falls on the room. All of the men look around at each other, but no one leaves. After about a minute, the General gets up, looks over the group of men, and says, "Okay, I gave all of you a chance, and no one left, so here we go. This is going to be the plan. First, I will break you guys up into three groups of fifty. Each member of each group will get the name and address, along with a picture of the target, and then have two days to travel individually to a designated city and town in that city. Once there, each individual member will get himself some sort of boarding and settle in. Then he will search out his target and determine the best time and place to take out the target. All this will be done on a specific time schedule that will be the same, for all three groups and that will be strictly adhered to, with no exceptions. Each group will have their own go-to man in the event of a problem. The time schedule will be to take one to two days to get there. On the third day, you will start the search for your target. You will have three days to do this. Then, on the seventh day, you will take out your target. After the completion of your mission, you will call your go-to man. He will give you an address, where you will meet up with him. It will be in a room that he will rent under an assumed name. It will be set up as some sort of a technical meeting for a company, about cutting the cost of shipping, etc. That's just a sample. The meetings will be all different, but will serve to give all fifty men the information that they will need for their next mission. He will then give you your next destination, along with all the information that you will need, and again, you will have two days to get there. The rest of the time frame will be the same. As far as where you will be going next, that will be determined by your go-to man. Back here at the headquarters of Eight, we will have every name of every child molester in the USA. We will give you their names, addresses, and pictures. All these names will be randomly picked according to the town they live in. There will be fifty names picked for each town, so each member will get his own individual target. We will be doing this so that we will not set up a pattern for anyone to predict where we will strike next. Okay, that would be it in a nut shell, so I will stop now and see if any of you have any questions."

One man holds up his hand. The General acknowledges him, and the man asks, "Am I to understand that we will be compensated for our expenses?"

"Absolutely. You will be reimbursed for every penny you spend. Before each mission, you will be given enough cash and then some for the mission. If you run out of money, just get in touch with your go-to man, and he will meet you at your mission nest and give you more cash. One important thing: make sure you get and keep all receipts. Any other questions?"

No hands go up.

"Now, before I end this meeting, there is one very important question I need to ask all of you. In the event any one of you get caught, you must be willing to give yourself up and be taken in by the police. I do not want any one of you getting shot and killed by the police, and if anyone does get caught, you have my word that you will be represented by one of our lawyers and all your expenses will be covered. Any questions?"

Again, no hands go up.

"Okay, then the next step will be Eight getting in touch with you when we are ready to get this thing going. Also, I want everyone to know that in the meantime, I will be doing everything I can to get the lawmakers to do what we want them to do and not bring us to the point that we need to implement this plan. Is there anyone here who does not know who John Harrison is?"

No hands go up.

"Okay, so everyone knows who he is. This is the rest of the story. Right now, John is working with a Senator Adams to get the child molester laws changed. The Senator went back to Washington, but that was a while ago, and so far, we have heard nothing from him. So what I am going to do is anonymously get in touch with the Senator and give him a heads up about what we are planning to do, without giving him any specific information. Maybe the Senator will see the light and get his ass moving. I hope that we will not have to do this thing. Anyway, that is it. Are there any questions?"

Again, no hands go up.

"Okay, then, if need be, Eight will get in touch with you. Thank you for attending and have a safe trip home."

The next day, the General, using a throwaway phone, puts a call in to the Senator's office. He gets the Senator's secretory and asks to speak to the Senator, but the secretory informs the General that the Senator in not in, but she can take a message for him.

"Okay, but please understand that it's extremely important that you get this message right. And make sure that the Senator gets this message; it is a matter of life and death, and not only one death, but hundreds of deaths. I hope you understand that this call is not a hoax or scam. I cannot express how important this call is. Do you understand?"

"Yes, I do. So, what is the message that you want me to give the Senator?"

"Okay, please give him this message, and he will not be able to call me back, because this phone is a disposable one, so that should tell you that I am sincere."

"I got it. So, what is your message?"

"Please tell the Senator that I am working on behalf of John Harrison, and that if there is no progress on the changes to the child molester laws, that I have a new plan: to kill many, many child molesters. And, just a reminder, I am the one responsible for the mass killings in Texas and Virginia, and if I don't see anything in the papers or on TV news, I will start my next operation, which will result in thousands of killings of child molesters, and that will be much more than the killings in Texas and Virginia. And seeing that the Senator cannot get in touch with me, the only way that I will know if he is doing something will be through the news media, papers or TV. So, that's it. Please, please give the Senator the message."

"I will do that, sir."

"Thank you."

"Your welcome."

The General then decides to sit back and keep his eyes and ears open, and give the Senator a week or so before calling the news media to push him.

Later that day, Senator Adams returns to his office. As soon as he walks in, his secretary hands him the message from the General. "Good afternoon, sir. I have several messages, but I think you should check this message out first. The man who called was kind of creepy."

"Ok, thank you."

The Senator takes his messages, goes into his office, sits at his desk, and starts to read them. As he starts to read the one from the General, he pops up from his seat. *That son of a bitch! What the hell am I going to do now?* He then tells his secretary to get Mike Santino on the phone.

"Ok, sir." She calls Mike's office.

"Mr. Santino's office. Can I help you?"

"Yes, this is Senator Adams's office. The Senator would like to speak to Mr. Santino."

"Please hold on." The secretary says to Mike, "Mr. Santino, Senator Adams is calling for you."

Thinking that it's good news, Mike says, "Yes, please put him through. Good morning, Senator."

"Mr. Santino, please hold."

The Senator gets on the phone. "Mike!! What the hell is going on? I thought we had an agreement about what I was trying to do."

"Excuse me, Senator, to put it in your own words, I have no idea what the hell you are talking about."

"I'm talking about the deal I made with you and John, about me trying to get the laws changed pertaining to child molesters."

"Yes, I remember that, but Senator, I still don't know what you are talking about. Did something happen that I don't know about?"

"I'm talking about some guy called my office today threatening to kill thousands of child molesters if I don't do something fast about the laws."

"Senator, please believe me! I know nothing about this. Let me talk to John to see if he knows anything about this."

"You know that I will work with you, but we don't deal with threats. I will stop everything in its tracks."

"Senator, please let me check it out and get back to you."

"Okay, but make it fast."

"You got it, Senator."

With that, Mike tells his secretary he is going to the prison to see John. When Mike gets to the prison, he is escorted into the same small room that they let him use, to speak to John.

John is surprised when a guard informs him that he has a visitor, because he was not expecting any. He asks the guard, "Who is it?"

"It's your lawyer."

"Oh, okay," John says. "I hope he has some good news for me."

The guard replies, "That, I would not know."

John is escorted to the small room where Mike is waiting for him. As John enters the room, he tells Mike, "I hope this is a good visit and that you've got some good news for me."

"Well, John, actually it's not a good visit. I have a little disturbing news for you that I hope you are unaware of."

"Well, Mike, now that you have my attention, what are you here for?"

"It seems that the Senator who is working with you got a call from someone threatening to kill hundreds and hundreds of child molesters unless a bill was introduced to get the ball rolling as far as changing the laws against child molesters. The Senator, to say the least, was extremely upset by this call. It seems that he doesn't take too kindly ultimatums or threats, and he threatened to call the whole deal off that he made with you as far as changing the laws. So what I'm doing here is trying to find out whether or not you know anything about this call."

"What?! I know absolutely nothing about this, but I have a pretty good idea who may be behind it, and I believe you also know who maybe behind it."

"I figured that it was not you, but I had to hear it straight from your mouth. So, who do you think is behind this, because the last time we spoke about things like this, did we or did we not determine that the movement has taken on a life of its own?"

"Yes, we did decide that, and whoever is in charge of that life is most likely behind what happened, and I don't know if there's anything I can do about that. I am hoping that if the laws get changed, the people behind this will listen to me and stop the killings. But Mike, truthfully, I have no idea who is behind this."

"Okay, John, like I said, I just wanted to hear it from your lips. I'll do some checking and get back to you. Also, I know you speak to Nick and Barney, and when you do, just for the hell of it, ask them if they know anything about this."

"Will do, but Mike, please keep me informed. This is serious. It could upset everything we've been trying to get accomplished."

As Mike heads back to his office, he keeps thinking to himself that he has a pretty good idea as to who made the call, and that person would be the General, because he is the only one associated with this whole movement that is capable of doing something like that. As Mike walks into his office, he instructs his secretary to try and get Judge Ghetto on the phone.

"Mr. Santino, I have Judge Ghetto on the phone."

"Good afternoon, Judge."

"Good afternoon, Mike. What can I do for you?"

"Well, Judge, actually, it's what I would like to do for you."

"Okay, I'll bite. What is it that you would like to do for me?"

"I would like to buy you lunch at Laduchies."

"Oh boy, that sounds serious. Can you give me a hint as to what you want me to do?"

"No, Judge. I would rather not discuss it over the phone, but I will at lunch."

"Okay, Mike, but you know how I feel about getting involved any further than I am."

"I understand, Judge. I am well aware of that, but it's kind of important that we meet."

"Okay, Mike. How about tomorrow at noon?"

"That would be great, Judge. I will see you tomorrow at noon."

The next day, Mike meets up with the judge at the restaurant, and they are escorted to their favorite table, nice and quiet in the corner. As soon as they sit down, the judge says, "Okay, Mike, what's this all about?"

"Well, Judge, how about we order something first. That way, if you don't like what I have to say, you will at least get a free lunch out of the deal."

"That sounds good."

The waitress approaches the table. "Good afternoon, gentlemen. Do you need more time to order?"

Judge Ghetto says, "No, I don't need more time. I am ready.

"Okay, and what can I get for you today?"

"I feel like having a BLT and coffee."

"And for you, sir?"

"You know what, that sounds good. I'll have the same thing."

"All right, gentlemen, two BLTs and two coffees."

"Okay, Mike, we ordered. So what is this all about now?"

"Well, judge, you know how long John has been in this fight to get the laws changed."

"Yes, Mike, I know it's been a long time."

"And you know all the sacrifices that he has made, and the many people who have also sacrificed a lot helping his cause."

"Okay, Mike, please get to the point. I know all of this. This is why I helped him out in the first place. But you've got to understand I'm a judge and I cannot get too involved in what is going on, so please let me know what's on your mind."

"Judge, you know about the meeting that John and I had with Senator Adams?"

"Yes."

"Well, things were moving slow, but nevertheless, they were moving. The Senator came back and asked John for some wiggle room, which John reluctantly gave him. I'm sure you know the way things work in Washington, very slowly, but evidently, there is someone in the movement who does not have the patience that we do and is sort of throwing a wrench into the gears that will stop everything in its tracks. All the heartaches and hard work that John and everyone else put into this movement will be for nothing. I believe that person is the General, and it seems that you are the only person who can get in touch with him and possibly reason with him, that is, if he is in fact the person to blame for this problem, to ask him to please stop and give the process more time to evolve."

"That is great, but you still have not told me what the problem is."

"Judge, the problem is that someone called the Senator and gave him an ultimatum, that if they did not see any movement as far as getting the laws changed, he will commence a killing spree on child molesters. And according to that person, the killings will go into the hundreds and hundreds."

"So you think that it was the General who made that call?"

"Yes, Judge."

"You know what, Mike? I agree with you. I think that he is more than capable of doing something like that."

"Well, Judge, the Senator called me and said that if there was nothing I could do to stop this person, then all bets would be off, and that would be devastating to John and everyone else who has worked hard to get that accomplished. So, to make a long story short, Judge, I am begging you to please get in touch with the General and, in fact, see if it was him who made that call and try to persuade him to back off. And you probably need this also. Try to please persuade him with the understanding that if nothing happens within a reasonable amount of time, then he will have our blessings to commence with his endeavors."

"Okay, Mike. I understand. I will try to get in touch with the General and see what I can do. Then I will get back to you."

"Thank you very much, Judge. I really, really appreciate this."

"No problem. Now, let's enjoy our lunch."

The two eat their lunches and then go their separate ways.

The judge heads back to his office, thinking to himself, *I thought that I was finished with all this, and now, here I am, right back in the middle of it.* As soon as he gets in his office, he informs his secretary that he is taking the rest of the day off, because he needs to take care of a few things. With that, he heads home. When he gets home, the first thing he does is look for the phone he uses to get in touch with the General. He gets the phone, grabs a chair, and sits, rethinking what he is about to do. Again, he thinks to himself, *What the hell am I doing? What am I getting myself into here? But then again, I still believe in John's plight. Something must be done about these child molesters literally getting away with what they get away with. So I guess I should help him out.* With that, he calls the General.

Back at the General's place, he is busy watching the news on television when his throwaway phone, which is in a drawer, starts to ring. At first, he doesn't hear it, but thinking that he hears something, he lowers the sound on the television. Tracking down the sound to the drawer where his phone is, he is shocked that the phone is ringing. He thinks, *Who could it be? The only one who has the number is the judge, but why would he be calling? The judge wanted nothing more to do with what was going on, so why would he be calling?* All this is going through his mind, and by the time he decides to answer the phone, it stops ringing. He finally picks it up and sees that, sure enough, it was the judge calling. Now there are more questions as to why he is calling.

Suddenly, the phone starts to ring again. This time, the General answers it.

"Hello, General?"

"Yes, Judge?"

"Yes, well, it's been awhile since we spoke."

"Yes, it has been awhile. So, Judge, what can I do for you?"

"Well, General, I'm in the mood for a plane ride. Would you mind meeting up with me at the airport?"

Still in shock, the General answers, "Well, okay, I guess, but may I ask what brought on this sudden urge to fly?"

"I will tell you, when I see you, okay?"

"I guess so, and when will you want to meet?"

"How about tomorrow morning, say about 9 AM?"

"Okay, Judge, I will see you tomorrow morning at the airport at 9 AM."

"Great, see you tomorrow. Just come over to my car. I will get there a little early."

"Okay, good."

The next day, the judge is at the airport by 8:45 AM. At about 8:55 AM, the General pulls into the parking lot and parks his car. He walks over to the judge's car, opens the door, and gets in. "Good morning, Judge."

"Good morning, General."

"Ok, Judge, you had me up all night thinking of what this could be all about."

"Tell you what; I will come right to the point. Did you call Senator Adams and threaten him about killing hundreds and hundreds of child molesters if he did not move faster to get the laws changed."

"You know what, Judge? I kind of thought that was what it was all about. As a matter of fact, I will also come right to the point. Yes, I did call the Senator, and as a matter of fact, I have everything all set to put my plan into action, and I don't expect to stop at this point. Look, Judge, so far, if it was not for me, we would not have come as far as we have, so I intend to go full speed with my plan if the Senator doesn't move his ass within two weeks."

"Well, General, Mike called me and asked me to talk with you and try to convince you to hold off and give the Senator a chance, and not screw up all the work that John and Mike have made. Mike got a call from the Senator about someone calling him with a threat and ultimatum, and he did not take to kindly to that call and told Mike that if we could not stop it, then he will stop whatever progress he has made in its tracks, because they, meaning all of his fellow Senators, do not work or grant any wishes to anyone threatening them in any way, shape, or form."

"Oh, really? Well, tell you what, Judge; you go back and tell Mike that there is no way, shape, or form that I will stop my plan. Whatever I did in the past for this movement worked. We at least got the Senators to talk to us, so I feel that my plan will push them to move a little faster. Also, you tell Mike that from now on, if he wants to talk to me, he can call me directly. There is no need for you to get involved anymore. So just go back, give Mike your phone, and I will deal with him. You take care, Judge." With that, the General gets out of the judge's car, walks over to his car, gets in, and drives away.

The judge heads back to his office. As he walks in, he asks his secretary to please get Mr. Santino on the phone.

"Ok, Judge." She gets Mike on the phone. "Judge, I have Mr. Santino on the phone."

"Good morning, Judge. Every time I find out that it's you on the phone, I get all tensed up. So, what can I do for you today, Judge?"

"What you can do for me, Mike, is buy me lunch at Laduchies."

"Oh, okay. How about tomorrow?"

"Sounds good."

"Okay then. I will see you tomorrow, Judge."

The next day, Mike gets to the restaurant first, get his favorite table, and waits for the judge to get there. Five minutes later, the judge gets there.

"Good afternoon, Judge."

"Good afternoon, Mike."

Before the judge even sits, he puts the General's phone on the table. Mike looks at the phone and then looks at the judge and says, "Okay, that's a cell phone. I guess you want to talk to me about this phone."

"That's right, Mike. That phone belongs to you now."

"Ok, Judge, I'm a little confused. Why are you giving me a cell phone? I already have one, but I guess that you are about to tell me."

"You guessed right, Mike."

"I can't wait."

"Well, let's order first."

"Okay, sounds good."

After the two order lunch, the judge starts to fill Mike in. "Well, Mike, you wanted me to go and talk to the General, to ask him if it was him who called the Senator, and that is what I did. And Mike, let me put it this way, I think the General is crazy and out of control. He, in fact, was the one who called the Senator, and he is steadfast in his resolve to go through with his latest plan. I tried to talk him out of his plan, or at least hold off for a while, and the more I tried to convince him to hold off, the more adamant he got. Then he told me that from now on, he did not want me in the picture. I'm not to call him any longer. Then he said, 'And you tell Mike that if he wants to talk to me, he can call me directly, with your phone, so when you see Mike, give him your phone. You know what, Judge? You guys, and I mean you, John, Mike, Barney, and Nick, you guys forgot all that I did for John's cause. If it were not for me and my plan, we would not have gotten as far as we did. All of a sudden, you guys don't need me anymore. Well, you go back and tell whoever sent you to talk to me that from now on, I am going to do whatever I feel I need to do to get the results that I started out to get, because I feel that it's a great cause, and no matter what, I am going forward with my plan.'"

"Did you explain to him, that he did a lot for the cause, but now it's time to back off and let the Senators do their thing. And did you also explain to him that the Senators don't like to be pushed or given ultimatums, that they will just stop everything?"

"I did explain that to him. But that just got him more upset."

"Okay, I will take it from here. I need to now come up with a plan of my own."

"Good, Mike. I would hate to lose all of the ground we made so far. If I can help you out in any way, just let me know."

"Thanks, Judge. You know what, Judge? I don't know if I can eat now. I sort of lost my appetite."

"Well, not me, Mike. And you should eat; you are going to need all your strength now."

"I guess you're right."

Both men eat their lunch and leave separately, with the judge leaving first. Mike then heads back to his office to try to come up with a plan to change the General's mind, or to stop him.

Back at his office, Mike contemplates a few scenarios, but comes up dry. He decides to go as see John, to see if he has any ideas.

Bright and early the next morning, Mike goes to see John. As usual, Mike is led into the same dull room, where he waits for John. After about ten minutes, the guard brings John in.

"I hope you're here with good news."

"Well, actually, I don't have good news. In fact, I'm here to see if you can help. I know that because of you being in here, there is not much you can do for me, but what I'm looking for more than anything is some sort of direction from you."

"Okay then, what can I do for you?"

"This is what is going on. You know that right now, we are waiting for the Senators to do something. You also know that they don't like to be pushed or given any sort of ultimatum. Well, it seems that the General called up Senator Adams and gave him an ultimatum, threatened him, and told him that if, he did not do anything in the next week or two, that he has a plan to go out and kill thousands of child molesters. The Senator called me and said that if I did not do something to stop him, then all bets are off. He pointed out to me the talks we had about them not working with ultimatums, threats, or terrorists and he told me talk to the General, or whatever, and just let him know how I make out. And just to let us know, he will not wait long before calling everything off. So that's what I am doing here, hoping that you will have an idea or two, because I have nothing."

"Wow! That would have been the last thing that I thought you would come to see me about, and right now, I also have nothing. Mike, I don't know what to tell you. I can't believe he is doing this, and not wanting to stop or wait for something to happen. What the fuck does he think all the rest of us went through? We all made sacrifices to get to the point that we are at. What makes him think that he can make decisions on his own?"

"I don't know, John. All I know is that we need to come up with something to stop him."

"Yes, we do, and it needs to be something fast."

"Well, Mike, all I can say is that I will sleep on it, and hopefully come up with something."

"Okay, John, and I will do the same, but I just don't know where to even start. The only way I can get in touch with him is with the cell phone that the judge used. I guess I'll try to come up with something."

"I hope so, Mike. I would hate to lose all that we gained so far. I can't believe this whole fucking thing came out of nowhere."

"John, try to calm down. We need to keep clear heads so that we can come up with an answer. If you do come up with something, call me, no matter what time of day it is."

"I will, Mike, and you do the same. Please let me know if you come up with anything. When I get a chance, I will talk to Barney and Nick to see if they have any ideas."

"Okay, John. I think I did enough damage for one day, so I'm out of here."

"Okay, Mike.

Before getting into his car, Mike call his office and tells his secretary that he is taking the day off and to reschedule all his appointments. He just needs to go home and think about what is going on. He feels really bad for John and thinks that this would be devastating for him, so he heads home. Once there, he hits the couch and starts thinking really hard, hoping to come up with something. Before long, he falls fast asleep. By the time he wakes up, it's after 10 PM. *Oh my God, I can't believe I fell asleep.* He makes something to eat and then considers hitting the bed, thinking that everything hopefully looks better in the light of day.

The next morning, he gets up, takes a shower, eats breakfast, and then heads to his office. Mike get his messages, goes into his office, but can't seem to concentrate on anything but the General, so he decides to call the judge. He tells his secretary to try and get Judge Ghetto on the phone.

"Mr. Santino, I have Judge Ghetto on the phone."

"Good morning, Judge."

"Good morning, Mike. What can I do for you?"

"Judge, yesterday I went to see John, and I explained everything to him, and between the two of us, we could not come up with anything, so I figured that maybe you might have something."

"Mike, I'm sorry, but I have absolutely nothing for you. But like I told you, if you do come up with something, and I can help you, please call me."

"Thanks, Judge."

"Okay, Mike, talk to you later."

The rest of the day, Mike finds it very hard to concentrate on his own work. All he keeps doing is trying to come up with some idea about what to do with the General. Short of killing him, though, Mike has nothing, and it's driving him crazy. He tells his secretary that he is taking the rest of the day off because he is not feeling too good.

On the way home, Mike nearly gets into an accident, and he says to himself, *You've got to get yourself together, Mike. You damn near wrecked your car. I think what I need to do is go home, and before I do anything else, go anywhere, or even talk to anyone, I need to come up with some kind of a plan.*

Finally home, Mike makes himself a stiff Scotch and soda and then heads to the living room. There, he resigns himself not to leave until he has a solution, but soon after finishing his drink, he falls asleep.

The next three days go by slowly because Mike is preoccupied with the dilemma that he and John have and need a resolution to. Then, on the fourth night, after Mike has gotten in bed, he is suddenly awakened by the sound of the telephone. Still half asleep, he searches for the phone, but can't seem to find it. When he finally finds it, it's too late, but the caller left a message. Mike recognizes the voice; it's John calling from the prison. John has left a message for Mike to call him. When he gets this message, Mike, still in a slightly tipsy, sleepy mode, decides to go wash his face and wake up before calling John.

Finally awake, and a little steadier on his feet, Mike calls the prison, only to find out that John was brought back to his cell, that it's too late to talk to him, and that they will give him the message to call Mike tomorrow. Mike tells them, "Okay, that's fine, but just make sure that he gets the message that I called and to please call me back. It's important."

"Okay, you got it. I will give him the message first thing in the morning."

"Thanks. Bye."

The next morning, Mike sits down and starts to do one of the things he hates the most: waiting for a phone call. He decides to put on the TV and watch the news while waiting for John to call him back. About an hour and a half later, the phone rings. Mike picks it up, and it's John. "Hi, John. I'm sorry I missed your call. I am so frustrated that I took off from work, and I came home and made myself a nice stiff drink, but I guess it got the better of me and I fell asleep. When you called, I could not get to the phone fast enough. So again, I'm sorry."

"No problem, Mike."

"Anyway, John, why did you call me?"

"Well, Mike, during my yard break, I had the opportunity to talk to Barney and Nick, and we sort of came up with an idea about my case, but you will need to come to the prison so that I can explain it to you in person."

"Okay, John. I guess I'll see you tomorrow."

"Okay, Mike."

The next morning, Mike is at the prison, in the same old room, waiting for John. After a few minutes, John is brought in, and he sits at the table. As soon as the guard leaves, Mike says, "Okay, John, so what is your plan? I can't wait another second."

"Well, we were out in the yard, and we figured that we would talk to one or two of the other prisoners that we made friends with, and one of them actually came up with an idea that we think is really the only way to get what we want. The three of us were up all night, thinking of some kind of plan. Barney came up with one, Nick came up with one, and I came up with one, but then, when we all got together and discussed the different plans, we all took each other's plan apart. Every time we came up with what we thought was a good plan, we found holes in it. Then, while I was in the yard, I was talking to one of the prisoners that I befriended who happens to be getting out in three days, so I decided to fill him in on our problem. He said, 'Just let me think about it, and I'll get back to you.' The next day, in the yard, he came up to me, and said that he came up with a foolproof solution to our problem. You'll probably think that this plan is foolish, crazy, and outlandish, but Mike, the three of us feel that it's the only sure way to go."

"Oh boy, I can hardly wait to hear what this plan is."

"I'll give you the short version of it. The way we figured it, the only alternative to this plan would be to kill him."

"Seriously? Are you kidding me? Killing him?"

"Yes, killing him."

"Okay, now that you have my attention, let me hear your plan."

"I told you about one of the prisoners we met."

"Yeah."

"Well, the one guy that is getting out has all kinds of connections, knows a lot of people that do a lot of crazy things, and Barney and Nick, along with myself, went over all our plans step by step and found them not to work. The plan this guy came up with, according to him, is foolproof, and the best part is nobody gets hurt."

"Okay, okay, so what is the plan?"

"It's really a simple plan. All we need to do is kidnap the General and hold him until it's all over and then set him free. He will not be harmed in any way. He will have comfortable accommodations with all the comforts of home, including a television, and be fed three meals a day, and for this, this guy wants $1000 a day. I have enough money in my safe at home to keep him there for a while. That's it in a nutshell."

Mike sits there, staring at John. "Are you serious?"

"I am as serious as a heart attack."

"Okay, and just how do you plan on kidnaping the General?"

"Well, that's where you come in."

"I figured that out, and just how do I enter the plan?"

"All you need to do is give the General a call and convince him to meet with you. Then all you need to do is get in touch with this guy give him the meeting place and time, and he will take it from there."

"And you don't think that the General is going to know that I set him up?"

"That's the other part of the plan. He won't suspect, because you are going to be kidnapped also, along with him."

"You know what, John? I always thought you were a little crazy, but now I know that you are really fucking crazy."

"Mike, this guy assured me that absolutely no harm will come to you or the General in any way, shape, or form. He will take you and the General to a place he has on the outskirts of town. He tells me he has a fully equipped storm cellar, again with all the comforts of home. As soon as you get there, the two of you will be separated, the General will be put into the cellar, and you will be let go. The General will have no idea that you were in on it, or that they let you go. I know this is all hard to swallow in one meal, but Mike, truthfully, you are the only person on the face of this earth that can help us do this, only because you are the only person who can get in touch with him. Again, I know this is against your better judgment, but Mike, I really think that this is the only way to go. In fact, I don't even want your answer now. Go home and sleep on it, and if you can come up with an alternative plan, I will be more than happy to listen to you."

"Okay, John, I'll do like you say. I will go home and sleep on it. I will come back tomorrow and let you know what I decided."

"That's all I ask for, Mike. Thank you, and I will see you tomorrow."

Mike heads back to his office to ponder the situation. He is torn between his friendship with John and his allegiance to John's cause, and his allegiance to his family, to provide for them and not do anything to jeopardize that, so he decides to call Judge Ghetto and ask his advice.

Mike is lucky, because the judge is actually available.

"Good afternoon, Judge."

"Good afternoon, Mike. What's up?"

"Well, Judge, what I would like to do is meet you at the restaurant so that I can ask your opinion about something.

"Mike, if it's about the situation with John, and some kind of new evidence for his case, so to speak, I really would rather not hear about it and would not like to advise you on any sort of a plan. Like I said, I will help you as much as I can, but I refuse to be involved in any decision-making. I am done with that part of this whole relationship. I'm sorry I can't help you out, but like I said, other than making decisions, I will help you out as much as I can. All I can say is let your conscience be your guide."

"Thank you, Judge. I'm going to have to decide this one for myself. Thanks anyway."

"Your welcome, Mike. Sorry I could not help."

"No problem, Judge. Have a good day."

"You to, Mike."

Mike spends most of the night awake, pondering the situation. Finally, at about 4 AM, he comes to a decision, though he thinks that this is not going to go down as one of the best he has so far made in his life. The next morning, Mike calls the prison and leaves a message for John to call him when he gets a chance. Later that day, John calls Mike back. "How you doing, Mike? What's up?"

"Well, about their new evidence that you were talking to me about and that I decided to pursue, rather than making an unnecessary trip to the prison, I figured I'd give you a day to get all the facts together. Then I will come up to the prison and get them from you."

"Okay, Mike, sounds good. I will have it all together for you tomorrow."

"Great, John! See you tomorrow."

The next morning, once again, Mike finds himself at the prison, in the same room, waiting for John. When John comes in, the prison guard leaves, and the two begin to talk.

"Okay, John, so how is this all going to go down?"

"The most important thing is you have to call the General and set up an appointment, but you must not take no for an answer. Setting up the appointment with him is imperative. Once you set it up, I will give you – let's call him Mr. X – I will give you his phone number. Call him and just give him the time and place of the meeting, and that's all you have to do. He will take it from there. Once they get you to the place where they are going to be holding the General, they will let you go. You will then need to go to my house. My wife will open my safe, remove $100,000, give it to you, and you then deliver it to Mr. X. That will be enough money to hold him for a hundred days."

"That's it?"

"That's it."

"Really? You make it sound so easy."

"Mike, it is easy."

"Oh my God, I cannot believe that I am about to do this. Never, not even in my wildest dreams. And when and if I set the meeting up, do you want to know about it?"

"No, just call Mr. X. Go to the meeting and try to act as normal as you can. Maybe you should take a tranquilizer or something before you go."

"That may not be a bad idea."

"Mr. X will go through the General's phone and see who he was talking to the most. Then he'll call them and tell them that he has the General, that if they don't pay him $100,000 dollars, they will kill him. and that he knows that they have the money because he was once a member of their organization. Then, once they have him, you can call up Senator Adams and inform him that the General will not be killing anyone, that he has agreed to hold off and give the Senator a chance to do something. So there. You now have all the information. Good luck, and don't worry; this will be a piece of cake."

"Yeah, I hope it's the kind of cake that I like."

"The only other thing is, after they release you and you call the Senator, please come back to visit and let me know how everything went."

Mike heads right back to his office to try and get in touch with the General and set up the meeting with him. Mike dials the General's number, and after two rings, the General answers. "Mike."

"Yes, General, how did you know it was me?"

"Well, I told the judge not to call me anymore and to give the phone to you, and for you to call me if you wanted to talk, so that is how I knew it was you. And frankly, I was expecting you to call and try to convince me to stop my next action. Well, Mike, let me tell you something; there is nothing that you can say to me to change my mind, because those sons of bitches in Washington just sit on their asses and twiddle their thumbs all fucking day, and someone needs to light a fire under their ass. That someone is me."

"Okay, with that said, and believe me, I understand you, but would you at least give me the courtesy of meeting with me face to face, and give me a chance to explain why I would want you to not stop completely but just postpone your action?"

"Well, if that's all you want to tell me, why do we need to meet in person?"

"That's the lawyer in me. I feel that I would have a better chance of changing your mind, if we met in person."

"Well, okay, but I'm telling you now you are wasting your time. When do you want to meet?"

"The judge told me that whenever you guys met, it was at Brookhaven airport out east, so I would like to meet you there, on Saturday, at about 3 PM. Would that be okay with you?"

"Okay, Mike, I will be in the parking lot. I will be sitting in my truck. It's a dark blue Ford pickup with a white cap. I will have a Mets baseball cap on."

"Great. I will see you on Saturday at 3 PM."

"Okay, Mike. See you there."

Mike next calls Mr. X and gives him all the information. "I've got to tell you I am extremely nervous about this whole thing."

Mr. X explains to Mike, "Please do not worry. This is not my first rodeo. First, no one will be hurt, especially you. When you meet up with this guy, just forget about what's going to happen, and just begin to have a normal conversation with him. Don't seem nervous or jittery, because, if you do, that will let him know that something is about to happen. If you are really nervous, just take a tranquilizer or a shot of vodka before you guys meet up. Just go with the flow, as though it is really happening. Like I said, this is not my first rodeo. I have done this many times before."

"Okay, I will do as you say. See you tomorrow."

It's Saturday morning, and after another sleepless night, Mike decides to get up early and try to do something that will occupy his mind and take it off the action that is scheduled for later on that day. The first thing he decides to do is eat the breakfast that his wife made for him, thinking that will kill at least an hour. But it only takes about a half-hour all together. The next thing he decides to do is work on some of his cases that he brought home, but that does not work, because, after an hour, he cannot comprehend anything that he is reading. The next thing is to take a long shower, but that does not do the trick either. After getting dressed, he decides to watch TV and catch up on the news, but nothing he seems to do is working.

His wife asks him, "Is anything wrong? You seem very nervous."

"No, I'm okay. It's just a big case I'm working on is on my mind."

"Are you sure?"

"Yes, I'm sure."

Mike decides to go to his office, thinking that it will kill some more time, but before he leaves, he decides to take a tranquilizer, and that seems to do the trick. He then heads to his office to take care of some paperwork he has to do. Finally, it is time to go to the airport, so he gets in his car and heads out. While driving there, he thinks that as far back as he can recall, he has never felt anything like the feeling that he is feeling right now, and he feels that he must calm down, because if he doesn't, the General is going to know something is up. A few minutes before getting to the airport, he decides to pull over and take another tranquilizer to calm himself down. Ten minutes later, while going over all the things that could go wrong, he feels that the only way that he is actually involved in the plan is that he knows about it. That is it. He had nothing at all to do with the actual planning of it. After that, and the second tranquilizer taking effect, he feels much better, so he continues to the airport.

Finally getting there, he starts looking for the General's truck, and eventually, he spots it. He looks at his watch and sees that he is a little early, so he decides to park and wait about ten minutes. He decides to wait until five minutes before 3 PM, and at that time, he walks over to the General's truck. Staying calm, he knocks on the window, and the General motions him to get in. As soon as the General does that, Mike get a knot in his stomach, but he opens the door and gets in.

The General speaks first: "So, Mike, what do you want to talk about? I'm telling you now, though, that nothing you say will change my mind. I figured, to be fair, I should at least give you the chance to do so."

"General, I have been with John from the inception of his plan, and I feel that we have come a long way, and a lot of the progress we made is because of you getting into the picture. Now that we feel that we are close to getting something done, I would hate to see that get messed up because of the Senator's stubbornness and why he is being so obstinate, but that's the way they work in Washington. They don't like to be pushed or given ultimatums. They consider that the same as negotiating with terrorists, and that they do not do under any circumstances."

"That's their problem, not mine, and as far as I'm concerned, I feel that we have given them enough time to do their thing."

Just then, a car pulls up behind them. Two guys get out and approach the car. One guy goes to the General's side, and the other guy comes to Mike's side. Both men are wearing police shields around their necks.

The General blurts out, "What the hell do these guys want?" He opens his window and says, "Hi, can I help you?"

The guy replies, "Yes, maybe you can. First, let me inform you that we are detectives and would like to ask you a few questions. Are you the guy they call the General?"

"What?! Who?!"

"You heard me the first time. Are you the guy that they call the General?"

"Officer, first off, I am not the General. I don't know who he is or where he is."

While this is going on, Mike has forgotten all about what was to happen, so it takes him by surprise and actually gets him extremely nervous."

"Sorry, officer, but you got the wrong guy. That's not me."

With that, the guy pulls out a gun and points it at the General's head. "I want both of you to freeze. One move by either one of you will result in a bullet in your head."

The General says, "Are you kidding me?"

The guy hits the General on his head with his gun, opening up a cut and causing it to bleed, and sort of stunning the General. "Does that look like

I'm kidding? Now, I want you guys to do exactly what I say. I want both of you guys to get out of the car, one at a time. You first, General."

"I'm not this guy, the General, you're talking about."

The second guy opens the passenger door and tells Mike to get out of the car. Both of them are told to face the car and to put their hands behind them. Then handcuffs are put on both of them, and they are searched. Everything they have on them is taken and put into a bag. Then they are led to the waiting car and helped into the backseat, with the men asking the General and Mike to please watch their heads.

The General says, "Where are you taking us?"

"We are taking you to the station. Now, shut up, or I will open up another cut on your fucking head. When we get to the station, all your questions will be answered."

The General glares at Mike and asks him, "Did you have anything to do with this?"

Mike looks back at him and says, to add credibility to his answer, because he hardly ever swears, "Are you fucking kidding me? Are you really asking me that question? Do you not see me sitting here beside you, also in cuffs?"

"I'm sorry. It's just that this came out of the blue, and I can't figure out where it came from or what the hell is going on."

"Well, I guess when we get to where we are going, hopefully, they will let us know." Seeing the General bleeding and hurting, Mike now feels bad, and he thinks to himself, *I hope this is all worth it.*

Before driving off, one of the men searches the General's truck, taking everything that is not tied down and putting it into a bag.

After about an hour of driving, the General asks, "Can I ask you a question?"

"Sure."

"Where is this police station?"

"That is none of your business. When we get there, all of your questions will be answered."

Another hour of driving goes by, and they finally come to a dirt driveway. They turn in and drive for five minutes down a winding dirt road, exiting the road at an opening with a small bungalow. They pull up to the bungalow, open the car doors, and tell the General and Mike to get out.

Once out of the car, one of the men grabs the General's arm and says, "You are coming with me." He escorts the General to a cellar door, opens it, and takes him down into the cellar.

"Why are you separating us?"

"Still, with the fucking questions. I'm going to give you that question free. One more question, and I will open up your head again. Is that understood?"

"Yes."

The cellar is set up with all the comforts of home: full bathroom, bedroom, TV, and full kitchen, including a pantry full of food. The only thing that seems to be missing is a telephone.

"Okay, General, I am now going to tell you what you are doing here and who I am, and I am only going to tell you this once, so pay attention. I know who you are and exactly what you do, because I was once a member of your underground organization. So what I am doing here is holding you for ransom, because I know the organization can afford it, and I feel that you are worth at least $100,000. If they don't pay it, I will kill you. As far as your friend goes, I have no idea of who he is. He was just at the wrong place at the wrong time, but I'm sure that he is worth something to somebody, and that I will figure out later. Now, do you have any more questions? This will be your one and only time that I will answer any of your questions from here on out. So, do you have any more questions?"

"I guess not, now that I know what I'm doing here. By the way, what club were you in?"

"Sorry, you said you had no more questions. I will check on you a few times daily to see if you have any needs. Once your ransom is paid, I will give you money for a bus ticket and drive you to the nearest bus station, and you will never see me again."

In the meantime, Mike is upstairs getting all his stuff back and getting an apology from the second guy. "I hope we didn't scare you too much, but we had to make it look real. We will drive you back to your home or office, or wherever you want to go, but there are two things you must agree to. First, you will get us our money and, second, be ready and willing to come back here whenever we need you to make an appearance to the General."

"Yeah, I guess I could do that."

"Okay, then. What we need now is your contact information, and if you have everything and are ready to go, we will drive you to wherever you want to go."

"The first thing I need to do is get my car and then go and get your money. Then I will call you to find out where to meet to give you your money."

"Okay, that's good, because we have to go and pick up the General's truck anyway and bring it back here so that it's hidden. We don't want the police to start looking for the driver of this truck, so we'll keep it hidden here."

With that, they drive Mike back to his car and pick up the General's truck.

Mike gets into his car and drives straight to John's house. John's wife, Mary, opens the door. "Hi, Mike. John called and told me that you would be paying me a visit and to have the money ready for you, so here it is."

Mike then drives back to his office. As soon as he walks in the door, he instructs his secretary to get Senator Adams on the phone. Surprisingly, the Senator is in his office, and Mike gets him on the phone. "Hi, Senator. You know that problem you were having a few days ago with that phone call that you got from that person trying to give you an ultimatum about a bill that you are trying to get passed? Do you know what I'm talking about?"

"Yes, I do."

"Well, let me assure you that problem has been taken care of, so try to forget about it. Although it may be a hard thing to do, try to make believe that you never got that call and just keep working on getting that bill passed."

"Okay, Mike, I will do that. And just how did you convince that person to stand down, because he seemed extremely steadfast on his quest? Are you sure that he will stand down?"

"Senator, I am absolutely sure that this person will stand down. The only thing I cannot tell you now is how long he will stand down, but if anything changes, I promise I will let you know. But please, if you can, promise me that you will finally pursue the passing of the bill that we are talking about."

"Well, okay, but I just hope that person knows just how close he came to me forgetting about the whole deal we had, because, as I said before, we don't negotiate with anyone who threatens us in any way."

"Senator, I understand that, and I'm sorry. Let me apologize for that phone call you got, and please be assured that it will not happen again."

"Okay, Mike. I hope so."

"Thanks again, Senator. Just keep working on that bill, and please let me know any time you make any progress on it, no matter how small."

"Okay, Mike, you got it, but I need some help from you also. I need the name of this General, because he confessed that he was the one who was responsible for the two mass killings. Part of this deal now is you getting me his name."

"Senator, I don't know his name, but I will try and get it for you."

"I don't understand, Mike. You say that this guy is not going to be a problem, and yet you tell me that you don't know who he is. How is that possible?"

"Because I never spoke to him. I did this through a third person."

"And who is this person?"

"He is an informant who calls me from time to time with information, about some of my cases, and I pay this guy whenever he has something good that I can use. But like I said, if my informant calls, I will try to get the General's name."

"Okay, Mike. I will hold you to your word."

"I understand, Senator."

"You take care now."

"And you too, Senator. Bye for now."

Then Mike calls Mr. X, informs him that he has his money, and asks him where he would like to meet to get it. Mr. X informs Mike that he will pick it up at Mike's office. Mike, a little surprised, says, "Oh, okay, that is fine."

"So can we come over now?"

"Sure. I'm here working."

"Okay, great. See you in a little."

Mike hangs up and thinks to himself, *I hope this all works out.* Thinking how much work he has put aside because of all the drama that has been going on, he realizes that now it's time to get back to his business and earn some money. Just as he is in the middle of working, his secretary come in and tells him that there is a man there to see him and that he says Mike is expecting him. "Oh yes, please have him come in."

Mr. X walks in, and Mike hands him the money. "I will count it later," says Mr. X. "I trust you."

"Oh yea, believe me, it's all there."

"Great, Mike. See you later. And remember, if we should need you, you are willing to meet with us, right?"

"Right."

"Okay, then. You take it easy."

Five days go by. Mike is busy earning money and is finally calming down and settling into his work when his secretary knocks on his door. She tells him that there are two men in her office who seem very nervous and who are demanding to speak to him. Mike thinks to himself, *What the hell is going on now?* "Ok. Send them in."

"Okay, sir."

When the guys walk into his office, Mike nearly has a heart attack, because, of all the people to walk into his office, these two would not even be on the list. It's Mr. X and his friend. Mike just stares at them and asks them to please close the door. Mike looks at them and says, "Excuse me, but what the fuck are you guys doing here?"

"Well, Mike, we have some bad news for you. This morning, we went to check on the General, and he was gone."

"What!"

"He is gone, and so is his truck."

"His truck too?"

"Yes."

"Oh, and I guess you just had the keys hung on a nail right by the door, right?"

"No, we still have the keys. We left nothing of his there. He broke the truck window, and I guess he jumped the wires to start the truck. Plus, we are sure that he looked for you before he left the area."

"I don't understand what happened. You guys were supposed to know what the fuck you were doing. First off, how the hell did he get out?"

"Well, it seems that he somehow broke some water pipes and used them to break through the two-inch solid wood door. He made a hole just big enough to put his hand through and lift off the bar that was holding the door closed, but we can talk about that later. Mike. Right now, we are just concerned that with him not finding you there and him putting two and two together, you are in danger, and until we can find him, we think you need to get out of town. We came here to protect you and help you get out of town."

Mike's head is now spinning. He feels that he is in a bad dream and wants to wake up, but can't. "I can't believe what you guys are asking me to do. I just can't drop everything and leave town. I have a business to run, and what do I tell my wife? She doesn't know anything about this. I just don't know what to do."

"Well, we do, and that is for you and your wife to get out of town for now, until we have a chance to try and find him."

"And how do you plan on doing that?"

"Well, we do have all of his personal belongings, including his cell phone and wallet, so we have his address and know someone who can get an address from the phone numbers on the phone. We also have some people who are helping us, because we also still have the $100,000 you guys gave us and were able to hire a few guys. But Mike, right now, you really need to think of a place to go, and you need to do that right now. That is what we are doing here. We will work the other details out later. Please think of a place to go."

Mike is now also thinking about the phone call he had with the Senator, and he thinks he now has to let the Senator know what the hell is going on, so he realizes that he should probably go to Washington. Also, he thinks that he should let John and the judge know. There are so many things to do, and too little time. Mike thinks, *The first thing I need to do is, like they said, get the hell out of town and worry about letting everyone else know what is going on.* "Okay," he says to Mr. X, "let me tell my secretary to get me a ticket to Washington.

"Absolutely not. What you need to do is go with us right now to the airport, buy your ticket, and go, and buy everything else that you need when you get there. And talk to no one else but us. We have a throwaway phone for you to call us with, and we will do what needs to get done, so just tell your secretary that you need to go with us. And as far as your wife goes, you can call her when we are on our way to the airport. Tell her to get ready and to just take what she can carry, and we will pick her up. But for now, let's get the fuck out of here. Everything else we can do later."

Mike tells his secretary, "I need to go with these guys, and if anyone asks, you have no idea where I'm at or when I left, and you don't know when I will be back."

"Sir, is everything alright?"

"Yes, it is. I'm perfectly fine. Don't worry. It's just something that I have been working on, and it came up sooner that I thought it would, and I don't know how long I will be gone."

"Sir, are you sure?"

"I'm absolutely sure. Don't worry."

With that, all three men leave and head for the airport. On the way, they pick up Mike's wife. It all goes well: they get to the airport, Mike gets his tickets, and an hour later, Mike and his wife are on the plane, heading to Washington, D.C., with Mike's wife's head spinning with a thousand questions. While Mr. X and his friend leave and get to the business of finding the General, Mike is on the plane, trying to wrap his head around what has just happened.

One of the first things Mike does when he gets on the plane is to use the plane's phone to book a room in a D.C. hotel. With that done, Mike now starts thinking about how he is going to break the news to his wife, and he needs to come up with some sort of a credible bullshit story for her to believe. On top of that, he needs to decide how and when he will get in touch with the Senator and exactly how and what he will tell him.

They finally arrive in D.C., and since the only luggage they have is his attaché case and one suitcase that his wife brought, he heads right over to the car rental area and rents a car. Then they head for the hotel.

Once checked in, Mike goes to his room to unwind and gather himself, because his head is spinning like a top. He is having a hard time trying to figure out what to tell his wife. Finally, in the room, his wife grabs him, sits him down, and says, "Okay, now you must let me know what the hell is going on."

Thinking fast, Mike tells her, "Well, it is about a case that I'm working, defending someone who killed someone. I think he did it, and he thinks that I am not doing such a good job of defending him. He broke out of jail, and the police decided that the best thing that I could do was to get out of town, so here we are."

"And you expect me to believe that cock and bull story?"

"Yes, I do, because it's the truth. Why would I lie to you?"

"Okay, it better be the truth, so help me God, because if you are lying to me, we are going to have a big problem."

"It's the truth, I swear."

With that, Mike decides to call for room service and order a few drinks to calm the two of them down. When the drinks get there, Mike grabs his and takes a huge gulp, and that instantly calms him down.

Mike's wife asks him, "Are you sure that we will be okay?"

"Yes, I am."

"Okay."

"What do you say that while we are here, we turn it into a vacation?"

"Are you sure?"

"Yes, I'm sure. So, why don't you decide where you want to eat tonight. But even before that, what do you say to a little shopping spree, seeing that you and I did not get a chance to pack much stuff. We will go out, and you and I can get a few new outfits, come back here, pick a nice restaurant, and then we will go out tonight and start our vacation."

"Okay, that sounds great."

"Good. Get ready, and we will go shopping."

"Okay, but let me say this. I'll accept that story for now, but I have to tell you I am not one hundred percent satisfied."

"Then what percentage of satisfaction are you at?"

"Ninety-eight percent, so you still have two percent to prove to me."

"That's okay; I'll take that ninety-eight percent. That's close enough. Go take your shower, and let's go and have dinner."

"Good idea, Mike. I will be ready in a few minutes."

Later, at dinner, Mike is trying to act very nonchalant, as though everything is normal. His wife makes small talk and tries to make plans. Mike asks his wife what she would like to do on their so-called vacation. In the meantime, while trying to hold a normal conversation, Mike's brain is smoking, thinking about when he is going to call the Senator and what he is going to tell him. He's also wondering about what the hell is going on back home in regards to the General and when Mr. X will call him. The rest of the evening goes well, with the two of them making some plans.

The next morning, which is now the third day that Mike has been in Washington, after he and his wife finish breakfast, they head back to the room. Once in the room, Mike decides to call his office and see what's going on there.

Mike's secretary seems surprised to hear from him. "Mr. Santino! Where have you been? I've been concerned about you. You took off so suddenly."

"I'm okay, just some business I had to take care of."

"Okay, I was concerned. Senator Adams has called twice wanting to speak to you, and he would like for you to return his call."

"Great! I will get in touch with him as soon as I can, and don't worry; I'm fine. Are there any other calls?"

"No, sir."

"Okay, great. I will call you tomorrow."

"Thank you, sir."

Mike is now really concerned. He thinks that the Senator may know something, and he is reluctant to call him for fear of not knowing what to say. Finally, he decides that if the Senator does question him about the General, he will deny everything and say that all he knew was that the General was going to hold back with whatever plans he had; that is, unless he can come up with a better story to tell the Senator.

Mike and his wife decide to go out, and check out some of Washington's points of interest. While doing all of this, Mike's mind is on calling the Senator and what he's going to tell him. Four hours later, and back in the room, Mike has no idea what points of interest he saw. Mike explains to his wife, "I need to make an important call to a Senator here in Washington about the case he's working on, and I'm going to need quiet. Since you are watching TV, I will need to go into the bathroom to make the call."

Mike's wife tells him, "No problem, Mike."

Mike goes into the bathroom and summons up enough courage to call the Senator. Finally, when he's finished arguing with himself, Mike dials the phone number.

"Good morning, Senator Adams's office."

"Good morning. This is Mr. Santino, returning the Senator's call."

"Just a moment, Mr. Santino. I will see if the Senator is in."

Mike nervously waits for the Senator to get on the phone, but instead, the secretary gets back on. "Mr. Santino, I'm sorry, but the Senator is busy right now. He said that he will call you back ASAP."

"Okay, great. Please have the Senator call me on my cell phone." Mike gives her his cell number.

"Mr. Santino, I will give the Senator your message and phone number."

"Thank you. Bye."

Mike thinks that this is a good thing because it affords him more time to come up with some kind of a story if the Senator questions him about the General. Mike comes out of the bathroom, and his wife asks, "So how did your talk with the Senator go?"

"He wasn't there. He is going to call me back on my cell. So what we have to do now is think about dinner and what we'd like to eat."

"You know what, Mike? I think I feel like eating Chinese tonight."

Mike replies, "That's fine with me. I'll check with the front desk to find out where there is a good Chinese restaurant. I'll be right back."

Mike heads down to the front desk to ask about the Chinese restaurant. When he gets there, the clerk asks, "Can I help you?"

"Yes, you can. I'm trying to find out if you could recommend a good Chinese restaurant in the area." As soon as the words come out of his mouth, Mike's cell phone begins to ring. Mike looks down at his phone and sees that it's the Senator calling. "Oh, excuse me. I need to take this call."

Mike answers the call, and it's the Senator's secretary. "Mr. Santino?"

"Yes."

"Senator Adams would like to speak to you. I will put him on the phone now."

"Thank you."

"Mike!" said the Senator. "Where have you been? I have been trying to reach you for two days."

"Oh, I'm sorry, Senator, but I've been really busy with a few of my cases."

"That's all good. Anyway, the reason I've been trying to reach you is that I have great news for you. I spoke to my fellow Senators about the bill that I was about to introduce, and they all seem to have no problem with it, so I am going to introduce the bill this week to be voted on. Between you and me, I don't see any problem with getting the bill passed. The other great news is that I spoke to the president, explained the bill that I am trying to pass and all of the heartaches that John and his cohorts have gone through, and the president agreed that if the bill goes through and is passed, then it would indicate that it was a good bill and that the cause that John and his cohorts are fighting for is a just cause. He would get John, Barney, and Nick released from prison by having their sentence reduced to time served."

Mike is stunned does not know what to say. There is silence on the phone. The Senator says, "Mike, are you there?"

"Yes, yes, I am, Senator. I'm just flabbergasted that this day has finally come, and it's put me in the position where I am at a loss for words."

"Well, don't get too excited, Mike. This is only the beginning. As a lawyer, you know what this bill has to go through before it becomes law. First, it needs to go to the appropriate committee. There it will be studied, and there is where we may have a problem, because there is where changes will be made if any. Then, once they make all the little tweaks, it goes to the floor for them to debate. After that, both the House and Senate must pass the bill. If there's any problem with it, then a conference committee made up of Senators and representatives will work out any differences. Once finished, the final version must be approved by both houses. Then, and only then, it will go to the president for him to sign into law. And even then, if the president does not like the bill, he can veto it, and the only way around that would be at least two-thirds vote in both the House and Senate to override the veto and for this bill to become law."

"I understand that, Senator, but to me this is a large step, a great, large step, and I cannot wait to let John know what the latest news is. Thank you very much, Senator. I cannot find words to thank you enough."

"No need for that, Mike. As a Senator, this is part of my job. I will keep you informed as to the progress of the bill, but before you enjoy the moment, there is one final thing that I must discuss with you. What about this so-called General who called me? Like I told you before, remember, he actually confessed to being the person who was responsible for the two mass killings in Texas and Virginia, and part of this deal is for you to cooperate with us in finding and prosecuting this General. And remember, Mike, I'm starting the process of passing this bill, and I can also stop it anytime I want before it's put into law, so I want you to start investigating this General at your end and help us apprehend this guy. Is that understood?"

"Yes, it is, and I understand."

"I will try to get as much information as I can so that you can catch this guy."

"Okay, Senator, and again, thank you and bye for now."

Mike hangs up and stands there in a state of euphoria, thinking that he needs to pinch himself to make sure he's not dreaming, but the state of euphoria quickly fades as Mike's thoughts now go back to the General: *Where is he? What is he doing? And is Mr. X still trying to track him down?* Mike hopes that the General isn't doing anything to fuck things up. Next, Mike thinks that he needs to call John and give him the good news, but that also fades, because now his next thought is to try and get in touch with Mr. X. In Mike's mind, the next logical step would be to make absolutely sure that the General can't mess anything up, so the next call Mike makes is to Mr. X.

Mr. X, doesn't answer, so Mike leaves a message: "Hi, this is Mike. I really need some good news. There's been new developments, and I don't like it that the general is running loose out there and has the ability to fuck things up all of a sudden."

Mr. X answers the phone. "Hi, Mike. I was just getting ready to call you. I have a little good news. We are pretty sure we know where he's at, and we will be closing in on him later on today. If anything changes, you will be first person I call."

"That's a little good news, but please, keep me updated and let me know as soon as you have him."

"You got it, Mike. Don't worry; we will get him."

Mike then goes back to his room. As soon as he enters the room, his wife asks, "So, did you find a good Chinese restaurant?"

Mike thinks to himself, *My God, with the phone call that I got, I forgot all about asking the clerk about the Chinese restaurant.* Thinking fast, Mike tells his wife, "The clerk is going to check and call me, or I'll check back with him in about fifteen minutes."

Twenty minutes later, Mike's wife informs him that she is getting hungry and wants him to check on the Chinese restaurant. Mike picks up the phone and calls the front desk. He explains that he was there earlier inquiring about a good Chinese restaurant and that he never got an answer. The clerk informs him that he actually has a brochure on a good Chinese restaurant and that Mike can pick it up on his way out. "Okay," Mike says, "I will do that. Thanks."

He turns to his wife and says, "Okay, sweetheart, the clerk has a brochure on a good Chinese restaurant near here. We can pick it up on our way out."

His wife looks at him and says, "Why do you seem so jovial? Your whole demeanor changed when you came back from downstairs."

"Well, it's because I got a call from the Senator that I was trying to get in touch with, and I finally did get in touch with him, and he gave me some great news about John's case, which I've been working on, so that's why I'm in a good mood."

"That's great. I'm happy that you got good news for you and John and the rest of the crew."

"Thank you, honey. Now, let's go out and eat, and also have a drink to celebrate the good news I got." With that, Mike and his wife go down, pick up the brochure, and then proceed to the Chinese restaurant.

When they finally get to the restaurant, Mike and his wife are surprised and pleased with how nice the place looks. Mike's wife remarks, "If the food is half as good as this place looks, we should really enjoy our meal."

Once seated, they check the menu and order their food and alcoholic drinks to celebrate the good news that Mike got. Two minutes later, the waitress serves the two drinks. Mike and his wife clang their glasses in a toast to the good news. As soon as they each take a sip, Mike's phone rings. He checks his phone and sees that it's Mr. X. Mike excuses himself from the table, informing his wife that he is sorry, but that he needs to take this call, that he needs absolute quiet, and that he'll be right back. Mike walks over to the lobby, seeking a quiet corner so that he can answer his phone.

"Hello, Mike, this is Mr. X."

"Tell me you got good news for me."

"No, I don't have good news for you. I got great news for you. We tracked down the General and have him secured in a place that he cannot escape from again I wanted to get this information to you as soon as I could so that you can make plans to come back home."

"Great! I thought I had good news earlier, but this news supersedes that. Right now, I'm having dinner with my wife, but as soon as we are finished eating, I'm going to make plans to come home. Also, when I get home, we need to talk so that I can decide what my next move will be."

Back at the table, Mike breaks the news to his wife. "Good news, honey. That call was about my case, and they settled, so we are free to go home. That is, if you are ready to go home."

"Mike, I was ready to go home on the first day I got here. This is not really my town."

"Okay, when we get back to the room, I will make arrangements to get us home."

"Good, Mike. It will be great to get home, the sooner the better."

"So, eat up, and let's get out of here."

Back in the room, the first thing Mike does is get on the phone to make arrangements to go home. Off the phone, Mike turns to his wife and says, "Well, that went well. We are booked on the second flight home. We need to be at the airport by 9 AM tomorrow morning."

"I can't wait, Mike."

At 8:30 the next morning, Mike and his wife are at the airport. A few hours later, they are in a cab and on their way home. Once home, Mike tells his wife that he will need to run to the office later to tie up a few loose ends.

"Ok, Mike. I'm just happy to be home."

Later on that day, Mike heads to his office. His secretary greets him with a big smile and a pile of messages that came in for Mike over the few days that he was gone.

Mike says hello, grabs the stack of messages, and tells his secretary, "I'm going to be on the phone for a while and do not want to be disturbed."

Mike heads for his office, closes the door, reads some of the messages, and thinks to himself that he has got to get on the ball. He needs to remind himself that he still has a business to run, with clients that are counting on him, so he decides to take care of business first before he calls Mr. X.

After taking care of business, Mike calls Mr. X.

"Mike, how are you doing today?"

"Well, I called to see how everything is going there and to see how the General is doing."

"The General is fine. He was not harmed and is comfortable where he's at. The only thing he keeps asking is what's going on, and I keep telling him the same story: that we kidnapped him for ransom, but he's not buying that story. Anyway, Mike, what's going on at your end?"

"Well, I got good news from the Senator, that he is introducing the bill and thinks that it will pass, but my biggest problem now is explaining to the General why I did it, and asking that he understand why I did it so that he doesn't want to kill me. What I would like for you to do is break the story to him while you have him captive, and hopefully, after he settles down, I would like to have a face to face with him and explain. If he is willing to forgive and forget, he will be free to go."

"Okay, Mike, I will fill him in on the whole story and get back to you and let you know how he is taking it."

"I'll wait for your phone call. Thank you. Bye."

Mike puts a call into the prison and leaves a message for John that he will be up to visit him tomorrow with some news. Then he decides that after the stress of the past few days, he just needs to go home and unwind for the rest of the day.

Early the next morning, Mike is on his way to the prison to see John. Again, he is led into the small, dull room that he is always led to when he meets up with John. After a few minutes, John is brought in by two guards. They chain John to the table and leave.

"So, Mike, what brings you here? I hope you got good news for me."

"Good, John. Let me put it this way: I have good news, great news, and some problem news. What would you like to hear first?"

"Give me the good news first. I need some."

"The good news is that I got a call from Senator Adams, and he has introduced the bill to change the child molester laws."

"You're not kidding me, are you?"

"Absolutely not. He introduced it a few days ago and doesn't foresee any problem with it, as far as his fellow Senators go."

"Okay, that's good. Now, what's the great news?"

"The great news is that the Senator spoke to the president, and the president said that if the bill goes through and is passed, he will consider it a justified bill, with changes that were needed to the current child molester laws now on the books. Also, he will amend your sentences, for all three of you, to time served, but only if the bill is passed."

"Mike, if you're kidding me, I swear I will kill you with my bare hands."

"John, I would not kid about anything this important."

"Oh my God! I can't believe this is happening. I can't wait to see Barney and Nick and give them the good news. So, now, what's this problem news? Now I'm afraid to listen to it."

"Well, there's a problem with the General."

"Oh no. What is he up to now?"

Mike looks at John and smacks his forehead. "My God, all this was going on, and I forgot that you don't know what was going on with the General."

"What was going on with the General?"

"Well, first of all, you know about the General calling the Senator and threatening to kill thousands of child molesters if he did not introduce the bill, and on top of that, the General confessed to the Senator that he was the one responsible for the mass killings in Texas and Virginia. Because of that call, we had to take the action that we did, but what you don't know, is that the General somehow escaped. Mr. X feared for my life and suggested that I leave town until they recaptured him, so I went to Washington, D.C., for a few days, even had my wife come and stay with me. But since then, the General has been recaptured and is now being safely held again. Now, this is where the problem comes in. Part of the deal for introducing the bill and helping it get passed is that we give the Senator information about who the General is and where he can be found."

"Oh boy, that's going to be a tough pill to swallow. I mean, the General is responsible for bringing us this far. Do we now throw him under the bus?"

"Well, John, we have to think of the big picture. I'm not saying to hand him over on a silver platter. We could just give them some tidbits of information, just enough to appeal to them, but also warn the General to stay low, or even possibly get out of the country for a while. I don't know what else to do. We've come so far; I would hate for the Senator to kill this bill now."

"Okay, Mike, let me sleep on it. I'll talk to Nick and Barney tomorrow, and between us three and you, we should be able to come up with some sort of a solution. I am really pissed at the General for doing what he did. Just remember, he put himself into this bind by going all maverick on us, so no matter how we look at it, he has dug his own hole and is going to have to try to dig himself out."

"Okay, John, well I gave you the good, the bad, and the problem news, so let's all sleep on it and hopefully come up with a good idea, because there are still children being molested out there."

"Did you hear about the two sisters that disappeared on their way home from school last week? They are ten and thirteen years old. That was last week, and there's still no sign of them, and I can almost guarantee you that it was a child molester that should not have been walking the streets."

"No, I did not hear about that, but then again, I was kind of busy. But for now, try to think about our present problem, and hopefully, what we are doing here will help with situations like that."

"Okay, Mike. Thanks. Talk to you later."

It's two days before Mike hears from Mr. X. "Good morning, Mike. Well, I spoke to the General, and to say the least, he did not take the news very well. Let me put it this way: it's a good thing that there was a barrier between us, because I think that he would have killed us with his bare hands. And you don't want to know what he said about you and your family. We may have a huge problem with him. I spoke to him for over an hour and calmed him down a little, but he is still really agitated. In my opinion, it is not safe to let him go right now. I spoke to him again this morning, and he seems a little calmer, but he's still not ready to be released. If you want to try to talk to him and get him to see the reasoning as to why you did what you did, and maybe calm him down enough to set him free, you are welcome to try and do that. While you are trying, we will keep you safe, but just a note, Mike, the money you paid us is running out. You have two weeks left before we walk away or get more money, so if you decide that you want to speak to him, let me know, and I will set it up."

"Well, at this point, I think I need to speak to him, and hopefully, I can calm him down enough to set him free, because there is something I know that the General does not know, that because of his big mouth, he has gotten himself in big trouble. I can warn him of this, so that may carry a little weight to sway him over to see the light, bite the bullet, and see the big picture. I would really like to try to calm him down."

"Okay, Mike, I will set it up for tomorrow. What time would be good time for you?"

"How about 3 PM?"

"Okay, I will pick you up at your office at 3 PM tomorrow. I want to drive you there, because I want at least three of us there with you."

"Then I will see you tomorrow at 3PM."

"Good."

Three PM sharp, the next day, Mr. X is at Mike's office. Both men get in the car and drive off. One hour later, they are at their destination. Mike is slow getting out of the car and walking kind of slow.

"Are you okay, Mike?" Mr X. asks.

"Yea, I'm just a little nervous."

"I can understand, and let me say this, Mike: I have seen a lot of tough guys, but this guy seems like the real thing, so before we go in, let me give you one more option. For $20,000 more, I can fix it so that you never have to worry about this guy again."

"What!! Oh no, I would never think of doing anything like that."

"I just wanted to give you that option."

With that, Mike and Mr. X enters the building. Mike looks around and does not see the General. Mr. X says, "He is downstairs. Let me go down first and let him know that you are here."

Mr. X goes down. The General is seated at a table, and he seems calm. "General," says Mr. X, "Mike is here to talk to you. Are you going to remain calm while he talks to you? And General, just for you own information, you left Mike little choices as to how to handle the situation you put the whole movement in. Just keep that in mind when he speaks to you, okay?"

The General glares at Mr. X and says, "Bring him down."

Mr. X brings Mike down. The General is still seated at the table, and between him and Mike are Mr. X and two more men built like, as the saying goes, brick shit houses. They had to be at least six foot four and 300 lbs. each, with about two ounces of fat between the two of them.

The General speaks first: "Good afternoon, Mike."

Half frozen, it takes just about all of Mike's energy and concentration to speak, but he managers to get out a "Good afternoon, General."

"So, tell me, Mike. Let me hear all your good reasons that you had to do what you did to me, and to quote your Mr. X, how I gave you little choices to choose from. Come on, let me hear them. I'm listening!"

Mike stands there, quiet and shaking a little. Finally, he gathers himself together enough to speak, and starts by saying, "Good afternoon, General." Then he pauses, thinking of what he wants to say. "First off, let me say this."

At that, the General blurts out, "Yea, yea, you are very sorry. I know what you're going to say. Let's get past that. I know how sorry you are. Let me hear the rest of the bullshit, why you did what you did to me after you tried to convince me not to do anything, yet never gave me a chance to change my mind. Instead, you had these two goons kidnap me and, in the process, drew blood. Why didn't you give me a little more time?"

Mike, now getting a little more comfortable talking to the General, says, "First off, General, you did not even want to meet. You said more than once that it was a waste of my time to try and talk you out of what you had planned, and you seemed very adamant about it. So now you are telling me that I did not give you enough time. If I thought for one second that I could have changed you mind, I would have given you every opportunity to do so, and also, I did not want you to change your mind about doing it. All I was asking for was for you to postpone what you planned to do, that's all, not to cancel it, but you were not hearing anything I was saying. You were steadfast and hell-bent on going on with your plan, even though I told you that we were close to having the Senator introduce the bill, which was the sole purpose of the whole movement, and that if you started doing what you planned on doing, that you would put a stop to everything. But you just did not care. You had a closed mind and did not want to hear anything, and that is why I had to do what I had to do. And the key word here is had, and yes, I am extremely sorry for what I had to have done to you. You left us absolutely no choice."

"And just who is us?"

"Well, us is me, John, Barney, Nick, and the judge. We all decided that this was the only way, short of killing you, to stop you. That is why we did it."

The General blurts out, "Well, I was doing it for The Club."

"Yeah, but you forgot who started The Club and who is currently in jail because of it. I thought that these were the people that you were ultimately trying to help, not just The Club itself. And while we are at it, I do want to give you credit for bringing us to the point that we are at. I don't know if we would be here if it wasn't for you, but just when we were about to take a big step, you lost your patience and almost fucked everything up."

"What do you mean almost fucked it up?"

"What I mean is that last week, the Senator finally introduced the bill, and it looks like it is going to pass. And on top of that, Barney, Nick, and John stand a good chance of getting out of jail with time served. That's what I mean. Do you now understand what I mean?"

"Yes."

"And do you want to hear what the worst part of your fuck up is?"

"After what you have been saying, I don't know if I want to hear it."

"Well, that's too bad, because I have to tell you."

"What do you mean, you have to tell me?"

"I have to tell you because the bill getting passed is predicated on you."

"I don't understand."

"Well, this is it. When you called the Senator and tried to give him an ultimatum, you also confessed to being the person responsible for the two mass killings in Texas and Virginia, and because you opened your big mouth, he wants us to help him capture you so that you can be tried and convicted. He thinks that we have information about you that will help him catch you. I have been telling him that we do not know anything about you, that you are simply a maverick, working on your own, picking up from what you read in the newspapers, but I don't know if he is buying it. Also, he wants to know how it was that I was able to stop you from implementing your plan. I have not told him anything yet, but if he pushes me, I am going to tell him that I have a confidential informant that helped me out, that this person calls me from time to time and helps me out with different things, and when I asked him about a general who was talking about killing child molesters, he knew of him, and was able to get in touch with him. I asked him if there was any way to persuade him from something that he was planning on doing, and he told me that there was always something someone could do for anything, so I asked him to try to stop the General, or at least ask him to hold back. He said to consider it done, and that he would send me a bill, of which I have not seen or know of yet, or even know what it will be, but I will cross that bridge when I get to it. So if he does push me, that is the story that I will tell him, and hopefully, he buys it."

The General is now just staring at Mike. "You know what? Hearing it the way you are telling it, I guess I could have waited a little longer, but I just hate waiting for anything. And now I can see that you did not have much of a choice in doing what you did to stop me. You know what, Mike? I'm sorry. I really am, and I hope that I did not fuck it all up."

"Hopefully, you didn't."

"Okay, Mike, so where do we go from here?"

"Well, General, if you give me your word that you will not retaliate on me or my family, the judge, John, Barney, or Nick, I will have these men release you."

"You got it, Mike. I swear, no retaliation on anyone."

"Okay, but General, I would suggest that you lay low or maybe get out of the country until this whole deal quiets down, or until the Senator is assured that I do not know who you are or how to get in touch with you."

"Okay."

With that, the General extends his hand out to shake with Mike. Mike hesitates for a second and then reaches out his hand, and both men shake. Then Mike asks the General, "Can we give you a ride back to wherever you want to go?"

"Yes, that would be fine. I would like a ride to my truck."

"No problem, General. Mr. X, the General, and Mike get in one car and leave. They drop off the General at his truck, and then Mr. X takes Mike back to his office. Mike thanks Mr. X.

"No problem, Mike, and if you should need us again, for any reason, you got my number."

"Okay, thanks."

Back at his office, Mike thinks it's now time to get back to work for his clients, hopefully thinking that the worst is behind him and that all he has to do now is wait and hear from the Senator, with good news, so Mike grabs a few files and gets down to work.

A week goes by with not too much happening, just everyday activities. Then, while deep in thought on one of his cases, Mike's secretary lets him know that he has a call from Senator Adams.

"Good morning, Mike. How are you doing?"

"I'm doing fine, Senator. How about you?"

"I'm doing good also."

"So, Senator, I hope you have good news for me."

"Well, that depends. Do you have good news for me?"

"As far as what, Senator?"

"As far as the General. Do you have any information as to who he is?"

"Sorry, Senator, but I don't. If you remember, I told you that the only way that I even knew about the General was from a confidential informant who calls me from time to time. I pay him for any information I can use, and there is no way for me to get in touch with him. But Senator, I promise you that if he calls, I will ask him about the General and forward any information I get on him to you."

"Mike, I hope that you're being honest with me."

"Senator, I promise I am being absolutely honest with you."

"Okay, Mike. Anyway, I called you, because I have some good news for you, and a little bad news also."

"How about you give me the good news first."

"The good news is that my bill passed through the committee, and the bad news is that they made one change to the bill, and remember, I warned you about that."

"Yes, I remember."

"Well, anyway, the one change they made was that they took out the clause about the death sentence being carried out within thirty days and changed it to one year to give the suspect a little more time to submit an appeal, just in case there was a mistake somewhere. So the first thing I need to know is if you are okay with that change, and to tell you the truth, I thought that they would have made more changes than that, but you got lucky. So, what do you think? Can you live with that change? If not, I can still pull the whole bill, so you need to let me know now. What do you say?"

"First, Senator, I need to speak to John about this. Can I call you back?"

"Sure, you can call me back, but don't wait too long. You have two days to get back to me, because the next step is that it goes to the floor for general debate, and if John is not happy with that change, then I want to pull it before it goes to the floor."

"Senator, I will get in touch with John today and get back to you."

"Okay, Mike, talk to you later."

"Bye, Senator."

Next, Mike puts a call into the prison and leave a message for John to call him back ASAP. One hour later, Mike gets a call from John.

"What's up, Mike?"

"Well, I got good news and a little bad news."

"Tell you what. Give me the bad news first."

"Okay, the bad news is that the bill went through committee and they changed the thirty-day rule about the death penalty to one year. They did it to give the suspect a chance to appeal, just in case there was a mistake somewhere in the case. The good news is that it went through committee, and that was the only change they made. I got a call from the Senator today, and he wants an answer ASAP as to what you think about the change. He said that if you don't like it, he can pull the bill and forget about everything, so I need your answer, John. What do you think?"

"Man! I told them I would not stand for any changes, and they went and did it anyway. Those people are a piece of work. What do you think, Mike?"

"at this stage in the game, John, if that's the only change they made, I would be happy and go ahead with it because, if they wanted to, they could have ripped that whole bill apart, and you would have ended up with nothing that you wanted. So my educated opinion would be to accept that change and let the bill go forward."

"Well, I guess you're right, Mike. Okay, call the Senator back and tell them him that I will accept the changes. So, is that it? Can they make any other changes?"

"John, this bill still has a long way to go, and there are many stops along the way with changes that will be suggested or made, so let's keep our fingers crossed and cross one bridge at a time."

"Okay, Mike. Let's go with it, and hopefully, that'll be it for changes."

"Well, John, cheer up. It's still good news. The major portion of the bill hasn't changed. I'm happy with it."

"Okay, Mike. I hear you. Let me know if anything else changes."

"You got it, John. Take care."

Next, Mike calls the Senator, and luckily, the Senator is in.

"Hello, Mike. So, how did you make out?"

"Well, I spoke to John. He was not too happy, but he said that he was okay with the change."

"Good, I'm happy to hear that. Now it will go to the floor, and we'll see where it goes from there. And Mike, don't forget about the information about the General."

"No, Senator, I will not forget. If I hear anything, I will let you know."

"Okay, take care, Mike."

"You too, Senator."

Three weeks go by with no call from the Senator. All caught up on his work, Mike decides to go and see John. Once there, John comes into the room all smiles.

"So, what's the good word, Mike?"

"Nothing so far, John."

"What! I thought you were here to give me some good news."

"Oh, I'm sorry, John. I just came by to see how you were doing. I didn't think that you would think that I was bringing good news. I'm sorry, John. I should have realized that you would have thought that. Again, I'm sorry."

"That's okay, Mike. It's partly my fault. I should not have jumped to conclusions. Not to worry, Mike."

"Okay. Anyway, how are you doing?"

"Well, I told Barney and Nick about the change in the bill, and they were not too happy about it, but I convinced them that it was still a good step forward."

"I just wanted to let you know that these things sometime take a long time, and not to give up. You know what they say, no news is good news, and I promise as soon as I hear anything, you will be the first one to know about it."

"You came here to cheer me up, and you did, because I was starting to think negative thoughts about the whole thing, but I feel better now that you came to see me."

"Okay, then, my job here is finished, and I will now leave. Take care, and I will see you later."

"Yea, later, man."

On the way home, Mike thinks to himself, *I feel like kicking myself in the ass. This was a stupid thing to do. What was I thinking? I can understand why he would have thought that I was there to give him good news, and I hope John was not lying to me about me cheering him up.* Mike decides to go to his office and do some work, and try to forget what he just did.

Another week goes by with no news. Mike is trying to do some work, but he can't seem to concentrate on anything. He just keeps thinking about what is going on in Washington and why he has not heard anything about it. Then Mike's secretary comes in and tells Mike, "There is a gentleman here to see you."

"Is it one of my clients?"

"No, sir. I have never seen this man before today."

"Okay, send him in."

To Mike's surprise, it's the General. Mike walks over to his office door, closes it, and then turns around and says, "What the hell are you doing here? By now, I would have thought that you'd be out of the country. Are you crazy, coming here? They may be watching me."

"No one is watching you. Please, give me some credit. I made sure of that. You are too paranoid."

"Well, I don't think so. Anyway, why are you here?"

"I'm here to let you know that I'm going to go to Canada, and I thought that it would ease your mind."

"Yes, it will, but I would have appreciated this information, in a different form, not in person. When are you leaving?"

"I'm leaving tomorrow morning, right after I meet with my landlord and give him my keys, and I just wanted to give you my information so that you could get in touch with me if needed."

"Boy, I don't know if I even want that information hanging around here. Look, you know where I am and how to get in touch with me, so why don't we do it this way: buy yourself a throwaway phone and call me from time to time. I would really like that better."

"Okay, Mike, you got it, okay."

"Have a safe trip and call me when you get settled in." The two shake hands, and Mike says, "Thanks for being understanding."

"Ok, Mike. Take care."

Five minutes later, Mike's secretary calls him and tells him that John is on the phone.

"Hello, John, what's up?"

"Just wanted to give you a call to see if you heard anything."

"No, John, sorry. I heard nothing, but like I said, no news is good news, and these processes take a while to finish, so don't get yourself down. Just keep thinking positive."

"Okay, Mike."

"So, John, is there anything new there?"

"No, not really, except for a few new books that the library got, but otherwise, no, nothing new. Sorry to bother you, but sitting over here, time moves by very slowly."

"I understand, John. Just try to keep yourself busy. Start writing a book or something."

"Yea, good idea. I'll start on one as soon as I hang up on you."

"Okay, take care, Mike."

"Take care, John."

The next morning, the General is getting ready to leave and waiting for his landlord. After a while, his landlord shows up, checks the apartment, gives the General the okay, and the General hands him the keys.

"Well, you were a good tenant and took good care of the place, so if you ever decide to come back, and I have an apartment available, I would be more than happy to rent to you again. Thank you, and you have a safe trip.

"Thank you."

With that, the General gets in his truck, but before he gets on the road, he decides to make one more call. He calls Eight. There's a pause on the other end. "Is this the General?"

"Yes, it is."

"Oh my God! Where have you been? The last time I spoke to you, we were ready to order all the stuff that you needed from that stealth action that you were getting ready to do. We all had no idea where you were. You just seemed to disappear off the face of the earth. I tried calling you a few times, but there was no answer. So, how are you, and is everything all right?"

"Yes. As far as the items that I needed for that stealth action, I will not be needing them anymore."

"Are you sure?"

"Yes, I'm sure. Like I said, everything is all right, and I got some good news for you and some bad news. The good news is Senator Adams has introduced John's bill, and it's looking like it has a good chance of passing."

"Oh, that's great news!"

"Yes, it is, and what I would like you to do is keep an eye on the news, and if you can help in any way, try your best to help."

"Okay, I will do that, but that still doesn't answer the question of where you were."

"That's not important. What I want to know is how everything is going with The Club."

"Everything is going great. We've added a few more lawyers here and there, and we are averaging about one case a month defending clients. There are still children being molested, and hopefully, if this bill is passed, it will help stop that or slow it down at least, but everything is good here, General. So, what's the bad news."

"Well, the bad news is I have to leave town for a while, and I don't want you to try and find me. I will not be getting in touch with you, and I don't know how long it will be, so I just wanted to let you know that I'm okay and I will get in touch with you when I can."

"General, you can't leave me hanging like that. If there is anything wrong, maybe we can help."

"No, you can't help. I have to help myself. But don't worry, it's not a big deal. I just need to get away and clear my head, and I don't want anybody to bother me, so you guys just keep up the good work. Don't worry about me, and I promise I will be in touch once I clear my head. So, please, thank everyone for me who gave or volunteered, and I will talk to you later. And remember, part of the deal John made with the Senator was his release from prison, along with Barney and Nick. If that happens, John can pick up where he left off with The Club. And by the way, if you need to get in touch with John, call his lawyer Mike at this number." The General gives Eight the number. "He can get in touch with John. So, like I said, thank everyone. Take care, and I will be in touch."

THE CLUB

The next morning, bright and early, Mike gets a call from Senator Adams. "Good morning, Senator. How are you today?"

"I'm fine, Mike. I've got some great news for you."

"Great! I could use some good news."

"Well, the bill flew through the general debate session with flying colors, with no changes. I got to tell you, Mike, now I am starting to get excited about this bill. I'm telling you now that if it keeps going the way it is, I am going to make a really big deal of this, so be prepared. Now, remember the next step: it goes to a conference committee made up of Senators and representatives. There, they will work out any differences that they run into, but if it's made it this far, I cannot foresee any problems with it, so keep your fingers crossed, and I'll keep you updated. By any chance, has your informant called you?"

"No, Senator, but he is due to give me a call any day now."

"Okay, Mike, let me know if that changes, and I will let you know if there are any changes on my end."

"Okay, great, Senator. Bye."

As soon as Mike hangs up, he calls the prison and leaves us a message for John to call him back ASAP. Two hours later, Mike gets a call from John. "Good morning, John. I hope you're sitting down."

"No, Mike, there are no seats by the phones. They are just phones hanging on the wall."

"Okay John I will make this short and sweet. Great news! The bill flew

351

through the general debate session with flying colors, and that is verbatim from Senator Adams. According to the Senator, he cannot foresee encountering any problems from here on in, and he also told me that he was starting to get excited about the bill and that if it does go through, he is going to make a really big deal of it. I don't know what he meant by that, but it sounds encouraging. I figured I would call you as soon as I could and give you the good news. I will not keep you on the phone, because I know that you want to go and give Nick and Barney the good news. I will talk to you later."

"Okay, thanks, Mike. Talk to you soon."

Mike tells his secretary that he is taking the rest of the day off. He feels like he must celebrate. He doesn't know just exactly how he plans to celebrate; all he knows is that he needs to, so he heads home. As he gets in the house, he tells his wife to get dressed, that they are going out to dinner tonight to celebrate.

His wife asks, "And just what are we celebrating, Mike?"

"We are celebrating the case of John Harrison, you know, the man whose daughter was molested and killed and the guy got away with it. John tried to kill him when he ran into him and ended up going to jail for it, and that guy has not been seen since. He just disappeared off the face of the earth."

"Yes, I do remember, but John is in jail now, right?"

"Yes, he is, along with Nick and Barney, but the good news is I am very close to getting them all out and getting John's bill passed into law."

"Oh my God, that is great news!"

"Yes, it is, so that is why we are going out tonight and celebrating. So, go and get ready."

The next week, everything seems to be going good for Mike. He has three court dates, two of which are settled in his clients' favor. The third is adjourned, but it looks good for Mike, so right now, he is in a good place and is a happy man. Sitting at his desk, thinking about what is going on with John's case, he can't help but think about all the years that he has been working with John and all that has transpired, that he was actually involved in a kidnaping scam to help John's cause, and that everything now seems to be coming to a head and working out for him, Barney, and Nick. Just as he is deep in thought, his secretary calls to let him know that Senator Adams is on the phone. "Hello, Senator."

"Hi, Mike. I've got some really, really good news for you. It went through the conference committee in record time. I have never seen a bill move this fast, and now we are at the final step. Now it must be approved by both houses, and from there, it goes to the president to sign. Once it gets there, it should move through fast, because at this point, it has been scrutinized by just about everyone who has anything to say about it, and we don't have to worry about anyone adding any pork to it, because it's just a law change, and there is no money being appropriated to it. So kid, we are just about there, but remember, I'm not letting you off the hook for the General."

"Okay, Senator, I understand."

"And one last thing. Remember what I said about making a big deal about this. I may need your cooperation with it."

"Anything you need, Senator."

"Okay, Mike. I'm kind of busy, so go and enjoy the good news, and I will talk to you later. Bye."

Mike immediately picks up the phone, calls the prison, and leaves a message for John to call him back. Later on that afternoon, when John calls back, Mike gives him the good news.

If John could do backflips, he would. "Great! I will give Barney and Nick the good, no, great news! Thanks, Mike!"

"Okay. Bye."

೨೨೨

It has now been three weeks since Mike has heard from the Senator. Then, one day, while putting a brief together for one of his cases, his secretary informs him that Senator Adams is on the phone. Mike thinks to himself, *It's about time! And I hope it's good news.* "Good morning, Senator."

"Good morning, Mike. Well, I got some more great news for you, Mike."

"Good, Senator, and again, I could use some good news."

"Okay then, here it is. The bill has passed both houses, and all it needs now is for the president to sign it into law."

"Oh my God, that is good news, but I will not celebrate until the president signs it into law."

"You're right, Mike, but I would not lose any sleep over it, because it is very rare that a president vetoes a bill once it passes all of the steps that it needs to go through before it becomes law. I also told you that I spoke to the president about this bill, and he is thinking of releasing your three friends on the bases of time served, so I would not worry. From here on in, as they say, it's in the bag. But what I really want to talk to you about is how and when it will all go down."

"Okay, Senator. I'm listening."

"Great. This is how it's going to go down. Do you remember that I told you that I wanted to make a big deal of this, and I asked you if you would give me your cooperation in this matter?"

"Yes, I do, Senator."

"Okay, great! So this is how I want to do it, and Mike, I know you are well aware of how politics works in Washington."

"Yes, I am, Senator."

"Anyway, Mike, this is what I want to do. As I said before, I want to make a big deal of this bill signing by the president, and the releasing of your three friends, so once more, this is how it will go down. First, I will issue a news release to all the media that the president will be signing in a new law regarding child molesters, because of how lenient the existing laws are and how this new law will fix all of that and make our children much safer. The president will also fix an injustice done to three men who were jailed with paid-for evidence that the president feels could have been artificially created, releasing them under the time-served law. This will all take place on the steps of the U.S. Capital building in Washington, D.C.

"The bottom line is that I helped you, and now, I want you to help me to get as much benefit as possible from this by cooperating with the news media when they get in touch with you and giving me as much praise as possible. Tell them how compassionate and caring I was in helping you to get this bill passed, and how it will save and protect a lot of children. As a politician, I want to get as much exposure as possible so that it will help me and my party in getting re-elected. I also want you to let John know about it so that he can get the word to his followers to show up there. I will even go so far as to offer free bus transportation for them to Washington, D.C. So, Mike, do you have all that?"

"Yes, I do, Senator."

"And are you okay with all of it?"

"Yes, Senator."

"Okay, Mike, that's good! The president, my fellow Senators, representatives, and I want to make as big a deal as possible with this. You're a lawyer, so I don't need to remind you how things work in Washington, D.C."

"No, you don't, Senator. I know, and I will do all I can to help you out. So don't worry; I have your back on this."

"Okay, Mike. Just wait until you hear from me with a date. Then you can start to do your part and spread the word, and I will get things started on my end as soon as I get a date for all this, and all that I need to get from the president."

"Okay, sounds good. Bye."

Again, Mike calls the prison and leaves a message for John to call him back. By late the next afternoon, Mike still has not gotten a call from John, so he calls the prison back and asks them if they gave John the message. They inform Mike that they gave John the message one hour after he called, so he asks them to please give John a new message and to include that it is important to call him back ASAP. They tell Mike that they will give John the message ASAP. "Okay, thank you."

It's the next afternoon before Mike gets a call from John. When Mike gets on the phone, the first thing he asks John is, "Where the hell have you been?! Didn't they tell you to call ASAP?"

"First of all, Mike, please calm down and give me a chance to explain."

"Okay, so explain."

"This is what happened. Yes, I got you first message, and your second ASAP message, but what these assholes didn't tell you was that I was in the hole, in protective custody, because of a problem I had with another prisoner."

"Oh my god! You should not be getting yourself into trouble while all this is going on. I am breaking my ass for you, and we are so close to getting you and your guys out, and you go and get yourself in trouble."

"Mike, will you please let me finish my story? You are flying off the handle without me telling you the rest of the story."

"Okay, you're right. Go ahead and finish your story."

"The day before you called, I went to the yard to get some exercise, and when I got back, the guy in the cell next to me told me that Pete, who is a prisoner on the other end of my tier, went into my cell and took some food that I had there. When I saw Pete, I questioned him, and he pushed me and said that if I did not walk away, that I would be very sorry. A guard saw and came over and put a stop to what was happening, and he saw Pete punch me and heard him threaten me, so Pete was cuffed and taken to a hole, where they take prisoners who get in trouble. As they were taking him away, he said that I was a dead man, that he would not be in the hole forever, so think about that. So they put me in protective custody, and while you are in the hole, you are not allowed to make phone calls. But then they finally figured out that I was only in there for my own protection and gave me my messages an hour ago. I called you the first chance I got."

"Okay, I'm sorry. I guess I did jump off the handle, but only because I had really good news and could not wait to tell you."

"That is now past us, so what is the good news?"

"Well, actually, it's great news, not just good news. Senator Adams called and said that the bill passed all the necessary steps. It's now considered a slam dunk to be signed into law, and that all that is needed now, for the president to sign it."

"Oh my God, that is great news! I am actually tearing up right now, Mike. I can't believe that we are this close to my goal."

"Well, believe it. We are there, and again, I'm sorry."

"Don't worry about it, Mike. I forgive you."

"Okay, enjoy the good news. I do have another question for you, though. The Senator told me that he wants to make a really big deal out of it, and he wants to know if you have any ideas on how to get as many of your followers to go to Washington, D.C., for the signing of the new law and to see the release of you guys. In fact, he is going to offer free transportation to all of your followers."

"Oh my God, that is great! But unfortunately, I don't have any way to get in touch with any of my followers. All I can think of is maybe for you to put an announcement of the signing in the newspapers and hope that my followers will see it."

"Okay, if nothing else, I guess that would be one way of letting your followers know. Enjoy the good news, and I will talk to you later."

Things quiet down for a while, and three weeks go by with Mike not hearing anything. Then, just when Mike thinks that he probably has to settle in for the long haul, thinking that it's the last step and is predicated on the president's agenda, and knowing that the president is busy and that it will take a while, his secretary informs him that the Senator is on the phone. Mike grabs the phone, excited in anticipation of what he is about to hear. "Good morning, Senator."

"Good morning, Mike. Well, we have a date. It is now April, and this event will take place on July 10, at 1 PM, on the steps of the U.S. Capital Building in Washington, D.C. One of the best things is that the president himself will be there to sign the bill into law and to give a short speech about it and how significant it is, and how it will save our children, etc., etc. Then he will introduce me. I will give a short speech, again about the new law, etc., etc. and then introduce a few Senators and congressmen who all worked on the bill and who will all give short speeches about the new law. Then they will give the podium back to me. I will give another short speech and officially release John, Barney, and Nick. Then I'll introduce John so that he can give a speech, and between the two of us, I hope that we can get a few thousand people there. On my end, I will issue a several news releases and give a few interviews promoting the event, and hopefully, you can get some people to attend. Like I said, I am willing to offer free bus transportation to people. To explain how to get tickets and where to get the buses, I will be sending you the full itinerary on the event. We have two months to get this done. Do you think we can do it?"

"Absolutely, Senator."

"Okay, great! I will be sending you the itinerary via a courier service. I don't want to use e-mail or the U.S. mail."

"Okay, Senator, I understand."

"Well, as soon as you get it, please get started on it."

"You got it, Senator."

"Great! Bye."

Mike next calls the prison, and while doing that, he thinks to himself, *As often as I call this number, I should have it on speed dial.* When they answer, he tries to leave a message for John to call him back, but the person on the other end of the phone gives him a hard time: "You know, this is not a hotel. You just can't call and leave messages for the inmates anytime you want. There are procedures you must follow."

"Well, I guess what I should have said first was that I am his lawyer and that it's very important that he calls me back."

"You got it."

"Okay, thanks."

Two hours later, John calls Mike back.

"Good afternoon, John."

"Good afternoon, Mike. I hope you have more good news for me."

"I absolutely do. I got a call today from Senator Adams, and everything is a go. I will give you the short version. The final step is that the bill will be signed by the president himself on July 10th, in front of the U.S. Capital Building in Washington, D.C., and the Senator told me that the president himself will give a speech about the new law, etc., etc. He will then introduce Senator Adams, who will give a speech, then some more Senators and congressmen, who will give speeches, etc., etc. You know how it goes. Then Senator Adams will bring you guys out and officially release you. Then he will introduce you. Then you can give a speech."

"Oh my God! Oh my God! I can't wait to tell Barney and Nick. Oh, and I need to write a speech!"

"Yes, you do. Okay, go tell the other guys and write your speech. The Senator and I will take care of all the rest. And by the way, celebrate now, because when you get my bill, you are going to cry."

"I'm sure I will. Mike, we owe you our lives."

"Yea, yea, go tell the guys, and I will talk to you later."

After Mike hangs up, he thinks to himself, *Oh boy, I've got to get started, but I don't know where the hell to start.* Then he thinks about a friend of his who is the public relations guy for a large company, and he decides to give him a call. He tells his secretary to try and get Tony Franklin on the phone. Mike's secretary tells Mike that Tony is busy and will call him back. Mike decides to try and get some work done, but can't, so he decides to just make a list of what needs to be done for July 10th. He starts working on the list when his friend Tony calls.

"Mike, how are you doing?"

"I'm doing great. And how about you?"

"I'm doing great also. So, what can I attribute this call to?"

"Well, I've got this situation. I have this case that I've been working on for a while now, and it's coming to a head on July 10th of this year. There are going to be Senators and congressmen involved, and the president himself will be there, signing in a new law, in front of the U.S. Capital Building in Washington, D.C."

"Oh, so it's a big deal."

"Yes, it is. Just to let you know, there will free bus transportation afforded to people who would like to attend, and this Senator wants me to try and get as many people as I can to show up, and I don't know where to start."

"Okay, Mike, tell you what. Just write everything down and give me a copy of it, and I will take it from there."

"Okay, that I can do."

"Good. I'll talk to you after I get the list."

"Okay, Tony. Take care."

"Talk to you later."

Mike now feels a little better, knowing that his end of the work will be handled by his friend Tony, who is a professional and who should have no problems. Again, Mike settles in, getting some work done. Even then, time passes slowly, and he can't get over the fact that the big day is finally coming.

Time passes, and it's two weeks before the big day when Mike's secretary informs him that there is a gentleman on the phone who wants to speak to him and who says it's important. Mike picks up the phone. "Hello?"

"Hello, is this Mr. Mike Santino?"

"Yes, it is, and who am I speaking to?"

"Well, let's just say that my name is Eight."

"Just Eight?"

"Yes."

"Well, Eight, if you don't want to give me your real name, I don't think I want to talk to you."

"Well, please hold on and give me the courtesy of hearing me before you hang up."

"Okay, you got one minute before I hang up on you."

"Thank you. First, let me drop a name on you: John Harrison. Is that name familiar to you?"

This perks Mike's interest, and he says, "As a matter of fact, I do, but what does that have to do with you calling me?"

"Well, I also know that you are his lawyer."

"Again, who are you, and what do you want?! You know what? I really wish that you'd get to the point and stop wasting my time, and if I don't like the answer, I'm hanging up."

"Okay, okay. Hang on. I'm not trying to be mysterious or anything. Please, give me a chance to talk."

"So start talking."

"Well, first off, I can't give you my name because I am a member of an underground group that helps defend anyone who has killed a child molester. There is one name that I would like to mention, and that is the General. I know for sure that you know him, because he called me, and asked me to get in touch with you and see if I could be of any assistance to you. And just for your information, we are one hundred percent behind John and his cause, and the reason we exist, is because of what John started. The reason I called you is I saw in the papers and heard on TV about a huge rally in front of the U.S. Capital Building on July 10th for the signing of a new law about child molesters. They said something about free bus transportation to the event, so I'm calling you to see if you need any help, and how to find out about the free buses. They gave a phone number to call about the buses, but I used this excuse to call you and let you know who I am and how to get in touch with me. And remember, the less you know about my organization, the safer it is for you."

"Okay, I can understand that."

"Now, the second reason for my call is about the buses. Our clubs are located in eight states, and we will need buses for each state. We'll also need to know where the pickup locations are."

"Okay, Eight. I'm sorry I was so short with you. I thought you were some sort of crackpot."

"No problem, Mike."

"Okay, that's good. Give me your phone number and what states you need the buses for."

"Mike, I'm also sorry for being so mysterious."

"No problem, Eight."

"Anyway, Mike, I need buses for Texas, California, Illinois, Florida, Ohio, Massachusetts, and Virginia, and if you're looking for people, I'm sure that I can fill all the buses."

"Okay, great. I will check it out and get back to you. Talk to you later."

Next, Mike asks his secretary to call Senator Adams. As usual, she informs Mike that the Senator is not in and will return his call ASAP. It's late afternoon by the time the Senator calls Mike back. "Good afternoon, Mike."

"Good afternoon, Senator."

"So what's up, Mike?"

"Well, I got a call from someone who heard about the event in Washington, D.C., and is a member of an organization that has about eight clubs in different locations across the country. He wanted to know how he could make arrangements for buses for the clubs."

"Oh, that's an easy one, Mike. There is an 800 number that he can call. All he needs to do is give them the states he needs the buses for, and they will give him all the locations, with the pickup times. One thing to keep in mind with these buses: they will only be available for a maximum of a four-hour ride. Otherwise, my party would go broke if we did not have some sort of cutoff point. But that, also, is explained in the news article and the ads on TV."

"Okay, I will let him know, Senator. By the way, how is everything going?"

"It's going great, Mike. You will be there, right, Mike?"

"Absolutely, Senator. I will be getting there the day before. I already booked a room."

"That's great, Mike. When you get here, come over to my office, and I will give you a VIP pass."

"Oh, thank you, Senator. I will do that."

"Okay, Mike, I will see you there, unless I'm in my office when you come to pick up your VIP pass. In that case, please make sure you say hello."

"You got it, Senator."

Mike then calls Eight to give him the 800 number and tells him about the four-hour ride limit.

"You know what, Mike? Forget about it. I will make my own arrangements for all my clubs to get there."

"Okay, that's great. Then I will see you there."

Often in life, whenever you are waiting for an important event to happen, the days and hours seem to drag on forever, but then, when the day finally comes, you can't believe that it's really here. That is exactly how Mike feels. In his mind, he has been preparing for this day forever, and now that it's here, Mike feels like he is not ready. He needs time to pack, to make sure that he has his airline tickets, to make sure he leaves in time to catch his flight, etc., etc., but even with all the things Mike has to do, he somehow manages to get his wife and himself to Washington, D.C., a day early. He goes straight to his room and makes sure he has all his paperwork, which he really doesn't need but brought anyway, just in case. Once sure that he has all his ducks in a row, he takes a shower and he and his wife get in bed.

While all that is going on with Mike, John, Barney, and Nick are on a plane about to land in Washington, D.C. Once there, all three will be put up in a local hotel, where they will stay until they are officially released tomorrow, at the ceremony. At this point, all three are in a state of euphoria and can't believe that this is really happening. Once at the hotel, they each find clothing that was pre-ordered, in their sizes that, which each gave to the authorities. Now that it's late, all three take their showers and get in bed, hoping to hasten the passing of time until the next morning.

The next morning, Mike and his wife are up early. They get breakfast, go back to their room, Mike gets his attaché case with all his paperwork, again, that he really doesn't need, and Mike heads to Senator Adams's office, to pick up his VIP pass. Then he heads to the U.S. Capitol Building for the big ceremony. Once there, he heads to the VIP section, where he meets and greets the wives of John, Nick, and Barney. Although it's only 11 AM, there are about 1,000 people there already. There is still about two hours to go before the ceremony begins, and all of the news crews are busy setting up their gear. Mike is impressed by the assortment of media that are represented, and he thinks that this is really going to be a big deal, just like the Senator said it would be. Back at the hotel, John, Barney, and Nick are all ready to go and are waiting for the marshal to accompany them to the ceremony, where they will be officially released.

At 12:30 PM, with a half hour to go, there are now about 5,000 people outside the Capitol Building, with many street venders selling all sorts of political propaganda, and people handing out free literature extolling the Senator's party. There is even music playing; it's a real party atmosphere. Then some other members of the Senator's political party arrive. Mike sees Senator Adams and waves to him, and the Senator waves back to Mike and then gives him the thumbs up.

Finally, it's 1 PM. A strange gentleman walks up to the podium, and the crowd quiets down. He taps the microphone to check if it's working, and then he says, "Hello all, and without further ado, ladies and gentleman, the president of the United States."

With that, the president comes walking down the steps to tumultuous applause and heads to a table with the papers for the new law that he will be signing. Amidst whistling and yelling, he raises his hands. As the music stops and the crowd quiets down, he stops at the podium and says, "Hello and welcome. First thing I want to do is welcome all of you and thank you all for coming. Today is a very special day, not just for me and a few more people; it's also a very special day because, this morning, I will be signing into law a bill that was introduced by my good friend Senator Sam Adams. It was his perseverance that brought this new bill into focus, and he followed it through all the steps it had to go through to become a law that will protect all of our children, and I am extremely proud to have been a part of the process. Now, without further ado, I will now sign the bill, putting the new law into motion."

The president sits at the table and uses several pens to sign the new law, again to tumultuous applause. He then stands and returns to the podium. "With that done, I would now like to bring Senator Adams up to explain the new law. So let's have a big hand for Senator Sam Adams."

At this point, the president waves to everyone and turns to leave. Mike is already thinking to himself, *I hope they don't drag it on and on with speeches. I want to see the three guys get released already.*

Just then, the Senator starts to speak: "Okay, in short, what this new law does is change the all-too-lenient laws in regards to child molesters. This new law will be a lot harder on them, giving them food for thought and ultimately saving the lives of many young children. But I did not do this alone. My fellow Senators, and members of both houses, also helped move this bill along to become law." Then he proceeds to introduce a few Senators and congressmen, who all had their speeches that seemed to go on forever. Finally, Senator Adams, is back at the podium. "Okay, and now I would like to introduce the three men who started this whole thing and who were very instrumental in putting this bill together."

At this point, Mike is starting to get bored and rolling his eyes back, but as the Senator is talking, the crowd starts to cheer, whistle, and applaud. Behind the Senator, Mike sees John, Barney, and Nick coming down the steps. This is a great sight to Mike, because now he knows that most of the people are here for them.

The Senator, with his arms, motions to the people to quiet down, but they keep going on with all the whistling clapping and yelling out, "YOU DID IT! YOU DID IT! YOU DID IT!" Finally, the Senator manages to quiet the crowd down. "Okay, yes, they did it, and now, before you guys start throwing things at me, let me introduce the three men standing behind me. They are John Harrison, Barney Cicale, and Nick Alesi. These three men are solely responsible for this new law. So, without further ado, here is Mr. John Harrison." Again, the crowd goes absolutely crazy, still shouting out, "YOU DID IT! YOU DID IT!!!"

John steps up to the podium. He has trouble quieting the crowd down, but eventuality they do, and John says, "Thank you, thank you, thank you all for coming here today and showing your support for our cause. It's been a long, tough road, but we persevered and forged forward, and it payed off, because today, we got a new law that will save a lot of children. The child molesters out there will now think twice before they do anything. As far as I'm concerned, I would have made the laws more severe, but this is a great start to the new law. It is ten times better, and the best part is that it is now a national law, not just a state law, so we are happy with what we got, and our thanks to Senator Adams for spearheading the bill, to all of the Senators and congressmen who pushed it through, and to the president, who signed it into law."

Then, as John is speaking and looking at his audience, he recognizes a face in the crowd. It's none other than Jim Tally, the man who raped and killed John's daughter. He stops talking and is overcome with rage, to the point that he can't control himself. As their eyes meet, John thinks to himself, *That son of a bitch has got a lot of balls showing up here, smiling at me. I don't give a shit if I go back to jail. I'm going to kill him.*

With that, John takes off after Jim, and all bedlam breaks out; no one knows what is going on. Barney and Nick instinctively follow John without even knowing what he is doing, Jim starts running and pushing through the crowd, knocking some people down, while John, Barney, and Nick are hot in pursuit. John loses sight of Jim from time to time and needs jump up and down to catch sight of him again; then he continues his pursuit. By now, Mike and the wives of John, Barney, and Nick, along with security personnel and the police, are all involved in the chase, still not knowing what it's all about.

For a moment, Barney and Nick catch up with John, and Barney asks him, "John, what the hell are you doing? What's going on?"

"That son of a bitch Jim Tally had the balls to show up here!"

"What!"

"Yes, he was here in the first row, smiling at me."

"But John, if you touch him, you will end up back in jail."

"I don't give a shit. I'm going to fucking kill that son of a bitch." John jumps up again and catches a glimpse of Jim. "There he goes!"

All three take chase, with everyone else following them. As only John, Barney, and Nick know what's going on, it's like Armageddon, with people running in all different directions, screaming, some people crying, some parents protecting the children, and all because no one knows what is going on.

Finally, Jim breaks out from the crowd, and at this point, he feels that he is running for his life. He is constantly looking back over his shoulder while running. Barney, Nick, Mike, the wives, the police, and security are all chasing John, and John is gaining on Jim. Jim is running as fast as he can, again constantly looking over your shoulder, tripping as he's going. He approaches a large street and starts to run across it while looking over his shoulder, not noticing a school bus full of children on a day trip to Washington, D.C. The school bus hits and kills him instantly.

Now there is more chaos, as a crowd gathers around the scene of the accident, with Jim lying motionless on the ground. Slowly, everyone catches up with John, and now the police and security have this to contend with.

One of the cops asks John, "What the hell is going on, John? Who is this guy?"

"This is the guy who raped and murdered my daughter years ago and got away with it. I've been looking for this guy ever since, and I promised myself that if I ever saw him, I would kill him with my bare hands, regardless of the consequences.

The cop tells John, "Well, I guess you can cross that off your bucket list. Fate took care of it for you."

By now, John's wife is alongside him, as are Barney's and Nick's wives alongside their husbands. Mike walks up to John and says, "Well, look at what we have here."

John asks Mike, "Do you know who this guy is?"

"Are you kidding me? I know exactly who this piece of shit is. It's Jim Tally, the man who killed your daughter. John, stand back and take a look at the big picture. He was a child molester, and here he gets killed by a bus full of children. If this is not poetic justice, nothing is."

THE CLUB

John, Barney, and Nick, decide to open up clinics to help children that have been molested, beaten, and abused. After a few years, they get enough money through donations to open up clinics across the country, helping many children.

The end.

The author, Barney Alesi, is a man of many hats. He retired
as foreman after working thirty-three years in the Department
of Public Works, Town of Islip, N.Y. he has been married to
his wife, Rose, for the past sixty years. Together, they share
four children, six grandchildren, and three great-grandchil-
dren. In 2004, he appeared along with his wife on a reality show on Fox
for eight weeks called The Complex: Malibu. He is a private pilot, rides a
Harley-Davidson motorcycle, likes ultimate fighting, and played drums in
a band for over twenty years, with the most recent band being called The
Cousins Three. In addition, he likes to sing karaoke. Along with his wife,
he enjoys camping in their trailer. He has been told that he has hands of
gold because he can build or fix just about anything. He loves all children
and is very passionate toward them, and his family and friends agree that
he is an all-around nice guy who would offer a hand to anyone who needed
help.

What prompted him to write this book was an incident that occurred
years ago to a member of his family, and ever since that happened, it has
weighed heavily on his mind and has progressively taunted and stressed
him. Rather than him going out and taking the law into his own hands, he
decided that the more prudent thing to do was to write a book about it.
Even though it's a fictional story, there are parts of it based on fact. The
truth of it is that the laws are too lenient against child molesters to act as a
deterrent. Convicted molesters often do not serve a sufficient amount of
time incarcerated, allowing them to go out and do it again and again. On
top of that, the laws are different in each state, to the point that some of
them are ridiculous, with some states leaving sentencing in the hands of
bleeding-heart judges who set the molesters free, sometimes with nothing
more than a slap on the wrist, allowing them to go out and molest more

children. He wrote this book to open the eyes of the lawmakers, to have them see what's going on regarding child molestation in this country, and to make the appropriate changes in the laws so as to discourage molesters and to try and stop them from doing what they do. The fact is that each year, sixteen percent of children across this country will be molested, and another proven fact is that the child molesters cannot be rehabilitated, and they themselves will attest to that fact.

www.ingramcontent.com/pod-product-compliance
Lightning Source LLC
Chambersburg PA
CBHW071153020726
47502CB00002B/396